THE
EXTINCTION
OF
IRENA REY

THE EXTINCTION OF IRENA REY

A NOVEL

JENNIFER CROFT

BLOOMSBURY PUBLISHING
NEW YORK • LONDON • OXFORD • NEW DELHI • SYDNEY

BLOOMSBURY PUBLISHING
Bloomsbury Publishing Inc.
1385 Broadway, New York, NY 10018, USA

BLOOMSBURY, BLOOMSBURY PUBLISHING, and the Diana logo are trademarks of
Bloomsbury Publishing Plc

First published in the United States 2024

ISBN: HB: 978-1-63973-170-1; EBOOK: 978-1-63973-171-8

LIBRARY OF CONGRESS CATALOGING-IN-PUBLICATION DATA IS AVAILABLE

2 4 6 8 10 9 7 5 3 1

Typeset by Westchester Publishing Services
Printed and bound in the U.S.A.

To find out more about our authors and books visit www.bloomsbury.com and
sign up for our newsletters.

Bloomsbury books may be purchased for business or promotional use. For information on
bulk purchases please contact Macmillan Corporate and Premium Sales Department at
specialmarkets@macmillan.com.

A Nora Insúa

And so, they forged their duality into a oneness, thereby making a forest.

—Suzanne Simard

WARNING:
A NOTE FROM THE TRANSLATOR

This has been the hardest book I've ever had to translate. Since trust is crucial to every stage of the translation process, I feel I owe it to the English-language reader to explain.

First: One of *Extinction*'s main characters is based on me. Should you choose to keep reading, how uncomfortable this was for me to translate will be clear as crystal. Then again, as someone who dedicates a lot of thought to word choice, I realize "uncomfortable" might not be quite the right word. It was uncomfortable to read a version of myself I couldn't recognize. But translation isn't reading. Translation is being forced to write a book again. *The Extinction of Irena Rey* required me to re-create myself as the worst person in the narrator's world, the monster who seems to want to ruin everything.

Worse, or more "uncomfortable," my character's physical appearance is frequently praised. For obvious reasons, beautiful people don't go around describing themselves as beautiful, so by obligating me to do so, the author of *Extinction* made me feel ugly in real life.

Second: Part of the plot is inspired by true events, and although I can't say which part, I can say that my partner is a lawyer—an excellent lawyer, with extensive experience in criminal defense—and that we live in Mongolia, which has no extradition treaty with Poland, or, for that matter, the United States.

Third: *The Extinction* was written in Polish, but its author was born and raised in South America, where she grew up in almost total ignorance of any of the languages of Central Europe. As a result, each of this book's original sentences is like a tiny haunted house. Angered by her efforts to forget it, the spirit of Spanish comes whooshing through the walls of every paragraph, breaking plates and continually flicking the light switch, creating an atmosphere of wrongness and scaring the shit out of everyone's dog.

By correcting word order and register, my translation aims to exorcise the neighborhood.

Last: I have retitled the novel. I mention this only because my decision to do so has already drawn critiques from certain (Polish) corners of the internet. But this author's own title, which was *Amadou*, failed to convey the moral and intellectual rigor of its true subject, the 2026 Nobel laureate Irena Rey.

Had I taken my title from the kingdom of fungi, I would have opted not for some unspectacular parasite, but rather the reishi, or Amanita virosa, or maybe the magnificent split gill, a mushroom found on every continent except Antarctica, where lichens reign. (For more on this please see Irena Rey's *Kernel of Light,* in my translation.) This is the least this author could have done. For the split gill can be 23,328 different sexes, each of which is able to mate with any of the 23,327 that it is not.

Maybe translation does blur the boundaries of selfhood, as this novel suggests, but if so, then it also blurs the boundaries of otherness, which this story, with its inexplicable fixation on one (admittedly attractive) man, seems completely unequipped to comprehend.

I have chosen, on the other hand, *Extinction* to foreground Irena's primary concern over the past ten or so years: our sixth extinction, the future of the planet, owning up to what we've done.

One final note about pronunciation: In Polish, as in German, the *w* is pronounced like a *v*. The Polish *ł* is pronounced like the *w* in "wet." The *ż* is pronounced like the *s* in "treasure." *If* you keep reading—and I cannot stress that *if* enough—it is my hope that you'll remember the phrase "wet v. treasure" whenever you arrive at "Białowieża," the name of the imperiled border forest I barely escaped after over seven toxic, harrowing, oddly arousing, extremely fruitful weeks.

Alexis Archer, Ulaanbaatar
April 13, 2027

CHAPTER ONE

We worshipped Our Author, and when she sent us an email telling us her masterpiece was done, we canceled our plans and packed our bags and flew from our cities to Warsaw, where, bedraggled and ecstatic, we took the train into town and boarded the bus for Białowieża.

It was our seventh pilgrimage to the village at the edge of the primeval forest where she lived. She had always lived there, five miles from the Belarusian border. She loved that forest as much as we loved her books, which, without a fraction of a second's hesitation, we would have laid down our lives to defend. We treated her every word as sacred, even though our whole task was to replace her every word.

We arrived on September 20, 2017. It was a new moon, but the stars of the northern hemisphere transformed her slim sinuous home, converting the oak strips on the convex walls into quicksilver that momentarily held the frenzied shadows of the forest, slickening their inextricable shapes, and then engulfed them.

There were eight of us. Swedish was new, handsome as a red deer, and we knew at first sight that he would be her favorite. Not only because of the prestige of his language, a conduit to her inevitable Nobel Prize, but also because of his saunter, his stance, that gratifying invitation in his hot blue eyes. Because somehow, that evening, Our Author's unshakable husband, Bogdan—whose lust, we believed, worked like kerosene on her authorial imagination—wasn't there.

With Bogdan gone, she was different from how we'd ever seen her. She was ghost-white. She remained immune to shadow, but her eyes were black holes, and it hurt to look into them directly, like we were being torn apart. So we kept our eyes on her crossed arms, but even her arms weren't her arms anymore, exactly— more like twigs half inhumed by her too-heavy, sludge-colored dress. Her neck lacked the onyx amulet she'd been given by her grandfather, the local black magician; without it, her collarbone jutted out like it wanted to break.

She didn't say much; she said nothing about Bogdan. We chalked up all these departures from our routine to the toll of finishing a magnum opus. We felt certain we could help her. Not only because of Swedish, but also because we always had. Now we'd have to: Besides Bogdan, we were the only ones she truly trusted. If he was gone, that meant that all she had was us.

That night we simply tried not to tax her. Soon we adjourned to our usual rooms, while Swedish stayed downstairs with her. We assumed she would put him in Czech's former place in the shed in the backyard. Perhaps if she had, there would have been no fire, no Tempelhof, no old revolvers. But back then we were still in possession of our greatest luxury: never questioning her choices, transmuting the form without so much as touching the substance, or so we believed.

Her staircase was a spiral of oak that dawn brought back to life; the third step up had a knot that brought good luck. We held many superstitions, which we'd teach Swedish in the coming months. We'd learn in turn that he had expert knowledge of much of what was hidden in the forest, underground networks, electric, that we never even knew were there, although we had always belonged to them.

On the third floor, Serbian and Slovenian shared the bedroom with the slanted ceiling and the skylight, two twin beds, and the balcony overlooking Belarus; English occupied the second-floor suite with the sleek tiled stove and private shower, a glass case in the middle of the room; German got the cot in the winter garden, where he'd sleep beneath the upside-down constellations and the Czech chandelier, surrounded by prayer plants and ferns.

The Czech chandelier was made of ten little skulls and too many bones for us to count. The house was filled with storied objects: dark portraits of her ancestors in scalloped, gilded frames; a grand piano, never played; massive chests with cavernous keyholes; a Bozdoğan mace; a solid-bronze candelabra, three feet high, with nine tendriling, gravity-defying arms. Around the living room hung suits of armor that fortified our feeling that her home was our fortress, our defense against the wrongheaded world.

When we were translating, which we did every day except for Sunday, we worked at a table for ten on the third floor; we took all our meals together at an identical table downstairs. When we had time to socialize, we did so in the other downstairs room, the one with the Lotto-like carpet, thick and bloodred with indecipherable black-and-white calligraphy. Atop the carpet were a mustard chaise longue and a ring of seven barrel chairs, bedecked by Bogdan in the orange and pink and blue Punjabi patterns from Our Author's 2007 world tour. That was the room with the fireplace, where later we'd erect her shrine.

Along the mantel, pictures of her as we had known her until now: regal insouciance in a soft red dress, sleeveless, worn without a bra; crouching to nuzzle a rescued bear cub (which legend had it she had rescued herself), her visible cheekbone aglow; gliding through a concrete passageway like a last black orchid bursting into bloom, a splendid endling in some abandoned factory, hurtling into eternity alone.

Pictures of her mother, lost to cancer fifteen years earlier, when Our Author was just twenty-eight. A picture from a winter hunting party, devastating in its desultory black and white.

Her home stood in the village's center, surrounded by red glowing currants, a gigantic stork's nest on its roof. We always wondered, since storks were symbols of fertility, why Our Author and Bogdan never had kids. But we put it down to the demands of stitching up the world's wounds with language, which left no time for any other forms of care.

That night our sleep was heavy, and when she roused us in the morning at a little after five, our dark march toward the strict reserve bled back into our dreams. We passed through an expanse of weeds that reached up to our knees. The birds at that hour were deafening, mustering the forces of the sun. Rumpled from our journeys, our clothes soaked up the dew.

The strict reserve was the most protected part of Białowieża, off-limits to the public. But nothing was off-limits to Irena Rey. At its entrance she turned and pressed her trigger finger to her mouth. Then we all turned in silence to look out over the field. A pale halo on the horizon revealed pine islands, pinkish, awash in a web of fog; the field was filled with tiny starry flowers. We stood stock-still.

The field responded to our quiet in kind, and, satisfied no one was following, we went in.

She'd been convoking us here, on the periphery of Poland, since 2007, the year after she published her third book. A hit in its original language, *Lena* soon gave rise to translations, first into German, then into Czech. That was how we were born, from the foam of a novel called *Lena*.

For the first time since she dropped out of college in Kraków after only a couple of weeks, Our Author started to circulate outside her native voivodeship. She was thirty-two years old. Enchanting at festivals, at conferences, at readings, she was often compared to a żar-ptak, the luminous peacock-like creature of Proto-Slavic myth that offered hope to the beleaguered and guidance to the lost.

Many tried to describe her indescribable aura. Some said it was akin to fine filaments of strummed silver that hovered over her dark cascading hair. Others were reminded of the southern lights, brilliant streaks that hissed across her deep-sky eyes. Still others said her fingers were like holy spinnerets, that her every nimble gesture was an act of brilliant, captivating love.

Irena Rey became a household name. But the more households she entered, the more rumors arose. Some people said she stole her ideas from an obscure Kashubian philosopher; others, from Wikipedia and Bogdan.

Her first book, *Still Life with Still Life*, short stories about the guards at Kraków's Czartoryski Museum, had sold so few copies when it came out in 2000 that almost no trace of it remained, just a low-res image from the "Archives" section of the publisher's website of a cover depicting flames that were devouring a portrait of a woman, likely da Vinci's *Lady with an Ermine*, the most renowned object in that eccentric Polish collection, which also included mummies and an armory until unsolved thefts in the late 1980s forced the folding of those wings.

Published by a different house in 2004, her next book, *Ad Nauseam*, did not fare better. Then she got married, changed the spelling of her last name from the semi-Polish "Rej" to the more international "Rey," wrote an action-packed, heart-wrenching tale of an Albanian girl named Lena trafficked to London whose desperate quest for freedom was hailed by critics as both "scorchingly real" and "chillingly allegorical," and suddenly, everything changed.

A movie was made, and the movie made a fortune. It had everything: sex, guns, scenery—and even more importantly, Irena looked and sounded fabulous promoting it on TV. That was when she built the tallest house in Białowieża. She commissioned an architect from Yokohama to create a home in perfect harmony not with the village, but with the forest, and the result was a jigoku-gumi wonder, a three-story masterpiece of undulating, unscathed oak. It was alive, and it made you feel more alive just to look at it, let alone reside inside it. She never said it in so many words, but we always knew her house had been designed for us, for our work together, as a family.

The reduction of that wonder to rubble and ash, ineluctable in hindsight, was inconceivable that morning as she led us down a curving path deeper into the forest. On either side of us were stinging nettles, a couple of feet deep; past that, slender trunks that bowed under the weight of their fresh foliage. Some of the older trees were fallen, spiked, half covered by mosses, lichens, slime molds in bubblegum pink and neon yellow we could just make out in the escalating light.

Suddenly the tallest trees started to crackle and lick. We felt no wind—down where we were, besides the tits and woodpeckers, the nuthatches and siskins, there was only the quiet drone of tiny insects always on the verge of getting stuck in our eyes. We were ceaselessly swatting at mosquitoes; being in the forest, just like being with Our Author, meant always being on our guard.

In the wake of *Lena*, especially the movie version, trolls went after Our Author's every word. Her next book, 2007's *Kernel of Light*, told the story of a nonbinary scientist who tries to steer clear of corruption at a research station in Antarctica where symbiotic communities of fruticose lichens already taxed by climate change are being decimated in the interest of pharmaceutical research. By this time, everyone either hated or adored Our Author. There was no in-between. *Kernel of Light* prompted thousands of death threats, rape threats, and threats of deportation. It also got her nominated for every literary prize in existence; with the money from the ones she won, she finished furnishing her house, our summiting place, and created a communal account for us to use to pay for flights and trains and bus fare. To Czech and German were added English, Serbian, Spanish, and French. And Catalan, but somewhere between Barcelona and Białowieża, that translator disappeared.

We came to a fork marked by a ragged stump. In Polish, these vegetable wrecks are known as złoms. They are created by rime—the frost formed by fog—or by very strong winds, or by hail. The word "złom" can also mean an old car no one wants, one bound for the scrap heap, or any useless piece of junk, like a washing machine that won't work or a hefty home phone. It is related to the word "załamanie," meaning fracture, crash, collapse. A person who is załamana is psychically broken—like Irena Rey, who stood stooped over the stump as though scrambling to decide how to proceed. Stress shot through our bodies and made our extremities ache; she'd never hesitated in the past, especially not on an opening day, and she had certainly never gotten lost or confused in her own forest.

At last she went left, and we passed through a swamp we knew well, our footsteps resounding on the primitive bridge, unleashing splashing and scampering that shook the primordial ferns. We took deep breaths and were soothed by the scent of urine and stinkhorns and rot.

If you take away the *m*, "złom" becomes "zło," the Polish word for bad, or evil, which would start to feel more apt to us over the coming weeks, when we'd happen on these and other rough-hewn ruins in all the phases of the moon, praying we would find her, leaving no snail, no stone, no scarlet elf cup unturned. We'd come to understand the forest wasn't a place that could be searched like any other place. It was a million unconnected events in the process of connecting, some advancing in time, some going backward. It was as many unentanglings, unpredictable and unstoppable. It was all time condensed into a moment at once so fleeting and so unfathomably vast that if a person wished to disappear in it, there would never be anything anyone could do to recover her.

Unless, of course, she'd never been there in the first place.

But none of that could have occurred to us that morning. We were book people. We had yet to truly concern ourselves with earth.

We came at last to a little clearing, and Our Author positioned herself in front of a massive, ancient oak. Our eyes moved from grass, dirt, and our feet to her feet, and from there up the scant remnants of Our Author's body, past her caved-in face, entering the crevices and ridges that formed the bark's great maze, up, and up, and up, and up, twenty meters to the beginning of its branches, which then shot out in all directions, swerving and spiking and exploding into leaves. Our Author bent and rustled a bundle out of her small olive green backpack, then straightened up and flicked her hair back, leaned against the tree, and cleared her naked throat.

"*Szara eminencja*," she said in a disconsolate gurgle, yet in our minds we invested her voice with our own ecstasy and vigor, made it pronounce this new title in our languages: *Éminence grise, Siva eminenca, Graue Eminenz. Grey Eminence.*[1] But then she didn't read.

When we had translated *Kernel of Light*, and then *Perfection, Matsuura, Sedno I: The Sacher-Masochists, Future Moonscapes of the Eocene, Sedno II: The Hopefuls,* and *Pompeii Catalog,* we had kept to a certain routine. As we had taken our places around our table on the third floor of her home, Irena at its head, presiding, Bogdan had placed a spiral-bound copy of her new manuscript before each of us in turn and pronounced a few discreet words—of welcome, of praise—before leaving us alone together. First she would divulge the title of her latest work. Then she would wait a little for the title to sink in, and we would marvel over it. Then she would read us the first paragraph, which ranged in length from just a couple of words with a semicolon (in the case of *Pompeii Catalog*) to thirty-five pages (in the case of *Perfection*).

She wanted us to translate fresh, uninfluenced by any reviews or propaganda we might read, whether for her or against her. She refused to send her manuscripts to her editor, now at the largest publisher in Poland, until our translations had passed the halfway mark. This meant that Our Author did not write rough drafts, only final ones, and that gave her work an appealing unevenness, akin to the oak bark behind her, that other literary figures' slicker coproductions lacked.

On every previous occasion, after she had finished reading the first paragraph, Our Author would drink. Near her left hand she always kept a glass of mineral water into which Bogdan would release three drops of some dark tincture before leaving us each morning, a procedure he repeated at four in the afternoon. The tincture would sparkle and unfurl, a liquid galaxy, and we'd watch Bogdan watch it with reverence for exactly six seconds before turning sharply toward the door and gliding out of the room to clean or cook or garden, chores he performed with obsequious, lascivious joy, even making our beds despite our protests.

But now there was no tincture, and there was no paragraph, and there would be no made beds, and the absence of a manuscript was a sudden precipice in the forest, as if a fault had yawned open and would swallow us. With her thumb and

---

1 A sizable excerpt of my translation of Irena's novel *Szara eminencja* first appeared in a Romanian magazine that adopted U.K. spelling for all words, including the first word of the title, *Grey*. Perhaps due to the outsize success of that excerpt, the U.S. publisher made the unusual decision to preserve that spelling here (Trans.).

forefinger, Irena made the slightest movement over the oddly shaped bundle she had extracted from her backpack, and the fabric that had covered it fell away, becoming a miniature tablecloth draped over her skeletal hand. Upon this broken table lay a severed hoof.

The air in the clearing, formerly abundant, thinned. We held our breath. We scrutinized her object. It was hideous: deformed and inexplicable.

She said a word in her language—in our shared language—and our minds scrambled, fumbled, failed. We dedicated our lives to understanding her. But all of a sudden, we didn't understand.

She said another word, similar to the first one—something like "hoo," something starting with "hoo"—and then a phrase, but it wasn't a Polish phrase, and none of it made sense to us.[2]

Then she went on, saying something about mushrooms and something about fire. But because we had panicked, we didn't see the connection, however unbelievable it seems to us now, given what came later: the pyre that sank into the snow, the loss of every line from her majestic library; how we took Białowieża's fate into our own hands, creating an ending Irena could never have written, or wouldn't have.

Unless, of course, she did.

When she stopped talking, we all looked around, blinking back confusion. The sun was higher, a white light between the birches that arched and bared their lenticels, shimmering their leaves. The chill in the air had dissipated; the general cacophony had broken into hushes and occasional incontestable shrieks. Then, in the distance, a brief roar became a rumbling, followed by a crash, and to our utter bewilderment, Our Author strangled a sob.

She knelt and rummaged around in her backpack. We tensed, praying she wouldn't reveal a horse's severed head. Instead, she took out eight red velvet pouches and distributed them to us. Each pouch featured a miniature version of the executioner's axe of her family's coat of arms, a familiar symbol that whetted our anxiety now. When she had gone all the way around the circle— when all of us were holding tiny axes embroidered in gleaming purple thread— Irena moved to stand at our center and wait.

---

2   Here I will refrain from making any significant comment, but perhaps it will be useful to the reader to know that the author liberally employs a *very* royal "we" throughout (Trans.).

We tugged at the pristine white cords until they gave. Inside we found lumps of a hard substance the color of sawdust. We looked up at Our Author, at her perfect profile, or her once-lustrous hair, now scraggly, playing host to gray. She didn't offer any explanation. She bowed her head and shed two tears that crashed into the humus, and although we worshipped her, and although we rejoiced in the forest because it was her forest, we were then overtaken by terrors.

First there was the fear that she would fire us, replace us with younger, smarter, faster translators able to supply her the elixir of being fully understood. But then there was something even worse. What if there wasn't any magnum opus? What if the novel *Grey Eminence* was just a hoof and some nuggets of compacted sawdust, and nothing more?

That would mean the end of literature, maybe even of language, at least for the eight of us.

Just then, Swedish turned his back to her. All of us, including Irena, stared. He got down on one knee, making a fist over his red velvet pouch, and with his other hand, he drew back some ferns to reveal a split elm lying rotting on the ground. We squinted.

"Come," he said over his shoulder, smooth. "I can't believe it."

There was a pleasant lilt to his Polish, but as a rule, we rarely ventured comments on anything other than Our Author in the presence of Our Author, and on opening days we didn't usually say anything at all. We glanced at Irena and saw she didn't know how to react, either. Her renewed hesitation made our toes curl up inside our shoes.

Somewhere in the middle distance something snapped. She nodded us forward, but just when we were about to come close enough to see whatever he was enraptured by, Swedish looked up. He smiled at Irena, and we felt her thrill. He held her gaze for a beat, and then another, then reached out blindly for the cadaver of the elm.

He leaped back with a gruff and provocative howl, dangling a snake from his free hand. It was enormous—from head to tail it must have been three feet long—with links like black diamonds up and down its skin, and its belly was bulbous like it had just finished innocently gorging itself on some innocent thing. We screamed and then were paralyzed. After what felt like an eternity but must have been no more than a beat, the viper dropped, coiled with its head cocked back and its jaw still open, hissed, then shot off into the undergrowth.

As one, we rushed to Swedish's side, some of us seizing his uninjured wrist. Someone said, "Let's go," and we all raced back through the forest the same way we'd come. Swedish kept saying he was fine, and it was true upon inspection that the two small points between his right thumb and forefinger barely even bled. But by the time we reached the meadow, large white discs had formed around them, and the back of his hand was swollen, and he told us it was tingling, and then it went numb, and by the time we reached the house, he could no longer move his fingers.

He doubled over in pain in the living room. Two of us stood on either side of him and helped him to the chaise longue, where he reclined while we debated what to do, savoring his emergency proximity. Given what had happened to his predecessor, Czech, we had every reason to fear for his life. Irena had disappeared into her room, and we were looking up clinics and cursing the village's cell service when she returned with a wicker basket of purplish flowers with spiny, ethereal centers and bright floppy leaves.

Irena knelt before Swedish and ordered us to bring her a bottle of sunflower oil, a large bowl, a pestle, and a dish towel. We flew off in all directions after her instructions; when we reassembled, we observed that his whole forearm was swollen, all the way to his elbow, but that he and she were calmly conversing, so softly none of us could hear. She barely broke eye contact with him as she slid her glistening paste over his inflamed and gilded skin.

"Does it hurt?" we finally heard her whisper, and in that moment, she was achingly beautiful, beautiful almost beyond belief: She was warmth, she was moisture, she was light, she was the adamant perfection of a million billion snowflakes in a split second's descent, she was tender, she was eternal, and she was memory, she was love. She was everything we'd ever wanted, all anyone could want in the world. And she was kneeling before him, and he bit his bottom lip and moaned a breathy "mmm."

And yet, at this, Irena fled. We heard her lock her office door. A few minutes later we heard a crash and then a muffled yowl.

We never meant her any harm. How could we have? All we wanted was to follow in her footsteps, making them our own. We were all in love with her. I was in love with her, too.

CHAPTER TWO

It was noon now. After our unsettling meander in the forest, we were hungry, but we didn't mention it. I had searched for "hoo" words all over the internet and consulted the ancient volumes on her living room shelves, but so far the only thing I'd found was an entry for "huba," which meant polypore, and that seemed to be a red herring, because according to Google a polypore was a "fungus that releases its spores through its pores" which sounded both disgusting and irrelevant.

Yet it was soothing to be sitting at our working table at the top of Our Author's curving house, Swedish in Czech's seat to the immediate left of Irena's, waiting for her to emerge. We all clung to the hope that our summit might yet resume its usual course. We didn't speak, and we didn't look at one another, but we were nonetheless unable to keep from sensing the throbbing of Swedish's hot, pomiform hand.

We were affected by Our Author's style, which coursed through us as though it were our own, and as we felt the beat, beat, beat of Swedish's blood, we made the connection Irena might have made if this had been a scene she'd written: Swedish's engorgement reignited our grief over Czech.

Our colleague Czech had been killed in a freak accident in 2014. Something to do with electrocution, we never found out what. It wasn't in the papers in Prague or even Uničov, where—as we learned upon his death—Czech was from. Irena was the one to let us know, in person, when we gathered together to embark upon her *Pompeii Catalog*.

It was a major blow to us, and although she never so much as hinted at it, we didn't doubt it was a worse blow to her. If anything, Irena wanted more translators, never fewer. She most earnestly desired translation into Japanese. Many of her favorite writers, the people she considered her peers, hailed from that country where she had never, she told us one evening over delicate cabbage-swathed groats, existed. After losing Czech, we tried to recover our equilibrium by reaching out to our Japanese colleagues, inviting them to our next primeval summit, but in the end, alas, none came.

It was in the midst of *Pompeii* that Our Author issued her famous ultimatum (made famous by an interview that English gave): either we could translate her and no one else,[3] or we could draw upon the whole of Polish literature, with the exception of any of her past or future works. According to Irena's teachings, intelligence is the ability to choose between, and on this point we were instantly intelligent, or at least as smart as slime molds, whose pulsating pathfinding is able to rival the accomplishments of human engineering, despite the fact that slime molds don't have brains.

We knew something about slime molds because Irena had described them in *Perfection*. They were gooey, variously colored beings that formed expert maps over tiny serpentine terrains, including here in Białowieża, where many slime molds existed that existed nowhere else. They were a favorite of Japan's longest-reigning emperor, who, born just two years after Borges, shared with my compatriot a love of labyrinths. Borges wasn't in Irena's book, of course—no other authors ever were. But what was mentioned—I remember when I first came across it, sitting at our working table between English and French, because I read it again right away, in wonder—was that if you tear apart a slime mold, even if you shred it into a thousand tiny pieces, it will always coalesce again. All it takes is time.

Even now, I sometimes picture the emperor, alone in his lab, sundering his slime molds just to watch them heal. I wonder if he ever hoped they wouldn't— if he wanted to invent an unsurmountable rupture, if that seemingly impossible achievement might have made him feel more whole.

---

3 I would note (as I noted in the interview alluded to here) that Irena almost immediately softened this sentence to permit us to translate two poets: Miron Białoszewski (1922–1983), known as the Polish "poet of linguistics," and Bolesław Leśmian (1877–1937), the forest-worshipping mythmaker and renewer of sacred and secular lore called by one critic "the ultimate and overwhelming proof of the untranslatability of poetry," an assessment that, for some reason, no one has disputed in the decades since (Trans.).

Perfection was the first book we had all—aside from Swedish—translated together. Only sitting waiting for Irena on September 21, 2017, did it occur to me that even if there was a magnum opus, someday, there would have to be a last book, too.

But all of a sudden Our Author was here—she'd come up out of her office and blown into the room, smelling pleasingly like petrichor—and she appeared more collected, or sturdier, at least; her ribbed brown dress that hit just below the knee even seemed to fit her better, as if it issued from her instead of merely overhanging her, although its ballerina neckline continued to emphasize the absence of her grandfather's black magic ring. She might have been in crisis, but some people flourish in crisis, and we had always assumed that she'd be one of them. She was holding three thin pages that were covered in words. So there *was* a book to translate—here was its beginning—and our bellies' anxious rumblings were quelled.

"Over the course of its more than ten-thousand-year lifespan," she proclaimed, "Białowieża Forest has offered shelter not only to Europe's sole surviving megafauna and the royals who legislated its exclusive use, but also to boreal owls, dwarf marsh violets, black storks, gray wolves, snakes (as we have witnessed), the world's only population of *Agrilus pseudocyaneus*, around two hundred types of moss, two hundred eighty-three kinds of lichens, and over eighteen hundred fungal species, of which nine hundred forty-three are classified as being at risk. Of which two hundred can be found nowhere else in Poland. I am *saying* that there are *two hundred* different kinds of fungi here in Białowieża that are, everywhere else, probably already extinct."

She scanned our faces. "This is not the novel," she admonished us, and our gazes scattered, and the thick glass distorted the shapes of the small objects in the cabinets arranged around the room, turning seashells into goiters, little books into hunchbacks, teacups into death caps. Swedish's hand was on the table near the loose coil of beige gauze it had just shed.

Scowling, she went on: "What I am trying to tell you is that Białowieża lost its last endemic bison to German soldiers, Polish poachers, or Soviet rogues in the winter of 1919. This has everything to do with the novel, but it isn't the novel." She wrung her once-beautiful hands, looked back up at us, and squeaked, "I never should have written the novel."

And yet at this there was general elation. She had openly admitted it: The novel existed. She simply wasn't ready to share it with us yet. All that mattered was that we wouldn't return empty-handed to the clamoring world.

None of her previous books had ever elicited half as much eagerness or speculation. The Polish press had been host to vicious disputes over whether Irena's new work would be poetry or prose (this despite the fact that she had never written poetry). Critics from around the world had conjectured: Maybe it would be a VR drama! Maybe a sculptural sound piece. Maybe an exhibit of radical textiles at a museum she'd once mentioned in Makassar, Indonesia, or maybe just a handkerchief.

Readers favored simpler explanations. Perhaps, they hoped, confiding in Twitter, Irena's next project would be *Sedno III*, the volume that would finally resolve the many tensions between the Hopefuls and the Sacher-Masochists at the end of *Sedno II*. But we knew *Sedno* was no trilogy. And the last time we'd seen her, she had shared with us the thrilling secret that she was writing something pertaining to art and extinction. "Art and extinction," she had said—we all, aside from Swedish, recalled her putting it that way.

Strictly speaking, as her translators, our part was to wait, and not to hazard guesses. But we were defenseless against discussing other people's guesses in our Team Irena WhatsApp group.

Irena had always taken legible pleasure in the connections between text and textile, so we knew the new book could have to do with fabric, as the critics had said, and that it was possible to combine prose (or poetry) and fabric, and even to combine this combination with art and extinction. She might, we thought, be writing about fast fashion's long-term tolls on the environment, or embroidering Sumerian words like "bir" (to wreck, to weep, to murder) onto corrective canvases in madder and myrobalan threads.

German, who could be a bit of a provocateur, suggested in our group chat that Irena's next work might be about extinct techniques from other forms of art—daguerreotypes or Mayan trumpets—or that she might be making huge new cave paintings of woolly mammoths: "A translation," he added, "of sorts."

I answered at once that Irena would never knowingly engage in translation, or in any other way conflate our idyllically defined respective roles. No one responded to me until several days later, when Slovenian sent a picture of a hideous frigate bird, which Ukrainian, for some reason, called "cute."

We all believed Irena could be working on something about warfare.[4] She had always been curious about biological warfare, berserkers, and, to a lesser extent, chemical warfare. Then there was tectonic warfare, but that subject struck us as unlikely for a few reasons, not least of which was her recent ban on any talk about the weather.

In spite of ourselves, we came up with a variety of notions, from screenplays to ceramics to terrariums to haiku, examples of each of which have since been attributed to her. But what we had always hoped for, for the sake of our careers and hers, was the Great Polish Novel,[5] and now that we were sure she'd written it, our cares burned off like fog from the forest at dawn.

Yet now she stood, ripped up all her pages, threw them in our faces, and screamed: "Białowieża isn't a place! Don't you get that? It's a network!" She was pacing, wringing her hands. "Remove the trees, and you sever every link! I haven't slept once since they started chopping down the spruce trees in the spring! Are you not aware of what's been happening? Have you not been moved?" She grabbed her head, and I grimaced since it looked to me like she was going to rip her hair out. But then she sank back down into her chair and whimpered, "What are we going to do?"

Perhaps there had been times we wished her husband wasn't there, but this was not one of them. We'd been jealous of Bogdan, though not exactly in the way people would conclude nearly a decade later, after some unfledged U.S. journalist happened on our Instagram and took it literally and reposted our video from Halloween in an article on literary sex scandals, no doubt in desperation to add a woman to the list. But we were her translators; everything was metaphor, was transference, with us.

---

4   I will also note that by the date of this novel's original publication, Irena's book-length analysis of Russia's full-scale invasion of Ukraine had already been released, in its entirety, by means of Substack, although for some reason the author of *Extinction* (or *Amadou*) chose not to acknowledge this (Trans.).

5   The "Great Polish Novel" had, by 2017, already been written, repeatedly, by Bolesław Prus (for instance, *The Doll*), Witold Gombrowicz (for example, *Pornografia*), and maybe even Stanisław Lem (although I haven't really read his books), as well as Nobel laureates Henryk Sienkiewicz (*With Fire and Sword*), Czesław Miłosz (*The Captive Mind*, which isn't a novel, but which offers the intellectual and emotional satisfaction of a novel), and Olga Tokarczuk (*The Books of Jacob*), who received her 2018 Nobel in 2019, when we were sure it would go to Irena, in light of her harrowing journey in 2017 (Trans.).

It is true that we had coveted her husband's access to her. We'd wished we could be by her side at every moment, maybe especially when she lay in the dark, defenseless, submitting to her dreams—to the parts of her that even she could not fully write. Some of us had gone so far as to say they couldn't see what she saw in him. That he was crude and undeserving and already losing his hair. Yet how all of us longed for Bogdan now, to deliver her tincture, to reassure her, restore her to the voice of reason and consistent and coherent inspiration she had always been, at least since *Lena*.

"Think of the lynx," Our Author exhorted us, and we dutifully pictured bright eyes and ornamented ears. But we couldn't figure out what to do with the lynx once we had pictured them, and, like morning fog, little by little, they evanesced.

For a long time she said nothing, and none of us knew what to say. Some of us had put our hand-stitched executioners' axes in our pockets; some of us held them on our laps. German later told us that he had silently played himself four songs from an album by a punk band called Planlos, inwardly rocking his body and mouthing the words while outwardly remaining as still as an origami crane.

Serbian said she'd imagined us emptying our pouches one by one onto the middle of the table, making a pile of sawdust lumps that our touch would transform into nuggets of gold, creating a radiant, dazzling Babel that would scatter her sentences, make them one with the air. That the air would be thick with heat and ruin, but that eventually, it would clear, and that when it did, Our Author would be gone, or rather invisible, shooting up to the height of that great oak inside the strict reserve, through the roof, snapping the wires, vaporizing the stork's nest, becoming a hovering, haunting omniscience, a thunderstriking cloud.

I told everyone that I'd imagined something similar, but really what I thought about that day was Swedish, how if he and I were alone in that room, I would perch atop the table right in front of him and take his hand in my hands and suck his swollen fingers, keeping my eyes on his.

"Think of the fungi," whispered Irena, and our gazes returned to her face. "Fungi are the epitome of evil, feasting on—rejoicing in—the deaths of everyone and everything around them. How many species of frog have been led to the brink of extinction by some fungus?! How many species of bat?" She looked at me, and I didn't know if I was supposed to answer, and I didn't know the answer, and then she looked at French.

"Many?" French ventured. "Many species?"

Seemingly satisfied, Irena went on: "Yet they are a necessary evil because fungi *consume death*. Fungi make the forest possible. Without them, death would amass, death would obliterate life, leading to far more extinctions, perhaps a mass extinction; but now, without the bodies of the trees to eat—without the dead-wood—how will the fungi survive?"

Most of us were paralyzed, terrified of saying the wrong thing. Most of us were disoriented, too. Yet German, deferring to his inner punk perhaps, managed to speak. He cleared his throat, brought his thumb and middle finger together over his mustache, and, in a tremulous, half-muffled voice, ventured: "Is *Grey Eminence* about . . ."

We watched him watch her. We watched her, too. She didn't move, didn't take her eyes off the ring-stained surface of our table, the place where we'd performed and compared our performances of seven of her brilliant prior works. At the same time, Swedish's disfigured hand rose slightly, and ever so slightly, it ventured toward hers. An electric charge ran through us: Suddenly one of us was holding her hand.

Then German finished: "Białowieża?"

Around the room went a sigh of relief: He hadn't mentioned the daguerreo-types or asked about the Mayan trumpets—hadn't betrayed our illicit specu-lations. But at the same time, we were stunned that one of us was guiding her, helping her search for her own words. It was the opposite of translation—it was an unthinkable act—yet for a moment she looked grateful, and the world was on the verge of overturning, but then she recoiled, releasing German from her gaze and Swedish from her fingers as she leaped out of her chair, sending it crashing backward, and then she cried, "I can't! Can't you see I can't?" And she ran out of the room and down the spiral staircase and back into her office, slamming the door.

Our hearts were pounding. For a few beats we sat perfectly still. Eventually, we blinked at each other like we'd just been released from a spell.

CHAPTER THREE

All of us were racked with guilt. It was the second time in a span of only hours that we, or Swedish, had driven her away. It was more power than we should have had, more than we had ever had before, and we yearned for the bright unmistakable commands she had so magnanimously issued over the course of summits past.

We worshipped her. That was the truth. The other truth was: This was our job. If she didn't give us her novel to translate, it would mean that we were unemployed. Some of us had other mouths to feed: Ukrainian had a wife with a penchant for misadventures, not to mention a dog; Serbian's profligate daughter was now at the University of Niš. I had parents who would never let me hear the end of it if I became a failure, and if I failed, I would be forced to move in with one of them, probably my mom, and my mom would keep haranguing me with diagnoses—depression, anxiety, *malaise*—stock the fridge with probiotic yogurts, lettuce heads, Rutini chardonnay, and nothing else.

For a while we stayed at the table, praying for forgiveness or refreshing her semisecret personal Facebook page. She hadn't posted in three weeks. All her official social media was paused, as it always was when she was writing or preparing to launch a new book. Finally we googled "spruce Białowieża 2017."

This was the kind of investigation we knew how to conduct. Our lives away from her were spent almost entirely online, researching and double-checking, and sure enough, we soon turned up an explanation, or at least a set of facts.

First: On March 25 of the previous year, Jan Szyszko,[6] Poland's minister of the environment, announced a plan to triple Białowieża's logging limits; prior to our investigation, none of us had realized there was logging in Białowieża at all. According to Greenpeace Poland, the 3,100 square kilometers of the forest were divided on the Polish side—which was 41 percent of the total forest—into 17 percent national park, 19 percent nature preserve, and 64 percent government-managed forest that could be cut down within limits that had been all but eliminated now.

By contrast, in Belarus, Europe's last dictatorship,[7] 100 percent of the Białowieża Forest was a national park. The strict reserve section, where you couldn't go without a guide, was nine times larger than its Polish counterpart. Our understanding of all this would be completely transformed four years later, when Belarus would turn their strict reserve into a slow killing field for mostly Kurdish refugees and migrants, but on the day of our investigation, that other side of the border struck us as a kind of promised land we couldn't believe we'd never visited or even known about before.

Second: The reason, or the pretext, for the policy change was that spruce bark beetles had overrun the forest. Their remarkable proliferation wasn't in dispute. What people disagreed about was how it had happened and how to handle it.

According to the Szyszko camp, infestations were eternally recurring, and they were best confronted head-on: All affected trees and any trees liable to be affected—in other words, the whole of the spruce population in the forest—would be cut down. Without anywhere to live or anything to feed on, the beetles would simply disappear. Oak, a symbol of the Polish people, more resilient and more beloved, would be planted in the spruces' stead. It was a simple, routine operation that would produce immediate results.

According to the small but vocal opposition, however, this particular infestation was new, the result of a changing climate that was drying up the local swamps. Spruces fend off insects by crying—that's how it looked to

---

6 Pronounced "Yan Shishko," the second as in "shish kebab" (Trans.).

7 Unless you count Russia, which this author does not (not because she thinks of Vladimir Putin as anything other than a dictator, but because she doesn't think Russia counts as being *in Europe*, she says because the bulk of it is physically in Asia) (Trans.).

us—terpene-laden resin that was toxic to spruce bark beetles, not to mention
sticky enough to trap smaller insects that might be trying to get inside their
trunks.

But spruces can't protect themselves this way if they're dehydrated. By 2017,
Białowieża was hotter and drier than it had been in ten thousand years. Thus,
the opposition argued, the infestation. But according to them the solution
wasn't—couldn't possibly be—to eradicate all spruces from the forest. The forest
had always found a way to heal itself, but in order to do so, it had to have biodi-
versity: a variety of plants, animals, and fungi that only in cooperation with each
other were able to perpetuate the cycle of life. No one species could do this on
its own; no two or three species could, either. The opposition alleged that the
government knew this, and knew that the only meaningful actions that could
be taken were long term—with nothing immediately resulting—like reducing
dependence on energy derived from dead plants and animals that was slowly
ending life on Earth. The government claimed it knew no such thing, that like
everybody else it was already working on sourcing sustainable energy, and that
no one was buying spruce wood, which was too soft and too susceptible to rotting,
and so the debate went around and around.

At approximately three P.M., we admitted we were starving, and we heaved
ourselves downstairs. Bogdan had always overseen our meals, and there had
always been three of them, with an afternoon tea. We did not yet feel authorized
to make a meal, so we scrounged around Irena's kitchen for the ingredients for
tea. In the back of the pantry we found two packages of rice crackers, some pickled
beets, and an enormous container of bright green powder we hoped was matcha.
All along the counter there were tulip jars with grayish mushrooms floating in
icy water—but where had she gotten the ice? We took the crackers and the pickles
pickles and put the kettle on.

Then we sat around the living room and waited, wilting in the wildly inap-
propriate late-September heat, not that we could talk about the weather. The
armor gleamed beside the fireplace, like the silver escutcheons on the giant
wooden chests behind our barrel chairs that kept our arms stiff and extended,
and the thick sheets of glass that every afternoon shielded the portraits of her
ancestors from view.

At seven, German said we couldn't go on like this, and we needed to at least
make dinner. Such was the speed of our early metamorphoses: In four hours, we

had gone from deeming dinner completely and totally out of the question to believing it the least we could do, to even imagining it was *what she would have wanted*. Yet such changes were invisible to us: We were too turned around, too hot, like our true selves had melted and our molten selves were too preoccupied with finding a new form.

While Swedish rested, and English rested for some reason, too, German charged Serbian and Slovenian with slicing up the mushrooms from the counter while French made a sofrito and German and Ukrainian folded up German's cot and spread a simple white cotton cloth over our dining table. I hovered and hesitated, unintelligent, helpless until German instructed me to set out the silverware.

Let the record show that we did not serve wine. We never drank alcohol in Białowieża because we found Our Author intoxicating enough, and because she herself did not drink, and we wanted to follow her in everything as best we could. She was a vegetarian, so when we were with her, we also ate no meat. We shared almost all of her opinions since it was mandatory not to disagree.

We scoured her spice rack for paprika. We hoped the aroma would reach her, making its way under her door, and when our plan worked, we got giddy. At eight we were serving her the socarrat, which was the only part of a risotto she would eat, even at restaurants, even when it meant Bogdan having to have words with the waiter, or the manager, or the chef. As we chattered merrily we noticed, despite being oblivious to our own alterations, that she seemed changed again: Her hair was still pulled back, but it was looser, and her cheeks were flushed. Her eyes didn't seem to want to focus, and she ate with unusual appetite, like an animal, instead of elegantly absorbing her meal the way she always had before.

One by one we fell silent as she regaled us with gossip from the upper echelons of world culture: the feud between the famous painter and the famous dancer; the mind-numbing receptions; the cigarettes; the sycophants; the Polish snails they'd tried to serve her at the Palacio de Cristal in Madrid. The Hungarian author of melancholy novels whose reputation for complexity would be ruined if the public ever got a glimpse of him guffawing in the greenroom, sniffing his schnapps and spitting pits into a portly woman's palm; the skinny Egyptian violinist who tore off his clothes—every last scrap of fabric—and dove into the ice-cold Atlantic; the woman from *Ham&High* who followed Irena back to her hotel room one night after a gala, stroking Our Author's lustrous black hair and trying to say something meaningful about Chernobyl, repeating words like "regrettable" and "doomed."

Irena had never talked to us this way, so heedlessly, and on such mundane topics; although we felt uncomfortable, we hung upon her every word. She'd never asked us to go with her to any important ceremonies or other events—but what if, without Bogdan, she would want us to accompany her now? Bogdan hadn't made a single appearance in her stories that evening, which made it seem like she might be in the process of erasing him from the living draft of her biography—unless he really hadn't gone with her to London or Cartagena or Jaipur.

Over ice cream she and Swedish had a hushed conversation while the rest of us clanged our spoons against her heavy Bolesławiec stoneware, glaring at each other and the careening and convulsing shadows that overpopulated the winter garden's panes. Then Swedish—although it seemed impossible—quietly began to cry, and Irena swiveled in her chair and flipped her hair and called across the table to German, whose eyes darted from Ukrainian to Swedish to me and then at last to her.

"You mentioned your partner," said Our Author, leaning back. She reached behind her and took an African violet off the shelf. She set it down on the white cloth in front of her, still immaculate but for a couple of dots of reddish oil. Then she put the pot at English's elbow, produced a pack of cigarettes, lit one, and leaning in over the filthy wet clay saucer, began to smoke.

This was the most shocking action she had taken yet. Until now, Irena had always been immune to peccadilloes. Only weak, only sad people—only people like, occasionally, in general in secret, me—still smoked cigarettes in 2017. I looked back at German, who was nodding wide-eyed. None of us knew a thing about his partner. None of us was able to fathom the direction this might take.

"Am I remembering correctly that he's a well-placed official in the city of Berlin?"

"Yes?" German said, squeezing in his shoulders.

"That he holds keys, various keys, keys of strategic significance—isn't that also correct?"

German nodded again, but his eyes, which were greenish, flecked with gold, betrayed a dense perplexity.

Irena transferred her cigarette to her left hand, exhaled emphatically in Swedish's direction, and plunged her spoon into her ice cream.

"Is there any invention more deleterious to the forest than that of lock and key?" asked Our Author, pulling the clean spoon upside down from her mouth. Her lips shimmered in the light of the Czech chandelier.

That she was simultaneously eating ice cream and smoking a cigarette was almost too much for us to bear. But also: Was she suggesting that German's partner was responsible for the logging in the Białowieża Forest somehow? Or was she saying that he was the one who would somehow save the forest, with his strategically significant keys?

"In the Neo-Assyrian Empire, a key was a shaft of wood," Our Author continued, her gaze settling on Slovenian. "It looked like an *F*, but with more cross strokes. It could 'unlock' a set of wooden pins by simply forcing them out of the way. Our keys are cards, or strings of numbers and letters. With any luck, perhaps the key—the concept of 'key'—will go extinct someday." She took a drag off her cigarette and watched her small remaining globule of vanilla as it slumped into a pond. Then she shook her head three times quickly, and, to my terror and to my delight, she looked at me.

"Yours is a director," she said. I had no idea how she knew this.

"Oh. He—he was. I mean, he is. My ex-boyfriend. We broke up."

It was as if her former spirit reentered her wasted body. She rose in her chair, enveloped all of us in the resurrecting gaze that was one of her hallmarks, and clapped her hands. "Ars nova!" she said as she stood, stamped out her cigarette, and exited the winter garden.

In the vacuum she left in her wake we looked at each other as though one of us might know what to do. I was glad to be able to parse the two words this time, to identify the boundary between them, although that didn't mean that I knew what she meant. Someone got up, and then all of us did.

Irena stood aglow before the empty fireplace, and I saw for the first time the dust on the mantel, in between and on top of the photographs she again resembled, but for the fact that she was taller, suddenly more definite, almost more herself now than she had ever been before.

"Stay," she told us and left the room again! The sounds of wind and heavy hooves, maybe elk hooves, filtered into the room through a slim upper window.

I was closest, but I couldn't decide if I should shut it or not. I folded my hands
and spun my thumbs four times. The first thing I saw when I looked up again
was the mace that faced the stairs. Carefully skirting a wobbly stack of old boards,
I went and shut the window.

Then Irena was back, handing out pieces of paper, sheets of music only some
of us could read:

> Sans cuer dolens de vous departiray
> Et sans avoir joie jusqu'au retour
> Puis que mon corps dou vostre a partir ay
> Sans cuer dolens de vous departiray

As a Spanish speaker, I was able to piece together the gist. Someone (the narrator)
was having to leave (for some reason) someone they loved. I imagined Irena had
chosen this song for our choral debut because of Bogdan, but there wasn't time
to puzzle out the clue because already she was raising a little black rod.

"Ukrainian, piano please," she said tightly, and we became aware that we
should have arranged ourselves already, and as we shuffled and turned and
bumped into one another, not knowing how to be, Irena started singing.

We had never heard her sing before, but if anyone had ever asked, we would
have answered that hers would have to be the magical, mellifluous voice of an
angel, or a delicate, energetic soprano, or the Demiurge on beholding the freshly
fashioned world. In reality, however, she sounded wobbly, frail, uncertain of the
tune and of the words' pronunciation. She held notes at random and skipped
over half of the second line. Her voice broke at the end of the fourth line, which
was also the first line, but she didn't seem to notice because when she was done
she picked up her rod again and waited for us to stand still and watch her, then
stabbed at the air.

Ukrainian, it turned out, could play the piano, which stunned us by working
and by being in tune. Slovenian was the one with the angelic voice, and the more
we heard her, the quieter the rest of us fell, even when Our Author was pointing
right at us.

Oh, Irena. At first our disobedience was just confusion. I've always wondered
if you, in all your wisdom, realized that.

The piece was polyphonic, or at least it was intended to be, as I learned when I googled it later that night. But our performance wasn't polyphonic so much as completely uncoordinated, a collision and collapse of voices, then a solo by Slovenian, normally the quietest of us all.

When we were finished, Irena bowed her head, and there was another long silence, and I wished I hadn't closed the window, but to open it now would be to admit I had misgauged the situation, misunderstood once more. Then Our Author *lit another cigarette*, announced she was going to *give Swedish a tour of her office*, and wished us a good night.

We—all but Slovenian and Serbian—scrubbed the dishes, including the saucer, which disgusted us, and threw away the unused mushrooms, which had turned from white to black and gotten sticky on the cutting board. We scraped the chairs against the walls. We had never seen the inside of her office. We dragged our feet. Some of us had jet lag. None of us could sleep.

At 2:37 A.M. we all got an email from Our Author with a subject line of "Do not open." The message's body was blank. Attached was a document ninety-three megabytes in size.

CHAPTER FOUR

O n Borges Street, in the heart of Buenos Aires, amid the tipa and lapacho trees and the low sea green and baby blue and canary yellow buildings frosted at the top like fancy colonial cakes, amid the whoosh of buses and the whir of failing motorbikes, amid parrots and rats, there stands a cold gray compound called the Casa Polaca, or the Polish House. Throughout my late twenties, my favorite place in the city was not the thrumming auditoriums of the university where I was learning a history of literature (one that included no Polish), or the little cinemas where my friends and I camped out each Saturday, or any of the many apartments in Recoleta or Belgrano or Villa Crespo where I'd go through the motions of one- or two-night stands, but rather that imposing institution, a house like a colossal spaceship that managed to preserve its extraterrestrial gravity by keeping itself almost hermetically sealed.

To get inside the heavy gate, you had to ring an unmarked, solitary bell, and most of the time, no one answered. The summer of my parents' divorce, I went three humid crumbling afternoons in a row, rang the bell again and again without having any clue what I would do if admitted: where to go once I got past the gate, whether anyone inside would want to speak to me and whether they spoke Spanish, and most of all, what I would tell them if they did. All I knew was that I would have sold my very soul for peace and quiet, for rest, for shade, for gray, for stillness. On the third day I went to the Casa Polaca, a pale middle-aged woman stepped up in kitten heels and unlocked the gate with a look of stern displeasure, and as I walked inside that frigid courtyard under her reproving gaze, everything quieted inside me, and all the tension I had been carrying around with me, the headache I had had since December, dissolved.

That was how I fell in love with Poland, with Polishness, with Polish. Polish washed over me, and I emerged absolved. It was barely six months later, on one of the rare occasions I was allowed into the library after my grammar and vocabulary lessons with that reassuringly disagreeable woman, that I came across the novel *Lena*, by a writer no one in Argentina had ever heard of named Irena Rey. On the basis of the author photo alone, I admit, I borrowed it.

We must have all had stories like this about how we arrived at Our Author. But when we were together, we didn't think of ourselves as individuals with histories—not yet. We had always been connected to each other by fine, feeling filaments that had no origin, and we had no stable hierarchies or particular ambitions beyond translating her work. It was as though we were a single organism—Irena's entourage—whose sole purpose was to conquer eight new realms in her name.

But now, with the exception of a moment before the fireplace the previous night, Irena Rey seemed to be breaking down, and Swedish knew things that we didn't and didn't know things that we did, and the sparks I had detected between him and Our Author—who belonged to us all—as well as the document she'd sent named "BEZ TYTUŁU," or "UNTITLED," were unnerving, and they unraveled us into separate sets of questions.

The next day Swedish was still swollen and clammy and pallid with bright crimson patches, and he said he thought he needed "actual medical care," but it did not occur to us to take him to the doctor. Our Author had told us he'd be fine. He said the pain came in waves, and that he hadn't slept. He also said, to our astonishment, that in the middle of the night Irena had communicated to him *through the wall* that she was sorry but that she wouldn't be able to join us that morning, or at any other point that day. He then admitted that he didn't remember for certain if she had specified "that day."

Czech had always been a little bit of a liar, but we hadn't held it against him at the time. As we understood it, that was just who he was. He was a goofball, and our memories of him—his striped polos that were always a size or two too big, his lousy jokes,[8] his shiny head—were fond. For all we knew, he'd died the

---

8   In light of the fact that puns are the one category of language that is truly untranslatable, I have had to remove this author's subsequent examples (Trans.).

way he'd lived, meaning that even the story of his electrocution had been some kind of harebrained lie. Perhaps he'd had a heart attack, or skydived with a faulty parachute, or been run over by a bus.

But we did hold those lies against Swedish that morning as we examined and cross-examined him and wondered how we could compel him to tell us the truth. Had he not slept because of his snakebite, or had he not slept because he'd been in bed with her? Had she communicated to him through the wall, or had she whispered in his ear?

Heightening the tension was the fact that we were now facing the biggest decision of our professional lives: Were we going to open the document or not?

What if it was *Grey Eminence*, the book we assumed was going to change and maybe even save the world? Shouldn't we go ahead and get started, particularly if it was as complex and magnificent as its file size seemed to suggest? *Kernel of Light*—the original and our translations—had led to the EU-wide Lichen Protection Act of 2010; *Pompeii Catalog* had ushered in a mass movement across social platforms on behalf of the written word, in all its forms and all its vulgarity, in our languages and many more thanks to grassroots translation efforts that included Norwegian and Nahuatl.

But we couldn't say that. We couldn't say any of it. As translators, we were accustomed to muting our own voices. But after what had happened in the forest and at our working table and at the dinner table and when we had tried to sing, after we had consistently failed to comprehend her, our shame crept into our silence, and our silence seemed to drag on and on, gathering in angst. So began the longest day of our lives.

Finally English, with her bracelets that glinted and clanged as she spoke, offered, "It's so hot today already."

Needless to say, it was the worst thing she could have said. Some of us had been affected by floods since the last time we'd met, some of us badly. German's Datsche had been destroyed by a derecho. Serbian and Swedish had experienced earthquakes, Slovenian a drought followed by multiple mutations of a bird flu that had done nothing to dampen her ornithological zeal but that had almost prevented her from being here with us. Out of compassion—or so we believed—Irena had forbidden all talk about the weather several months before.

It would have been odd for English to forget something like that, an outright ban. But it was too early in our fracturing to think it was deliberate, that she hadn't forgotten it at all.[9]

Serbian made a fist over her mouth and retched. Then we resumed our dread-filled silence, mitigated only by the buzz of a housefly as it attempted to penetrate a windowpane, until one of us lashed out and killed it. Another metamorphosis: We had never killed anything here before. The people we were today might already be unrecognizable to the people we had been two days ago. I felt for the tiny wings of my right earring, pressing its spiked post into my thumb.

At around eleven A.M., we all wandered up Stoczek Street toward Palace Park, where there was a small store that sold berries and essentials, a pizzeria we had never visited or ordered from, and the village's one bank. Somewhat dazed, we lingered at the entrance to the pizzeria before entering the store. Serbian, Slovenian, and Ukrainian busied themselves pondering the fruit, while French and I perused the shiny wrappers of the different cookie brands, and English reached around us for ugly whole-grain crackers and tiny cereal bars, sounding her gaudy wrists. German and Swedish were still standing in the alcove with the beer fridge when French and English and I stepped back out onto the street.

When we opened Irena's front door again, we found a clump of jagged spikes on the floor before us—English nearly pranced directly onto it, but Serbian stopped her by lunging for her foot and wrenching it away from the danger. English howled as though Serbian had ripped her whole foot off. I rolled my eyes and squatted down to investigate. It was rusty and gnarled, with one spike sticking straight up from a rough tripod made out of additional spikes.

"How did this get here?" I asked. I was about to say something else, but then I worried they might think I was the one who had installed it—worried I had been too hasty in speaking in the first place.

"Did it fall?" asked Ukrainian, glancing around with his hands partly covering his face.

"I have never seen any such artifact here before," said German. "Have any of you?"

---

9   I actually had forgotten, but honestly, I don't know which this author would consider worse (Trans.).

We shook our heads and squinted.

"Maybe we just didn't notice it," said Slovenian, who had been more talkative since starring in our bad rondeau. "Maybe there was always a caltrop in Irena's entryway, and we forgot about it *because* it was always right here."

"You think we forgot there was a thing that skewers feet in front of the *front door*?" English snapped, still a little flustered. Slovenian pursed her lips and bent down, touching the twisted iron with a single fingertip, then picking it up between two fingers like it was a piece of trash. Slovenian smelled oddly masculine—I caught a sudden whiff of her then—like cedar and allspice.

For reasons unbeknownst to me, English started laughing.

"Wait," she said. "Don't move." She wiped the lens of her phone off with her flouncy purple skirt, took a picture of Slovenian and the Roman caltrop, then submerged herself in a barrel chair and opened Instagram.

"We're not supposed to post until the book is done!" I shrieked. English had narrowly avoided one peril only to hurtle toward another much more dire: Our Author was the sole member of our household who was allowed to post to social media in the middle of a summit; breaking this rule—which we had never done before—would be like asking to be banished. English sighed, set down her phone, and rolled her eyes.

We ate, in pairs or individually, and waited for Irena to emerge. All kinds of paranoid ideas deluged us. What if we had already been banished, and we just didn't know it yet? What if, as we were waiting, strewn across our unmade beds or slumped over ottomans, Irena was summoning translators better versed in ecological horror—translators who knew whether that was a genre or not—and at any minute they'd burst in and send us packing, back to Belgrade, to Paris, to Ljubljana, to Berlin?

I pictured myself slinking down Borges Street, coming to the gate of the Casa Polaca, ringing to no avail. It was *barely* spring in the southern hemisphere, and Buenos Aires was not yet soft, or sumptuous, or purple.[10]

What if we never saw Irena again?

It was the longest day of our lives until the following day, when no one heard from her at all. We spent the whole morning, and then the whole afternoon,

---

10   I wasn't sure what this meant at first, but when I asked this author to explain it, she sent me a picture of a city that resembled a cross between Little Rock and Paris awash in jacaranda blooms (Trans.).

sitting around, repeatedly peeling our clothes off our skin, the weight of our muted inertia pressing in on us from everywhere and squeezing out more sweat, until English organized a Bikram yoga session in the winter garden, and I went upstairs. Or until the day after that, when the crows woke us up with such a raucous frenzy that we all ran out onto the sidewalk trying to identify the cataclysm. Soon we spotted them on a wire, fifty or so screaming at the tops of their lungs.

It appeared to be coordinated, like the chorus in a tragedy. We looked at each other, but by that time we'd refused to say so many things that it felt almost impossible to speak at all. Slovenian would later explain that crows sometimes staged funerals when a member of their murder fell, that she had checked, and there was no other known cause for such behavior. When out of nowhere the crows all took flight, the beating of their wings rough and deafening, we noticed that Our Author's neighbors had put up signs across their fence.

All the signs were warnings against trespassing, images of German shepherds or revolvers with different Polish versions of KEEP OUT! The words were written in white or black letters on navy or bright yellow backgrounds, some of them emphasized in red. As translators, we were aware of already interloping, and as foreigners in a small but prideful nation, we took these warnings to heart.

We flew back inside Our Author's house like a murder of crows. I couldn't say which of us banged on her office door first; in the blink of an eye, it was all of us. We had never said her name to her before. Now we wailed it.

"Irena!" we cried. "Irena, come out!"

"Irena Rey, you come out here right this instant," one of us said, while someone else said, "Please, Irena, please, we beg you." Meanwhile, Swedish loped over to Our Author's bedroom and in one fell, masculine swoop—heedless, graceful, hot—he simply turned the doorknob.

It hadn't occurred to us to take him to the doctor, but it had occurred to us by then that Swedish was essentially a snake. He'd been bitten by a snake; he had survived; all we'd seen from him since were bizarre actions like this one. The door swung open, and the weresnake went in. As one again, as if bewitched, we followed.

There were clothes in heaps with shoes on the floor, and the slivers of a mirror that only recently must have been propped against the wall. A slight breeze whispered through an open window. Slowly, we expanded into every corner of the room, treading lightly, almost imperceptibly, we hoped. The shattered mirror was not a good omen, but worse would have been for her to return and discover we'd trespassed upon her sanctuary.

There were seven mugs, some with moldy contents, scattered over both the bedside tables (as if some were left over from Bogdan) and on top of the dresser and one of the bookshelves. We examined the bookshelf: It was all Japanese books. It was all of her peers: Yōko Ogawa, Mieko Kawakami, Aoko Matsuda, Sayaka Murata, even Yoko Tawada, an author Our Author said she'd never read on account of her decision to write in German as well as Japanese. Turning your back on your mother tongue was the worst and most unforgivable of all betrayals, Irena said, especially but not only if you were an author.[11]

There were maps, too, and guidebooks to Tokyo, Osaka, Kyoto; a Japanese-Polish phrase book; Barthes's *Empire of Signs*; anime we attributed to Bogdan; an anthology of ghost stories; and a bowl covered in a piece of black muslin slightly smaller than a dish towel. The bowl was empty and perfectly clean.

We sniffed the musky European summer air. But our sweat and our perfumes—which were becoming mutually hostile—along with the forest's own aromas masked any trace of her that might have remained.

We went back to her office. We couldn't believe it, but its door, too, was unlocked. A red womb chair faced away from her giant computer screen, which was black, with no fingerprints on it, seemingly pristine. The walls were all bookshelves. One wall was green, which meant that Our Author—likely the greatest author in the world—had organized her books, at least in part, *by color*?

On the floor, on a pile of loose papers, lay the bulb of a lamp that was on and had been overturned; it was a miracle there hadn't been a fire. Whatever had happened, whatever she had done, could have killed us in our sleep, so that when

---

11   Nota bene: In writing this novel, my colleague has of course turned her back on her mother tongue. But is "mother tongue" still in any way a valid category? The implication is that we are born into a certain language the way we're born into a body. But even our bodies can be modified, and families move into new linguistic territories, and some families fall apart. Our colleague Chloe Diop's mother is Polish, but does that make Polish Chloe's mother tongue? Is she not fluent in French, the language in which she has lived most of her life—almost all of her life outside her home? I suppose I support this author's implied (though perhaps subconscious) suggestion that fluency and belonging are more complex than was once thought, though I do not support writing bizarre books in garbled versions of languages you don't speak half as well as you assume you do (Trans.).

she returned—and we still considered her return to be inevitable then, even imminent—she would have found that all that remained of her translators, her torchbearers, were embers and scorched parts, not much different from the little bits of sawdust in the pouches she had given us three days before.

But where there could have been a fire, there was nothing, not even insidious smoke, and where Our Author should have been, there was only that gauzy beige curtain that whipped fitfully against the window in the bedroom we now returned to, gathering around her rumpled sheets.

"What do we do?" said Ukrainian finally, pressing his hands together over his nose and mouth, and we all started talking over each other as some of us went around and inspected the closets, her dresser drawers.

English said, "Call the police?"

Swedish seemed about to say something, but German was already saying, "Maybe we should track down Bogdan." Then he grimaced like he had bitten into something sour. In fact, we had no way to contact Bogdan. He had always simply been there, and in the past, he had answered her emails and her cell phone, too.[12] But as we were soon to learn, no one answered her emails or her cell phone anymore.

In her plain, clear way, with her hands on her hips, Serbian said, "She can't have gone far, so she must be in the forest. Why don't we go back into the strict reserve?" Yet no sooner had she finished speaking than she ran into Our Author's private bathroom.

Slovenian said, surprising us, "Don't you think we should wait here?" Her opinion had never differed from Serbian's before, and for a moment, we all just stared at her. But she was undeterred. "She could be back at any minute. We wouldn't want her to find us missing when she arrives."

"Are there other rooms we haven't searched yet, in the house?" Swedish said at last, and the way his Polish rose and fell was entrancing, but then we heard Serbian throwing up. We looked at each other as if somehow we could just make a decision to stop all this—to travel back in time, to do everything all over, this time right. But the only thing that happened was that the toilet flushed.

---

12 Perhaps this is true of the author's contact with Irena. I always received direct responses to my emails and heard only her redoubtable voice when I called (Trans.).

When Serbian returned, her eyes were bulging. Shaking, she sank down onto Our Author's unmade bed. Her hand hit something hard under the covers, and sure enough, Swedish reached out for it valiantly or stupidly and held it up.

It was the amputated hoof from her welcome in the forest. Here in her house it was even more awful than it had been under that hulking oak. Our silence swelled, no longer made up merely of shameful questions hushed, but also charged with the insurmountable power of the unspeakable; never had we truly confronted it before.

CHAPTER FIVE

Dusk was creeping up, and the forest was crepuscular. Its floor pulsed as we made our way; it rustled; it buzzed. Echoes from its canopies beat, then faded.

We had waited until Serbian absolutely insisted we go, and now the glare of her blood-orange hair was almost blinding in the precipitously dropping sun. We'd left notes for Our Author all over her house, telling her where we were going. We wouldn't have the heart to take these down at any point over the coming weeks, so that her home would be littered with our scribblings, childishly forlorn.

We entered the strict reserve two by two: Serbian and Slovenian in front, followed by German and Ukrainian, followed by English and Swedish, with French and me bringing up the rear. As usual, German and Ukrainian chatted with exuberance, mostly about soccer, not quite letting Swedish in, despite his repeated efforts. Maybe he was showing off for English, who was the most beautiful person in our group besides him, and maybe French, who was also (though not by much) the youngest.

Everyone in Our Author's entourage was attractive, of course. I know I'm no abominable snowman. Men often compliment and stare at me back home, and they do so even more in blond places like Poland. It was almost as if Our Author's spectacular beauty had bathed us, her most faithful followers, in glory enough to make us semi-spectacular; just an eighth of her splendor would have sufficed.

As if it were a safety blanket, Slovenian was carrying a purse that looked like it was made of woven plastic, black that had faded in places to gray. She had been an archaeologist before becoming Irena's Slovenian translator, and she retained a penchant for dusting off junk and carting it around. We had all had different jobs before Irena chose us. Czech had been a physicist, or so he'd said, at least.

Serbian seemed preoccupied; I assumed it was her stomach flu. We weren't worried about it being contagious, I can't say why. I suppose we all assumed that whatever happened to one of us had to happen to us all, meaning it would have been pointless to take steps to prevent the spread of a virus that had already made its way into our fold.

As we crossed the bridge over the swamp, English began to boast about English. How the speakers of her language had an ancient respect for collectives and how we should invent a new word for ourselves. She gave examples: a murder of crows, a swarm of bees (we all had that, we muttered: essaim d'abeilles, roj čebel, Bienenschwarm), a shiver of sharks, a shadow of jaguars, a conspiracy of lemurs, a parliament of owls.

"What would we be?" she asked everyone in her high-pitched, slightly whiny voice, and her ugly English accent, and the stagnant slop of the swamp erupted into half a dozen wild boars screaming and ramming each other into the trees, detonating bursts of bats that seemed to graze our hair as they flapped desperately away. An owl dove into their colony, screeched, and withdrew.

"*Aegolius funereus*!" cried Serbian through the backs of her hands.

Slovenian, who was shifting her weight back and forth at the bridge's rail, seconded her friend: "That's a very bad omen," she said. "Boreal owls mean death."

I glanced at French, expecting an eye roll at the very least. But our alliance had been disrupted by this chaos, these creatures, some of which she clearly feared, and in fairness to her, the boars were enormous, charging toward the bridge as if unaware of our existence. One brushed against English, who let out a jagged keening. By the time she opened her eyes again, it was gone.

Swedish, German, and Ukrainian ran to her side. Overhead, steely clouds raced to cover the moon, rolling and whitening into foam, then darkening along with everything else.

Suddenly we heard a stranger's voice. "What are you people doing here?" it shouted. We all fell silent. Then came the sound of very rapid steps.

Nonetheless I couldn't take my eyes off Swedish, who had his good arm tight around English's waist. He was whispering something to her, moving his hand over her knee. I noticed I was shaking: The boar had missed me by a hair, and I couldn't stop hearing their horrible screams, and now here was a shaggy-looking ranger with his hands on his hips.

No one said anything. We hadn't designated a spokesperson yet.

"Please, people, you're absolutely not allowed into the strict reserve without a guide," the ranger huffed. "It is prohibited." He had a willowy quality about him, the way his hands hung, the way his body swayed.

"We"—Ukrainian started, pushing his glasses back up to the top of his nose—"We were looking for our guide."

"How did you lose your guide? There are no public tours at this hour! What can this mean? It is against the law to enter—"

"Irena Rey," said French, pronouncing the syllables gently, as if she were addressing a skittish animal of some kind. She was the only one of us whose mother tongue was Polish. "Irena Rey is our guide. But we can't find her."

Swedish straightened and said, in his singsong Polish, "We ought to go, we need to leave, right away, let's go home!"

But the ranger said, "Who are you?[13] Where is she?"

We stared at Swedish for a second. But it was night now, and we could barely make out the expression on his handsome face. German said something in German under his breath. We never did that—we never spoke our own languages out loud when we were here in Białowieża, not even Serbian and Slovenian when they were alone in their room (so they swore).

Then German said, in our shared language, in a disturbingly chipper tone, "All right, you're right—let's get out of here." He clapped his hands together.

At this we fled from the strange ranger, English limping a little but having regained much of her strength, toward what we thought was the exit that would release us into the wide field. But in the darkness, with only a couple of cell phone flashlights streaking over the black path ahead, we must have taken a wrong turn, because instead of the exit we found ourselves at the foot of a tumescent piece of land, a hump with saplings sticking out of it, and French said, trembling, "That's a kurgan."

---

13 In Polish, there are various words for "you." This particular "you" was directed exclusively at Swedish, as though the ranger already knew the rest of us, despite the fact that we had never set eyes on him before (at least not that we realized) (Trans.).

We stood there as if we, like the trees, were rooted to the ground. Swedish went up to it with his old Nokia. I followed and stood very close to him.

I had never seen an ancient burial mound before—I'd only read about them. I wondered what people had entrusted their departed to this earth. This area had always been a borderland: between Poland and Belarus, and, before that, between Russia and Prussia, not so much changing hands as hovering. Before that, way before that by human standards, it had hovered between Baltic tribes like the Yotvingians and the Lithuanians to the north (a direction the ancient Slavs had represented with white), Masovians to the west (represented with red), the Lendians and the Vistulans to the south (black), and to the east (green) the Volhynians, the Dregoviches, and the Drevlyans. Being from a comparatively new civilization, I had always been fascinated by what my country didn't really have: territory haunted by millennia of recorded battles, hunting expeditions, a slave trade, and pogroms—things that might change the soil by saturating it with blood.

I thought I saw a pair of antlers poking out of the far end of the mound and shined my cracked old iPhone on it; it was just some spruce branches. But on the spruce was a strange symbol, and as I examined it, I realized the symbol was repeated on several of the other trees. It was a white line, an inch or so wide and a foot or so long, with a yellow line underneath it of the same dimensions, and below that, more white. Could white still mean north here, I wondered, in this hovering forest? But what direction was yellow? Up? Down?

"What is that?" said French, coming up to me.

I shook my head. I don't know which one of us took the other's hand. I know only that when we let go and turned around we found the others gathered around an oak. English was standing inches away from it, *petting* a hoof that was almost identical to the hoof Our Author kept in her bed. Out here it made the tree look like a mutant, rooted yet ready to rove. A chimerical creation that was both and neither. From somewhere came the sound of the willowy ranger, whose screeches and creaks were getting louder as he came closer and closer to where we were.

I don't know which one of us took off first, only that all of us ran.

A TRANSLATION IS a new experience of something that is essentially, fundamentally the same. Twice in one week we had run home from the forest: once with her, and now once without her. It was the ultimate example of loss in translation, a catastrophic dereliction we couldn't yet begin to comprehend.

Back at her house, we fell upon the document inside our emails like a pack of ravenous wolves. Irena had sent us *Grey Eminence*, the novel she'd been working on over the past couple of years. That was what was written on the document's first page: *Grey Eminence* (*Szara eminencja*). It would be hard, if not impossible, to overstate our rapture. No matter where Irena was, her magnum opus was right here.

Nine months earlier, when Irena was arrested for protesting the suppression of the Polish press, we were the ones who wrote the open letter that got published in German, English, Spanish, Serbian, Ukrainian, Slovenian, and French. Normally all but invisible, we did get some credit—in her country and ours—for her subsequent release.

We had even saved her life once, back when Czech was still with us, in 2008. That was my second summit, and when we were done, Bogdan had rented a van and driven us six hours to Gdańsk for a conference called "Adaptation, Perfection, and Irena Rey." At the closing reception, at a rooftop sushi restaurant, a waiter with a bearlike build had charged her, like a bear. Irena had been occupied, gazing out at the toxic, torpedo-laden Baltic, and Bogdan had been pestering her editor under the artificial cherry tree, blinded by its bleached frayed blossoms. But we had been paying attention. We had perceived the ursine onslaught in time. We had instinctively tightened our circle around her, shuttled her sideways, and saved her, so that her attacker flew off the roof and into the marine alone.

We did love her. We wanted to make her eternal. We had been sworn to shuttle her sideways, into our other languages, new worlds where she'd be increasingly sought after, talked about. Protected. Desired.

But as we ensconced ourselves in her living room, with its sooty fireplace, cluttered mantel with photographs in black and white, and its library of forbidden Polish literature, whole centuries of which we weren't allowed to touch, its piano, and its probably impenetrable chests, all we really wanted was the novel. We wanted to possess it, to stake our claim to it, to make it our own before anyone else even knew of its existence.

We emailed her back. Each of us sent her an email. With a trembling hand, German texted her, too. But he, too, received no answer.

We knew this must be some kind of test. We also knew it was a test that we were probably failing. But that didn't stop us from continuing on to the next problem set.

Ordinarily, we never read ahead. Irena didn't want us to be contaminated by critics, and she also didn't want any of our pages to be contaminated by the pages that would follow them. However, that night, in desperation, between the eight of us, we read it all.

German read the first hundred pages, Ukrainian the next, and Serbian and Slovenian together took the three hundred after that. I wanted the end, but so did English, and as always (so it seemed to French and me) English won. I took 511 to 630, and French took 679 to 798, while Swedish was assigned the forty-five pages between ours (since we weren't sure how much he could handle). We set a timer for three hours and when it went off, we went around in a circle and recounted our parts.

The protagonist of *Grey Eminence* was Amália, the world's first true climate change artist[14] and the first person to exceed a billion followers on Instagram, making her a sort of global empress, unprecedented in the history of Earth. She was also Portugal's foremost performer of fado, a gold medalist in rhythmic gymnastics, excellent at baking, and capable of taming the aurochs she summoned back from extinction to revivify Lascaux. Her ample accomplishments that occupied 902 pages in Polish were sure to exceed that in certain other languages, such as mine, with its slower, steadier rhythms, or even English, with its phrasal verbs and mostly unbendable rules about word order.

Yet we agreed the novel didn't feel long at all. If ever it registered as heavy, it was only because of Amália's sole foe, Nikau, who sat in his bunker for 869 pages, plotting at the other edge of the map from Amália in pursuit of the world's end.

Maybe it was our harrowing forest crawl, or the black hole of Our Author's absence, but Nikau's gravity was the last thing we agreed on. English insisted Amália was an alter ego of Irena Rey. Swedish, who had read ahead, into French's section, asked us if we didn't think that all Our Author's work had a distinctively

---

14   What the author means here is that Amália was the first to view climate change itself as an art. Her oeuvre was above all a radical reinterpretation of the still life. She practiced extinction as well as large-scale action sculptures that undid or outmaneuvered natural processes such as decomposition and promoted catastrophes when opportunities—weather-related or other—arose (Trans.).

feminine flavor, which both enraged and excited me. I was enraged because it didn't and excited by the suggestion of a struggle between the sexes, which in turn suggested sex. I glanced at French and could see that she felt the same way. Serbian and Slovenian expressed the sacrilegious as well as seemingly irrelevant opinion that Our Author's essays were not quite as finely crafted as her book-length works, which shocked us, since we'd never considered such possibilities before.

Responding to English, Ukrainian pointed out that Our Author had no legitimate foes, no one who could be classified as an archnemesis—no one worthy among all the critics, the would-be competitors, the trolls. She was the literary version of an apex predator, a preternaturally gifted grizzly bear, a crocodile genius.

"I mean, who could possibly be her Nikau?" he asked.

"Barbara Bonk?" German suggested at last, and we all looked at each other, holding our breath. But then we released it in a kind of collective deflation as we shook our heads: surely not Barbara Bonk, the popular Polish pianist and essayist whose output consisted of annual memoirs she called novels about cheesemaking and snorkeling, fashion in the People's Republic of Poland, concert-giving and fifth dates.

"Her husband?" said French, who was sitting cross-legged at the coffee table, leafing through Our Author's coffee-table books. Her fingernails were luxuriously, immaculately pink.

We thought about this for a while. What if English was right, and French was right, and Irena Rey was Amália, and her husband had wanted to destroy her all along? Could Bogdan have kidnapped Our Author, dragged her into the woods, or even driven her beyond Białowieża somewhere?

"Definitely not," said Serbian. "She's never written about herself. Bogdan is like a fruit fly. What could he ever possibly do to her?"

"I think she did write about herself this time," said English, unnecessarily, since she was the one who'd brought it up. "And I think Nikau could be Bogdan."

"This is typical of writers," pontificated Swedish, "to sublimate. To channel their secret desires into fiction. We do it all the time."

It stunned us that he categorized himself as a writer; it was like a bolt of lightning down the center of the room. It left us numb. Another hush fell, and in this one we heard something scrabbling in the kitchen, or the pantry; I glanced around in the hopes that someone would go looking for ghosts, intruders, or even Our Author, but evidently none of us could budge.

At last German asked: "Is everyone familiar with the Leshy myths?"

Ukrainian nodded with vehemence. His lips were ashen. He was staring at Slovenian, who nodded, too.

"That man we ran into at the strict reserve," German said, "do we all agree he looked like . . . ?"

"Leshy!" cried Serbian, smiling the broad smile she normally reserved for the birds of Białowieża, which she and Slovenian went on long walks to watch.

But German wasn't smiling. He looked around the room. "You know about Leshy," he prompted Swedish, whose face was blank. "You were the one who urged us to get out of the forest. I assumed it was in order to protect us from—in case it was—him."

Swedish looked down at his French Brazilian sneakers that were largely unmarred by the swamps and then looked up at me and shrugged. "I didn't feel we were ready to speak with the officials just yet," he said.

English scoffed and said, "It's not like he was the head of the ISA."[15]

"I don't think we should speak to anyone," Swedish said. "Regardless."

"Regardless?" asked French, cocking her head.

"Why?" I asked.

"Well, after all, we haven't even searched the backyard," Swedish said.

It was a reasonable point, even a helpful one. At the same time, I thought I detected a kind of lie in his blue eyes, miniature Baikals, with that depth and that clarity. But I told myself that I was being oversensitive, on account of his handsomeness, as well as our earlier conclusion that he was probably a snake.

Whatever our qualms, we followed him out the back door with cell phone flashlights and Bogdan's pistol-grip spotlight that English and I both grabbed, then dropped, then grabbed again. Her hand was colder than it should have been, and she scratched me; as soon as I drew back in pain or surprise, she leaped up with it clutched in her fist and was gone.

We had never seen inside Irena's shed before. From the outside, it was less sleek and less Japanese than her home. We had always assumed it was where she,

---

15   I hate to footnote myself, but the ISA is the Polish equivalent of the FBI. Also I doubt I *scoffed* (Trans.).

or Bogdan, kept their gardening supplies when we weren't there—since when we were summiting, Czech's lodgings were the shed. But we were surprised to find a padlock on the door.

"I don't remember this being here before," said Serbian.

"Maybe the village got more dangerous," offered English.

"Or," said Ukrainian, clearing his throat. "What if someone locked her inside?"

We shuddered, but French stepped forward and laid her hand on the pine siding.

"Irena," she said softly. She rested her forehead against the shed. "Irena, are you in there?"

Across the yard, there was a rustle in the trees and the tall grass on the empty lot behind Irena's property. It sounded like a human-size animal, or something even larger, and we spun around and shined our lights on it. The shadows of the shrubs were gargantuan, whirling and trembling and flinging themselves up and then down upon the evening breeze. We had not yet experienced a serious storm in Białowieża, but we knew that plenty of people had been killed by hundred-year-old trees abruptly cracked in half, or uprooted, and we had always prayed for clement weather, and we would have done so now had we been allowed to talk about the weather. Slowly, we moved in the direction of the rustle. But it died down, and if there was anything to see, we couldn't see it.

Even on Irena's property, we couldn't really escape the forest at night; it was an all-pervasive thing that gave the sensation of being surrounded by hundreds or thousands of pairs of gleaming eyes. Bats flapped unsteadily over our heads, and hoots and howls punctured our attempts to concentrate, and before moving I had to shine my flashlight on the ground to keep from crushing any of the enormous Roman snails that came out after dark to forage and continue growing their shells. Their slimy ends contracted when I sighted them, then only slowly relaxed.

"What is Leshy?" English asked, sidling up to German with her pistol-grip spotlight partially illuminating her face. I didn't need to see it to know it was the face she always made when she wasn't embarrassed not to know something but was aware that less beautiful people in the same situation might be. It was not a face she'd ever made when speaking to Our Author, but it was one the rest of us knew well. German ignored her, too intent upon the nothingness just past the chain-link fence.

It was Serbian who said, "Leshy is the guardian of the forest, according to the ancient Slavs. As the forest changes with the seasons, so Leshy changes, too. He can shape-shift into just about any animal, from the tiny louse to the giant bison. But often when he takes a human form, his skin is rough, like bark, and his hair is long and shaggy and tinged with green."

"You're saying that was the guy in the strict reserve?!" I exclaimed, but English burst out laughing. I was either the last person in the group to make the connection or a fool for taking the bait. Were they joking or serious?

If there was anywhere forest spirits might be real, of course, it was here. Leshy did not sound less probable to me than hot pink slime molds. But English was still sucking in air after all that laughter, and before I could think of anything to say in response, French called out:

"Hey! I found the key."

We turned around again.

"Not in my eyes!" she howled, and on lowering my phone I saw a pair of earthworms thrashing intertwined. An animal trundled past in the near distance. I scanned the yard, hoping for a hedgehog, but whatever it was had already disappeared.

French popped the padlock of the door to the shed, and English stepped in first, holding her spotlight on her shoulder. Not everyone could fit at once, so German and Ukrainian, who were closest, stepped aside for Serbian and Slovenian, and the remainder of Irena's entourage waited and listened for clues.

When they came out, Serbian and Slovenian moved slowly, stiffly, seeming not so much shaken or haunted as confused. Swedish nudged me forward, and, thrilled to be touched by him, I took French by the arm.

The walls were covered in postcards, and a bed occupied most of the space in the room. On the bed were elegant cream-colored sheets, with a russet linen throw folded neatly at the base. There was a faint indentation in the center of the mattress where someone's body had been, seemingly recently—certainly more recently than three years ago, when Czech was here last. There was a small wicker basket in the corner that held a wadded pair of boxer shorts and a wrinkly T-shirt from Jagiellonian University in Kraków, the very institution Our Author had dropped out of after only twelve days.

Along a shelf built into the wall over the head of the bed there were candles and vials. Without thinking, I picked one up and opened it. It smelled like honeysuckle, and a little bit like mint. When I set it down, I saw that my fingers were covered in dust. I looked up and saw, through a skylight, the dark barreling clouds. French and English knelt on the bed to look at the postcards, and I got in between them, my eyes traveling from hunting scenes (bare-breasted women on horseback) to Istanbul (dolphins in the Bosporus).

From the doorway, Swedish was watching us kneeling three in a row like penitent schoolgirls. Serbian said, seemingly to Slovenian, though all of us heard, "Bogdan must have been in here."

"The bed," Slovenian said solemnly.

"The boxers," Serbian said. "She must have kicked him out of the house. He must have stayed in the shed until he went wherever he is now."

In spite of the rondeau, it hadn't really occurred to me to wonder where Bogdan, as a separate entity from Irena, might have gone. I couldn't actually picture him anywhere but by her side. Was there anywhere in the world where he could be, as merely Bogdan?

But I had also never seen him in a Jagiellonian University T-shirt, and I couldn't imagine him in one. I couldn't imagine him smelling like honeysuckle, or mint. I didn't have the courage to register my doubts—not yet—but it struck me that most likely, despite the sheets that were perfectly crisp and symmetrical, Bogdan had never set foot in this shed.

There were three postcards lying on the bedside table. The first was plain brown cardstock, with no picture, postmarked in Warsaw (written in the Cyrillic alphabet) on November 3, 1887. It was in a language I didn't recognize, something like Romanian, but I couldn't be sure.

The second postcard showed a photograph of Tempelhofer Feld, the former airport. There were people rollerblading down a runway that had been cracked open by weeds. On the back, in ink that was strange, thick, somewhere between gray and brown, the postcard was dated August 30, 1978. There was no address and no message.

The date didn't make sense: I'd flown into Tempelhof in 2007 on my first trip to Białowieża because a ticket from Buenos Aires to Berlin had been cheaper than a ticket from Buenos Aires to Warsaw. Not long after that, the airport was indeed shut down, becoming a public park in 2010, but in 1978, it was definitely still an airport.

I started to reach for the third postcard, a skinny painting in the saturated shades of early twilight, when English whispered, "Whose amadou is this, I wonder?" She was holding a handful of sawdust-colored nuggets, just like the ones Irena had distributed three days before. She said it like that: half in Polish, half in whatever language "amadou" might be.

"Hubka," French corrected or reminded her.

"Whose hubka is this?" said English. It was right under my nose now, her palm and those worn-looking vegetable lumps, and before I had time to stop myself, I was holding her hand—to keep it still, to keep her from reaching across me, to keep Irena's gifts intact. My fingers forced hers into a fist.

I let go. I jumped up. "That's the word Irena was saying on our first day in the forest. Huba? Hubka? Right?" But English and French did not seem to share my sense of epiphany. They merely blinked. I kept my eyes on the empty space between them where, three seconds earlier, I had been. "Why didn't you tell me you knew?" French's face was blank. "You knew what 'hubka' meant all along, and you didn't tell me."

"I didn't know you didn't know," said French.

"It's not like it's super important," English said. She looked from me to French. "I don't think."

"What were the first words you used? Ama? Do?"

"Amadou," French said. "It's one word. They couldn't come up with their own term in English so they just borrowed ours. As usual." She stuck out her tongue, and English grabbed the pillow from beneath her knee and swung it around, but before it could make contact with French's face, I grabbed it. I couldn't believe that this was their behavior—here. Was all of this—everything that I held sacred, understanding Irena, doing her language justice, giving her what she deserved—just a game to them?

I stumbled outside. The lights at the front of the house next door—the one with the crows and the warnings against trespassing—had been switched on. But as translators it was our lot in life to arrive after the fact, and by the time we'd cautiously crossed the yard again, the windows had gone back to black. Almost all of them had spiderwebs in the corners, littered with little bodies, trembling in the unstable air.

CHAPTER SIX

I'd planned on searching social media for traces of Our Author, but by the time I got upstairs, I was too worn out to disentangle Polish letters on a screen. I googled "amadou," but all I found in my language was a long list of Senegalese writers and soccer players and a Guinean man who had been murdered in 1999 by New York police. I concluded from this, first, that there was something so sick about U.S. society that it was no wonder English had turned out the way she had, and second, that the contents of the red velvet pouches had something to do with French, whose father had been Senegalese.

French must be involved in some way in *Grey Eminence*, I realized, but why hadn't she said anything to me? Not even when I confronted her in the shed had she admitted it. I removed my shoes without untying their soiled laces, then my jeans with my underwear and socks. I took off my tank top and bra, and my earrings, which I set down on the desk next to my laptop.

When I woke up in the middle of the night from a nightmare about staring down the barrel of a gun—I couldn't see who was holding it, maybe no one (maybe it was just a floating, all-encompassing gun)—I couldn't remember getting into bed, like I'd fallen asleep standing up and just dropped in, naked. My whole body was slick with heat and worry. I got up and crept downstairs, silently paying homage to the knot near the bottom. Directly in front of me, the head of the Bozdoğan mace glinted in the starlight, its gold leaf feathers like the fletching of an arrow, but for their turquoise studs. I went into Our Author's bedroom. I turned on the light.

The underside of the hoof was a labyrinth of pores—not exactly a hoof, but also not anything else I'd ever seen before. The top was hard, keratinous, but the inside was softer, almost as if you could reach in and scoop it out. I held it up to my ear and closed my eyes to see if it could make the sound of the ocean.

A large palm made contact with my upper back, and when my eyes opened, I discovered the light had gone off. As I was discovering this, I was spinning around with the instrument that wasn't a hoof still raised in my hand, and with it, striking a torso.

"Forgive me," whispered Swedish, rubbing his chest with the hand that had been on my back. "I'm so sorry to have startled you."

His voice sounded like honey, and I felt like I had melted.

Nevertheless, I hissed, "Qué hacés acá?" Those words in my language, which had escaped against my will, cozied that room and made certain impossible things feel less far-fetched. "I'm sorry," I said. "I got scared. I was wondering what you were doing here."

"I saw the light come on," said Swedish. My eyes had adjusted, and his face was so close to mine that I could see it clearly, even inhale his exhalations.

"Of course, you're next door," I breathed. "I just—I'm sorry. I just . . . I couldn't sleep."

"Of course." He moved his hand from his face to my waist. I didn't or couldn't move.

"What is your name?" he asked, and inside me something blazed. The question was intimate, even illicit—we had never called each other by our names in Białowieża before.

"Emilia," I whispered. "Emi."

"Emi," he whispered. I could feel all up and down my body the way his lips pressed together in the middle of my name.

"What is yours?" I ventured, my eyes remaining shamelessly on his.

"Freddie," he whispered.

"Freddie?" I asked, like he might have made a mistake.

"Freddie," he whispered again. "Listen, why don't you come to my room? I can make you some tea." I fell back into my trance and surrendered the not-hoof, which he set down on Our Author's dresser among the mugs and the small conducting rod, the shaggy halves of coconuts with tarnished five-, ten-, and twenty-groszy coins in them, the two sharpened, blackened bamboo reeds, the porcelain moonflask, and the ostrich feather. Some of these I would remember later because they'd come up on page 272 of *Grey Eminence*, in a passage about things Albrecht Dürer brought back from his travels in 1495; some of them we were about to put to use. That night, I noticed they were there only because I had to grab a coconut that Freddie inadvertently shoved off the edge. I restored it, stooping to gather several tiny cupronickel coins. Then he guided me out into the hall and through the door to his room.

Like mine, it had a medium-size wooden bookshelf, though Bogdan's books were all in German (since before marrying Irena, he had been a translator, too). Like mine, it had wood siding, lightweight floral curtains, a small sitting area with a glass bowl on a coffee table, and two single beds pushed together and covered in one big blue duvet. There were only three significant differences between Bogdan's room and mine: first, that he had a relatively large, relatively flat TV screen in his sitting area; second, that his low-pile gray carpet was covered in one spot by a lumpy navy rug; and third, that French was currently sitting on his bed.

I stared at her. She was flipping through a little red notebook. She didn't even look up.

"Chamomile?" Swedish said, and when I didn't answer, he added, "I also have mint."

"What difference does it make?" I said, laughing as if some part of what was happening—their sophisticated European rendezvous, a luxury bike to my third-world wheel; the notion that Our Author might be in some kind of danger, even grave danger; the Sisyphean task of the translation; the (fictional) disintegration of the inhabited and uninhabited earth and the (real) violation of the earth's most sacred ancient corners—amused me.

He brought me chamomile.

"I was just telling Chloe," he said, and suddenly I loathed him with every fiber in my body. I loathed him, but not Chloe, who had been my friend for too long now, since what felt like the beginning of the world, and who was also uncomfortable, uncrossing and recrossing her legs on the bed, and who must have been about to tell me what she had to do with amadou, and *Grey Eminence*, must have just been waiting for the right time to talk to me in private, since she was my closest, truest friend. I had known her since *Kernel of Light*, ten years, but until now, I had always called her French.

Freddie smiled at her and turned back to me, motioning for me to sit on the small blue couch with his good hand. The other one was working better now, but it was still splotchy, and he had kept his bandage on. "I was just telling Chloe about how I decided to become a poet. So anyway. You guys must know Eleanora Fagan."

We looked at him blankly.

"Most people call her Billie Holiday," he said. "I was eleven when I learned the meaning of—how do you say it in Polish? *Lincz?*"

I had the same mental lag then that we all had at the table with Our Author our first day, when Irena had run out of the room. I had never heard that word before in Polish.

"Lynching," said Chloe, in English, to me. Chloe might have been European and therefore more cosmopolitan than I, but she hated the English language as much as I did, if not more. She looked like she'd just bitten into a lemon. "He means like in America—sorry, the United States—when white idiots rounded up people who looked like me and murdered them collectively and left their bodies hanging from the trees. Among other incidents."

"Why would he mean . . . ?" I looked from her to him, then back to her. She shrugged.

"This is about poetry," said Freddie. " 'Blood on the leaves and blood at the root.' Do you guys know it by heart?" Neither of us said anything. He took a deep breath and moved so that he was equidistant between us and recited, in English, gazing at the phosphorescent blue window: "Here is a fruit for the crows to pluck. For the rain to gather, for the wind to suck."

He looked at me and then at Chloe. He almost looked like he was waiting for applause.

"You're talking about 'Strange Fruit,' " said Chloe, finally.

"Yes!" he cried. "Just think how different the world would be without that song."

"Okay," she said, narrowing her eyes a bit.

"The song comes from a poem, don't you see? A Jewish schoolteacher named Abel Meeropol wrote that in 1936. 1936!"

"Abel Meeropol," Chloe repeated.

"I bet you didn't know that!" Freddie said triumphantly. He strutted over to the edge of the bed and sat down next to her. She snapped the little red notebook closed.

"I'm tired," she said. But he didn't seem to hear her.

"Of course, then you wonder: Which was the deciding factor, the performance by Holiday or the song by Meeropol? But that's a chicken-and-egg problem. Like your translations of—what was the name of it? The one that made Irena famous all over the world?"

"*Lena?!*" asked Chloe, and I alone could hear her unspoken follow-up: How could one of *us* not know all of Our Author's titles?

"What kind of poetry do you write?" I asked him, to change the subject.

"Some people call me Sweden's social conscience." He shrugged. "I guess that doesn't really answer your question."

"Can I ask you an unrelated question?" Chloe said to Freddie, who peered at her closer, sweetly, attentively. "Why would you want to pick up a snake?"

His face clouded, and he cocked his blond head and said, "What do you mean?"

"Our first day, when we were in the forest. Why would you reach out for the snake like that? Didn't you think it might bite?"

"I did not reach out for the snake, of course," said Swedish. "I'm perfectly aware this kind of snake—*Vipera berus*—is poisonous."

"What do you mean?" I said.

"Common European adder," he clarified.

"No," I said. "That's not what I mean."

"Then what do you mean what do I mean?"

"How did it happen?" I asked.

"Yes, what were you doing?" said Chloe.

"I was trying to show you all a *Rhodotus palmatus*," he said.

"In Polish?" Chloe asked.

"It has a number of names," said Swedish. "Rosy veincap, wrinkled peach."

Chloe and I looked at each other.

"It's a fungus," he said.

"Another fungus?" asked Chloe. I judged from this that fungal topics were among his favorites. Since Irena had called fungi "necessary evils," my feelings about this were mixed.

"Another fungus, yes," he said. "I only mentioned the first one in the hopes of . . . ensuring her safety."

I didn't know what to make of this, either, but I did understand from his tone and his eyes that now avoided us that he was no longer enjoying our company. Night was ebbing away, and his curtains had gone from crystal blue to peach.

"The rosy veincap is rare and beautiful," he said. His gaze fell on me, and I shivered, although the air in the room was still warm. "One of the most beautiful fruiting bodies I've ever seen. I was surprised to see it there because it can't really happen in such heat—"

"That's okay," said Chloe. "We're not supposed to talk about the weather."

He looked from her to me.

"So you were trying to harvest a mushroom when you were bitten by the snake?" I asked him.

"I wasn't trying to harvest it!" Swedish said, definitively losing his patience with us. "I just wanted you to come and take a look. Then I was attacked by a heavily pregnant snake." He took a deep breath. "All animals are beautiful when pregnant, then again. Wouldn't you say?" he asked Chloe.

"Right," said Chloe, and, clutching her notebook, she slid off the edge of the bed. "We should go."

"We have to translate tomorrow," I said mechanically. Then I realized I didn't know if that was true. I turned to Chloe. "Right?!" I said. But Chloe only shrugged.

"Today," Freddie said. I looked at him. He smiled.

"Today," I said and smiled back sadly.

Chloe walked out the door. I followed. But I felt sorry for Swedish, and at the same time, my desire for him hadn't evaporated. I knew that part of it was just that viaje de egresados thing[16] of briefly and intensely falling in love with people you wouldn't look at twice in the day-to-day world. Part of it was the idea that Our Author had felt attracted to him, too. I'd witnessed it: She had. And perhaps something secret had transpired between them, perhaps something so intense and overwhelming it had driven her away.

---

16   Apparently a tradition in Argentina, "viaje de egresados" involves dispatching recent high school grads en masse to the imitation-Alpine city of Bariloche, near the border with Chile, where they may maraud and smoke pot and have sex with one another for a week (Trans.).

I wanted his body that could have been in hers to make me into her, or at least to instill in me some of her power. But I was also just drawn to him, in that chemical way things in the forest come together. I found him irresistible, despite his flaws or due to them.

For a long time I lay in bed, staring at the crack in the ceiling. I'd never noticed it before; perhaps there had been cracks in the past that Bogdan had covered, or perhaps the recent extremities of temperature had finally caught up with the house. I realized that Chloe and Freddie and I had just had a whole conversation without mentioning Our Author, and the idea that this was possible made me tremendously sad. At around six fifteen, I got up and went to the window.

Outside on the street Slovenian and Serbian were standing clamping binoculars to their eyes. I couldn't see what they saw because the window cut off at the roof of the house that faced Our Author's, with its crooked gate and unusable letter box. I smoked a cigarette, then walked over to my desk and started working on my translation, alone. We'd never done it this way before. It felt forbidden. And since she hadn't officially authorized us to break ground on our translations, maybe it actually was. I fingered the grooves in the corduroy cover of the huge old Polish-Spanish dictionary I'd taken from downstairs. The first sentence of the prologue went something like this:

> Amália died not when she was supposed to, when all the florists in Portugal would have found themselves suddenly stripped of their wares, and the botanical garden and even the natural history museum would have been ransacked, when roses would have flooded in from Spain, and paperwhites come from Morocco, when the population of Lisbon would have doubled, or even tripled, as her coffin hovered over white streets soft as down, nor did she die in childhood, like her little sister, Celeste—no, by the time Amália finally got around to dying at the age of twenty-eight, it was in a manner befitting a goddess: no trampled petals, but the erasure of a city; not the end of one life, but the end of almost all life, and almost every way of life the earth had known since the dawn of its civilizations, ever favored, ever ungrateful.

I wrote and rewrote it in Spanish, but I couldn't come up with a version that satisfied me. I had never written a first sentence that didn't change once I had more of a feel for the whole book. I knew, too, that the first sentence would never be the most important sentence, and that it wasn't worth the agony of these revisions. Perhaps it wouldn't end up being just one sentence in translation; maybe translations shouldn't have to bear that kind of weight, that many paperwhites. Maybe the final version of the first sentence of her masterwork would simply read: *Amália didn't die when she was supposed to.*

Or: *Amália died at the wrong time.*

It was as I was typing these alternatives that I noticed my earrings, tiny gold bees, a gift from my father, were gone.

CHAPTER SEVEN

While the storm was gathering, blackening, releasing intermittent downpours, we turned on all the lights in the house and sat down around our table and did research. Chapter One kicked off with flips and splits and leaps and pirouettes, and we needed to know what those looked like if we were going to re-create the proper atmosphere. Serbian pulled up the 2016 Olympics, and we all clustered around her old, off-brand laptop to watch.

Although the competition was obviously over—Russians had taken gold and silver, a Ukrainian bronze—we were nervous every time an athlete kicked a hoop. Serbian in particular would suck in her breath through her teeth when anything was very airborne, and she would moan when a woman stumbled or fumbled as if each of them were her miscreant daughter in Niš. Slovenian clapped her hands at the most impressive feats, holding them together after, as if in prayer, while Freddie explained the replays to us, and German growled when scores were shown, no matter what they were.

"It's a little bit sexist," English said as we watched a Belarusian French woman undulate over a golden ball. Serbian hit pause. "I mean, these women are practically naked. Like literally jumping through hoops."

"Venerating balls," said Chloe.

"Exactly," said English. "It's not like there's men's rhythmic gymnastics. Is there?"

Very tentatively, Ukrainian said, "Could that be part of her point? Chapter Twenty-Three, from my section, is a fencing match. Perhaps we could turn to fencing now, unless . . . ?"

Because we'd never read ahead at any previous summit, we'd never researched ahead, either. I assumed this was the reason for Ukrainian's "unless." But no one tried to stop Serbian as she typed in the search.

I'd never seen anyone fence before—the Argentine Fencing Foundation was only a ten-minute walk from the Casa Polaca, but I had never paused on my way to take a peek inside. So it took me by complete surprise that fencing gripped me, instantly, and that my body started moving in tandem with the bodies on Serbian's screen. We watched a match between Ukraine and Russia, both of them in silver space suits, their faces veiled by flag-colored mesh. The Ukrainian woman (bright blue and bright yellow) leaped forward, graceful as the rhythmic dancers but vicious, too, desperate to plunge a saber into the Russian woman (silver, blue, red), who skittered backward, then ruthlessly attacked.

Chloe lunged at me and, laughing, I lunged back. English said, "Isn't there anything we can fight with?"

Chloe and I froze. Freddie said, "You know, this is an interesting idea, like method acting but for translation." He started explaining the Method, but Chloe and English and I were already spiraling down the stairs in search of arms.

"There's this," Chloe said, gesturing at the mace.

"And the bullet-shooting crossbow! Remember?" I said, seized by sudden inspiration.

But Chloe just said, "No."

"Are there any actual swords?" asked English.

"Maybe hidden," said Chloe. Then she asked a question that had never occurred to us to ask before: "What's inside the chests?"

"Ooh!" said English.

"We can't open those," I said. "You know we can't."

"Why," said English flatly.

"Because it would be like breaking into her computer or something. Like reading her emails—"

"Yeah but isn't that exactly what we should be doing while she's gone?" asked English. "Shouldn't we know *everything* about her if we're going to translate her well?"

"No—?" I said, but then I had to stop to think it through. In the past, we had only known what Irena herself had decided we should know. That had made sense to me: She was the authority on her own books, after all, and she knew what we needed to know in order to do our jobs as she wanted us to do them. If we knew more than what we strictly needed to know, would it make our translations better? Or would it make them worse?

But before I could figure out the answer to that question, Chloe said, "They're probably locked anyway."

English shrugged.

"The tools by the fireplace?" I said, hoping to distract them. English picked up the poker.

"Ladies, we're not really trying to kill each other, are we?" Chloe said.

I cocked my head at English, who sighed. Casually, she loped over to the middle chest and reached down to grip its sides. It didn't open. She tried the next one. She knelt, cocking her head before the keyhole.

"Keys!" cried Chloe, and English sprang back up, nearly knocking over the pile of old boards.

"Yes," said English. "All we have to do is hunt down the keys. Easy! Like what we did with the shed."

"You mean what I did," Chloe said, but she seemed to be teasing Alexis, judging by the look they exchanged.

"Please stop," I said. "Let's just find something in the kitchen we can use. Then let's go back upstairs and keep working."

Freddie had drifted down the stairs and was watching us, or maybe me. He was wearing a dusky pink T-shirt that looked like it would be nice to lie down on, and his arms were a little less pale under the gleam of his fine blond hair.

"The two reeds in her bedroom?" said English, and she and Chloe raced down the hall. I stayed where I was, massaging my temples, and I thought I made meaningful eye contact with Freddie, although I wasn't sure what the meaning of it was.

Chloe and English came back with the blackened bamboo reeds, and we started up the stairs. We were just past the second floor when Our Author's electricity went out. It was the middle of the afternoon, but we were plunged into darkness. Slowly, awkwardly, keeping our hands on the banister, we made our way back down.

We spent the rest of the day, and much of the night, half expecting to be crushed by the roof caving in, or those sinuous walls blowing over. We sat in a circle on the floor, inside the circle of barrel chairs, with Our Author's store of candles lit in the fireplace and around the room, one small one in front of each of us. Despite their size, they cast weird shadows that danced violently up and down the creases in our foreheads, our distorted noses, our witchy chins.

"Maybe we should tell ghost stories," Chloe said into a lull in our talk about *Grey Eminence* and how to hold our editors, many of whom were expecting installments, at bay. Her suggestion was punctuated by an all-illuminating flash of lightning—across from me, I saw all of Serbian's sickened, stricken face—and then, almost immediately, a roar of thunder.

Serbian gagged but kept herself from throwing up. Each of us was rooted to our spot on the floor. The abstract shapes on the carpet were animated now: The red and blue rows of spirals were whitewater rivers, the strange motif in the middle bursting open into an army of giant-eyed monsters all advancing with their wings in fight mode, their beaks ajar.

"Chloe," I said, "maybe now is not the time to haunt the house." I looked around, expecting the others to agree with me, but the others only stared, their faces flickering.

English cleared her throat. "Are we going by our names now?" she asked.

Chloe nodded, casting a quick glance at German, who hesitated, then said, "I suppose it's true that without her here we could be more than just our languages."

"Or we could each select an alias?" asked Ukrainian. German, seated next to him, nodded vigorously at this.

But English was already waving and putting her hand to her heart. "I'm Alexis!" she said. "It is so wonderful to meet you new people with names."

"In that case," German said, "I go by Schulz."

Ukrainian said, "I go by Ostap. That is, my name is Ostap."

"Ostap, Schulz, Chloe," said Alexis, pointing at each of them, and then pointing at me.

"Emi," I said, but it didn't feel good the way it had with Freddie. Alexis was playacting—the truth was we all knew each other's names because we followed the fates of each other's translations, and translators don't publish under pseudonyms.[17] But saying it aloud in front of everyone felt like lying naked on an

---

17 I've published translations under pen names. The Xander Bowman who translated the award-winning musical *Swiss Cheese* was me. I no longer have any reason to conceal my identity, but plenty of translators— I know two women, for instance, who translate controversial works from Persian—do (Trans.).

operating table under seven oversize fluorescent lights. I folded my hands, closed my eyes, and clarified: "Emilia."

"Ostap Schulz Chloe Emilia Alexis," she said, then pointed at Serbian.

"I'm sure she had—I'm sure she *has*—a reason for calling us by our target languages," said Serbian.

"But what was it?" said Alexis.

Serbian gazed into the flame of the candle she was keeping on the carpet in between her hands. "Petra," she said. She looked at Slovenian. "Renata," she said, no doubt to spare her friend the turmoil.

"Freddie," said Freddie, although no one had asked.

Something crashed into the room then, a darkly shimmering presence that trembled the air.

"It's a ghost!" cried Petra.

"Irena!" Renata howled, like she was pleading for forgiveness.

"Is it a bird?" Ostap asked Renata, but Renata just gave him a look, and in the low light and our panic I couldn't interpret it.

The presence passed over our heads. Chloe dove into me, pressing her head into my side. Alexis blew her candle out, as if to make herself invisible, as if someone like her could ever escape anyone's notice.

"This is bad," said Schulz.

It careened around again and flew over my head at a remove of what felt like mere millimeters. I screamed. Chloe screamed with me.

"It's a bat!" I said. "How did it get in here?"

"How do we get it out?" whined Alexis, covering her head.[18]

"Don't bats carry Ebola?" Petra said.

"Bats may carry any number of diseases," Freddie said. "Those of you who are scared should go up to your rooms. Those who can should stay and help me catch it."

Fleetingly I pictured everyone running upstairs except for Freddie and me, me catching the bat in a net and flinging it out the front door, Freddie shoving me up against the door as I was shutting it, picking me up as I wrapped my legs tight around his waist. I wanted that. But what I did instead was run upstairs with everybody else.

---

18 Notwithstanding that this is, obviously, fiction, I nonetheless remember this differently: I was the one who pointed out that the bat was a bat, and Emi was the one who whined and covered her head.

I knew in my bones that it was English Alexis who had let in the bat. But when I entered my room, I was hit by a blast of moisture, and in wet horror, I saw that my own window was open—I had forgotten to close it after my cigarette. The carpet was sopping—it squelched underfoot—and the wood of my two single bedsteads was slick and dark, and my sheets, exposed where they weren't wadded up, were soaked, littered with little bits of trees.

I didn't want to admit what I'd done, but I didn't think I had a choice. I went to Chloe's room. Her door wasn't shut yet, or rather, it was only half closed. It creaked when I pushed it fully open.

Chloe didn't notice me, too busy rummaging around in the drawers of her unfinished dresser.

"What's wrong?" I asked.

She gasped and spun around, then saw it was me. "I can't find my notebook," she said.

There was a crash downstairs. For a second, we looked at each other.

"It has all of my ideas in it," she continued anyway. "Sketches for a project I've been working on. So much of it is in that notebook—I've had it for *years*."

"You mean the one you had in Freddie's room?"

"Yeah, that's why I was there, or at least I thought so. He wanted me to show him the cover of my graphic memoir. I mean, it's like a prototype. I don't know if they'll let me keep it yet."

"I'm sure it's here somewhere," I said, trying to conceal my shock. Chloe was a writer, too? A graphic memoir? About what? She was younger than I was (if not by a lot). And what did she mean, she *thought* she'd gone to Freddie's room to show him the cover? If that hadn't been the real reason, what had the real reason been?

But instead of those questions, I managed to ask, "Can I help you look for it?" And then, once we'd searched everywhere and found no trace of it, once we'd agreed to scour the rest of the house in the morning, beginning with Freddie's or Bogdan's room, I also asked, a little squeakily, "Can I sleep with you tonight?"

"Of course," she said. "That way if the bat squeezes in under the door, surely one of us will notice."

On the verge of telling her the real reason, I sat on the loveseat in her sitting room. In the glass bowl on the table was the red velvet pouch from Irena that held the amadou.

"Chloe," I said, "is there anyone in your family named Amadou?"

"Emi, no," she said. "I mean, yes, Amadou is a name in West Africa. But I don't know anyone by that name—not personally—and there's no connection between West Africa and Irena's little gifts."

"Are you sure?"

"Emi! *Yes,*" she said, undressing. "There's nothing there. It's a complete coincidence."

I always loved the way to say "coincidence" in Polish: "zbieg okoliczności," literally a place where circumstances meet. I liked to picture a stream junction in the mountains with a street sign that read HERE. Not the wide black-and-white signs we have in Buenos Aires, but the thin green ones you see in U.S. movies. That was coincidence to me when I spoke Polish.

In my language, the word sounds more casual, almost pointless. Although I suppose that was what Chloe was saying: that she had nothing to do with Our Author's opening present, and by extension, nothing to do with her being gone. That the connection could and should be thrown away.

Chloe fell asleep quickly. I could tell by her breathing. It took me a long time. As always, I filled the time with research. If amadou wasn't connected to Chloe, I reasoned, it had to be connected to something else.

I googled "ama," the first two syllables, without the third. In Basque, "ama" meant "mother" or "origin"; in Garo it meant "mother"; in Kamayurá it meant "mother"; in Lolopo it meant "mother"; in Eastern Huasteca Nahuatl it meant "now"; in Sidamo it meant "mother." In Romance languages like my own, of course, it was the third person singular of "love."

In Old Norse—the ancestor of Freddie's language—it meant "to wound." In a number of Austronesian languages, spoken by indigenous Taiwanese people and in Madagascar, as well as throughout Maritime Southeast Asia, "ama" meant "father." In every case, it seemed to suggest a primal referent, something a human speaker literally couldn't do without.

But what could we, Irena's translators, not do without, that hadn't already been taken away from us?

WE WOKE SURPRISED by the clarity of the air and our continued existence, only to remember we were still in Białowieża, still being terrorized by a bat that was no doubt lying in wait for us somewhere, still not sure how to approach *Grey Eminence*, still clinging to the slippery hope that Irena, our essence and necessity, might, if we guessed right, return.

In a way, I think we were also disappointed: The storm hadn't torn down hardly anything, other than some leaves. It had slightly sapped the extreme heat, but it had quelled none of the forest's natural chaos and revealed no ugly but essential truths. If anything, the rain had been good for Białowieża. It might help the spruces, we agreed, in their battle with those deadly bugs. Then again, none of the government-wrought destruction Irena had urged us to imagine was perceptible to us yet, which made us feel like we were missing something, maybe everything.

The exception was the shed in the backyard, which must have been struck by lightning, because when Schulz (formerly German) went out the back door that afternoon, looking for his keys, he saw that the mysterious structure had been reduced to black rubble, singed shards. I was sorry not to have stolen any of the banal or erotic postcards; I assumed they represented some component of some project she'd been working on, an epistolary novel or an album of ambient ballads or an exhibit on the history of women and hunting and traveling or just an essay about sheds. But we agreed it was better to have glimpsed it once than to have never been inside it at all, and we only hoped she would forgive us upon her return for having permitted it to vanish.

After breakfast, Petra (formerly Serbian) captured the bat in a laundry basket as it napped on the skull of a set of armor, releasing it on Stoczek Street. We took this as a good omen, and we climbed back up to the third floor to translate Chapter One together. By nightfall, we had finished Chapters Two and Three.

The next day it got hot again, and we translated five chapters, moving through the manuscript at unprecedented speed. But the day after that was two local holidays: the Solemn Commemoration of the Battle of Hajnówka and Saint Wenceslas Day. In point of fact, Saint Wenceslas was a Czech, not Polish, holiday, but since it appeared on the calendar over the sink, we determined to mark the occasion somehow.

For these were the kinds of cultural activities Irena expected us to take part in. Language and culture were conjoined, she argued, and without some comprehension of her region's traditions, her words would carry no real weight when we remade them, and our translations would slide right off the page.

We decided that Chloe, Freddie, Alexis, and I would attend the patriotic picnic in the nearby village of Hajnówka, while Schulz would take Ostap (Ukrainian), Petra, and Renata (Slovenian) to mass at a church he said he'd been to before, in an even smaller village that was just up the road. Although Irena could not have been said to be religious, she was able to work miracles with words, and although she was vehemently anti-nationalist, Chloe said she had recently taken up archery again, and bows and arrows were pictured on every poster for the patriotic picnic.

The big black Toyota was gone from the garage, and we were ashamed not to know if it had been there when we'd first arrived—not to know whether Bogdan had absconded with it, or whether she had used it to make her escape. (Although we'd never seen her drive before.) Public transportation in this area was scant, and there were no official taxis, nor, of course, more avant-garde options like Uber, which we didn't really have in Buenos Aires, either.

The sky was a pale perfect blue again, and I decided to wear a red dress. This was the first time we'd be going out into society, and it felt right to take the opportunity. It was the dress I had packed for our customary groundbreaking dinner, when, after Irena had welcomed us our first night and read to us our first full day, we broke ground on our translations, solemnly yet in the spirit of openness to feral experiment that characterized all her work. It was a sleeveless dress that hit just above the knee, a bright red with broderie anglaise, and it tied in the back leaving triangles of skin exposed on either side. I had bought it specifically for this occasion, from a nice store not too far from my family's old apartment, where my father and his new family lived, with the money I'd set aside from *Pompeii Catalog*.

Since I'd never worn it before, aside from in the fitting room, I had forgotten it was impossible to tie without assistance. I stood facing away from my mirror trying to see over my shoulder until my neck started to hurt, my fingers unwilling to work upside down. Finally I tiptoed out and knocked on Chloe's door. But the door that opened was Alexis's, and she came tripping out in her yuzu perfume, in her espadrilles that looped gracefully around her perfect ankles, in her green gingham jumpsuit that fit her perfect body perfectly with its spaghetti straps that clung to her shimmering golden skin. It almost seemed as if she'd grown more beautiful since Our Author's disappearance—she'd let her light brown, almost blond hair down, and it swept over her shoulders and shone. The bow around her waist made her look like a gift from a generous, distractable god who'd meant to make me, too, but who had instead cast me aside, half slapped together, at the kickoff of some angelic or demonic soccer game.

"Need some help?" she asked, acting as though she hadn't noticed my mortification, stepping carefully around me and placing all her fingertips in the middle of my back. "You can let go now," she said, and I dropped my hands awkwardly to my sides. Chloe opened her door to find us in this quasi-embrace, and I could feel her fighting not to raise her eyebrows, and then Alexis let me go. I tossed my hair back over my shoulder; it was still wet, and it had dampened the material of my dress, leaving a dark circle overlapping almost exactly with my breast.

We heard Schulz calling to us from downstairs that we were going to miss our bus, and we were off, racing past Freddie, who hurried after us without a word.

It was 8:35 in the morning. The PUK Trans bus—the only one for the next four hours—was just barreling down Stoczek. Freddie waved at it from the middle of the street with both hands. For a moment I thought I would see him get run over. But the bus stopped, and we clambered onto it, trying not to fall into the laps of the locals—all apparently bemused by us—as we went by them to the back.

There wasn't much but forest along the way; a stretch of it did seem to be undergoing a cull—the word in my language is "sacrificio," which strikes me as more honest—but the three yellow bulldozers that were apparently being used for this purpose were sitting idle in the middle of that horizontal grove, with none of Szyszko's henchmen anywhere in sight. Past this, Chloe and I chatted about Amália, debating whether Irena intended her to be evil or secretly, somehow, good, and Chloe mentioned something strange about her fiancé—not boyfriend, *fiancé*—some connection between her fiancé and *Grey Eminence*'s Nikau, but it was complicated, the fiancé seemed to be at some serpentine remove, and I overheard Alexis telling Freddie about her professorship in California, the patent eagerness or need in her voice so exhausting I slumped down in my seat next to Chloe and rested my head on her shoulder and was about to drift off when all of a sudden we were at our stop.

CHAPTER EIGHT

On the opposite side of the street sprawled Hajnówka's cemetery, four or five times the size of Białowieża's; I was scanning it for moving figures, thinking that after all Our Author could be anywhere, when I heard Chloe exclaim, "You're not even tucking in your thumb!"

"What would that entail?" asked Freddie, and I turned to see his twinkling crystalline eyes darting to meet mine, and then, I thought, perhaps, to my wet breast.

"Irena taught it to us," said Alexis. "You have to hide your thumbs when you pass a graveyard because the Japanese word for 'thumb' means something like 'parent-finger,' so by tucking in your thumb, you're protecting your parents from death."

"My parents are dead," said Freddie. At that Chloe seemed to warm to him again, or at least to feel a fleeting interest, which surprised me a little, although I knew she had a fondness for true crime.

"How?" she asked him.

He looked at her warily now, or so it seemed to me; I wondered if this was because of the question or because Chloe had rebuffed him the other night over herbal infusions. Was Freddie in love with Chloe or Irena? Or worse, were they somehow interchangeable to him?

"An accident," he said. "A long time ago."

We each mumbled we were sorry, and then no one said anything for a while, until Alexis stumbled over a crack in the sidewalk. While trying not to laugh, I glanced at Freddie.

"What about your parents?" he asked me, and it was clear from his expression that he was only asking to help me mask my mirth or schadenfreude, and the fact that this was our first conspiracy suffused every cell of my body with joy.

"My mom is a therapist, and my dad runs a condom company," I said.

"Seriously?" said Alexis. "I didn't know that." I shrugged. Alexis seemed to doubt her Polish. "You mean condoms like—"

"Like for dicks," said Chloe, nodding. "She grew up helping the Bolivian women who work at her dad's factory stretch out latex on a conveyer belt."

"I'm glad your mother is a therapist," said Freddie.

"So am I," I said, smiling although everyone always made this joke. There was still a little bit of joy left in my cells.

We reached the corner, where we turned and untucked our thumbs. We had a little time to kill before the picnic, and Alexis determined we should kill it with coffee. As we walked, Chloe told Freddie the story of her parents' first encounter in Paris, back when they were both eighteen, how her Senegalese father, a first-year student at the École normale supérieure, had swept her Polish mother, the latest assistant at *Kultura*,[19] off her feet, and Alexis made a brief attempt at a rousing account of a strong single mother who sounded even more unbearable than my own.

Freddie said nothing more about his origins or life.

The Anastasia Café was decorated exclusively in the top halves of matryoshka shells that gaped at us—we were that establishment's sole customers—from around the blue walls. There was a silence as we settled in at our wobbly red table. Then Alexis said, "Where do you suppose she is? Do you think she's coming back?"

"Of course she's coming back!" I heard how shrill my voice was after "of course," but I was unable to calm myself by "back."

"What if she isn't, though?" asked Alexis, wrinkling her perfectly symmetrical nose.

---

19 *Kultura* was the most important Polish émigré journal in existence from 1947 to 2000, covering politics and literature and advocating for intellectual freedom not only for Poland, but also for Ukraine, Lithuania, and Belarus. Located in the Paris suburb of Maisons-Laffitte, *Kultura* published, among others, Czesław Miłosz, Wisława Szymborska, and Witold Gombrowicz (Trans.).

It was the first time any of us had uttered that possibility out loud. Perhaps it would have been impossible to broach it, or even think it, in her home, surrounded by her belongings, in the presence of a still-warm trail we nonetheless could not follow.

"She did look bad," said Chloe. "Something was wrong, that much we can say for sure."

"Do you think it could have been the book?" asked Freddie. "There've been so many rumors regarding her new novel, maybe she grew worried it wouldn't—or couldn't—quite live up to all the hype."

Chloe put her elbow on the table and cradled her cocked head in her hand. "How did you end up here?" she asked Freddie.

"What do you mean?" Freddie said.

"I mean why are you here? Have you even read all of her other books?"

"Not all of them, no," he said, smiling his thanks to the waitress as she deposited our cups on their saucers, sloshing slightly foamy off-gray liquid everywhere. "I've read *Matsuura*, which I liked, and some of *Sedno I*, and the one about the warring amber-mining gangs, which I liked more."

"*Future Moonscapes of the Eocene*," I said, tamping down my disbelief that verged on disgust at his blithe ignorance.

"Anyway," Freddie continued, "one day I got an email from Irena inviting me to participate in a—how did she put it?" There was a pointless, frustrating pause. "Summit. A translation summit in her forest home. I believe what she said was that she'd researched me, and I'd be perfect."

"Perfect," I repeated, while Chloe was saying, "Researched?"

"So wait," said Alexis. "So you didn't, like, apply to translate her?"

"How do you mean?" asked Freddie.

Chloe let out a long sigh into her fist. The waitress had turned on a soundtrack of old Polish tangos, and the scratchiness of Wiera Gran's 1937 "Gdy odejdziesz" sizzled its way under my skin: "If you go," sang that woman's deep, doomed, desperate voice, "if you leave me, I won't complain, I won't tell you my heart's bloody and broken, I won't say I'm in pain."

Alexis said, "What if she was taken by Putin?"

"Taken?" asked Freddie.

"Could have been Russia," Chloe said. "Also could have been Poland. Or Belarus?"

"So nothing like this has ever happened before?" asked Freddie. "She's never gone anywhere while you were here?"

"Definitely not," said Chloe, at the same time as Alexis said, "No," and I bleated, "She would never leave us!"

"She has, though," Chloe said to me with sympathy, covering my hand with hers.

"Unless," Alexis said. "Unless she was kidnapped."

"The thing is," said Chloe, "Irena needed—needs—our summits as much as we do. She conceived them as a way to expand her writing process and connect with the various stages of the life cycles of her books. Including afterlives."

"It also gives her full control," said Alexis. "Over us and our translations."

My heart started racing. Full control?! That wasn't why she did it. She did it because we were a family.

"It's not exactly common," Chloe said, "but it's not a new idea. Günter Grass used to do it."

"Murakami does it," said Alexis—but we weren't allowed to mention Murakami.[20]

Chloe said, "Bestsellers in the U.S. and the U.K. do something similar: They make their translators sit in a bunker for six weeks without internet. In order for the book to be published in every language at once, and not to run the risk of spoilers."

I pictured us locked in a basement in the middle of nowhere, our ties to the world snapped and scattered across the cold hard concrete floor. In the forest, we were swimming in life, almost drowning in it, fleetingly but eternally bound to every being on Earth.

"It isn't similar," I said. "Their author isn't even there."

"Emi's right," Alexis said and grinned at me. Her white glinting teeth were among my least favorite of her perfect features. It was terrible, too, when she agreed with me. It made it impossible for me to trust my own thoughts. "But," she continued, "Our Author's gone now, too."

---

20   Murakami doesn't do it. His translators, it turns out, organize their own meetings, to which the author himself is not invited. For more, please see Nitesh Anjaan's documentary *Dreaming Murakami*, which I enjoyed (Trans.).

"No words will help," moaned the controversial, unknowable Wiera Gran over the speakers in the four corners of the room. "Nothing and no one will possibly help."

I glanced at the time on my phone. "Should we go?" I asked.

"What if," Chloe said, "what if—and hear me out—all of this is a performance piece to get us in the mood for *Grey Eminence*, what if she's doing, bah, something like what Freddie was talking about, like method writing, like she's becoming Amália and staging this big drama for the sake of our translations—"

"Does she really care so much about your translations?" said Freddie. His chair made a scraping sound as he scooted it back.

"*Your* translations?" Alexis laughed. "Aren't you translating her, too?" She downed her coffee in a big, uncomfortable-looking gulp.

"Our translations," he corrected himself. "Does she care so much about our translations?"

To me, and I believe to Chloe, the suggestion that Irena might not care that much about our work was hurtful. Unsurprisingly, it didn't seem to faze Alexis, who was too excited by the idea of a kidnapping to genuinely care.

It felt like we'd each started writing our own story about Irena now, each in the genre that suited us best. Alexis was writing a mystery novel, Chloe an illustrated psychodrama taking major cues from true crime, Freddie Nordic autofiction, more understated and more boring. I wondered what kind of story mine would be.

AS IT TURNED out, the picnic on the grounds of the Park of Monumental Miniatures was more of an open-air market where you could buy camouflage skullcaps and gloves, cotton candy, gas masks, and spiral-bound "books" on preparedness and histories of martial law. We browsed the stands and the mostly proportionate replicas of local landmarks until we came to a stand that sold toy swords. Chloe raised an eyebrow, and I gave her a nod: Although we had, on our vain hunt for Chloe's graphic notebook, turned up a third reed in Irena's room, it felt obvious that swords would be better for three-way fencing than that blackened bamboo.

"How much do you want for this?" Chloe asked a man in camouflage as she grasped a gold-toned pommel, and I saw there was a series of pictures that ran down the rest of the hilt. The man squinted, looking at her as if she'd asked him what year it was, or who was the president of the United States. Sometimes Poles reacted that way to a Black woman speaking their language, but it tended to be less of a problem around here, an area that had long been mixed, if not with Africans, then with Jews, and Belarusians, Lithuanians, Ukrainians, and Tatars.

Then again, it occurred to me that some of these vendors might not be from around here—they might have come in from Elbląg or Lublin or Łódź. There was no telling how their patriotism might affect their dealings with us: three obvious trespassers, only one of whom, Alexis, might look close enough to Polish to pass—*if* she kept her mouth shut, which with her was an enormous if.

"This is Szczerbiec," said the man. "This is the symbol of the greatness of the nation of Poland and of the bravery of the Poles."

"Fantastic," said Chloe. "How much does it cost?"

He looked scandalized, either by her crass insistence on putting a price tag on the greatness of the nation of Poland or simply by her presence at his stand, but in the end, he said an amount, which was low, about the same as a half-liter bottle of Żubrówka, and I opened my little silver pouch and took out one pink and one blue bill. When I looked up, Alexis was standing right in front of me, giving me another face.

"Fine," I said, taking out a green bill. Then we were all armed with three-foot plastic swords.

We had just begun to look for Freddie when the picnic's emcee announced that the battle's featured guest Pan[21] Igor Dembowski would be delivering his address now, and would we all please take our places near the miniature Church of the Transfiguration of the Lord on the Holy Mount of Grabarka. Alexis and I started to follow the crowd, but after a few steps I realized Chloe wasn't with us either anymore.

I turned and saw she was frozen in place. "I'm sure he'll be there," I called back to her, although it was hard to imagine her worried about Freddie, and indeed, it felt like I'd said the wrong thing because she did not unfreeze and maybe even froze a little harder. Behind her, Freddie loped up.

---

21   "Pan" means mister in Polish. In general I translate this, but I decided to leave it in the original here because the name comes back frequently later as Pan Igor, and Mr. Igor sounds unnatural in English (Trans.).

"Nice swords," he said.

"Where have you been?" asked Alexis—almost flirtatiously, I thought.

"At that stand over there by the miniature fortress." He tilted his head toward a pond with two ducks in it. "I bought this," he said, and he held out a round hat made of something that looked like suede but also not like suede. When none of us reached for it, he put it on. "What do you think?" he asked.

I wanted to tell him he looked gorgeous and ridiculous, that no one but me could love him in that hat, and even I wasn't sure if I could, unless Alexis did, but Chloe said, in French, "Is that amadou?"

He nodded brightly. "Wait—" I started to say, but just then an old man began speaking, his voice crisp over the loudspeakers nestled in the trees. He was telling a story about the time he was arrested by the Gestapo when he was twenty, and oddly, right away, I felt as invested as if I knew the old man somehow. In truth I knew hardly any Polish people other than Bogdan and Irena and the sour-faced woman who had taught me the language back home. Yet the tempo of the war story, the rises and falls and the switchbacks in each sentence, sounded so familiar I forgot about the amadou, forgot about the hat, forgot even the existence of Freddie, although he was close enough to me to touch.

He would have been put to death had it not been for a friend of his who burst into the old tsar's power station that the Nazis had turned into their headquarters with a picture of the now-old man as a young man arm in arm with Hermann Göring.

"Of course, as everybody knows," the old man said, "Hermann Göring was the founder of the Gestapo, one of the most ruthless men in history. And here these boys had evidence that I, a mere villager and humble Pole, was friends with their big boss."

"What does this have to do with the Battle of Hajnówka?" I heard Alexis whisper to Chloe, bursting the spell.

"Nothing," whispered Chloe. "The Battle of Hajnówka was a Polish Thermopylae."

"What's a Polish Thermopylae?" I asked.

Alexis placed her hand on Chloe's other shoulder like one parent relieving another. "A Polish Thermopylae," she said, moving around behind Chloe to stand next to me, "is when Polish troops fight to the death despite being vastly outnumbered. Almost no one survived the Battle of Hajnówka. In fact, historians can't say for sure whether anyone survived. And at this point, even the couple of people who claimed to be survivors are dead."

"So who's the old man?" I asked, leaning across Alexis to catch Chloe's eye.

"No one," said Chloe, forgetting to whisper. "As far as you or anyone else is concerned, there is no old man."

This seemed like a strange assessment, but I couldn't inquire because now it was time for the archers, and we joined the crowd as it flowed toward a cordoned-off part of the park with a slim track down its center. My dress, I realized, was attracting too much attention. I could feel eyes boring holes into my sides where the skin was exposed. Freddie seemed to feel it, too, and he moved to stand close behind me.

A few children in traditional outfits were ushered out and oohed and ahhed over as they shot arrows that dropped limp into the grass a couple of feet from where they were standing. Then the emcee, who I could now see was a man in a red hat with four crisp corners, announced two representatives of the Polish Horseback Archery Association in Białystok, and Chloe and Alexis and I stiffened in excitement, hoping against hope: Irena could be one of them. I turned to Chloe, whose hands were together in front of her face as if in prayer, her toy sword at her side. When it toppled, she didn't even notice. I picked it up with my free hand.

As we waited, I saw in my mind's eye: a beacon of enlightenment on horseback, power incarnate, Irena in a cascading blue-green dress, her hair streaming behind her like a black-glittering river as she galloped toward us, her eyes brighter and more forceful than a thousand suns, and my version of Our Author's story, I realized, would definitely be an epic, a new ancient adventure that we could all intone together, singing her praises in our disparate languages to form a perfect homophonic narrative as we shouted from the rooftops tales of her feats—the feats of a centauric goddess whose words would staunch calamities, hold our apocalypse at bay. Neither a tragedy nor a comedy, it would end in an act of great salvation, a renewal of the life of something larger than ourselves. I watched the field for her coming and felt against my naked back Freddie's hot silver belt buckle.

Or maybe my story was a love story, I thought then, too.

But no sooner had I thought of this than two horses rode out, neither one bearing Our Author, just two men with beards and hats and feathers. At first I was disappointed. Then a third man galloped up out of nowhere and raced ahead of the other two, turned his horse and pulled back his bowstring and aimed at the crowd by the pond with the two ducks in it, then swiveled in his saddle until he was aiming directly at us.

"Cleo!" cried Freddie as he pulled me and Alexis down. But since Chloe's name wasn't Cleo, she didn't move. I was marveling at his stupidity when Alexis elbowed me in the face, then stretched to grab Chloe by the hem of her black shorts and pull her down into the pile of us, cluttered with swords. As Chloe crouched, the arrow flew directly over her head, into the arm of the stranger standing next to her.

I don't know what happened after that. Everyone panicked. Everyone ran.

CHAPTER NINE

By the time we got home, the shrine was all but done. There were drawers open everywhere, books splayed over the coffee table and floor. Freddie had locked the front door behind us, and he stayed standing there while I ran down the hall to lock and barricade the back door. It was when I ran back into the living room, glancing wildly from window to window, that I understood what they had done. It was a bookcase in front of the fireplace, facing the fireplace but decorated all over with photographs and paragraphs cut out of—I understood as I approached—*Sedno I* and *Sedno II*, and *Future Moonscapes of the Eocene*, and *Lena*. Kneeling down between it and the fireplace I saw that all her books were there, *Matsuura, Perfection, Kernel of Light*, and in the middle were some squat little candles—new candles—and votive offerings including three wedding rings.

I would never have thought of building it—her whole house was already a kind of shrine—but even exhausted, even fearing for our lives, seeing it gave me a rush of awe. Like everyone, I had no idea how Our Author did it, how she always came up with the exact right words to say in the exact right order—that was her genius, irresistible and inimitable, no matter how hard we tried to recast her every spell.

I looked up. Renata, who had lined her eyes with black and emerald, explained forlornly, tipping her head toward the wedding rings, "I have never been married."

"Yet," Petra said, but this word of encouragement seemed to sadden Renata even more.

"What happened to you?" asked Schulz, looking at me and then at Chloe, who was half dragging Alexis across the carpet to the chaise longue, little clods of earth sullying their wake.

"Is everyone okay?" asked Ostap.

I unclenched my first from around our three swords for the first time in hours and said, "I think someone might be trying to kill us."

I was as surprised as anyone to hear it, and I flushed. What if I'd imagined the whole incident? What if after only eight days in the forest I was already losing my mind? I was an urban girl. I didn't know how to handle myself robbed of concrete, robbed of sirens and exhaust.

"Who?" hooted Renata, exactly like an owl.

"Who?" Petra echoed. "Why would anyone kill want to kill *us?*"

"The patriots," panted Alexis. "The men in camouflage." She slumped down onto the mustard cushions. "The archers." Then she put her legs up, and all of us gasped. Both her feet were bleeding, covered in dirt and twigs and leaves that stuck to her skin because of the blood.

"Camouflaged archers shot at your feet?!" cried Ostap.

Freddie said, "No. What happened was that we were enjoying the patriotic picnic at the Park of Monumental Miniatures when a rogue archer rode out and started shooting into the crowd, possibly at random. Possibly not."

"At Chloe," said Alexis. "Does anybody have any painkillers?"

"I do not know whether or not he was shooting expressly at Chloe. Maybe he was. I simply do not know. In any case he was shooting, and we fled, and then we walked all the way back, since the holiday bus wouldn't have come until evening, and we didn't want to risk asking someone for a ride, under the circumstances. This is how our colleague's feet became damaged, from our twenty-kilometer walk."

"What circumstances?" Schulz asked. His voice was louder now. Petra hurried into the kitchen and returned with two glasses of water. As soon as I started drinking, I felt an unquenchable thirst.

"We should wash your feet," Ostap said to Alexis, who gave him her frightened kitten face.

"Yes," Freddie said, and before Alexis could resist or even understand what they were planning, the two of them had lifted her up.

But I was not about to stand idly by while they showered with Alexis, so I said, "I'll bring towels," and ran after them empty-handed, with no idea where Our Author or Bogdan kept spare towels.

The only shower on the ground floor was the one in Irena's master suite. As they tested the water and rolled up the green gingham of Alexis's jumpsuit, I pried back the mirror over the sink. There was Our Author's wrinkle-reducing retinol; there were her acids: salicylic, azelaic, lactic, hyaluronic. There was her sensitive-gum toothpaste. There were all her human things.

But if Irena was merely human, then what did that make us? And if she had really been kidnapped by Russia or Bogdan or one of her trolls or even one of her superfans, was it too prideful or too paranoid to think we might be next?

"Can I turn on the news?" I whispered to Freddie, touching my fingertips to his forearm, with its golden down.

"Good idea." He smiled at me, and I temporarily forgot my own mortality—and worse, the limited lifespan of our translation work, which would need to be redone, unlike Irena's originals, which were eternal—and leaving the actual cleansing of Alexis to Ostap, he ushered me into his room. We sat down together at the foot of his bed. Even on recalling that we might all be killed soon, I was able to appreciate the fact that I was sitting on his bed. In literally one fell swoop I could be in it. I looked at him. His face was sweetly focused, like a child's. He flipped down until he reached a local station.

Ostap brought in Alexis, and Freddie leaped to his feet to make room for her, and then she was lying on his bed, an *on* that was closer to *in* than my *on* was, and her feet were wrapped in fluffy towels that I hadn't provided for her.

Renata entered the room with the severed half leaf of an aloe oozing its juices into her cupped hand.

"Do you mind?" she asked me, practically shoving me aside as Schulz and Petra sat down in Freddie's sitting area, and Chloe walked around me and positioned herself next to Alexis's head. Suddenly we were all in Freddie's bedroom, half of us on his bed, and I wasn't even a part of that half.

"What happened to her shoes?" Petra asked the air, which was uncomfortably humid.

"She took them off," Alexis answered. She was just the type to speak of herself in the third person.

"Why?" asked Petra. "Where?"

"In the woods," said Alexis, folding an arm over her eyes. "They were killing me."

Renata set her half leaf on the pale blue duvet. Then, very slowly, she unwrapped Alexis's feet. We sucked in all the air in the room through our teeth. Even after being washed in the shower, they were covered in hideous marks, scratches, cuts, sickly yellow splotches, blisters from before she had shucked off her espadrilles.

That the most beautiful thing we had left—Alexis—had been marred didn't give me as much pleasure as I would have predicted.

"Should we contact the police?" asked Schulz.

"No!" Freddie said at once. "We'd need to get our stories straight. We really do not know what happened."

"Well," said Chloe.

"We know that someone tried to murder Chloe," Alexis sighed. Renata was rubbing aloe into her feet. But Alexis must have been accustomed to all kinds of people massaging her feet because she never so much as glanced down at Renata.

"Someone screamed 'murzynka,'" I said. It was an antiquated Polish way to say "Black woman," controversial at best. I didn't know if what I was saying was in support of what Alexis was saying or not. I tried to replay the memory with limited success. It was a woman who'd screamed it. Had she been accusing us of something, or trying to warn us? Or simply striving to provide a play-by-play to those in the audience who weren't close enough to see? I couldn't summon what she'd said before or after, if she'd said anything else. "People had been staring at us," I said, "before the archery began."

"Why?" asked Schulz.

"That's the thing," said Chloe. "It could be because Emi and I look foreign. But I doubt it—despite the new conservative regime. People don't necessarily even think of themselves as fully Polish here. They think of themselves as from here. It's not a national identity. Some skinheads beat me up in Kraków once, and in Warsaw a guy tried to run me over with his car."

"Jesus," said Petra.

"Chloe," said Alexis, drawing out the *eee*.

"In several cities people have accused me of shoplifting or at least followed me around the store. People call me a murzynka constantly. If I tell them it's racist, they simply tell me that it isn't, and that's the end of the discussion with them. Men and women have assumed I am sexually depraved. I've had people grope me in public, just walking down the street. You'd be surprised. Not like it's paradise in France. It's not—at all. But."

Alexis rolled over and screamed. We waited for her to say something. She sat up and said nothing.

"My point is," said Chloe, "this picnic felt different, but I'm not sure exactly why. I could tell Emi was anxious. I felt strangely anxious, too. Well. Maybe not so strangely, I mean, in my case."

"What do you mean?" asked Renata.

"Nothing," Chloe said.

"We used to have Our Author for protection," noted Ostap, looking tenderly at her.

Chloe shrugged. "Honestly I thought people were looking at Emi more than they were looking at me."

"You do stand out as well," said Freddie.

"Emi's complexion is no darker than Our Author's," said Petra.

"It's not just darkness," Schulz said.

"Emi looks sexy," explained Freddie, and I was swept up by euphoria, but then he went on: "Polish women carry themselves differently. My wife is Polish."

I gaped at him. "Your wife?!" We'd just talked for hours, the whole way here, sharing our life stories with the threat of death over our shoulders, and yet he'd failed to ever once mention the single most important thing about him: that he was married.

Freddie nodded like I'd just asked him if he wanted pizza for dinner later. Carefully, so no one else would notice, Chloe shook her head at me. I tried to think what we'd been talking about before. I took a look at the TV screen. It was an ad for cheese. I took a step out into the hallway, where my eyes drifted up the trail of sylvan filth Alexis had left on her way to be showered. I thought I saw, on the floral runner rug, a luminous beetle, dusting itself off, beginning to check out its new surroundings. It glimmered a russety green; from here it was magnificent, and I thought that if my story was a folktale, that beetle would turn out to be Irena.

I was about to go investigate when I heard Chloe say, "What was that?" I stepped back into the room to see her rising ever so slightly from Freddie's bed, eyes wide. Then the rest of us heard it: a knock at the front door.

"Okay," said Schulz, peering at his phone in his outstretched hand. "I'm calling the police."

"No!" said Freddie. "We shouldn't bother the police. It's likely just a neighbor dropping by."

"A neighbor dropping by?" Chloe repeated like he had lost his mind completely now.

"Do the neighbors not drop by?"

Chloe looked at me. Did Irena have *neighbors*? Had we ever seen her or even Bogdan speak to anyone in town? The knocking resumed, a little heavier.

"I'll go," Ostap said, puffing up his compact body.

"We'll all go?" I said uncertainly.

"Safety in numbers!" Alexis said brightly, in English, which she blithely assumed we'd understand.

Petra pulled a handful of acorns from her pocket. "For luck," she said, passing Chloe and me one each.

Alexis had the audacity to stay behind while the rest of us approached the door, slowly, some of us on tiptoe. Chloe and I picked up our plastic swords. Schulz ripped the Bozdoğan mace out of its rack, and as we moved past, the rack, too, came off the wall, leaving a ragged patch of scores and gunk in the wood.

I had the wild idea that if it was Our Author at her own door, she would be displeased to see her home disfigured. I folded my hands and squeezed them together until it felt like all my bones were about to break and looked up and saw Ostap putting his ear to the door.

But—why would Irena knock at her own door?!

"Who's there?" Petra said, holding her stomach like she might throw up again.

"InPost," sang a voice from the other side of the door.

"It's just a courier," Chloe said. "Whew. Open the door."

"What would you expect him to say? Isn't that exactly what a murderer would say?" Petra asked, but then she had to sit down because she wasn't feeling well, and in any case, Ostap had already opened the door.

On the doorstep stood a young man in a cheerful uniform holding a package and a little clipboard with a pen attached.

"Which one of you is Irena?" he asked, untroubled by the swords or the mace or the sheer energy and quantity of us.

"I'm Irena," Chloe and I both said at the same time. We looked at each other and laughed. But then I took a quick step forward, and I signed. My mind drew a blank on her actual signature, although all of my copies of her books were inscribed. Rather than getting it wrong, I decided to sign my own name, just more floridly than usual.

"What if it's a bomb?" Ostap asked.

"Should we open it?" Chloe asked. "It's not a bomb. Why would it be a bomb?"

"We could place it at the base of Our Lady of Literature," Renata said. "Like an offering. Or just to keep it out for her until she comes back."

I walked the package over to the shrine. I set it down. As I was rising, I saw another of the sentences they'd chosen from her works. This one was from *Kernel of Light*. Helplessly, I remembered where I was when my Spanish version was published, in a little apartment by the beach in La Pedrera. I'd planned it as a celebration and distraction from the towering fear I'd had of not doing her justice in that very first translation; my ex-boyfriend was there, drinking an Uruguayan beer straight out of the bottle, like they do on U.S. television. That was a nice time in my life, before he'd moved to Mexico. Before he'd met the up-and-coming actress with the curvy, baby-ready frame.

The sentence my colleagues had chosen read: *The fight against death is the dullest contest, taking place in gloom, in gray, in solitude, inglorious, absent any will to victory, and yet: It is a battle daily won.*[22]

It felt like a prophecy, except that our fight against death had taken place out in the open, on a sunny day and on purpose.

"We told you what happened on our excursion," I said to Petra and Renata, dragging myself out of my trance, forcing myself not to think about that Oaxacan witch my ex-boyfriend loved instead of me now. "What happened on yours?"

Ostap had backed up and was standing in the kitchen. Schulz was getting down on hands and knees to *sniff* Irena's package, as though he were a bomb-detecting dog.

---

22   This is Irena's take on Joseph Conrad's famous lines from *Heart of Darkness*: "I have wrestled with death. It is the most unexciting contest you can imagine." Much of *Kernel of Light* was like this, her takes on things that were written in English, which made my job much more difficult than anyone else's, not that anyone else even cared (Trans.).

"We started missing Czech," said Renata, not taking her eyes off Ostap, who seemed to be trying to lure her in to where he was, although she didn't move.

"Yes," said Petra. She glanced at Schulz, who was at her feet. I actually thought she might be about to kick him, but she just said, "Because Saint Wenceslas, before his martyrdom, was the Duke of Bohemia, none of us was able to resist remembering our fallen comrade."

"Poor Czech," Renata said.

"It got us thinking," said Schulz, leaning back against the base of Petra's barrel chair. "In particular about one of the verses the father read, Corinthians 15."

"Which says?" Chloe prompted him.

" 'Death is swallowed up in victory. Behold, I tell you a mystery: We all shall not sleep, but we shall all be changed, in a moment, in the twinkling of an eye, at the last trump: for the trumpet shall sound, dead shall be raised incorruptible, and we shall be changed.' "

"What does that mean?" I asked. "Catholicism is a little more relaxed in Argentina."

"It means that the faithful must resolutely accept the doctrine of life after death," Schulz told me. "In a way, what it means is this: There's no such thing as death. Nothing ends. Everything only transforms."

"Hmm," I said. I was doing my best to stay calm, but the day was beginning to take its toll on me. I needed to think about something—anything—other than death. I sat cross-legged on the floor next to Schulz and reached for Irena's package.

"No!" cried Ostap from the kitchen. I pulled the cardboard strip. Everyone was watching me. I reached in. I held the thing inside, a little bottle, and relished the knowledge that everyone was watching me, that what I had in my hand was the most important thing to us right now, even though I also knew that revealing what it was would put an end to its importance (and mine).

"Okay," said Chloe. "What is it?"

"Maybe the four P.M. tincture?" I said.

"Just take it out," said Petra, and I did.

It was a bottle of glycolic acid, for wrinkle relief. It was just Irena's missing toiletry, another useless little tool in her fight against time. It was nothing.

Unfazed, Chloe asked Petra, "But does that mean you think Irena might be dead?"

"Why would it mean that?" I asked.

"Irena isn't dead," Petra replied, "because she can't be."

"The only thing she could be is transformed," clarified Schulz.

"Transformed," I said slowly, letting the word melt in my mouth. "Hey, didn't you say Leshy could take on any likeness?"

"Leshy," Schulz repeated, in a tone that suggested I was the only one still thinking about tutelary deities. But that didn't stop me.

"What if it was Leshy when we got here, and not Irena at all?"

Chloe squinted. Renata was knitting, and the clack, clack, clack of that unseasonable project made my skin crawl.

"I mean the person who was waiting for us when we arrived last week was a pale imitation of Irena. What if it actually was an imitation? What if the real Irena—our Irena—had already left? What if, for example, she had already left *with* Bogdan, totally of her own accord? What if everything with Irena is actually totally fine, and this is all just the forest trying to trick us? To protect itself?"

"But then why did we supposedly see the Leshy in the strict reserve? Why did it stop impersonating Irena?" said Chloe.

"It?" said Petra.

"You guys, come back!" screeched Alexis.

The TV was playing a tense little jingle. "The Commemoration of the Battle of Hajnówka," said a woman with a man's haircut, "a glorious and ceremonious occasion at the Park of Monumental Miniatures, was spoiled today by the actions of an insane man who terrorized the crowd with his arrows, which struck three. There were no reported casualties. The authorities are on the hunt for the man, who was described by attendees as bearded, and who was last seen near Świnoroje."

"Bearded," Chloe said, laughing again. "That's all they got?"

"Then he's still at large!" said Petra.

Several of us were searching for Świnoroje on our map apps. It was north of us, but not so far north that we could rest assured he wouldn't loop back down to Białowieża.

"But if he hit three people, that means he wasn't only shooting at us," Chloe said.

"Not necessarily," Alexis said and gave an extended sigh.

"What should we do now?" asked Ostap.

Petra sighed. "Call the police?"

"Translate?" I suggested.

"Now?" said Freddie.

"Did anyone else think Chapter Nine didn't really add that much?" Alexis said. Her eyes were closed. She was fanning her stunningly beautiful face. "And like it's also a little"—she cupped her hands around her mouth like she was about to tell us some important secret—"overwritten?"

"Okay let's call the police," I said, seeing scarlet at this latest break with sacred protocol. Overwritten? Didn't really add that much? I wanted the police to come, and I wanted them to arrest Alexis.

But for the third time that afternoon, Freddie said, "No!"

"But—" Schulz began, and Freddie groaned.

"We can't call the police," he said.

"But why?" I said.

"She could be injured," said Petra. "She could—by now . . ."

"By now she could be dead," I said.

I didn't mean it, Irena. I never actually thought you could ever be dead. All I was doing was helping Schulz and Petra say what they wanted to say, now that Corinthians had transmuted what they wanted to say into pablum. But then Freddie said, "I think you might be right," and walked straight up to me. I felt hot and afraid and driven forward by a gust of intrepidity I wouldn't have been able to explain then and still can't.

Then he added, with a quiet intensity, moving his lips slowly, looking at me with a luxurious hesitation that could have preceded a first kiss: "And if she is dead, I think it's possible we killed her."

CHAPTER TEN

We were horrified and brimming with adrenaline and didn't want to want to eat. But Freddie and Chloe and Alexis and I had walked over twenty kilometers that afternoon, and Schulz, Petra, Renata, and Ostap had gone to the market on their way home and brought us bread and cheese and all of the ingredients for gazpacho. After what struck me as an unnecessarily long debate about whether or not I, as a native Spanish speaker formerly known to them as Spanish, should know how to make gazpacho, Petra and Renata made it, and we carried our chairs outside to Our Author's back garden, where Alexis created yet another toxic cloud around us to frighten the mosquitoes away.[23] Remarkably, Petra had not yet recovered from her gastrointestinal malady, and she threw up twice before serving our soup. I was eager to blame this on Alexis's repellent, but I also thought that maybe it was some kind of bird flu, some remnant of Renata's plagues, given how close the two of them were, or conversely, that it was psychosomatic, a panic reaction to the little wedge of daylight I was beginning to detect between them.

Then the sun's rays began to change colors and get fainter, and Freddie stood up. Pacing in front of the shrubs with their currants that glowed as though possessed by tiny individual demons, keeping his hands clasped behind him and his eyes fixed to the ground, he first enumerated what we definitely knew.

"As my French colleague has noted, upon our arrival in Białowieża—eight days ago now—Irena Rey appeared transformed. I quote Cle—" He paused. He

---

23   It's like they don't have insect repellent in South America. But I googled it. They do (Trans.).

continued: "I quote *Chloe* because as you all know I had never met Irena prior to that occasion—"

Here there was a murmur among the half of us who had attended the Saint Wenceslas mass at the Parish of the Assumption of the Blessed Virgin Mary and Saint Stanislaus the Bishop and Martyr. Freddie paused, then continued: "Or perhaps you didn't know. In any case, even to me she didn't seem to be herself. We can deduce from this that there was something wrong. Correct me if this is not the case," he said, looking us over, plucking a currant from the nearest shrub, "but none of us has any real information as to what that thing might be. For all we know, she might have been dying of cancer." Renata burst into tears. We were not allowed to *pluck* Our Author's currants. "She might not have been dying of cancer," Freddie added quickly, raising a steadying hand.

Chloe raised her hand then, too.

"Chloe," he said.

"Can we please try to refer to her in present tense? I don't think she's dead, although I don't know where you're going with this. I mean, I might, but I'm not sure."

"Sustained," said Freddie. "Where I'm going is this: We know something in her life must have recently changed, but that is all we know—apart from the issue of the government removing her beloved trees. Now. Petra, Renata, our chefs." He turned on his heels. "For Irena's last supper, if you remember, we were served an exquisitely smackfull mushroom risotto."

Chloe raised her hand again, and once more, Freddie called on her.

"This is where I thought you might be going, but just a small reminder that I am actually the one who made the risotto," she said. "And 'smackfull' continues not to be a Polish word."

"No," said Freddie thoughtfully. "However: Petra and Renata were the ones given the task of preparing the mushrooms to be added to the meal. Do you recall," he said to them, "how those mushrooms initially appeared?"

"In ice water," they said simultaneously. We considered it bad luck to say the same thing at the same time as someone; we believed our job was to create not identical utterances, but rather complementary ones: careful, artisanal upcycling, not mechanical reproduction. Petra and Renata looked at each other for a moment as though trying to decide how to handle this latest run in the fabric of Our Author's former entourage. Finally, Petra repeated the word "ice" and added that there hadn't been time to go to the forest and forage, and the little nearby stores would have already been closed, so that those mushrooms—which presumably Irena, in her infinite generosity, had supplied—had been the only option she and Renata had really had.

Renata pointed out that everyone had said the mushrooms were delicious—Our Author had made sure to comment on their flavor more than once. (Twice when her mouth was full, which served to emphasize her point.)

"Do you recall," continued Freddie, as though neither Petra or Renata had said anything, "how the mushrooms looked later on that same evening, when we took our dishes to the kitchen, and the rest of you—I being unable to participate, due to my . . . injury—cleaned up?"

"They were goo," said Ostap solemnly.

"They were goo!" said Freddie. "They were goo because those mushrooms were *Coprinopsis atramentaria*, also known as inky caps on account of the fact that they self-destruct after releasing their spores or being harvested. They digest their own flesh, which turns into a black viscous substance that can be—and has been, since ancient times—employed as ink. Irena grows her own *Coprinopsis atramentaria*," he continued slowly, methodically, "because Irena only writes in ink whose production she can personally oversee. I found several jars of it on her desk when I was poking around in her office. To be honest, it gave me a whole new respect for her."

These were all such bizarre things to say—our existing respect for her should have left no room for any new respect, let alone "poking around"—but to our shame we were almost accustomed to his inexplicable outbursts, and since we desperately needed to know what his point was, we allowed him to go on.

"Had I been my usual self, I would have realized what was happening in time. Due to my injury, however, I didn't get it until after she was gone. The use of inky cap mushrooms for culinary purposes can be quite dangerous, even lethal."

Petra sniffed. "Inky caps are only dangerous when they're combined with alcohol, and we don't ever drink here. You're not the only one who knows what they are."

"Of course not," he said. "But do you know what your Author is?"

For the second time that day, we issued a collective gasp. In hindsight, however, I'm not sure we all interpreted his comment the same way. Was he calling Irena a liar? Was he suggesting she had a well-concealed problem with alcohol (and possibly mushrooms)? Or were we mostly responding to the notion that we might not know her every thought, her every move, her every conscious desire, like we had always believed we did?

Alexis beamed, throwing back her shoulders. She had always worn a gold necklace with her initial on it; now the *A* was more prominent, as if she were becoming Amália, or a surrogate for Our Author herself.

"Honestly, I would love a glass of wine right now," she said. "Wouldn't that be good?"

"No!" I howled. "How can wine be your first thought on hearing Freddie's theory? No one's drinking wine, my God."

"Well, I would," Alexis said, "happily." Freddie nodded. Their eyes met and locked, lit up. I thought about how much he had touched her after the picnic, as we were making our way home,[24] how he had even fed her slivers of apple—the only sustenance we'd had—from his ratty Bob Dylan tote bag.

"She has a secret cellar," he told us. "That's where she grows her inky caps. It's underneath my room. There's plenty of wine down there."

"There's plenty of lots of things down there," Alexis chirped. "There's even a washer/dryer!"

Silence fell like a blade on Our Author's entourage. Even Freddie was flummoxed by this. Had Alexis been burrowing under his room?

"Oh, not this time," she announced, as if we'd asked out loud. "Before."

But the word "before" from her here was a wrench in the space-time vortex; could she mean that it was when Our Author's husband had occupied those quarters that she'd been granted access to their underbelly? And would that mean—I stood up, got dizzy, sat back down—that she and he had . . . ? But it couldn't possibly, they couldn't have—I violently shook my head, trying to expel the image of Alexis straddling that somewhat homely, thoroughly devoted-seeming man.

Unless it had been the three of them. Unless Alexis had seduced both Irena and Bogdan, betraying us all.

---

24 I really tried not to comment on this chapter, but the phrase "making our way home" in no way does justice to the more than *thirteen* miles we walked in terror after nearly being killed. I walked *barefoot* over bark and sticks that were still strewn across the highway from the storm and/or the invasion of the government workers. I stepped on a *bee*. I was in agony! Not to mention the fact that my eyes did not light up (Trans.).

"What I mean to suggest," said Freddie, looking a little disappointed to have been upstaged, "is that Irena did in fact drink alcohol, that because of her as-yet-unexplained novel problem—that is, new problem[25]—she indulged in a fair amount of alcohol, in fact, taken from her own well-stocked cellar and consumed in her room before and after our dinner."

"You have no evidence of that," said Schulz.

"I have the same evidence that you have. That you would have," Freddie corrected himself, "if you'd only open your eyes. You all know she was behaving strangely that night. You all saw her eat vanilla ice cream with a side of cigarette. You heard how horribly she sang. Surely it must be clear to all of you that Irena Rey was *drunk*."

At this we exploded, all talking over one another, and Petra threw up again in the corner of the yard. Alexis's cloud hadn't worked because in our soups on our laps now floated insects; I picked a gnat out of mine and flicked it, by accident, onto Alexis. She stood up and hobbled off. When she came back, she was carrying two bottles of wine.

"WWCD!" she proclaimed, pronouncing the letters in English. She looked around.

"What would," Chloe began, and Alexis flapped the bottles at her. "Christ?"

"Czech! What would Czech do! Czech!" screeched Alexis. "Now is the time to honor our fallen comrade. It is still Saint Wenceslas Day after all. Everyone: Finish up your soup. And someone get me a corkscrew."

Ostap stood and looked at me and then at her and then at me again. I rolled my eyes. He darted into the house. Renata followed.

"Even if Irena drank," I said, "although I'm not saying I agree that she did. But even if she did consume vast quantities of alcohol, would eating the inky caps really have killed her?"

"It is unusual," said Freddie, "but so is a wrinkled peach, aka rosy veincap, aka *Rhodotus palmatus*, at the end of September, so is being bitten by an adder—so is everything that has happened here so far. So is having arrows aimed directly at our heads. So is *Grey Eminence*. It is all unusual. It is all extremely unusual. And yet." He plucked another currant and popped it into his mouth. "It is my

---

25   Pun obviously mine (Trans.).

belief that Irena may have grown delirious on consuming those *Coprinopsis* and wandered off into the forest. This exposure to the elements, in her state, in this heat, followed by the storm, may have brought about her d—"

"We're not allowed to talk about the w—" Petra ventured queasily, but Freddie shouted, "Oh, come on! Wake up! She's not here anymore, and I have to say that even if she were, it sounds like an awful lot of rules for a handful of guests and colleagues."

"We are not her colleagues," I said and stood up again.

"Fine," he said. "Employees, then."

I stared at him. He stared at me. There was the sound of a cork coming out of a bottleneck. I drank down my soup.

INSIDE, UPSTAIRS, I took a shower. I had pocketed Irena's latest acid; now I smeared it all over my face. Squinting into the mirror, I thought I could detect a glow beginning to free itself from the confines of my body, about to become visible to all.

I never tried on purpose to become you, Irena. I don't even think Alexis did. It was just that our task as your translators was to fill in for you, and even Alexis, in her own, different way, was dedicated to that task.

At the end of the hall I found a linen closet. In my room, cross-legged on my bed that I made less expertly than Bogdan would have, but that nonetheless no longer smelled like forest mop, I checked Chloe's Instagram, but she hadn't posted in months. I checked Alexis's.

It was patently insane, the work of yet another deranged Archer.[26] Beneath a picture of her laughing with her head thrown back at some unbearable fake Latin American restaurant, a caption that read, *"end white supremacy #charlottesville."* I googled Charlottesville. It was a city in Virginia, a state in the eastern U.S. Yet the picture—I clicked on the location—had been taken in southwestern Australia.

I was overwhelmed by the incoherence of Alexis. The post was like a post-card of Mount Everest that said, "Greetings from Bangkok, Argentina." Or a

---

26 Ha, ha (Trans.).

postcard of an erupting volcano that said, "Beach vibes," or "Palais du Louvre," or all of the above. What did her East Coast have to do with Latin America and what did Latin America have to do with Perth? What did her own whiteness have to do with ending white supremacy?

I googled "Freddie social conscience wife" but got no relevant results. To soothe myself, I checked my ex-boyfriend's Twitter, and not seeing anything new about awards or invitations, I snuggled into my pillow and mentally prepared to go to sleep.

My phone dinged. Of course it was Alexis, drunkenly messaging our Team Irena WhatsApp group. I sat up again. "Salman Rushdie's Japanese translator Hitoshi Igarashi was stabbed to death in 1991," she wrote. "The case remains unsolved. Also in 1991, his Italian translator Ettore Capriolo was stabbed but survived. Then a mob tried to burn Rushdie's Turkish translator Aziz Nesin in 1993 by setting fire to his hotel. They didn't get Aziz, but they did kill thirty-seven other people. Rushdie just keeps writing!"[27, 28]

What was Alexis trying to say? That the archer was Irena's fault? Alexis was saying that by writing controversial novels, Irena was putting us, her translators, at risk. I let out a long exhale of hatred and frustration and checked Irena's semi-secret Facebook page. There was nothing new there, but I went through each of her photos and, when I came to my favorites, held my phone to my lips and closed my eyes. "Te amo,"[29] I whispered to the last one of Irena in Gdynia wearing dark aviator glasses and a black silk scarf. My lips were still on my screen, kissing it in the middle of the word, which I repeated.

"Amo," I murmured. "Amo. Ama. Amadou."

I got up again and went back to my notebook and wrote:

---

27   A friend, whom I shall not name, died by suicide earlier this year after her author doubted her motivations for translating her work. The unscrupulous house that was to publish the work then removed my friend's name from the translation, pretending it had been done by the author herself. People don't think about translators very much—I mean in general—and we often get less credit (and money) than we deserve. But I just want to note here by way of emphasis that sometimes we even get written out of the story, out of our own life stories. And sometimes we get implicated in crimes we didn't commit (Trans.).

28   P.S. Please remember that I wrote these words five years prior to the horrific 2022 stabbing of Salman Rushdie himself (Trans.).

29   "I love you," in Spanish (Trans.).

AMADOUAMADOU
MADOUAMADO
ADOUAMAD
DOUAMA
OUAM
UA

Then I ripped out that page and laid it flat between my skin and my pajamas, its center where my waistline was. I lay down on my bed on my stomach and mentally prepared to go to sleep.

When I woke up the next morning, a week after Our Author left, my amulet page was stuck to my skin, and when I peeled it off, I saw that AMADOU-AMADOU was tattooed onto my abdomen, but faintly, and in reverse:

UA
OUAM
DOUAMA
ADOUAMAD
MADOUAMADO
AMADOUAMADOU

CHAPTER ELEVEN

There were many ways to look for Irena, and the next day we hazily agreed it was now more important than ever that we exhaust them all, with the exception, needless to say perhaps, of calling the police. I did not buy into Freddie's theory, and I'm not sure anyone else fully did, either, but the detail with which he had explained it to us, coupled with our possible brushes with Leshy and definite brushes with the picnic archer, had brought to mind in all of us other, equally horrific possibilities, along with their attendant details, which lent our search an urgency it had not yet had before, when we were mostly scared of enraging her and waiting for her to decide on her own to come back.

I still couldn't shake the sense that none of us felt how we were supposed to feel—that collectively we weren't lost enough without her, even though some people were acting somewhat strange—but I made the decision to attribute our relative okayness to shock.

Schulz and Renata and Petra took *Grey Eminence*, which they would pore over in the hopes of tells or codes—whatever clues we might have missed on our first group and second individual reads. We'd already managed to translate ninety-two pages, but that still left 810 for the answer to all our problems to possibly be hiding in, like—according to Polish Wikipedia, which I foraged nightly now—Jews or Polish partisans in the Białowieża Forest during the war.[30]

---

30 I realize this author is of Jewish ancestry, partly, but still: This line disgusts and perplexes me every time (Trans.).

The forest fell, meanwhile, to Chloe and Alexis and Ostap. There were hundreds of miles of it where we had never set foot. In spite of the aloe, Alexis's feet were still marred and disgusting, but she insisted she'd be fine. As it happened, she wore the same size shoe as Our Author, so she had borrowed some comfortable sneakers and cozy socks, a turn of events I loathed. How were we supposed to track Our Author when there were others walking around in her shoes? But I kept my revulsion to myself because I still wanted Alexis to go hunting with Chloe and Ostap, and I knew there probably wasn't any other way.

That left Freddie and me. We were supposed to make small talk with anyone we could find in our immediate vicinity who didn't have a murderous look in their eyes. Although ours was the most dangerous assignment, it was ours— Freddie and I would spend the day together alone, without any distractions from the rest of the group.

Before parting ways, we stood in a circle around the shrine and held hands like we used to when we used to form circles around Irena, back when we were vine-like, a proper entourage. Freddie's hand was both soft and rough, and I tried not to hold on to it too tightly.

Petra cleared her throat. She and Renata had dark, puffy circles under their eyes, which gave me a glimmer of hope that maybe some of us weren't as okay as I'd believed. "Saint Anthony," boomed Petra, "perfect imitator of Jesus, who was granted by God the special power to restore lost things, allow us to locate Our Author, without whom we ourselves shall be lost, and allow us to honor, fully and appropriately, our fallen comrade, who translated from Polish into Czech, and who always amused us with his outfits, his stories, and his chronic lateness to work and to play."

We bowed our heads, and what began as a moment of silence stretched out into a few minutes of postponing the inevitable, until finally Freddie released my and Alexis's hands and clapped his together and said, "Onward!" It sounded like, "On guard!" But we all knew what he probably meant.

Freddie and Alexis and Chloe and Ostap and I tumbled outside, where it was starting to sprinkle. Alexis opened a sturdy American umbrella without so much as a half step away from our tight cluster under the roof. I ducked and saw the other three had also scattered to escape her. She didn't notice. How American, I thought, and how Alexis.

I hadn't brought an umbrella, but Freddie had found us one by rummaging through Bogdan's things in the basement.

As we set off in opposite directions along Stoczek Street, Freddie said, "You know, I told Chloe."

"Told Chloe what?" To our right were several houses that seemed to be abandoned, but two of them had new signs. Each sign displayed a ferocious-looking guard dog, although there were no dogs in sight, and I had never heard one barking.

"My theory," said Freddie. "The theory that it could have been the inky caps."

"When?"

"The night I met you by your name, Emi." For what felt like the hundredth time since the previous afternoon, I looked at his fingers, now wrapped around the handle of our or Bogdan's umbrella. As on previous occasions, there was no ring.

Chloe had come to my room the night before, not long after Alexis's harrowing WhatsApp, and together, on Facebook, we'd sleuthed out the identity of Freddie's wife. Her name was Bogdana—the feminine version of Irena's husband's name, immeasurably uglier than its masculine counterpart.[31]

It was a pleasant surprise to me, at first, that she herself was also ugly. (We both agreed she was.) In every picture she wore either a stern expression or an uncomely, too-broad smile; her dishwater blond hair coiled atop her head in a frizzy, desperate way that made me anxious just to see on my screen. But when my initial surprise wore off, and we finally found a picture of the two of them together, my delight was overshadowed by confusion: Why would *he*—handsome as a red deer, with his Baikal eyes and his muscular arms and shoulders—have married *her*?

"I should have told you, too," Freddie said, misinterpreting my silence. "But she dismissed it—I believe she called it 'extravagant'—and for a few days I felt, I have to say, a bit embarrassed about having told even her, or having thought of it. So I swore her to secrecy."

I wasn't sure if Chloe would want me to or not, but I couldn't restrain myself from making the accusation we'd quietly arrived at a few days before: "Is that why you stole her notebook?"

---

31   Why, I wonder (Trans.).

"Stole?"

"Her notebook?"

"I didn't steal her notebook, Emi."

"Okay." I wanted to believe him. "Honestly, she probably forgot about it until you brought it up again." Chloe did have a healthy habit of never dwelling on things she said weren't "furthering her journey." But Freddie still looked hurt.

"I know I don't really fit in here," he said. It was the first time I'd heard him sound vulnerable, or real, although I hadn't realized quite how unreal he'd remained to me before. I was also relieved that someone had finally said what was so glaringly, painfully true—that Freddie seemed to have almost nothing in common with the rest of us, and it was weird that he was here—and I let out a tiny moan of relief and threw my arms around him. He leaned down, and for a split second, I pressed my face into his neck. When we pulled apart, I was blushing.

"We would never have said anything," I told him, "because to do so would have been to doubt her wisdom—but Irena must have had her reasons for choosing you."

Freddie said, "Hmm," and turned to start walking again.

But I wasn't finished tackling tough subjects. I blurted: "Why don't you wear a wedding ring?"

"Ah. My wife has always insisted on each of us having . . ." He paused and turned to face the other side of the street. Having what? My mind raged. Having their own lives? Having unadorned fingers? Having this upsetting effect on any Argentine women they should happen to come across? "Should we go into the pharmacy?" he asked.

"Maybe," I said. I knew I couldn't force him. I needed to change course, make him feel comfortable enough to confide in me without my even asking. Also, we did need to find Irena. "If she was sick, then maybe the pharmacist would know about it."

"Exactly," he said.

It was very dark inside, with just a few things on the shelves, some soap and toilet paper, packets of pills called 2Fast2Thin, a lone pregnancy test, and no condoms (due to my upbringing, it was a reflex to check). There was no sign of life behind the counter.

"Hello?" Freddie called.

"Is anyone here?" I asked, walking up to the window. We heard a crash in the back, and the sound of a woman swearing. Then the shuffle of approaching footsteps.

"Hello," Freddie said after a silence, taking my place at the window. "We work for Irena Rey. She sent us to pick up her medication."

"Her medication?" the woman balked.

"Yes," I said quickly from very close behind Freddie, "she sent us to find out if it's ready yet."

The woman narrowed her eyes at me, and I moved even closer to Freddie, so that my whole left side was pressed against him, and I could feel him pressing back. I was pretty sure the pharmacist had seen right through us, that she knew we'd done something that had resulted in the loss of Our Author, and that she was about to report us to someone—Irena, Leshy, Veles, the police. Minister Szyszko. Freddie's ugly, frizzy wife.

Instead, she said, "You mean her father's medication." She said it fast, and loud, like it had dawned on her that we were foreign, but she hadn't figured out how to handle it yet.

Freddie turned to me. I must have looked surprised. The woman was watching us closely, and it occurred to me that this must be a kind of trap, a test to make sure we really knew Irena and weren't journalists or just crazed fans. So I ventured, "It isn't possible for her father to need medication. He died on the day she was born."

But the woman merely laughed at this and shuffled away. I judged from this that we had fallen straight into the trap she'd set—but how? How had I managed to make myself ridiculous *again?*

"Excuse me!" Freddie called after her, but I grabbed his arm and dragged him out the door. Until I understood why what I'd said was wrong, I couldn't have a way of knowing what to say next that might be right.

Back out on the street I tried to rein in my racing thoughts. The precipitation had picked up, and my legs were getting wet in spite of Bogdan's umbrella. We came to the village's other little grocery store, not more than what we would call a "kiosko" in Buenos Aires, and tried the door but found it locked. We huddled under the little corrugated roof, and I slipped a cigarette out of my secret pack.

"Don't tell," I said to him, although as I said it I remembered Irena smoking, wondered if it even made sense to keep my smoking a secret anymore.

But Freddie said, "Of course."

"Do you want one?"

"Of course."

As we stood there smoking in the rain, I told him the story of Our Author's origins. I had told it numerous times before—on a radio program in Buenos Aires, at the Book Fair in Guadalajara, on a podcast about Polish culture by a Madrileño living in Warsaw. She had been born, I began again now, in Hajnówka, to a beautiful twenty-two-year-old named Nina Rej, a woman Irena resembled so closely that had the pictures of her mother been in color, it would have been impossible to distinguish them from the pictures of Irena at that age. It was almost uncanny, I said, and Freddie raised his eyebrows and exhaled.

Nina and Irena's father, Aleksander, had been in love since they were children. The first time they made love, they were fourteen. It was a miracle, Irena always said, that she didn't come into the world several years earlier, and she often pondered what her fate might have been if she had. As it was, the couple married in 1973, and in 1974, they created Irena, who was born on December 3, the very day Aleksander was shot dead in the forest at dawn.

Out of habit, I paused. Always before, people had shown interest here, but either Freddie wasn't listening, or Freddie didn't care.

"The murderer," I continued, "was none other than Emil Wierzbicki, Aleksander's *best friend*. Emil disappeared that day, never to return or be captured—his whereabouts remain unknown, if indeed he's still alive—but their circle of friends later revealed a plot between the two of them to fight a duel. It had been planned, with seconds, for the following morning, but some premonition must have hastened it—since had they waited, surely Irena's arrival would have prompted Aleksander to call the whole thing off. Instead they absconded alone into the forest, and at however many paces, Aleksander was shot and killed."

Thankfully, the mention of a duel had piqued his interest. "I could never imagine how people fought duels," he said, sucking more violently on his cigarette. "I know it was so common—so popular, even—for so many years. But how could you look another human being in the face and then just shoot them? How could other people stand around and just . . . observe? What's the word for that in Polish? The combatants' friends who observe the murders?"

" 'Seconds'," I said, watching the smoke I breathed out wrap around him in a swiftly disappearing cloud.

"Seconds," he repeated. "I can't imagine it."

I wasn't sure I agreed. Surely there were certain moral truths still worth defending. What seventeenth- and eighteenth-century people called honor, what we might call integrity today. I could imagine that. But I was afraid Freddie would think I was weird if I said so. I dug my nails into the palm of my free hand.

"Were they fighting over Irena's mom?" he asked.

"No," I said. "Not at all. The duel was over the outcome of that year's World Cup. That was when they'd first stopped being friends: July 3, 1974, two days after the death of Perón, in my country, and the day of the game between Poland and West Germany."

"Oh, I remember that game," said Freddie. "I mean, I don't *remember* it, but I know about it. Die Wasserschlacht, right? In German."

"Right. The game on the water." As I said the phrase in Polish, the wind and rain picked up, and seeing me shiver or shudder again, Freddie draped his arm around my shoulder. I took a breath without my cigarette and let the words I had used in the past, in Spanish, come back to me in Polish now.

Every World Cup is political, I told him, but 1974's was especially charged: the USSR did not participate as a result of the Chilean coup d'état; Poland did participate for the first time since 1938. More importantly, the games were held in West Germany, with East and West facing off in the first round, on June 22, in Hamburg, before a crowd of sixty-two thousand. It was the only time they'd ever play each other on this level, and the Stasi was watching even more attentively than all those fans. East Germany won—it was a major triumph—but they were eliminated in the second round.

But that left Poland. They had beaten Argentina, Haiti, and Italy by the time of their match against the West Germans. The problem was the Cup had been plagued from the start by terrible thunderstorms, and at the official start time of the Poland–West Germany face-off in Frankfurt, there was a devastating downpour that left the pitch in standing water. The fire department was called to try to clear the field, but they could do only so much. When the game started thirty minutes late, the players had to contend with mud and puddles everywhere they turned, and it was hard for some of them to get their footing. To everyone's surprise, the Poles seemed to have the advantage, staying agile in spite of the deluge and keeping the ball on the West German half of the pitch.

"Ten minutes into the game," I said, "there was a minute of silence for Perón. I've always wondered how the players felt about those sixty seconds, whether they could have been thinking of anything other than mud and strategy. In any case, it was that moment of Peronism that changed the course of the game. When play resumed, the West Germans were less panicked, more deft, and although the Poles played well, they ultimately couldn't keep up their strength and lost, 0–1, to the West Germans."

"But what was the disagreement?" asked Freddie. "Between Aleksander and Emil? What made them want to kill each other after that?"

"Apparently, tensions mounted over the course of the game, minute by dramatic minute," I said, "and few of the intricacies have survived. We assume that offensive remarks were exchanged. That characters were called into question. That body language became increasingly hostile. The main thing was that in the end, when Poland was defeated, Aleksander, Irena's father, was willing to take a somewhat measured stance. He wasn't bothered by it the way the remainder of the circle was. He didn't think it was unfair, didn't suspect foul play or demand a rematch. He even went so far as to call his own nation's team 'fair-weather players.'

"It was the equivalent of treason as far as Emil was concerned. For two months, he didn't speak to Aleksander. Everyone thought it would pass, that they would reconcile, as they always had after a spat. But when they did resume their conversation, it was, if anything, on terms that were more antagonistic, more confrontational than before."

We were approaching the end of Irena's origin story, and the rain had relented, so I started walking again, outside of the umbrella, which he closed as he followed. Previously, when I had talked about Irena's father, I hadn't needed to say that in between the game on the water and the duel, Isabel Perón had taken over Argentina from her husband and ushered in a period of kidnappings and attacks; that soon there would be a coup and a military dictatorship that would torture and murder tens of thousands of my countrymen, including my father's rebel sister, the same year I was born.

I might have needed to say all that to Freddie, but I didn't have the strength. So I focused on Stoczek, but there wasn't much left of Irena's street now, just the souvenir store, which was always closed. We made our way to its display window.

Inside it were hatchets and varieties of knives, refrigerator magnets, thermal rifle scopes.

Freddie dropped his cigarette on the wet cement, giving it a courtesy tap with the ball of his foot. I had been so caught up in my narrative, or her narrative, that I had all but forgotten my own cigarette. I took a drag.

"I suppose the real question is," said Freddie, and I expected him to come up with some new conspiracy theory about the game, like Czech and Schulz had done before him, but instead he said, "what are we really doing here?"

I let out all the smoke from my lungs.

"If as we hope she was not poisoned by us," he continued, "then she could be anywhere by now. She could be in Brazil. She could be in Laos. Why are we walking around some godforsaken quasi-Belarusian village looking for someone who clearly isn't asking to be found?"

I bulged my eyes at him.

"She's not!" he cried. "Not by us, anyway. There is nothing stopping us from getting on a bus and heading back to Warsaw. We would be there in three hours, at either airport in three and a half. She's gone," he said firmly. "We came here to work with her. Think about how crazy it is for us to stay here. We've invaded her house, we're using everything she owns without permission—"

And that was when I kissed him. I did it to keep him from saying any more. That's the truth. What it later turned into is true, too. But that was how it started: I kissed him to shut him up.

He held me by the wrists, and he tasted like venom, and salt and fire and firs. As we pressed ourselves together, breathing each other's breath, I forgot where we were, and when at last I opened my eyes I was surprised not to see Buenos Aires—to see, instead, of a rounded bustling corner, drab angular concrete and a dark display window and the end of a road.

"I have an idea," I said and took off up Stoczek Street, nodding for him to follow. We passed her house and continued, past the pizzeria we'd never visited or ordered from and the Booted Eagle Hotel, turning at the big brick orphanage where the bulk of the Białowieża storks lived, passing the ponds that looked like giant primordial beasts in the sun that was still in the process of emerging, turning again at the old Palace Station with its humble, ornamental, eastern facade. It hadn't seen a train in thirty years. I took his soft, rough hand.

CHAPTER TWELVE

Freddie was right, and I was right: It was crazy to keep sleeping in her beds and scratching her pans and donning her footwear. But surely it was the best thing we could do for the novel, if indeed she intended for the novel to survive. Not only in the sense that being together would help us resolve slight misunderstandings, but also because every reading quickens in discussions, and it would be as a result of our talks that *Grey Eminence* would come alive and spread its wings and venture out into the Spanish-speaking, French-speaking, Serbian-speaking worlds.

I couldn't figure out if the insanity of it outweighed the literary value of it, and I was mulling this over, trying to see "insanity" and "literary value" on either side of a scale, but I couldn't quite envision it, and then, on our bikes, just a few minutes later, the scale clattered out of the frame, and, farther and farther removed from the village, as both future and past shed their relevance, Freddie and I became free.

The glare of the green landscape and the air, the air that was everywhere, in us and making way for us, and we rode and were aware only of each other and ourselves for those couple of miles, and for those couple of miles I was myself, back in the neighborhood of Chacarita, where I moved with my mom after we realized my dad was never going to move out first, that we would have to leave him, and I saw on either side of me the big ugly high-rises and squat goldenrod houses and fuchsia and blue and inscrutable notes scrawled on the walls, graffiti intermingling with the shimmering, shadowing little leaves of the tipas, and as I rode I slowed at the oleander at Facultad de Medicina, those delicate pink flowers that rose over the fence in utter opulence and the lush stiff leaves that reached out through the bars that were freshly painted bright green.

Then there it was: the Great Mamamushi.

I slowed, and Freddie slowed. We parked our bikes. I was out of breath and all the air on Earth was in my blood, and we kissed again, and I turned around, and he put his arms around my waist, and I leaned into him, and we beheld it: a tree that was almost too much to be true, that truly was incredible, with its trunk that was almost eight meters around, a staggering circumference, glittered over by dragonflies, heavy, petite, iridescent incarnations of Irena's genius, when suddenly a flock of impossible parrots exploded out of the alders, and we looked up to see them shattering the sky.

"All the oaks on this trail have their own names," I explained to Freddie. "This one is my favorite. Can you believe it's still growing?"

He put his face against mine. He didn't say anything. For a while we just stood like that, together, watching the Great Mamamushi grow.

Finally he said softly, "Are we still looking for Irena? Here?"

"I wanted to show you something you might like better than the village," I said, shrugging. "But also, you know how sometimes you search for something you absolutely have to find, like your keys, and you look everywhere and you still can't find it, until finally you just give up in frustration because it's impossible that your keys could be anywhere because everywhere has refused to have your keys?"

"Mmm," he said into my neck, releasing a charge that coursed through my body, reaching my feet on the dark hard soil.

"That's always when I find my keys," I murmured. "When I give up on finding them."

"I see. I'm not sure it will work if we're doing it on purpose. Doesn't it have to be an accident?"

"Yes—but now that I've told you I can try to forget."

"But either you forget or you don't," he said. "It's not something you can do by trying. It's like falling in love."

I looked at him. "Maybe," I said. And thought: If Freddie fell in love with me, he wouldn't want to leave. I smiled. I said, "Let's just enjoy the forest for a little while."

I took his hand, and we stepped onto the wooden boards that made up the trail that ran between the royal oaks. Thanks to Petra and Renata, I recognized the sweet squeaks of the firecrests in the spruce, and I knew that the hypnotic, nostalgic song we heard was a blackbird's—but a stampede of small children came up from behind us then and chased the birds away. As the children squealed and leaped, I thought in sad astonishment that there was once a time when I, too, could afford to expend all my energy, knowing it would all be restored, like an animal that can regenerate the parts of its body it loses in a skirmish. I'd be turning thirty-five soon. I'd be entering my middle age. What would happen if I couldn't convince Freddie not to leave?

Just then he cried, "How gorgeous! That's a four-footed earthstar. Fresh and perfect. Isn't it gorgeous?"

"What is it?" I said.

"It's a fungus. Cosmopolitan, but quite uncommon, I'd say—especially these days."

"What does that mean?"

"It means it could be found just about anywhere, but it probably won't be. And yet—once more, in an extremely unusual turn—*we* have found it."

He said "we" as if it were thanks to us that all these extremely unusual things were happening—or, I suppose, as if it were our fault. He knelt, and I joined him. The earth was blanketed with leaves. Atop them, Freddie's fungus was a couple of inches tall, and it looked like a chimera, a hideous distortion of my earlier vision of Our Author on horseback leading her epic charge. Instead of a noble centaur, this was a tiny, lumpy godlet with four fat white tapering legs, covered in what looked like bleached sashimi and topped with a tumor that could have been a cross between a chestnut and a date.

Freddie pointed at the tumor and said, "Here is where it produces its spores."

"Mmm," I said. It was ugly, and it horrified me. What if only ugliness appealed to Freddie, what if he had some sort of curious disorder, an aesthetic dyslexia—what would that mean about me?

Suddenly I saw us from above, from my ex-boyfriend's perspective, as though this were a scene in one of his films. How would *he* tell our story, I wondered—in the grainy, oneiric mumblecore of his twenties, or the grittier dramatic style of late? Would he be jealous of Freddie, or would he not even care anymore?

"Most of its life it spends as mycelium," Freddie said. He seemed to be talking about the mushroom to the mushroom, but it was hard to be sure, so I asked:

"What is mycelium?" It turned out to be the right next step in our conversation. He grinned.

According to Freddie, mycelium was the network of fine hyphae (little living threads) that coursed through the soil and stitched the plants and the trees of the forest into a united and communicating whole, a fabric that featured the beavers and the mole crickets and the moose—in short, it was the basis for the forest. Trees could share nutrients with one another through mycelium. On rare occasions, trees even poisoned plants via mycelium, if they posed some threat to them. But primarily the trees and plants received through the hyphae the minerals and water they needed from the soil, and in return, they offered the fungus the sugar that they, with their leaves, had the ability to produce through photosynthesis.

"Wait," I said. "But what are hyphae?"

Freddie beamed, and the light in his eyes and the release of all the concern from his features made him look even sexier somehow, if that were possible, and unlike on Stoczek when he was advocating for our individual escapes, I wanted him to keep talking, needed him to keep talking, to keep connecting with me, and it felt like he was on the verge of telling me some important secret, something that would actually lead us back to Our Author at last. Then I shook my head, to try to get her out of my mind, and Freddie noticed.

"Is this what the Americans call mansplaining?" he said.

I thought: Probably. But then I thought about Alexis. "Fuck the Americans," I said, even though technically, I was an American, too.

There was a horrible roar in the distance then. Freddie registered my horror; he put his hand on my arm again. He explained, raising his voice a little, that hyphae made up the circulatory system of a fungus, while at the same time interlacing with other organisms and with inorganic matter. Fungi didn't have strictly delineated bodies like animals or plants, Freddie nearly yelled: They were fully immersed in their surroundings. And it was this immersion that gave them a host of powers that we animals couldn't imagine, let alone imagine having, he said, and I loved how he referred to us as animals, and I thought it boded well, for sex.

"Think," said Freddie, "of all the alchemists in human history who wasted their lives trying to transform worthless objects into gold. Fungi do something like that every day. Fungi convert death and nonlife—convert what would otherwise just be waste—into life. Without fungi, none of what we know as our world could have existed."

"But you also think Irena Rey could have been killed by fungi," I shouted back, but in the middle of my sentence, the roaring ceased, so that the words "killed by fungi" blared needlessly down the walkway, and a middle-aged Polish couple turned and glared at me, and I covered my mouth.

"Yes," Freddie whispered. "Fungi don't have the kinds of ludicrous agendas human beings have. There is no veil of moral fantasy that distorts their view of the world and alters their behavior. Their behavior is their behavior. They don't discriminate between a supposedly worthless predator and a supposed future Nobel laureate. They simply do what they can to survive. There are fungi in Chernobyl"—he gestured southeast—"that can turn radiation into food. Just think!" He rubbed his hands together. "They are the planet's only future. Our only hope."[32]

"Do you think that might be what we do?" I ventured. "As translators?"

"You mean, turn radiation into food?"

"Yeah?" I said. "Maybe?"

Freddie smiled. "This is one of the reasons I agreed to come, in fact, when Irena emailed me. I consider it my duty to provide this service to the cultural ecosystem. Translation is a kind of recycling."

For the first time, I felt an intellectual connection to Freddie. I didn't know what to make of this, so I simply embraced him again. We had passed the Bona Sforza and Helena oaks and were coming up on Kazimierz the Great, a stunning four-hundred-year-old with a jagged, unspeakably green crown, magnificent, its branches extending in every possible direction, shimmering with birds' leaps and swoops. I thought of all the mycelium that must have been so busy on its behalf, all the mycelium across the centuries, fetching it nutrients.

"Do fungi always work with trees?" I asked, and I assumed he would say yes. I still remembered Irena saying that fungi were evil, but the notion of an

32   Yet another massive fungal exaggeration by Freddie—although at the same time, his Polish was never sufficient to express all this, so who knows (Trans.)?

underground indissoluble bond that made life possible appealed to my translator's view of the world and the circulatory system that was language—I just wanted to know that these translators of trees were unwaveringly faithful.

"You are asking all the right questions," said Freddie, and I was the one beaming now. But then he said, "Because no, they do not—fungi do not always work with trees. Plenty of fungi work *against* trees. Plenty of fungi are parasites."

Parasites, I thought, like Alexis, and that thought blocked out the option of an answer. I looked down at the boisterous ground. Hundreds of ants were carrying the broken body of a beetle across the trail. I took a showy step over their macabre parade.

"How did you become a translator?" Freddie asked, as though he, too, were thinking about Alexis.[33] "Are you a writer, too?"

"I never wanted to be a writer." At the time, it was true. "I feel the same way about people that I feel about literature. There are so many books out there already, so many trees, so much that goes to waste. The most wasteful thing of all is all the stories and ideas that exist in just one language, that only a few people can read."

"You don't want to have children?"

"I do want children. I just want to adopt them."

He gave me a look that felt familiar, and I realized I recognized it from other times men had decided they would change my mind. To distract him, perhaps, I said, "What was your first translation?"

"Ah," he said, smiling, "it was Francis Ponge. 'L'on ne peut sortir de l'arbre par des moyens d'arbre.'"

"Translation?" My school French had long since rusted, and Chloe, of course, spoke only Polish with me.

"There can be no escape of the tree by way of the tree."

"By way of the tree?"

"By means of the tree."

"Wouldn't the tree way be the only way to escape the tree?"

"You mean you have to become the tree to truly be free of it?"

"Maybe? Although I don't totally know what we're talking about?"

---

33 ?? (Trans.).

"I never thought of it that way," Freddie said. " 'Au printemps, lorsque, las de se contraindre et n'y tenant plus, ils laissent échapper un flot, un vomissement de vert, et croient entonner un cantique varié, sortir d'eux-mêmes, s'étendre à toute la nature, l'embrasser, ils ne réussissent encore que, à des milliers d'exemplaires, la même note, le même mot, la même feuille.' That's what comes before it. In the poem. Meaning the tree can't escape its treeness—that even when it thinks it's doing something new, intoning some thrilling, different hymn, it's just repeating the same note, the same word, the same leaf, over and over and over again."

"How do you know so many poems? I mean, by heart?"

He shrugged. "My mentor when I was first translating was a woman named Gunnel Vallquist, who translated *In Search of Lost Time* over a period of about thirty years, finishing shortly after I was born. She spent the nineties reworking it, making changes, adjusting her interpretations. I appreciated her obsessiveness, her passion for the project. She was a remarkable woman. She was chair thirteen in the Swedish Academy. She wrote a book of something like prose poems on her Catholicism that was really about fire, and about becoming inflammable, about the paradox of living with any kind of faith. Then when I moved to Oslo after university she put me in touch with Anne-Lisa Amadou, who had translated *In Search of Lost Time* into Norwegian in the sixties and seventies. Translators always have these networks, not like writers. Writers compete. In any case, one of the things both of them insisted on was learning poetry by heart. Reciting the poems I was translating almost as though they were prayers, in the mornings and before I went to bed. I was comforted, I suppose, by the ritual of that. I've never stopped."

I imagined Freddie reciting Proust at his bedside. It was pleasant, arousing, to think of him that way, murmuring in boxer shorts and a soft white T-shirt, on his knees, wallowing in words. But I was also startled by this mention of amadou, now as some Norwegian. How could everything be amadou now? Or had everything always been amadou, and I had simply never noticed it before?

We had reached a little clearing on the banks of the Łutownia, where the easy flow of the river made the mottled tree trunks sparkle and set the leaves' gray shivering undersides aglow. Freddie was talking about lichens, indivisible amalgams of fungi and algae and bacteria that can live for thousands of years. Too timid to take a picture of him, I took one of the water.

I am not and never have been a picture-taker. It simply isn't in my nature. But maybe because of my impending birthday, maybe because Irena was gone, or maybe just because of Freddie, I needed something to hold on to from that day, something with a beginning and an end and no guesswork.

It was only in the surface of the river on my screen that I noticed the clouds, or their reflections, beginning to gather again, and then the terrible noise resumed, louder than before, and we both cast around in a vain attempt to apprehend its source.

"Are they cutting down the trees?" asked Freddie.

"I don't know," I said. I felt for the acorn Petra had given me the day before, but it was no longer in my pocket.

He said, "Shall we go and see?" Ignoring all my inner warning bells, the bad omen of the missing acorn, I followed him as he rushed back to where we'd left our bikes. We retraced our steps, then rode past every part of Białowieża that I knew, past signs that said that we were leaving Białowieża, past a set of bison-crossing signs. Abruptly the chainsaw or the chainsaws stopped. Freddie pulled over by the side of the road.

"Let's try here," he said. Ahead of us, on the road, three enormous ravens scuffled over a flattened scrap of food. When a hawk soared overhead, they scattered. Freddie and I walked away from the road, toward a fluorescent yellow sign that absolutely forbade us from entering this section of the forest, and my feet hurt—my whole body hurt, from stress and from searching, and I wondered how Alexis had managed to overcome her footly wounds, whether it had been the aloe or some semidivine fortitude that would only make me loathe her more—and I would have preferred to be home, in my bed or in his bed, but I said, in spite of that or because of Alexis, "Let's keep going."

To our right there was a gentle burst of sedge grass completely surrounded by nettles, backed by a row of wild bergamot. Beech-trees hovered over every earthly thing in that direction, spiking into the regathering clouds. To our left were the spruces where the firecrests and the dunnocks and the three-toed woodpeckers lived. But I couldn't hear them. In fact, it was eerily silent, unlike on any of my previous visits to the forest, when there had never not been noise; even at night, there were the foxes and the moths and the wood mice and the crickets and, sometimes, the wolves, and the lynx if you were very lucky, and the wind.

But now it was still. Suddenly I thought I saw someone, and I grabbed Freddie's arm, and he spun around to look. But whoever it was was gone.

I was distressed, and Freddie sensed that, lowering his head onto my head and pressing my face into his chest. For a moment, we just stood like that, so tightly together I thought that maybe we were lichenizing. I thought it would be good if we could start a symbiosis—there were all kinds of things I felt I needed in order to live that I couldn't produce on my own. Then he released me, and we stumbled to our bikes.

CHAPTER THIRTEEN

We were a block away from Irena's when it began to rain again. I had ended up with the umbrella, and when I attempted to hold it high enough to cover both of us, I poked Freddie in the back of the head. I continued to feel superior to Alexis.

We tried the door but found it locked.

"Who is it?" we heard someone say from inside.

"Swedish and Spanish," I said without thinking.

"Who?"

"Me and Freddie," I said. "Open up. We bring not-great news from the national park."

"What's the password?" said another voice, and I thought I heard Alexis laugh that nervous, meaningless laugh.

I kicked the door.

"'Open the fucking door' is the password. I need to pee, and they're fucking cutting down the forest!"

The door opened. Just past it, the six of them were standing in a row like beech-trees, grinning like Freddie when he pondered the fungal world.

"You're here!" said Renata.

"Just in time for the wedding!" said Petra.

Alexis took a big step forward and handed each of us a strip of paper. I looked down at mine.

"You gave me yours," I said, holding it out to give it back to her.

"No, silly," she said. "You drew me from the helmet!"

"What are you talking about?" I said.

"You will marry Alexis," said Renata. "Freddie will marry Petra. She will be such a wonderful wife."

Apparently, because Alexis's feet had hurt, she and Chloe and Ostap had retreated to Irena's after only a block and joined Schulz and Petra and Renata in their search for clues inside *Grey Eminence*, which would have made me angry if it hadn't been for the fact that Freddie and I had made out. Also, they'd found what they hoped might be two clues. The first was more like an interpretation, but since that was what we did all day, under normal circumstances, they said, it made sense to trust their instincts and treat it like a clue. And besides, it was an interpretation that was predicated on an array of indisputable facts.

"Fact," said Schulz. "The climax of *Grey Eminence* and the end of the world take place on June 12, 2075, in Lisbon. Fact: June 12 is a major holiday in that city. Fact: That holiday is the Feast of Saint Anthony." He motioned to Ostap.

"Fact?" said Ostap, looking at Schulz. "Saint Anthony is the patron saint not only of lost items, lost persons, and lost souls, but also of marriages. It is a custom in that city to rely upon Saint Anthony for the realization of domestic bliss."

"The custom further stipulates," Petra jumped in, "that a statue of Saint Anthony should be buried until such a time as the burier has enjoyed her nuptials."

"So that's what we decided to do," said Renata. "That's the instinct part. We put everyone's name—the new names, that is, our actual names—in a hat and each drew at random. It's a way to renew our commitments to each other and to Our Author."

"We know it's just a ceremony," Alexis said, "but since we don't know what this is all about, we figured anything could help?"

"Not to mention," said Schulz, "that there is a long-standing belief in the Catholic Church in mystical marriages, like Saint Catherine's. She was mystically married to Jesus, with Mary presiding, so as to have a share—an intimate share—in all His sufferings."

"Think of nuns," offered Renata.

"Okay," I said slowly.

"I thought the whole thing was that you were already mystically married to Irena," said Freddie.

But if this was a protest, it fell on deaf ears. Petra scooped up the rings from Our Lady of Literature—the three from before and a new one made of wood, along with a purple hair band and three rubber bands—and headed out the back.

I wanted to entreat them to help us save the forest, to race back with us to where the spruces were being cut down, or to come up with a plan, at least, but there was something catching in their trance. So we just stood around a freshly exhumed patch of earth, rain streaming down our sides. At first it felt more like attending a funeral, but then we went pair by pair, orbiting the burial ground,[34] until the dirt that had sludged into mud had been circled a total of twenty-eight times, with twenty-eight pledges of allegiance, at which point Petra hopped across the yard to get the shovel and handed it to her new husband, Freddie, who dug.

Out came Agni, Hindu god of fire. I looked at Chloe, who had just married Schulz. Chloe said, "It was the closest we could find in her office," and Renata and Ostap, newlyweds themselves, turned and led the way back inside.

"Now," said Petra, clapping her hands together, "we go to the Tsar's Restaurant, to celebrate, and because of the second clue. Don't worry, it's just a few kilometers."

The very last thing I wanted to do was travel more kilometers, in the rain, to get to another Russian-themed restaurant. But their trance held—and anyway, what were my alternatives? Broach the subject of a protest knowing how dangerous a protest in Poland could be? I scrambled to conceive of other options—stealing the chainsaws while the government workers were having their lunch, bribing them, pleading with them, bludgeoning them with Irena's Bozdoğan mace—yet each felt less satisfying than the last.

We set out. I tried to walk with Freddie, but Schulz informed me politely but firmly that from now on my partner in all things would be Alexis. Making conversation with Alexis was not exactly hard—she spoke profusely—but I found it painful to concentrate on anything she said.

Soon, she said as she limped along by my side, all there would be in her life would be wildfires. She lived between Los Angeles and Sydney, as she had always

---

34 This was something we had learned about from Brides.com: "In North Indian tradition, [the couple makes] seven circles around a ceremonial fire, each round signifying a specific blessing they request of the gods." It is an example of the perfect portability of language and culture, in that we translated this tradition to our own Polish-based needs and, in so doing, were able to solidify our friendships (Trans.).

been fond of proclaiming, even though we all already knew. She omitted that she hailed from a small, god-awful-sounding town in Arkansas, and that she only "lived" in Sydney for two months of the California summer, missing the best weather in both hemispheres, and that her partner, Rosemary "Romy" Corona, was supposed to move from Sydney to Ulaanbaatar at the end of the year. These were things Chloe and I had learned from Facebook, before Alexis deleted that account.

I considered Our Author's ban on weather-inspired conversation, but even I now accepted it was no longer in effect. *Grey Eminence* was about a lot of things, but most of all it was about the weather, and we could hardly be expected to translate it if we weren't allowed to entertain the very subject. Plus, only hours earlier I had told Freddie all about the December duel that killed Irena's father, which, when you thought about it, went back to weather, too.

So I let Alexis talk—she seemed to need to talk—about the impending ravages of climate change, all the wildfires she predicted would scorch the Australian and Californian earth, and all the victims they would claim, how no one was prepared for it, and I began to hate her, in my bones and in their marrow, I hated her for picturing dead kangaroos and for making me picture them, kids suffocated in their pouches, I hated her for her incessant nervous laughter.[35]

I hated her for her *A* and her big hoop earrings and her destroyed, discarded espadrilles, and I hated her for being my wife.

But the rain let up again, and we got there, and the rays of the late-afternoon sun over the patio-platform of the Tsar's Restaurant and the nearby disused train tracks left over from a bygone era of some slight importance or potential for importance that had long since been forfeited and the trees were so honeying that I forgot some of my rancor and was able to sit between Freddie and Alexis and touch him again under the table, touching her by accident just once (she winked at me, and I hated her), and the dunnocks chirped and thudded minutely onto the peony-patterned oilcloths of the neighboring tables that were all empty, and from some hidden place a coal tit made high-pitched proclamations, and we all ordered big draft beers except for Schulz, who ordered kvass, and we made a toast to us, to our unusual, mystical, intellectual union, to our goal of translating

---

35   I have been trying to eliminate this habit (Trans.).

Grey Eminence, come hell, said Alexis in English, or high water, and although I rolled my eyes, I did understand that phrase, and it did feel true that no matter what, our purpose was to ensure Irena Rey's continued fame and even her infamy, because the only thing that mattered was that she be read, in every language, with love or hatred, and the garbled strains of Ukrainian folk music and the train car in the yard and the stork in the field and the long strands of butter on the white plate in the middle of our table were just what we needed to complete our task, of this we could be certain, and we watched as the plate of butter that looked like a plate of fettuccine slowly melted, each strand blending into the next until it was just one malleable blob, and Freddie slipped his finger underneath my knee, and I was wet and peaceful until all of a sudden, just as the sunset reached its almost sickeningly colorful peak, and the air grew heavy with the inexplicable fragrance of honeysuckle, a miracle occurred, and Petra threw up onto the railway, and Renata burst into tears, and Ostap choked on his porcini kopytka, as Czech, who had been killed in a freak accident three years earlier, waved and came around the table and extended his hand to Freddie and said, "Hello, my name is Pavel. I believe you're in my place."

CHAPTER FOURTEEN

H aving come back from the dead, Pavel had a lot of explaining to do. But to our credit the first thing we asked him was whether he would like some bread, butter, or beer, to which he responded in as easygoing a fashion as ever, merely saying, "Sure."

We began scooching our heavy chairs around, scraping the iron against the concrete, making several little spaces around the table but none into which a person could fit. Pavel, stronger than I remembered, picked up a chair from the birds' favorite table and hoisted it with pomp over his shoulder and came to stand behind Freddie and me. I inched my chair toward Freddie, but Pavel obliviously wedged his own chair in between us, then reached for Freddie's beer and took a big swig.

I looked around the table. No one seemed to know where to begin. So I said, in desperation, "You were killed in a freak accident in 2014. What are you doing here, alive?"

He chuckled, but almost immediately the smile faded from his face.

"Is that what she told you?" He drank a little more of Freddie's beer. His hands dwarfed the pint glass. I had also forgotten how lanky—how long—he was. The strips of stubble on his head had thinned. But he was wearing a white T-shirt that actually fit him, and he looked almost appealing in his Levi's and his New Balances that suggested travels around the West. "I'm going to tell you the truth," he said, looking around the patio-platform and lowering his voice. "But you have to promise you won't repeat a word of it to her. You have to swear you'll never say anything about any of this to anyone. Ever."

"I swear," I said.

"I swear, too," said Ostap.

"We couldn't tell her even if we wanted to," said Petra. "She's gone."

"What do you mean?" Pavel said, sitting up a little straighter and gripping the iron arms of his chair with both hands.

"Not until you explain," I said. "Everyone swears. Please. Go ahead."

He regarded me with wariness.

"The story of your resurrection," I prompted him.

"Talk," said Schulz.

"You may remember," said Pavel, "except for you, of course," he said to Freddie, "that as we were finishing *Future Moonscapes of the Eocene*, Irena was already working on *Sedno II: The Hopefuls*, and we all agreed that she was flourishing and at the height of her powers. Remember how beautiful she was in those polka-dot dresses, with the shoes with the laces and the little heels? She danced, she even sang—do you remember?"

It was strange, but until he said it, I hadn't remembered. Perhaps the most recent Irena had made such an impression on us that all previous Irenas were being erased. Now images came back to me, brief flickering pictures of Our Author and her perfect, almost avian movements, her infinite grace, floating more than dancing, rosy-cheeked and beaming, and it was impossible to believe that that woman who had left us here without any explanation was the same one who had drawn us here after *Lena*, who had shown such kindness again and again to each of us in the specific way we needed most. And I thought again that regardless of where Irena Rey had gone on September 22, she had—in a deeper, truer sense, and possibly even literally, if Leshy was real—already left by the time we'd reached her home again on September 20.

It often happens when I translate that I reword a phrase over and over, unable to get it quite right, only to realize that the problem lies earlier in the sentence, or even earlier in the paragraph, and that if I go back and solve that, the troublesome phrase will suddenly become perfect without requiring any alteration at all, and I thought perhaps that was the case here, too. Maybe we'd been searching for the wrong Irena.

But then Pavel said something that made me wonder if there was any part or version of Irena I had ever understood at all.

"She was happy back then—she was flourishing—because we were together."

It took a few seconds for the bomb to detonate. At first we thought he meant that Irena had been happy that we, her translators, were surrounding her with love and devotion and dedicating ourselves so fully to the cause of her creations. But that wasn't what he meant.

"Irena and I were in love," Pavel continued. "We snuck out into the forest every night at midnight to make love under the stars."

"What?!" Chloe and I cried in unison—another bad omen.

"Rain or shine," Pavel said.

Petra jumped up, and her chair fell back with a resounding metallic crash.

"How dare you?" she said.

"She started it," Pavel said. "What can I say? I'm a charmer."

Ostap cleared his throat. "You're saying that you and Irena were . . . dating, during *Future Moonscapes of the Eocene* and *Sedno II*?"

"Right up until *Pompeii Catalog*," he confirmed. "We were seeing each other until late 2013, when she found out she was pregnant."

"What?!" screamed Petra. A waiter peeked his head out from inside. Freddie motioned to him for more beer.

"She was with me in Uničov," said Pavel. "She'd told Bogdan she was writing a book about the conference between Frederick the Great and Joseph II that led to the First Partition of Poland. She'd told everybody that. Didn't she even tell you that?"

"Yes," said Schulz, very slowly. "Then she didn't say what happened. She just wrote a different book."

"What happened," said Pavel, "was that she got pregnant. I was beside myself with joy. I thought it meant she'd leave Bogdan and come live with me for good. I always wanted a child."

"Me too," said Freddie unexpectedly, and Pavel seemed to instantly forgive him for being there, clinking Freddie's former stein against the one the waiter had just brought.

"But where's the child?" asked Renata. Petra picked up her chair off the ground, then sank back into it. Her face was the white of a freshly laundered sheet that someone other than me had laundered. (My laundry always turns out beige or gray.)

"But Irena didn't plan on leaving Bogdan. She never had. She told me we had to stop seeing each other, that she was coming back to Białowieża, and that the baby would be his. Bogdan's. That I would have nothing to do with it at any point."

"Maybe it was his?" said Ostap.

"It couldn't have been," said Pavel. "Without going into too much detail, I can assure you that it couldn't have been his."

"Gentlemen never tell," said Freddie, and he and Pavel exchanged a kind of vile fraternal look, knowing and lascivious. All of this, I thought, could have been prevented; I could have been napping postcoitally right now with Freddie, and instead I was losing him completely, to a Czech idiot who until ten minutes earlier had been dead.

"It was awful," said Pavel, "but I had no choice but to let her go. Five weeks later, she wrote to me one last time to say that she had lost the child. She told me not to contact any of you, and not to ever so much as mention her name to anyone ever again."

"Then she wrote *Pompeii*?" I asked.

"Then she wrote *Pompeii*," he agreed.

Pompeii Catalog hadn't exactly been a book, I realized only now, three years after completing its translation into Spanish. It had really been a catalog, with descriptions, of household objects, food, and teeth preserved by the volcanic ash after the disaster at Pompeii: a pair of gold earrings, fittings from a medicine chest, bread, a giraffe bone, a mosaic of a dog with the warning inscription CAVE CANEM. She'd also had us translate a couple of her essays at that summit, including "Amber Exclave" and "Bakhchysarai," both of which became famous in most of our countries, but even still it had been meager—I now saw—in comparison with everything she'd done before.

"So wait," I said. "You mean you never got electrocuted?"

"That's what she said happened?"

We all nodded.

"If she was going to kill me off like a character in one of her books, you'd think she could have picked a nobler cause of death, at least. Like rescuing a child from the Morava, and drowning." He shrugged. "Something like that."

"That would be the least she could do," agreed Freddie.

"It did flood," Pavel persisted. "It has flooded. The Morava, I mean."

"Fire," said Chloe, "is her preferred finale. She is a Sagittarius."

"What does that mean?" I said.

"Sagittarius is a fire sign," she said. "Just like Aries, which is mine."

"That's true!" said Petra. "She does like to give her characters fiery ends. *Pompeii Catalog*, of course, but even going back to the beginning—think of the semitrailer truck at the end of *Lena*, or the Siberian fireball in *Future Moonscapes*."

"Electricity's not fire," noted Renata.

"True," said Chloe. "I just thought it was related."

"If it makes you feel any better," said Schulz, "Freddie thinks we killed her in real life."

"What do you mean?" Pavel said. "What did you mean before, about her being gone?"

Freddie swallowed. "No one believes me, but I thought she might have been drunk when we served her an inky cap risotto the night she disappeared."

"That's not possible," said Pavel.

"We told him that: She doesn't drink," said Schulz.

"Oh, she drinks," said Pavel. "But she would never combine alcohol with a mushroom that isn't supposed to be combined with alcohol. She knows more about mushrooms than anyone I know. What do you think is in her daily tincture? Fortifying *Cordyceps*, of course! If there is one thing in the world that actually interests Irena, it's fungi. Believe me."

"Didn't she say fungi were evil?" said Ostap.

"Yeah," said Schulz. "Why should we believe you? You've lied to us before."

"I mean, we can see that he's not dead," said Alexis.

"I know we can see that," Schulz snapped. "But about what happened with Irena—anything could have happened. She might have had a very good reason for firing Pavel."

"Firing me?" spat Pavel.

"Well," said Schulz, "isn't that essentially what happened? She didn't want you to translate her anymore. Maybe your translations weren't good. Maybe you were unfaithful. Maybe she was right."

Everyone, including Schulz himself, seemed dismayed by what he'd said. We had always feared disappointing her, and getting fired, but we had never questioned each other's translations, or each other's fidelity to her.

"Unfaithful?" spluttered Pavel. "Unfaithful? She was the one who was unfaithful! Did you not hear anything I said?"

"What about the time we were all supposed to go to Białystok, remember?" said Renata. "For the LGBTQ-plus march? When Schulz and Ostap ended up getting arrested, and Bogdan had to bail them out? We all met downstairs to go together, but you weren't there, and then Irena came out and told us to go on without you because you were behind on your translation of *Sedno*, and she needed the day with you to help you catch up. But then the next day, when we were sitting at the worktable, waiting for her, you said you had translated the last line of the novel the previous weekend. Remember? You said it was 'exquisite' and you couldn't wait to discuss it with us."

"It was," said Pavel.

Freddie started laughing.

"Who did she send in my place?" said Pavel.

"Fuck!" said Alexis.

We all looked at her.

"Nothing," she said. "Bogdan. She sent Bogdan. She tricked us. She lied."

"I was never a liar," Pavel said triumphantly. "But Irena always was."

"Then how did you know we were here?" said Schulz triumphantly.

"You left a note on the refrigerator, dated September 29, 2017: *Gone for dinner at the Tsar's Restaurant, join us if you get this!* With a little heart."

We all looked around. Renata reddened.

"I don't know if you should still be doing that," said Chloe. "It's starting to seem like she doesn't really care about us. Like she might not even want to come back."

Ostap stood up and threw his napkin on the table.

"I can't sit here anymore," he said.

"Me neither," said Schulz.

"Me neither," said Petra.

"So let's go," said Chloe. She motioned to the waiter, who'd come back out on hearing Alexis shout the word "fuck."

We walked home in the dark, in a hideous stupor. There was nowhere for Pavel to sleep except Irena's bed: The shed was in ruins, and even those had been partly washed away. I slept in my bed, and, as far as I know, Freddie slept in his.

CHAPTER FIFTEEN

At four thirty in the morning, when I believed I was the only one awake, I got dressed and crept down the stairs. I'd had a sex dream about Pavel and woken up hungry and confused. Before making coffee I wanted to loiter in the darkness in the hallway that linked Freddie's bedroom with his predecessor's, listening to the two of them sleep. I wanted to know if they snorted like boars. I wondered if they slept on their backs, or, on the contrary, on their stomachs, in relative silence. On the third step from the bottom, I paused over the knot and prayed.

Irena, just one word from you, I entreated the whitish stain in the wood where the mace had been, or even just a sign. I took a step forward and shined my cell phone flashlight on that map of gunk and scratches, scrutinizing it until I was so close I couldn't see it. Something in the living room stirred. I jumped back and spun around.

"No!" said the someone that was rising from the chaise longue and covering their face. I turned off my flashlight and squinted into the starlight and the light of the fast-waxing moon.

"Petra?" I whispered.

Petra switched on a lamp, and I saw as I tiptoed toward her that she was wearing, in addition to the silver cross she always wore, a black bra under a metallic tank top, but also sweatpants and teal socks: half clothes and half pajamas.

"Nightmares," she said, by way of explanation.

"Oh," I said, and I sat down beside her. "I'm sorry."

She shrugged. "I don't even usually remember my dreams. But ever since we got here I've been . . ."

I listened to the ticking of the grandfather clock that sat behind the piano. I repositioned myself atop her still-warm sheets.

"Visited," Petra finally said.

"Visited?" I asked.

"Visited," she repeated. She glanced around the room, her eyes lingering on the portrait of Irena that hung over the fireplace. "By ghosts."

"Ghosts?"

She nodded. "I've been sleeping down here not to keep Renata awake."

I'd never believed in ghosts before. But these days, given everything—all Freddie's extreme unusuals—I didn't know what to believe. Besides, I liked Petra, and what with her mysterious illness unsubsiding, the least I could do was give her the benefit of the doubt. "What do you think they want?" I said.

"I'm not sure," she said. "They all have something to do with the forest. Sometimes they're animals."

I thought of all the signs on everybody's fences, alerting passersby to dogs that did not seem to exist. Unless they existed in some parallel timeline, or in some way outsiders like us just couldn't access, like another layer of language our dictionaries didn't have the capacity for. Unless, of course, the dogs were just dead.

"Sometimes it's Leshy," Petra said. "Sometimes it's other figures from mythology. Veles, the god of the underworld and arts and crafts and magic. His nemesis is Perun, god of war and storms. In my dreams, Perun is always an oak tree, but he's also the bolt of lightning that explodes the tree and scatters its branches in every direction." We flinched when she said "explodes." "I must have a dozen dreams a night. Other times it's people from the cemetery here. Olga Smoktunowicz. Filimon Waszkiewicz. Sometimes it's people who were murdered in another forest. Georgiy Gongadze, do you remember? That journalist who was killed in the woods near Kyiv. You wouldn't remember—it was probably twenty years ago now. I guess I've always been haunted by that case: a sweet, brave, handsome young man, kidnapped by a corrupt Ukrainian government, murdered, left, lied about." She shuddered. "Sometimes the visitors are less definite than that. Sometimes they're presences. I don't know who or what they are. Premonitions, maybe. I mean," she said, thinking, "people who haven't yet been killed."

"Oh," I said. "You mean . . . Has my ghost ever visited you?"

"No." Petra laughed. "No one we actually know."

Since *Pompeii*, Petra had cut her hair boyishly short, which suited her, usually, but in that moment, it made her look like a lost child. For the first time it occurred to me that she was only a couple of years older than I was. She had always seemed so grown-up before, with her grown-up kid in Niš, and her seemingly bottomless knowledge of Polish literature and culture, and the way she talked, saying things like "it was probably twenty years ago now."

"Petra," I said. I hesitated because I wasn't sure how to broach the subject and didn't want to make her feel any worse. But her face was growing anxious, so I blurted: "I can't find the acorn you gave me."

"Oh," she said with relief. "I have a whole bowl of them, upstairs. I can give you more as soon as everyone else is awake."

"Oh, Petra," I said with a sigh. "How can I ever repay you?" I think I meant not only for the acorn, but also for not describing my ghost.

"Don't be silly. Although . . ." she hesitated. "Would you want to go on a walk with me? I was thinking that maybe if I went to visit the dead, they wouldn't have to come to me so much. But I've been a little afraid to go alone."

"Sure," I said. "Let me just grab something to eat—"

But at this, Petra bolted into the bathroom, slamming the door. Meanwhile, from one of the bedrooms, I heard the sound of someone rolling over or maybe sitting up, and I felt an urgent need to leave before I got caught wanting Freddie or Pavel by Freddie or Pavel—before I got permanently trapped in my perplexity—so when Petra returned and apologized, saying maybe she wasn't feeling well enough to go, I said, "Don't worry, I'll go for you."

Effortfully, she produced a pale, grateful smile, and without so much as a droplet of coffee, I slipped on my muddy shoes and stepped outside.

DAWN WAS IMPENDING; already the sky was bluish gray. I took Tropinka Street out of the village, east into the national park, walking carefully so as not to crush any of the infinitesimal frogs that burst from the pine needles half a dozen at a time; like translators, perhaps, they were invisible other than in motion.[36]

---

36   Here the author is referring to the old adage that translators should be neither seen nor heard, or, as the Israeli writer Etgar Keret puts it, "Translators are like ninjas. If you notice them, they're no good." In

I shuddered to think what bad luck it would be if I were to crush an infinites-imal being underfoot.

Because I didn't feel confident in my ability to detect the kurgans and other unmarked graves around the forest, I determined to limit my purview to the known dead. Still, I wanted to feel at least a little brave, so I set out for a place I'd never been but that I'd read about, a so-called place of national memory about three kilometers away.

As I walked, I saw that some of the trees wore more strange symbols, white lines with red in between them; their paint was fading, chipped. A massive sign at a crossroads listed all the things you weren't allowed to do inside the national park part of the forest: hunt mushrooms, smoke cigarettes, stray from the offi-cial path. Yet on either side of the official path the forest floor was soft with moss, opulent, beckoning, extending an almost opiate effect.

To my left, I saw smoke rising, and I strayed a little from the path. Beams of light that were so bright they seemed opaque, almost solid, embraceable, had touched down upon a mossy stump. The rest of the tree lay in the grass, the exposed wood rough as though after an explosion—just as Petra had seen in her dream.

I squatted beside it, searching for the fire. But there was no fire, and the smoke must have just been steam, abundant and unfurling, the metamorphosing dew the moss had gathered overnight. I watched it a while: It was beautiful, but it was also disturbing. I decided to take a picture, not to keep as a souvenir, but to study later, after I was fully awake.

When I pressed the shutter circle on the screen of my iPhone, the artificial click dispelled any lingering ease. I rose from the ground and felt wild as a hunted animal. Leshy or the archer could be anywhere, I realized—in the moss, in the mushrooms, in the trees. I thought I heard steps, or something that sounded like steps. It was deer, I told myself. Just red deer grazing.

I remembered the path, and then I saw it, and without thinking of the tiny frogs I leaped across the moss field and retook it. I began walking quickly without allowing myself to turn around. I knew that this was happening because I had

---

other words, she wants to say that only *while translating* can anyone see us—perhaps because she wants you to believe that this book contains some secret knowledge, exclusive access that lasts only as long as Irena's story does. Needless to say, I disagree (Trans.).

lost my lucky acorn, and because I had failed to understand Irena, and most of all because none of us had acted—had ever acted—in time. The steps got louder, and I took off at a run.

I must have gone a hundred meters down the path before I realized that I stood the best chance in the forest, where at least I could hide, unless what was chasing me was something that could smell me, in which case, no matter what I did, I would be doomed. I veered left and flew past a fluorescent yellow sign that read, KEEP OUT. After several more meters I stopped, almost toppling backward, as if I had run into something, but what it was in fact was nothing: a newly hewn clearing, hundreds of spruce trees (and other trees) raggedly slain, their bodies jumbled, some of them chopped up into smaller pieces a meter or so long.

That the cacophonous softness of the forest was contiguous with this ragged emptiness was so staggering I forgot to run, or hide, or listen, and when the thing that had been chasing me caught up with me, and seized me in its grip, at first all I could do was howl. Then I spun around to see a startled Freddie, and I pushed him, back into the still-standing forest, into a birch that knocked a granola bar out of his pocket and onto the splintered forest floor.

"Oh my God, what is wrong with you?" I moaned, burying my face in my hands.

"I wanted to bring you breakfast," said Freddie. He crouched down to pick up the bar and held it out to me uncertainly.

I closed my eyes and counted to ten, forcing myself to do it in Polish. But when I opened my eyes, the first thing I saw was the worst thing possible: another amputated hoof.

Protruding from a sickly oak, it was pale and pockmarked, misshapen—sunken in the middle—and foul. It was beyond bad luck. Like the chopped-up trees behind me, it was a terrifying guarantor of disaster.

Freddie had followed my gaze. "Yes!" he cried, seemingly forgetting I was furious with him, clapping his hands, sending a trio of starlings rocketing into the aureate sky. "*Fomes fomentarius.* That is it, exactly. I was trying to think of it when you asked about parasites. It was on the tip of my tongue!"

"When did I ask about parasites?" I said absently, suddenly thinking exclusively about the tip of Freddie's tongue.

"When you asked about fungi that work against trees."

"Wait," I said, still gawking at the hoof. "You can't mean—" My mind replayed the moment Freddie had lifted up an amputated hoof from under Irena's sheets, and I was overwhelmed by disgust. "You can't mean that thing is also a mushroom. Do you?"

"I do." He laughed. "Don't you remember? From our first day? The velvet receptacles filled with amadou? The ones she gave to us?"

I stared at him. For a moment, he stared back. A ladybug landed on my arm, which was good luck, I thought, but probably not good enough to get me out of this nightmare where either everything was connected to everything else by means of a word or everything *was* everything else, and the word was just the sequela of that staggering collapse.

Then Freddie reached out and took the ladybug between two fingers and set it on top of a birch branch. "Have you ever heard of Ötzi the Iceman?"

It should have gone without saying that I hadn't—that I didn't even know what an "Iceman" could possibly be—but I managed to make myself say, "No."

"Ah! He's a mummy, naturally formed, found in the Alps. He lived about five thousand years ago, until he was murdered. We don't know who did it, of course, or why. There've been all kinds of theories: He was sacrificed, he was killed in revenge, he sacrificed himself. We'll probably never know. Some think there's a curse on Ötzi, even now, and that this curse is responsible for the deaths of many of the people he's been close to since the discovery of his body in 1991. The man who found him was lost in the Alps. The man who put Ötzi's body in a bag was killed in a car crash on his way to give a lecture about Ötzi."

I was trying to decide if it would be rude to reach for the granola bar now, and Freddie must have sensed that my mind was beginning to wander. "None of this matters," he said, and I decided against it. "What matters is that when he was killed, he was carrying several pieces of *Fomes fomentarius*, which he would have used as tinder, and which were preserved by the ice along with him."

"So it's a flammable parasite," I said.

"A flammable parasite!" Freddie said, laughing like I'd just said the funniest thing he'd ever heard. "*Fomes fomentarius* rots its host tree. That is its biography, let's say. But it is also one of the oldest tools known to mankind. For thousands of years, *Fomes fomentarius* was harvested and chopped up and treated with potassium nitrate (which is easy to get, you can get it from urine). That's how

Fomes fomentarius turns into amadou. And amadou is, among other things, a portable fire-starter. People used to use it all the time, everywhere, as far as we know. It was a universal tool, like a knife."

"What happened to it?"

"The invention of the safety match—that is, a match that wouldn't explode or poison anyone—made it obsolete. Besides, the fungus had been so overharvested in Europe by the end of the nineteenth century that it was almost extinct."

"So amadou is tinder, made out of a mushroom that looks like a hoof."

"Yes."

I thought for a moment. "So you're telling me that what Irena was telling us that first day in the forest was just something else about fungi?"

"That I really couldn't say," said Freddie. "I found her impossible to follow. I don't think we were the only ones. I don't think she was making any sense."

But that could not be, I thought. Irena had always *made sense*. That was her whole job, as an author: to produce meaning, glimmering and glorious, for all her readers to behold. I reached for my phone. It had switched over to a Belarusian carrier, and Our Author's semisecret Facebook page took forever to load, long enough that I began to hope for some new clue. But then there it was, her post about the new archery range in Narewka, and nothing in the whole month since.

A red squirrel stirred in the arboreal rubble. All her favorite places must be gone now, I thought. She must be grieving and confused.

"Would you like to keep walking?" asked Freddie, squeezing my shoulder.

I remembered Petra, and I pocketed my phone. We made our way to the place of national memory, which stood behind a low brick wall, a concrete monument set back some twenty meters from the road. It was dedicated to 222 Białowieżans who were murdered by the Nazis here in 1942, on Christmas Eve. According to the inscription, their needlessly shed blood had sanctified the site, and I tried to attune myself to holiness, but the truth was I couldn't really tell the difference.

It was a monument, not a cemetery, but there were a few individual graves. I stood a moment in front of each of them while Freddie continued reading about the atrocity. I wasn't sure if I was supposed to tuck my thumbs or not. Just to be safe, I did.

The last of the markers was a tall, smooth block of black granite that read, "zg. śm. trag.," an abbreviation I assumed from context must mean "died a tragic death" or "was tragically killed." It struck me as an odd thing to abbreviate, but perhaps there had been too many tragedies here to merit all the letters it would take to spell each of them out fully. This man, whose name was Adam, had been killed at thirty-four, when he was the same age as me.

Irena had written that at the heart of nationhood lay necrophilia—it was the argument that set in motion the events of *Sedno I*—and although it was also true of my country, nowhere was it more evident than in the Republic of Poland. Or Białowieża: Even without the loggers, the whole forest was more death than life.

Then again, you couldn't really tell life and death apart in a forest like this. You could make life-sustaining fires out of deadly parasites here, where *Fomes fomentarius* wasn't extinct at all. The place of national memory buzzed with birds, and bugs, and tiny frogs, and Freddie, and me.

I cleared my throat. "Gentlemen," I told the cold stones and their lichens and flies. "I am here on behalf of my colleague Petra. I respectfully request that you make your intentions known to me, her representative, in lieu of visiting her at night."

Freddie's voice boomed back, "My intentions are honorable. My situation is weird."

I turned around. I didn't realize I was grimacing until he laughed. I tried to neutralize my face.

"I just wanted to tell you I'm in an open marriage, Emi. It can be an awkward thing to introduce."

I wasn't sure what to say to this. I presumed he wasn't introducing it at random. But was he saying we should sleep together? Or was he merely making excuses for what had happened at the Royal Oaks Trail?

"In fact," he said, glancing at his hipster Nokia. "I should get back. I have a Skype with Bogdana."

I grimaced again at her name, but I walked back into town with him. I don't remember what we talked about. My mind was on Pavel and ghosts. And when we got to Puszczańska, the street that led to Irena's curving house, I found I couldn't bear the thought of sitting around while Freddie cooed at his computer screen.

"I have to do something else," I told him and forcibly removed my fingers from his grip.

"Sure," he said. I didn't look back to see if he was watching me because I needed to believe that he was.

WE HAD BEEN to the Białowieża cemetery a few times with Bogdan and Irena. It was only a couple of blocks from their house. I had always considered it a surprisingly cheerful place, at least when it was overgrown with thick grass and waxy cornflowers, as it was now, and weeds as tall as trees with thick dark stalks. In the distance, a stork was returning to its scraggly nest. Near the base of the pole at the top of which it lived, I thought I saw a person, but I blinked, and there was no one there.

A new notice had been posted at the cemetery's entrance since the last time we'd come. It read: KEEP INVASIVE SPECIES OUT OF BIAŁOWIEŻA. At first I thought this must have meant the spruce bark beetles, but then I saw another sign that said, KEEP NONNATIVE SPECIES OUT OF BIAŁOWIEŻA, which surely couldn't have been in reference to them.

"Nonnative" couldn't mean the same thing as "invasive," unless I was missing something—unless there was some biological sameness between the two. I looked around for a place to sit and eat my bar. There was what sounded like miniature-machine-gun fire, and I turned again to the stork's nest. I could just make out the chicks' heads wobbling; if they were lucky, their breakfast would be bugs and frogs. I found a bench and sat facing away from them.

Out of nowhere I felt a hand on my shoulders. Freddie! I thought—he'd changed his mind—but then I put my hand over the hand on my shoulders and found it was scalier, almost ligneous, and I spun around and saw that it was not Freddie at all, but rather the strange ranger.

I sprang back from the bench and nearly choked on my granola. For all I knew, he was Leshy, or maybe even the archer who'd tried to kill us before—or maybe even both. But the man or the spirit in the collared olive shirt didn't seem to notice my alarm.

"I am Leszek,"[37] he said, pushing back his shoulder-length hair that hung in clumps with hints of club moss. His other hand was on a mottled leather satchel.

---

37 Pronounced "Leshek" (Trans.).

When he released it, I saw that it was fastened with a wooden disc engraved with a portrait of a mushroom. Leszek extended his hand.

I gulped. "Emilia," I said. Remembering that the Leshy of ancient lore wore his shoes on the wrong feet and cast no shadow, I stared down rudely or maybe just incompetently and confirmed that Leszek's boots were in the right place, and that faint black orbs were emanating from their toe caps.

"I know who you are," said Leszek. I pocketed the rest of my granola bar. Did he mean he remembered me from the strict reserve, or did he mean he knew who I was? And if the latter, how? "Allow me," he said.

He seemed to want me to stand up. "Am I not supposed to be here?" I asked him.

"Not at all," he said, but I found the meaning of this, too, murky: Was it not true that I was not supposed to be there, or was I not supposed to be there at all? "Come," he said, his voice creaking, and I stood. "I take it you're familiar with the Białowieża bartniks?" he asked, briskly walking away.

If I'd been thinking logically, I would have run—sought shelter at Irena's, warned the others, maybe finally called the police. Instead, I hurried after him, wanting to assure him that just as I had not known about Ötzi or hostile mushrooms, I wasn't even remotely familiar with the word he'd just said, but it was all I could do to keep up. He stopped, pivoted, and reached out to touch a tombstone.

"This is Filimon Waszkiewicz, 1879 to 1964," he said. "Filimon was the last bartnik of Białowieża. Surely you must have heard his name before?"

I shook my head. "I mean," I corrected myself, "I think my colleague Petra might have mentioned him this morning, but I don't know who he was."

"A bartnik is not the same thing as a beekeeper," Leszek said, swaying defensively for some reason, petting the stone. "A bartnik is a honey hunter." His voice took on a roller-coaster quality as he eased into a classic Polish storytelling mode. "It was a distinguished vocation that required enormous talent, risk-taking, and skill. Filimon Waszkiewicz learned to be a bartnik from his father, Józef, who learned from his own father, Omelian.

"Left to their own devices, you see, the bees will build their hives high in the trees, where they can be safe, not to mention more comfortable. Until the twentieth century, honey and wax were worth far more than timber, therefore bees were treated with respect. By the early 1900s, however, this was no longer the case. Wood was needed for war efforts. The Russian Empire made it illegal—just imagine that, *illegal*—to hunt honey in the traditional way.

"Nature survives only when it proves itself useful—to human beings, I mean; it is always useful to itself. By World War I, the Waszkiewicz dynasty was over. Filimon was forced to open an apiary, but after his son Włodzimierz was killed on the battlefield in World War II, he gradually got rid of all his bees."

He had made himself so sad I didn't know what to say. I thought of my father and the little gold bees he had brought me from somewhere, some condom conference in Europe, perhaps. A gift for my fifteenth birthday, chosen because "Emilia" sounded like "miel," or "honey," to him.[38]

"Wait," Leszek said. He pulled his phone from his bag, and as he tapped it with his index finger, I took another look at the leather of the satchel. I knew it wasn't cow leather, but I also couldn't figure out what animal it was.

Leszek thrust out his screen for me to see:

---

38 Over its *entire lifetime*, a bee makes one-twelfth of a teaspoon of honey. This isn't really related to the book at hand, I just thought it was interesting (Trans.).

"Filimon," he said. "That photograph was taken by Professor Jan Jerzy Karpiński." He snatched his phone back. "Instagram."

I nodded solemnly: Instagram.

"So," Leszek said, cracking his knuckles, "you still haven't found her?"

The question had a crushing weight. Coming from him, a strange ranger, and not a member of our entourage, it felt a little like an accusation. I didn't want to admit we'd made no progress in our search, but in order to make progress, we needed to turn every stone. Leszek could have leads—after all, his range was Irena's forest. Then again, I knew we didn't know if we could trust him—if he was anything like his mythological near-namesake, we absolutely could not.

And yet—we had already lost Irena. What else did we really have to lose?[39]

"No," I said. "We haven't. How did you know she was gone? Do you know where she is?"

"Have you tried getting in touch with her?" he asked, ignoring my question.

"Yes," I said. "Of course. We didn't want to overwhelm her, but we texted. We emailed."

"Earthlink?"

"Earthlink."

"There has to be another way," he said.

"You mean like send up a flare?" I joked. But he seemed to be considering.

"A flare. Yes. Maybe." He stopped swaying. "You know I went to high school with Irena."

"What? No."

"Yes. She is a very unusual person. I once saw her steal a postcard in Białystok. I never told anyone that."

"Why are you telling me?" I did not ask: Who cares? Who would begrudge the world's greatest writer one measly postcard—let alone from a run-down town like Białystok?

Leszek hesitated. "I'm telling you because the situation has changed now. The balance of the forest has been upset. And you must un-upset it."

"How do we un-upset—"

---

39   Our dignity, maybe (Trans.)?

Leszek raised his trigger finger and stuck out his hand. "You have to be careful. But like a bartnik, you may also have to risk everything in order to respectfully obtain your goals." He turned away from me. He seemed about to march off into the graves.

"Wait," I said, and he must have sensed my desperation because he spun back around on the balls of his feet. I hesitated, then blurted, "Do you know anything about ghosts?"

"Obviously," he said. "What do you want to know?"

"My friend is being visited. At night. I want to know how I can help her."

Leszek nodded sagely. "This is because of the logging. Cutting down the trees releases carbon, but not exclusively. Thousands of years ago, human beings cut down the forests because they didn't feel safe in them. If you level the forests, nothing can stalk you. Nothing can take you by surprise. You become the apex predator by virtue of being in absolute control of your environment. We cut down the trees out of fear," he continued, "but cutting down the trees releases our worst nightmares back into the atmosphere. This is a far more terrifying situation than before because now there is nowhere to hide. There is no way to run. There's no escape."

"So you mean," I said, inadvertently addressing his strangely captivating satchel, "that in order to help Petra, I'd need to stop the loggers?"

"You'd be helping the whole world, but especially our village," said Leszek. "Your colleague's not the only one who's being visited right now. Haven't you noticed all the new guard dogs around town?"

"Sort of. I mean I haven't actually seen any dogs."

"Of course not."

"Wait, what—"

"You may have to risk everything," Leszek repeated. "It is time for me to go."

"Wait! What does that mean?! Wait!" My hands flew to my mouth. I spread out my arms. "What is your bag made of?"

"Amadou," Leszek said, like it was the most obvious thing in the world. He patted his satchel. "Amadou will take the place of plastic soon." He turned around again, and within seconds I'd lost sight of him completely.

Amadou, of course, I thought. To no one, or to the dead, I moaned out loud: "What does amadou have to do with *Grey Eminence*?!"

I lit a cigarette. I hadn't forgotten about Petra—my plan was to retrace our steps and start with Filimon, tell him how sorry I was to hear about his son and his bees, but also, could he find it in his no-longer-beating heart to leave my colleague alone?

Wandering around, though, I couldn't find the path: the graves were a maze, and all along the edges of the cemetery, different species of trees jostled for sunshine in their various shades of dark and brilliant green, obscuring street signs and every other kind of landmark. Then something, some flicker, drew my eyes to the ground.

My match had lit one of the many desiccated weeds that festooned the cemetery's pathways on fire. Now I know that—at the time, my only conscious thought was: Fire. I think I screamed; I know I ran back to it and started stomping. I stomped and stomped as though stomping would bring back Irena, as though stomping would save the forest and resurrect the chopped-up spruce. I stomped until I heard, through the dull roar of my panic, the sound of a Roman snail shell cracking apart, of a native or a nearly native snail being crushed—sickeningly, devastatingly, by me.

CHAPTER SIXTEEN

Before I could see what I had done, before I could begin to grieve those slimy remnants, I took off. I ran and reached the tree line, and then the street, and then the steps to Irena's house where I scraped the tiny shards from my shoes before opening the door to see everyone already gathered at Our Lady of Literature, holding hands as if I didn't exist.

"Wait!" I cried, wedging myself in between Chloe and Alexis. Only when Alexis's yuzu-stinking fingers were interlaced with mine did I become aware how out of breath I was and try to catch it. "Wait," I panted. Everyone was looking at me. I couldn't tell if they were concerned or curious or just annoyed, but I did wish I had showered, or at least brushed my hair, or put on pants as opposed to terry short-shorts. "I was at . . . the cemetery . . ." I wasn't going to tell them about the fire, or the snail, but I was trying to decide if I should tell them about Leszek—a greedy part of me wanted to keep him to myself, to keep seeing him in secret to get more information and advice, but another greedy part of me wanted to explain something to them right now, rather than always allowing everyone to explain things to me. I blurted, "I saw the strange ranger."

I saw the balance tilt toward concern.

"It's fine," I hastened to add. "He's an ally." Alexis raised an eyebrow, but I went on. "He knows Irena. He didn't offer any clues per se, but he and Irena have known each other since they were kids. I think if we keep talking to him . . ."

"Hang on," said Freddie. "Why did we go to the restaurant last night?"

Everyone turned to him. No one seemed to know what he was asking. I wasn't sure if I should be annoyed by the Nordic non sequitur or grateful for it.

"Emi has been out searching for clues," Freddie continued. "Yesterday's search—conducted by all but Emi and me—"

"And me," interjected Pavel.

"Sustained, but even so, yesterday's search yielded two clues, if I am remembering correctly. The first, which led us to marry one another, had to do with Saint Anthony. But what was it that led us to our dinner? What was the second clue?"

"Ah," said Ostap. He took a deep breath and began to lay out their methodology.

We had always wondered why—since it was obvious how much she loved this place, by far more than anywhere else in the world—Irena had never written a book about Białowieża. She had never written so much as a page about Białowieża, and after our first and final—our only—day with her this year, we had come to believe that *Grey Eminence* was no exception. And yet, as it turned out, page 813—not surprisingly, a page that had fallen in Alexis's purview on our initial read—contained the following:

In the fourteenth century, Saint Albert the Great sang the praises of the fair, ferocious tarpan, first recorded eighteen centuries earlier by Herodotus in his depictions of Polesian swamps. That was a realm that had always, without exception, unlike anywhere else on that cursed continent, held off the vile troops of civilization, determined to doom every animal, every plant, in their brutal march toward a mirage of perfect happiness—toward an illusion of a home. Yet in the twenty-first century, the Polesian swamps remained self-sovereign, irrepressible, wild.

This, Amália recognized, and at the height of her powers, she set out to stage her most controversial still life yet: a Nazi-engineered pseudo-neo-tarpan fight on the rusted rails of an abandoned station at the edges of the forest, to the death—to the reextinction—amid the relics of a tsar and some of the only extant remnants of that mode of transportation, to the dark, silent delight of the billions who would watch it live on Instagram from their climate-controlled cells.

Petra and Renata had done the research: The last true tarpan had been driven over a cliff by a mob in 1879, the same year the bartnik Filimon Waszkiewicz was born. (I remembered this because I had just seen it on his grave.) But a man named Lutz Heck had tried to re-create the tarpan by breeding Icelandic mares with Central Asian steppe stallions in the years leading up to World War II. During the same period, Białowieża had become a beloved hunting ground for some of the most powerful figures in Germany, among them Holocaust architect Heinrich Himmler and Luftwaffe commander in chief Hermann Göring—the same Göring who'd been mentioned by that patriarch at the patriotic picnic. The sort-of tarpans, which weren't tarpans but which *looked* pure and authentic, were released in Białowieża—Nazi natural paradise—where they remain to this day.

As for Amália's day, the six of them surmised that the station Our Author mentioned wouldn't have been built after 2017, which left the two that had already been abandoned: the passenger station Freddie and I had passed on our way to the bike shop, and the freight station that had recently been converted into a Russian restaurant that featured relics of the tsars.

"But why now?" I said.

"What do you mean?" Ostap asked.

"I mean, she never wrote about Białowieża in any of her ten novels before *Grey Eminence*. So the question is: Why now?"

"Has anyone actually read *Ad Nauseam* or *Still Life with Still Life*?" Alexis asked. Everyone was silent, probably all agreeing with me that Alexis's question was, as was so often the case, irrelevant.[40]

"Well, let's just assume," I went on. "You know what I mean. Why would she write about Białowieża now?"

Everyone seemed to be thinking. Freddie turned to me.

"Remember when you said that by telling me something, you might be able to forget?"

I was blushing. It was a struggle to keep track of all the different timelines of the village and Irena's novels, along with the timeline of her disappearance, along with her secret life, along with my own inner existence, which I had always suppressed in her house until now, so I knew I couldn't trust my own estimates, but it really did feel like decades since a man (or a boy) had made me blush like this.

Then again, I was still wearing terry short-shorts and a tank top that was suddenly too soft against my skin.

---

40 So few people ever actually agreed with this author in those moments that this novel almost turns into a cautionary tale about interpreting silence as endorsement (Trans.).

"If, as some of you say, Irena maintains an absolute distinction between her life and her work, then such a mania would have to have its rationale. Perhaps the principle is similar: Once she puts a thing into words, that thing recedes into the fog of all the million other things that have already been resolved—the things that, so far as her brain is concerned, no longer require the energy of clarity as they are no longer nodes of active processing."

"What are you talking about?" said Chloe.

"I suppose I'm suggesting that Irena doesn't write about anything she can't risk losing," he said.

"She's never written about us," said Renata brightly. It was the sweet confidence in her voice then that would haunt me later on. But right then she glanced at Ostap and bit her lip *as her eyes welled up with tears*! Ostap and Renata must have had a fight while I was out, I thought—but over what?

I resolved to keep an eye on them as over the course of the rest of the morning we made lists of everything that was missing from *Grey Eminence* in the hopes of pinpointing what mattered to Irena most. From this list, we planned to deduce where she might have gone. It was like tracking a highly elusive animal, attempting to glean from a series of empty impressions in the earth what Our Author cared about and where her cares could have taken her from here. The list went like this:

Chloe: *astrology; illness; traditional royalty; national parks; anyone genuinely committed to the environment, social justice, etc.; acknowledgments*

Schulz: *political parties; specific political processes, such as elections; professions; any mention of class*

Freddie: *father; mother; more than a couple token dinosaurs; a meaningful consideration of outer space; real poems by real poets*

Petra: *books; developed characters other than Amália; seasons*

Renata: *references to other authors; volcanoes; character development for Amália*

Ostap: *humbler plants like weeds and humbler animals like rats and flies; onyx; amber*

Alexis: *poetry; internal logic; clothes*

Me: *sex; a spirit of beginning or discovery; a home; a dedication*

Pavel: *love*

Once we had put them all together, we stared at our screens for a while. As the temperature rose, our moods worsened. Chloe fanned her face in vain. Every few minutes, Alexis groaned and said, "My kingdom for AC!" Freddie was across the room, again acting as though nothing in particular had ever happened between us, and I couldn't make sense of a location, or even a direction, that would feature parents, weeds, books, and many kinds of dinosaurs.

Alexis sighed.

"Are you all right, Alexis?" asked Schulz, craning his neck to peer at her.

"I'm okay," Alexis said softly, gazing down at her blood-orange claws, which Chloe, I imagined, had painted for her.

I was becoming unbearably frustrated, and I got up, planning to pace in front of the fireplace until Freddie noticed me or until I figured something out about Our Author (whichever happened first). Seemingly by coincidence, Petra got up at the same time. She announced to the room that she was going on a walk. As a result of this, Renata got up and reached for her plasticky purse, but Petra said something to her, quietly and in one of their languages, or some South Slavic hybrid—in any case, I couldn't understand or even really hear it—and astonishingly, Renata, who had accompanied her friend on every single excursion throughout the whole history of Irena Rey's translation summits, sat back down.

Oblivious, as usual, Freddie started chatting with Pavel, and although I stared at him, he didn't so much as glance in my direction. Renata had lowered her head and put her purse down at her feet and was wringing her hands in her lap. I wanted Petra to sit down again, to apologize to her best friend, but instead, she left. I wanted Freddie to cross the room and take my hand and say that what had happened between us in the forest—at the Royal Oaks trail, or even on that morning's walk—had been important to him. I suppose if he had said it, by our own logic, we might have forgotten it and moved on.

"Why don't we all take an hour?" asked Ostap, seemingly out of consideration for Renata—but weren't he and Renata fighting, too?

We scattered. It was eleven A.M. I'd been up investigating for seven hours, and to no real avail. I lay down in my bed and tried not to think about anything, just to rest, but the harder I tried, the more the nothing was overshadowed by *Grey Eminence*. It seemed to me Irena's novel was suggesting that our current extinction event—in which hundreds of thousands of species, maybe millions, were dying out all around us, right before our refusing eyes—was the direct result of art. Painting, sculpture, literature—even language itself, a system of abstractions intended to stand in for the real world. That was the key: Every creation that served as a substitute for what was given in nature was art.

Art is the uniquely human impulse to relentlessly transform whatever we come into contact with, to undo in order to do or redo. To create, we first have to destroy. Architecture offered the clearest picture of this rule: An elegant home like Irena's meant razed earth and mutilated trees. Not, as we had previously believed, holy time together as a family.

As the members of Amália's family were killed one by one in gruesome, almost unbelievable accidents, Amália's reactions to their deaths became increasingly, though perhaps understandably, bizarre. Irena seemed to be saying our art impulse stemmed from our rejection of mortality, our abject rage at being fleeting. We were the only species so uncomfortable with passing away that we would sacrifice everything living to make anything permanent. Plastic was one of our arts, our greatest still life, and one of Amália's first fascinations, after the decapitation of her little sister in a freak crash that also mangled her father (soon to die himself) and (although concealably, even—by some accounts— appealingly) her.

But *Grey Eminence* progressed from plastic, lingering on nearly every medium until it finally arrived at Amália's sick performances that, surely, reinforced Irena's point: Every artwork, even something as sublime as a symphony, arose at the expense of a forest, or a tundra, or a desert, or a stream.

I knew that as her translator, whether or not I agreed with Irena's theory didn't matter. What was troubling was not knowing if she meant it herself. All the contradictions seemed to cancel meaning out. More than anything in the world she wanted to save Białowieża. Yet she had dedicated all her time, maybe at the cost of her health and sanity, to writing a huge novel that was the epitome of art, the kind of art that makes a major impact, that spends a century or several blocking out the sun. Did she not see the full implications of *Grey Eminence* until she had completed it? Was that why she had left us, because she couldn't bear to see us perpetuate her own extinguishing actions through our translations? But then why had she sent us the file?

I put on some perfume in front of the mirror, rolling the cool silver ball down the center of my neck, the insides of my arms, and finally my wrists. It was a slightly salty mandarin orange scent that reminded me of Mar del Plata, the couple of times I went to the Argentine seaside with my parents when I was very young, before everyone started going to Uruguayan beaches instead. Then I tiptoed back downstairs and knocked quietly on Freddie's door. He said to come in, and I did, quietly shutting the door again behind me. He was lying in bed, fully dressed except for his shoes that were marred more and more by the forest, with his laptop on his lap. He smiled. Only when I exhaled did I realize I'd been holding my breath. He patted the empty space on the bed next to him, and I walked around and sat down.

"Linda," he said, which means "pretty" or "beautiful" in my language, which I didn't know he knew,[41] and setting his computer aside with one hand, he repeated with the other the gesture of tucking my hair behind my ear. Our lips met and my tongue found his neck, and soon his mouth was on my nipple and his hand was underneath me and then he pulled me on top of him and I unfastened his jeans and he was inside me, and we moved in fervid waves and fused together, my fingers in his mouth and his hair, and he flipped me over and I was underneath him and my heels were inside his ankles, and they rose at the rhythm of sense without meaning to the backs of his knees, and higher, and higher, and he moaned into my ear and bit my throat and earlobe and was part of me, and I felt it in my shoulders and down my legs, electric in my fingers, on my scalp, and then we were breathless, lying facing each other, laughing.

\

---

41   Not to take away from this no doubt romantic moment, but is it not possible that Freddie actually forgot this author's name and called her Linda (Trans.)?

CHAPTER SEVENTEEN

Then the hour was over, and we seated ourselves for lunch—all of us but Petra, who (I might have been the last to notice) remained some distance from our table, in the embrace of a monstera, her hands balled into fists.

Ladies, gentlemen," said Petra, as if addressing some symposium of strangers, and not the only other people in the world who truly understood the most important aspect of her life, "I'm going back to Belgrade."

Even though we must have all felt something like this was coming from one of us, the table was momentarily submerged in an anguished wavelet of surprise.

Then Renata said, "No."

Inspired by her concision, I pushed back my chair and stood. I had conviction and bliss on my side; I would speak, I thought, and I would make Petra stay.

"If lichens can create life from surfaces without any life on them," I said, smiling at Freddie, "then surely we can translate her book without her here."

"Of course we can," said Ostap. He gave Renata a nervous glance. "In fact, this is the way translation is normally done."

"To be completely honest," said Schulz, "in a way, it has even come as a relief. Without Irena here, we can focus on the text."

Alexis had changed into yoga pants and a sports bra, and it was all I could do not to glance at her midriff as she chirped, "Plus we're more connected to the forest."

"No," Renata repeated. "None of this can happen. We need Irena. We need to find Irena, and in order to find her, we need to stay here. To wait."

Chloe and Ostap and Freddie and Schulz started and stopped talking at the same time. I took the opportunity. "In the end," I said, "what we do is mycelial. What we do as translators is stitch the world into a united and communicating whole."

"Excuse me," said Petra, raising her trigger finger, "but this is personal and has nothing to do with Our Author, *Grey Eminence*, or any of you. I will leave tomorrow, and from then on, I will be happy to remain in touch as we all continue to work on our translations, assuming continuing is indeed what we decide to do."

No one knew how to respond to this. I looked up at the garlands of ribs and the skulls dangling over our heads. I looked at Pavel, who was shoving forkful after forkful arugula into his already at-capacity mouth.

I think none of us believed Petra, not really. What could "personal" possibly mean? It was a mind-boggling word in this context—in the context of our single-mindedness and our devotion.

"But Pavel didn't get to marry," said Renata.

Pavel looked at her and tried to swallow. But then I looked at Renata and felt sorry; she was in despair, and like all of us, she was doing her best not to fall to pieces. I looked at Chloe's chipped pink fingernails, and I thought this had to be the very lowest moment of our existence together as translators, our Irena nadir. But then Pavel gave a throaty cough and said, "Alexis? What are you thinking?" And I realized we could go lower.

Alexis simply pursed her lips and shook her head, as though it was harboring so many fine, intricate thoughts that she could not possibly decide how to begin.

"Hold on!" said Ostap, turning to Freddie with a victorious grin. "We told you what we came up with yesterday, but what about Emi and you? Wasn't there bad news from the forest? Couldn't that have been a clue?"

It made sense to me that he would grasp at straws. Why would he want to go home to his misadventurous wife in Dubliany and his cobbled-together career of copyedits and composition classes at a university that couldn't even always pay?

"I'm afraid it wasn't," said Freddie. "It was just that the forest is being cut down. We already know the effect such news had on Irena. But we came no closer to figuring out what steps she took next."

At first, as Freddie spoke, all I could think about was the Swedish syllables he'd panted in my face before, how his face had tensed, how his hands had gripped my arms. But I forced myself to come back to this conversation, the winter garden, our entourage.

"The truth is we only managed to speak with one person yesterday," I admitted. "In the village. And that was almost the opposite of a clue."

"What do you mean?" said Chloe.

"Who'd you talk to?" said Schulz.

"The pharmacist," Freddie said. "We made up a story that we needed Irena's medication."

"We thought that maybe she could tell us if Irena had been sick," I explained. It felt to me like months ago that we had tried to search the village.

"Sick?" said Pavel.

"We don't know," Chloe said. "Maybe she's not. She just didn't look so good."

"How exactly did she look?" said Pavel.

"What did the pharmacist say?" said Schulz.

"She said something about Irena's father," I said. "I think she was testing us or something."

"Testing you?" Chloe repeated. "How? Why?"

"Like to find out if we were paparazzi or something, I guess?" I said. "I don't know. She implied that she had a prescription for Irena's father. I told her that we knew Irena's father had died on the day she was born."

Petra rose from the table with an unusual pallor to her face—the same whiteness that had ailed her the previous evening, at the Tsar's Restaurant. She turned and glided away. Chloe stood, appeared to consider, and then fell back into her chair.

"There has to be something else we can do," I said.

"I tried to break into her office computer," Alexis said. "I thought maybe we could check her email, or her calendar, or something—her FaceTime. I couldn't figure out the password, though."

"You've got to be kidding," I said. Breaking into Irena's computer would be the ultimate violation. It would be an unimaginable betrayal, not to mention it would likely be like staring straight into the sun. How could we, as mere translators, even begin to comprehend all of her notes, all her preliminary sketches, her drafts?

Of course I would have killed to read the very first version of *Lena*, or *Kernel of Light*. Of course I wanted to get inside her process, find out what she was thinking about writing next. But I thought then that I would never even have *dreamed* of opening Irena's files—not unless Irena had commanded me to do so herself.

"You don't really think we should read her private things," said Ostap. "Do you, Alexis?"

"We can't," said Renata.

"We can't," repeated Schulz. "Right? Even if Alexis is right that it might lead us to Irena?"

"It's moot," the English-language criminal observed. "We'll never figure out her password."

Pavel stood up. "Try my name."

Slowly, we floated into Our Author's office and stood staring at her desk. It may seem like a paradox that I was the one who finally sat down in Irena's red womb chair. But I thought that at least if I was the one in charge of our illicit foray, I could mitigate the damage we did. That is, if Alexis had commandeered her keyboard, who knew? Files could have been tampered with, even deleted. If I was overseeing our operation, I reasoned, at least the worst we could do was read. I entered Pavel's name where it said password.

The box shook, as if indignant, but Alexis leaned over my shoulder and whispered, "Try it all lowercase."

And we were inside her computer, inside her brain. Exactly where we'd always wanted to be, I realized, but no matter how hard we'd tried through our translations, we'd never quite been able to inhabit it till now.

Irena's inbox was rife with junk mail, special offers on cleaning sprays and credit cards and all-inclusive trips: slight variations on the noisome contents of our own inboxes, more hateful still in hers. There were a few emails from people: her editor, a well-known critic, people we didn't know. That there were people in her life we'd never heard of liquefied whatever remained in my mind of rational thought—made me feel like I was dissolving into my surroundings, the stacks of paper, the double rows of books, the shelves themselves, all of which were liquid, too. I made myself click on the most recent message from Bogdan, the subject of which was: "From Milan."

My kitten, please try and find it in your capacious heart to forgive me. I love
you, as always, and I would like to come home, but I won't until you tell
me I can.
Your B

"Milan?!" said Pavel. "I thought he was mopping up snot somewhere near here."

"Yeah," Freddie said. "Why Milan?"

"Let's write him back as her," said Alexis. "Maybe we can get him to come and help us find her."

"Yeah, but then Bogdan would be here," said Chloe, wrinkling her nose.

"I'm uncomfortable with this," Renata said. "I agree with Schulz. I'd hate it if anyone got into my private correspondence."

"Okay," I said, although I doubted anyone would care to read Renata's private correspondence. "Let's just look through her drafts and her trash and any folders she's created that might have to do with her whereabouts or work."

But just as I was about to move Irena's cursor, Petra burst into the room. For a second I thought she was going to yell at us for being in Our Author's office, at her desk, but instead she held up a small package and said, "Losec."

"Losec?" repeated Ostap.

"When I went to the pharmacy this morning, the pharmacist insisted on giving it to me," Petra said.

"What is it?" said Alexis.

"I thought you went for a walk," said Renata. For the second time that day, her eyes filled with tears.

"I walked to the pharmacy," Petra said softly. She put her hand on her friend's shoulder, which only hastened the flooding of Renata's floral blouse.

I was relieved, however, that Petra had gotten something that might make her feel better, and I said as much.

But Petra said, "It isn't for me. The pharmacist told me to give it to Irena for her dad."

"You accepted the prescription?!" I cried. "But wasn't it a test?"

Renata sniffed. "But, I suppose—what if it wasn't?"

We were inside Irena's computer and surrounded by her books, thousands of volumes jammed into shelves that reached clear to the ceiling, all of the styles and ideas that had shaped her, helped her become the greatest writer on the continent, maybe the world. Suddenly she wasn't remote—she was right here; we were closer to her than we had ever been when she was with us. And yet, I still couldn't understand what any of it meant: amadou, Pavel, her leaving us like this. Her forgetting Białowieża, as if it didn't matter whether it was sacrificed or saved.

"La puta que te parió!" I yelled into the bookcases, leaping up and lunging into them at random, coming, to my continued surprise, face to face with a shelf of self-help books: *Forty Ways to Feel Better*; *How to Stop Smoking in Thirty Days*; *One Hundred Rules to Follow for a Better, Happier Life*; *You're a Ten, Don't Let Him Get Away with It.* I couldn't imagine Irena reading a book called *You're a Ten.* Irena wasn't a ten. She was a goddess—a twenty, surely, maybe more. It must have been research for a new book, or an essay on the banality or futility of our times, not that I presumed to know her mind enough to know her future subjects.

"So you all finally know about Pan Igor," Chloe said. She released her shoulders. "To tell you the truth, it's a relief."

"Who is Pan Igor?" Schulz asked.

"Dembowski," Chloe said.

"Who's Dembowski?" I said, though something was tugging at my brain, some too-dim suspicion.

"The old man who spoke at the patriotic picnic," said Chloe.

"Ohhh," said Alexis, but then she looked confused again.

Chloe said, "Irena's dad."

I laughed a nervous laugh that might have been the beginning of a nervous breakdown. I said, "Is this a joke?"

"No. The story about the duel is made up. Irena's real father isn't named Aleksander, and he didn't die in a fight with his best friend Emil."

I looked around Our Author's office. If it was a joke, she was playing it on everyone. Schulz had started jumping up and down in place like he was at a concert. Freddie had lain down in what looked like a comfortable position on the floor. My eyes swept over his long legs, his broad chest and his shoulders, his beautiful, powerful arms crossed behind his head.

"Did she give you something for your stomach, Petra, too?" asked Ostap. I was astonished by his ability to change the subject.

"Funnily enough," said Petra, "Losec is for stomach ailments, but there's nothing wrong with mine."

"Wait," said Alexis, who was still too close to me, although I was standing in a corner now. "Are you . . . You're not—"

"I am," said Petra. "Pregnant."

A pile of papers gradually slid onto the floor at Freddie's feet.

"Given that my only other child is currently in college," she said, "I was as surprised as you are now."

"Congratulations," Schulz said automatically.

Renata's jaw had dropped, and now she just stood frozen. Alexis went over to Petra and gave her a big hug that Petra pointlessly struggled to resist.

"Wow," said Chloe.

"Great news," said Ostap. "Congratulations."

Petra looked at Renata, who had covered her mouth and nose with her hands and was gazing wide-eyed at the text-strewn floor.

"I'm sorry," she said. "I didn't think of it until Pavel said something about pregnancy last night. Even after I thought of it, I didn't believe it. I didn't want to mention it before I took the test."

Renata didn't say anything.

"Are you going to name it Irena?" said Alexis, but from her tone I couldn't tell if she was being ironic for some reason or not.[42]

"Probably not," said Petra.

"Amália?"

"Probably not."

"Alexis?" I said.

"Yes?" said Alexis.

"Probably not," said Petra.

Chloe said, "I'm going to take Pan Igor his Losec. If anyone wants to come with me, you're welcome. Now that it's out in the open I don't see any reason why you shouldn't meet him. He lives next door."

"What?!" I shrieked. "The house with the crazy signs on the fence?"

---

42   I was, as would have been obvious to anyone but this author (Trans.).

"The crazy signs were Bogdan's idea. Every October a bunch of journalists show up on the off-chance that Irena wins the Nobel Prize. And also every pub day. You know, we've never been here for that. We're here before the books come out, not after. Pan Igor said it gets pretty nuts. They didn't want anyone barging in on him. He's a hundred years old."

"That's right!" said Alexis. "They said that at the picnic, he's a hundred years old. Wait, what day do they announce the Nobel Prize?"

"How could Irena's father be a hundred years old?" Renata asked as Petra said, "October fifth."

"If you don't believe me," Chloe said, "the picture of him with Hermann Göring is directly behind the shrine."

At the mention of one of the world's most infamous war criminals, Schulz cried, apparently in his language, "What?!" He looked at Chloe for a second, then ran out of the room. Ostap took off his glasses and began to massage his face.

Petra whispered, as she sank into Irena's vacant womb chair, "My God. The ghosts."

"But in that case," I said, "who's Irena's mother?"

Chloe shrugged.

And at my own mention of "mother", it occurred to me that I, Argentina's condom scion, had failed to use protection during my morning tryst with Freddie. If any of his spores had launched their hyphae—but I couldn't bring myself to think of it, a fungus of a fetus whose cells would become mine, making me chimeric. Not centauric: monstrous and invaded, not even me anymore.

Then again, I was a translator. Wasn't not being me what I spent every day trying to achieve?[43]

---

43   No (Trans.).

CHAPTER EIGHTEEN

In the span of just twenty-four hours, Petra, haunted by a panoply of dead souls, had created life out of nothing, while two men had come back from the dead, one newly, confusingly alluring, the other in the company of a Nazi, one of the worst people in Western history, now seemingly tied to Our Author in some awful, incredible way.

We'd thought that whatever happened happened to us all. But what had happened to Petra had hopefully happened only to Petra, and to her unmystical actual husband, and, it could be argued, to their future second child.

What had happened between Pavel and Our Author had happened between only them, unless you counted what had happened between Freddie and me, and unless something had happened that first night between Irena and Freddie, not that Freddie would tell me, and not that I wanted to know, because what if something had happened, but also: What if it had not?

Pavel had been sleeping with Irena—extensively, repeatedly, definitely, and in depth—and that gave him powers that Freddie, regardless, couldn't have. Pavel could, if I so desired, do the same things to my body that he had done to Our Author's body, an idea that took my breath away. Yet to my shame I had begun to develop an inexplicable genuine fondness for Freddie, even though I assumed it would ebb once *Grey Eminence* was done. Unless it didn't, in which case: What would I do about his wife?

Questions spread like wildfire through my body, and it felt like the more I fought them, the harder and hotter they got.

Per Pan Igor's instructions, issued to Chloe via Nina, who was not Irena's possibly still-dead mother, but rather Pan Igor's nurse, we arrived at the house with the frightening signs at seven P.M., soon after his afternoon nap. Although Petra had packed her bags and set them at the foot of the chaise longue, she was still with us. Chloe opened the gate and, without the slightest hesitation, waltzed into the seemingly forbidden front yard. She led us to the door, knocked five times, and then, without waiting for an answer, led us in.

"As-salaam alaykum," sang Chloe as we swished through the vestibule.

"Malaykum salaam," came an ancient voice from within the semidarkness of the house.

It would be hard to overstate our confusion at this. I'd known Chloe a decade and never heard her use what I later confirmed was Senegal's most common greeting; how had she taught Irena's hundred-year-old father to respond to it, to greet her back, but not taught me?[44]

Something animal in me, something predatory, like the wolf that disrupts the mycorrhizae to bury the bones of its prey, turned away from Chloe then, instead of reaching out to her. I wondered if this was the same impulse that had led Irena to abandon the forest (if indeed she had), to give up the thing she treasured most *because* she most treasured it: I couldn't bear to watch my friend drift away from me, so instead, I shut my eyes.

But Chloe went around opening the curtains, illuminating the droops and crags in Irena's father's face, the bruises and abrasions to the thin skin of his arms, his white close-cropped hair. When every window had been bared, she went to his armchair and almost shouted, "Mr. Bison Keeper, these are Irena's other translators, the ones you've heard so much about."

Pan Igor smiled and greeted us by raising both his liver-spotted hands, which had a tremor that didn't go away when he refolded them.

"Pan Igor is the true storyteller in the family," said Chloe. And although I knew from the picnic that this old man was capable of a captivating yarn, to suggest that anyone was a better storyteller than Irena Rey was still a sacrilege.

---

44 As already noted by this very author, Irena didn't want us communicating with each other in languages other than hers—meaning it shouldn't have been confusing to anyone that Chloe knew whole phrases we'd never heard her use. In other words, this wasn't a secret that Chloe was keeping from Emi (Trans.).

But Chloe seemed proud to be the one to introduce us to this man she evidently admired, the grandfather she had never had—her mother's father had disowned her mother after she defected, and her father's father had died before Chloe was born—and so we let it go.

Distracted by his hands, we stood around not knowing what to do with our own. Finally I folded mine and spun my thumbs four times. The first thing I saw when I looked up was a postcard from Cairo on a side table. It must have been more recent than anything else in the room because it was much easier for my eyes to make out than its surroundings, which were dingy, somewhat faded, stacked. I was about to pick up the new postcard when Pan Igor began to speak.

"This young lady," he said, his voice trembling. His eyes were clouded by cataracts, and I wondered whether he was seeing us all as just one shape, with no real borders between our colors or our frames. "You are all very fortunate to have such a fine young woman as your colleague."

I thought this, too, but I also felt a twinge of jealousy: Some part of me wanted all that fortune for myself.

Pan Igor continued: "I know my daughter is honored that each of you has chosen to translate her work."

This was, of course, exactly what we needed to hear; now we knew where Irena got that ability, her preternatural gift for reading and immediately responding to all kinds of people at once. In Pan Igor's case, the gift seemed to arise from genuine kindness, and it puzzled me—and I assumed the others—that Irena should want to keep him a secret. But just then Schulz and Petra both advanced and started shouting.

Aghast at their audacity, I couldn't understand what each of them was talking about at first. Schulz was waving a framed photograph, and Petra was waving her hands.

Chloe stepped forward. "Petra," she said. "Schulz. I can explain."

Pan Igor kept his eyes on his hands as Chloe proceeded to retell the war story that Alexis and Freddie and I had already heard at the Park of Monumental Miniatures, enhancing it with details like the fact that Pan Igor had only been arrested by the Gestapo in the first place because he'd accidentally witnessed a Nazi officer illegally shooting and killing a bear.

"What does this have to do with the picture?" Ostap whispered.

"The photograph you see," said Pan Igor, "is from Hermann Göring's final hunting trip in Białowieża, three years before the bear. He had already killed enough of the birds and the boar to feast all of Deutschland, but what he really wanted was a wolf. At that time, I worked for the municipality. Everybody else was fearful to do it, so it fell to me, the youngest, to escort Herr Göring on that grisly quest.

"Białowieża is the most powerful place in the world," Pan Igor continued. "It's a place with a will of its own. If you weren't born in Białowieża, it can be very hard to get it to accept you. There were a few fellows in town who never gave me a chance because I came from a village up by the sea. One of them turned me in to the Soviets for collaborating with the Nazis on the basis of that photograph, which he'd taken from me without my noticing. There was nothing I could say or do then. I shouldn't have kept the photograph. I don't know why I did. I don't know why my daughter keeps it now. Maybe it's out of respect—not for the criminal, of course, but for the wolf.

"In any case, they sentenced me to ten years of hard labor. They sent me to Kazakhstan, where I worked building mines. The girlfriend I'd had here was killed, like a lot of the young people back then. If it wasn't for people like Olga Smoktunowicz, it would have been even worse. My only brother died in combat. I got off easy, but the mines were still hard work. Physically, but also spiritually. I know I only survived by remembering my bison."

"Did you serve the full ten years?" asked Schulz.

"Yes, sir," he said. "In Kazakhstan. And where do you come from?"

"Berlin," said Schulz. "Born and raised."

"Ah," said Mr. Dembowski. "A punk."

"That's right!" said Schulz.

Pan Igor laughed. He seemed genuinely happy to be having this talk with us, which led me to believe he knew something about Irena's disappearance that we didn't—unless he didn't know about her disappearance at all.

I was trying to figure out how best to word the question when Alexis said, extra clearly, insofar as her Polish was ever intelligible,[45] "Do you happen to know where your daughter is right now?"

---

45   Just wow (Trans.).

Pan Igor shook his head. If he noticed her condescension, he gave no indication of offense. "She was here with me until the storm," he said. "She took off as soon as it cleared."

"The storm?!" said Petra.

"She was here until Tuesday?!" Ostap screeched.

Pan Igor nodded.

"Where is she *now*?" repeated Alexis, and I was overjoyed to see Chloe rolling her eyes.

"She told me she was going over to Ukraine for a couple of weeks, starting out in Drohobych, but to tell you the truth I always take what she tells me with a pinch of salt. If you all don't know where she is, I'd say that means she might have finally done it." He gave another laugh and let his head fall to his chest.

"Done what?" Chloe asked gently, putting her hand on his shoulder.

He looked up at her and said, lightly, "Headed to Japan."

"Ohhh," said Alexis.

"Japan," Renata repeated under her breath.

"Japan?" asked Freddie, but it didn't sound like he expected an answer, and he did not receive one.

"What about Bogdan?" asked Schulz, glancing apologetically at Pavel, who shrugged.

Pan Igor nodded and seemed to be gathering his thoughts. "Bogdan's father passed away in July. A heart attack, out of the blue. He was fifty-three, if I'm remembering correctly."

"But how old is Bogdan?" asked Freddie.

Pan Igor pursed his lips. "I think he's my age," Chloe said.

"Really?!" squealed Alexis.

"How old are you?" asked Freddie.

"Well, you're not supposed to ask a lady that," Chloe said, and Pan Igor smiled. "But I'm thirty-three."

"Why would he be your age?" I asked her, barely refraining from pointing out that she was already thirty-three and a half, and I was only—for another month at least—thirty-four.

"Irena came to Paris once, supposedly for a meeting with her French publisher, although her French publisher is Geneva-based. In any case, she let me know she was going to be there, and we met up. She wanted to take a walk along the Seine and talk. She confided in me that Bogdan was actually still at university when they first met, and she said it wasn't a long courtship, just a couple of months. I did the math."

"I thought Bogdan was a translator before Irena," said Ostap.

"I guess he was *studying* translation," said Chloe. She turned back to Pan Igor. "Is that right?"

"I think so," he said. "Irena never tells me everything, but I remember he was young when he moved here. At first I thought he was just a secretary. He seemed to be working for her."

"What about the father?" asked Petra. "The heart attack?"

"When his father died, Bogdan learned he had a brother—a half brother, I suppose—who is only nine years old. A couple of weeks ago, Bogdan went to visit that brother."

"Nine?" asked Petra. "So his father had a baby with someone when he was forty-four." This calculation visibly relaxed her. If someone else had a baby when they were forty-four, I assumed she was thinking, then surely she and her husband could handle it at forty-two.

"Where does he live?" asked Freddie.

"That I don't remember," said Pan Igor. "Sorry."

"Do you think Irena might win the Nobel Prize this year?" Renata asked, addressing no one in particular, and then everyone started speaking at once.

"Did she ever mention anything we did to offend her?" asked Petra.

"Have you ever considered selling this house?" asked Alexis.

"Do you need anything right now?" asked Chloe.

"A glass of water?" asked Freddie. "Some tea?"

"Have you read her new book?" asked Schulz.

"Who is Emil Wierzbicki?" I asked. I needed to know whether Irena's tale had any basis in reality—whether Pan Igor had ever had a best friend turned archnemesis—whether, for instance, Pan Emil was the man who turned Pan Igor in after the war—or whether all of it had been Irena's own invention.

"Pan Emil?" he said, looking at me with a smile of confusion, and I was excited that mine was the question he chose to answer. "That's our dentist!"

If Irena had been trying to humiliate us, she had certainly succeeded. But why would she want to humiliate her own representatives, the people who faithfully and methodically distributed her ideas to the world?

"What about Irena's mother?" asked Petra. "Do you know where she lives?"

"Irena hasn't seen her mother since she was nine years old," said Pan Igor. "Neither have I."

"What do you mean," Renata ventured, "nine?"

Pan Igor turned to Schulz. "Do you remember the hijacking of LOT 165?"

"Wasn't that the plane that crashed into the mountain?" asked Renata.

"Oh!" exclaimed Alexis. "The one that's still classified. Where they flew past their destination, and everybody died, unless they didn't?"

"Yes," said Pan Igor. "But no. That LOT 165 flight was in 1969. This LOT flight 165 was nine years later, in 1978."

"I remember that one," said Freddie brightly. And addressing each of us in turn, in the stentorian voice he'd used to recite song lyrics and poetry, he told us a somewhat convoluted story—not helped by his own Polish—of two friends from East Germany named Detlev and Ingrid who'd used a toy starting pistol to overpower the Polish crew of a flight from Gdańsk to East Berlin, forcing the plane to land, instead, at Tempelhof Airport, in West Berlin. There, they, along with Ingrid's young daughter, claimed sanctuary.

"My husband works at Tempelhof," said Schulz. "It houses the central lost and found of Berlin now. He coordinates the finders."

"The finders?" asked Chloe.

"Yes," Schulz said simply. "Someone else is there to coordinate the losers."

"What do German people lose the most?" asked Pan Igor.

"Maybe there's a section for lost authors," Alexis muttered under her breath.

"Oh, cell phones, laptops," said Schulz. "Books come in a lot, but most of the time they go unclaimed. Thanks to that my husband and I have a massive home library of Bahn novels—our term for novels left behind on the train."

"Well," Pan Igor said, "Ingrid and her child were not the only people who claimed sanctuary at Tempelhof that day in 1978."

"There was also Detlev," said Renata with a nod.

"No," said Pan Igor. "I don't mean Detlev. I had married a young woman from a village near where I grew up, and I had brought her here, to start our family. I was in love with her, and I believe she loved me, too, but she could never reconcile herself to inland life, the swamps, the closed society. She was descended from Lipka Tatars—steppe people, people who craved an open vista, an illusion, at least, of freedom. She didn't care about the forest, not really, not like I did.

Whether she would have run away on her own, of her own initiative, I'll never know. But when presented with the opportunity—she was going to her cousin's wedding in Prenzlauer Berg, in East Berlin, just a couple of days, a change of scenery, a little liberation, but then—she left.

"I didn't know how to take care of a girl like Irena, not on my own. I never knew what she needed. I knew about bison. I was good with them. I was good with plants—even bees I knew my way around. About young girls, I'm afraid to say, I knew close to nothing."

Pavel covered his face in his hands and left the room. Perhaps this was why Irena had wanted to keep her father a secret. If it was true, this story made her sound profoundly human: vulnerable, afraid. But a human Irena—the Irena with five kinds of acid she used on her face, the Irena with (as we'd discovered) holes in some of her socks—wasn't the Irena we had dedicated our careers to, fallen in love with (except for maybe Pavel). A human Irena was as lost in the universe as we were without her. Everyone seemed uncomfortable; no one seemed to know what to say.

Finally, Chloe said, "We should get going."

"Please don't be too hard on her," said Pan Igor. "I know she can be tough. But I believe she does the best she can. It's the kind of thing—losing your mother—some people never get over." Even in the near-total darkness I could see how violently his hands were shaking now. He paused, then concluded, "People like my daughter."

CHAPTER NINETEEN

The next day was the first day of October, and Petra didn't leave, and all we did was translate and laundry. That evening, like every evening, Alexis insisted on "getting a run in" before dinner, which meant we had over an hour without her, since she also insisted on taking a shower in the freestanding cube in the middle of her bedroom before wafting down the stairs to where we were in the winter garden, her hair perfectly towel-dried. Those hours without Alexis were our golden hours, the only time we were truly a team, although we never said so.

That night, once Freddie and I had torn each other's clothes off, I flipped him over and held him down by his wrists. I wanted him to see what was written on me—the scant remainders of my amadou tattoo—because I wanted Irena to be with us in bed. The stronger her presence became, the harder I fucked him until all of a sudden I was stunned by my own orgasm, an all-encompassing explosion, so that then when he turned me over and set me on all fours I felt like my body was just a shell that was bursting. But afterward, lying beside him in the moonlight, I didn't feel shattered or crushed. I felt like I was free.

The next morning I flew through Chapter Nine, Chapter Ten, Chapter Eleven of *Grey Eminence*. I no longer cared where the rest of them were. I was perfectly in sync with Our Author. All I had to do was touch my fingers to my keyboard, and the text would wash over the screen. This feeling lasted until around six P.M. on October 3, when Schulz returned empty-handed from the store.

"I saw two guys from TV out there. Two reporters," he explained.

"Then it's starting," said Alexis like a rabid puma, and I knew she was thinking only about which of Our Author's outfits she should wear in case she accidentally fell into the frames of many cameras.

"Where were they?" asked Freddie with captivating nonchalance.

"They went from here to their hotel," Schulz said. "I followed them."

"So let's go out," said Freddie.

"Out," Chloe repeated, as though "out" were a nonsense word.

"Yeah," Freddie said, putting his arm around my waist. "I'm hungry, and our clothes are clean. Let's take advantage of the fact that not all the reporters have arrived, and those two guys are probably still getting settled. Tomorrow we might have to remain inside."

"Yes," said Alexis. "Meet back in five." I sneered as she ran upstairs to change. Then I sauntered up and also changed.

THERE WAS A pleasant breeze, and in the unseasonable warmth, it made us giddy. I assumed then that we all believed Irena could and should win that year's Nobel Prize. The impending onslaught of reporters only bolstered that sense. And we had had just enough time since our visit to Pan Igor's to accept that Irena was, as he had said, simply in Ukraine or Japan—both places that felt logical to us, and both places she would obviously come back from as soon as she heard the good news.

We bounded up Stoczek Street and sat in the back garden of the pizzeria, which we hadn't tried before. It felt a little forbidden, but Irena had never actually issued a decree about pizza, so it also felt fine. I was about to place my order when Alexis asked, apparently without embarrassment, for a pizza *americana* without the chicken; I checked the menu again and saw that that would leave corn, bell peppers, and oregano. Chloe ordered the four-cheese pizza, Renata and Petra both got vegetarianas, and I got the margherita.

Then Pavel said, "I'll take a cztery smaki." I rushed to check the menu again. Sure enough: The cztery smaki pizza was mushroom with sliced hot dogs and ham.

"Don't you want it without meat?" I said softly to Pavel across the table, but Pavel simply shook his head.

"I'll take the salami!" said Freddie.

Not to be outdone, Schulz ordered the country pizza, which—I checked—had onions, pickles, and bacon.

"Have you all lost your minds?" I said, quite a bit louder now, and our waitress froze.

"Is something wrong?" Freddie asked me, in a sweet tone that reminded me we had recently had sex but that did nothing to diminish my bewilderment or panic. I looked to Chloe, who merely shrugged.

"I don't know that Irena's rules apply if she's not here," she said. "For now, anyway, maybe we can do whatever we feel like?"

"We've already had alcohol," Alexis pointed out.

"Alcohol and meat are two completely different things," I said.

"Why?" said Schulz.

"Are you serious?" I said.

"It's okay," Alexis said to our waitress with a lecherous grin. "You can go. We'll all have beers."

"What!" I shrieked. "We won't have beers! I won't have beer."

"No beer for me," said Schulz. I tried to smile at him in thanks.

"Six beers," Alexis said, and smiled, and the waitress went inside.

"What the fuck is happening?" I said. I was glad there were no other parties in the garden that evening; it meant I didn't have to pretend to want to lower my voice.

"It's the cycle," said Freddie, making a huge circle with his arm. "Life requires death. Even the men and women who were murdered in this forest during World War II: Białowieża's many fungi would have converted their corpses into useful foodstuffs. Some of those fungi would have offered minerals to plants, while others created nourishment for animals through mushrooms, the fungal form of fruit. In a roundabout way, the deer here were nourished by those who perished in the war, and perhaps subsequently, the villagers themselves, in eating the venison put on their plates by the hunters who stalked and killed and carefully dressed those deer."

"Wait," said Chloe. "What?" I hated how she looked at me when she was annoyed with him.

"Are you telling us we're cannibals?" joked Ostap, but the joke didn't land, or landed without laughter; only Petra was able to muster an uncomfortable smile, which vanished when she looked at Renata.

"I think what Freddie wants to say, really," said Alexis, "is that ultimately everyone in Białowieża is infected by violence—by the war, but presumably by all kinds of violence, even the ordinary kinds."[46]

"Well, yes, you could put it that way, I suppose," Freddie said. "It does feel like a haunted place here. Does it not?"

"Yes!" said Alexis, slamming her phone down on the table. "Extremely. Haven't we all been having a hard time sleeping at night?"

"Though what I also meant," said Freddie, before anyone else could respond, "was that those deaths might not have been in vain, exactly. As they provided for an ecosystem to come."

"A toxic ecosystem," Alexis said. "Think of all the chemicals your body produces when you're scared."

"Glutamate," suggested Chloe.

"What?" I said, as Alexis said, "Exactly," with so much satisfaction I wanted to slap her face off.

"That's the neurotransmitter," Chloe said to me, "that gets produced in higher quantities when the body is afraid. In such quantities, it can damage neurons and neural networks."

"How do you know that?" I asked.

Chloe's face clouded, and she didn't respond, and worst of all she exchanged a look with Alexis that made me want not so much to slap Alexis as to kill her, and then the waitress came back with a tray of half-liter glasses that sloshed and dribbled onto the concrete, leaving disappearing ellipses. I lit a cigarette.

"What are you thinking, Alexis?" asked Pavel. "You seem lost in thought."

Alexis glanced at Chloe again, then bit her chipped orange nail and shook her head. "It's not my place to say," she said.

I exhaled in her face. Gratifyingly, she coughed, and when she was done, there were tiny streaks of mascara around the undersides of her eyes.

---

46   I have here taken the liberty of correcting a statement of mine that my colleague clearly misunderstood, whether willfully or because of her Polish or due to the vicissitudes of memory that every now and then befall us all (Trans.).

NONE OF US was able to find our keys after dinner. I was sure mine had been in my pocket—as sure as I was that my little gold earrings had been on my desk.

Fortunately, with all that had been happening—to each of us, to our various pairings, and to all of us together—we had forgotten to ensure that every possible entrance to our stronghold was secured. So that when we went around through the site of our mystical nuptials, we found the back door perfectly unlocked.

"That's how I got in," said Pavel, and I hated him for pointing out our carelessness. The rogue archer had not been caught yet, and already reporters might be marauding, and Leshy or maybe even Leszek could slip through unblocked keyholes, yet here we were, acting as though things were how they always had been, when Irena had been with us, and we had protected her, and she had protected us.

We shuffled through her bedroom, depositing Pavel there. But as we were entering the hallway, we heard a scuffle, seemingly coming from the living room. There was no mistaking it this time: Someone was there.

"What was that?" said Chloe.

Freddie put his arm around me. I thought I could feel Alexis's eyes on the shoulder that was encircled by his hand. What *was* Alexis thinking? I wondered—but I knew I couldn't let myself fall into her trap.

Schulz commanded us to stay back. Almost silently, he stepped into the hall. He shut the door behind him. He switched on the light.

"No no no!" he shouted. Renata ducked down between the far side of the bed and the wall, and Ostap followed. Astonishingly, I saw him press his mouth to the top of her head.

"Petra!" Schulz yelled. None of us moved or even breathed.

"Petra!" he shouted again. "It's an emergency!"

Freddie said, "You're pregnant, I'll go."

My fear was becoming indistinguishable from my arousal. Freddie went. Given the way things had been going, I knew I might never see him again, unless it was a journalist, in which case, we might never see Irena again because he might be inclined to open his powerful mouth. But then he started laughing, and he came back and opened the door and left it open.

"It's a bird," he said.

"A bird!" said Petra and Renata in unison, Renata rising just enough to peek her head, freshly sniffed by her sworn enemy, over the bed. She locked eyes with Petra and, as though this were the moment they'd been waiting for, marched down the hall locking their arms as well.

It turned out the back door wasn't the only way to sneak inside Irena's house. Apparently a parrot had fallen into her chimney, and when we'd come in, he had panicked and fluttered and banged against the legs of the furniture until Petra swooped in and grabbed him and held him still against her chest. She and Renata exchanged another wordless look and carefully escorted him upstairs. A few minutes later Petra came back down looking fully ten years younger than she had over the past nine days. She told Chloe to chop up a banana and me to fill a measuring cup with cool water. She took the last raspberries out of the refrigerator and put them on a plate.

I let the water run over my fingers, pretending I was awaiting some perfect temperature. I was calming down, and I noticed the calendar that hung over the sink was still on September, and I dried my hands on my shirt and flipped the page. September had been elk grazing, green and brown. October was blindingly bright, an aerial portrait of fall foliage that in no way matched our current October.

"Look," I called over my shoulder. "October 5 is completely blacked out." Chloe leaned in.

"What does that mean?" asked Freddie.

Without missing a beat, Alexis said, "Maybe she figured it's the day she'll lose another Nobel Prize."

"Lose?!" I said. I spun around. "Lose?" I felt like I was choking. The knives hanging over the stove were blotched by the shadows of skulls and tall plants.

"It probably would not go to Irena Rey this year," Freddie said, offering me the can of beer he'd just cracked open. It was bitter. I gulped down foam, then turned around again and spat what was left in my mouth into the sink.

"Did her real mother maybe die that day?" asked Schulz. "My guess would be that—that it's the death of someone."

"Could it have been the child?" Renata asked.

But Pavel shook his head. "That was in the spring. An April day. She didn't tell me exactly what day so now I mourn the whole of April."

"It's not like it happens all at once," said Chloe.

I looked at her. "What doesn't?"

"A miscarriage," she said. "Depending on where you are in your pregnancy—"
Petra floated out of the room with her fingers in her ears. Renata followed with
water and banana. "It takes more than a day, is all I'm saying," Chloe finished,
hushing her voice so as not to discourage the fetus upstairs.

I thought that Chloe must be referring to the experience of a friend, that
surely she would have told me if she had had a miscarriage, if she had gotten pregnant in the first place. But then I thought: She never told me about Irena having
a father. I hadn't even known she was engaged.

THE FOLLOWING MORNING, compounding my mistrust, Chloe was inexpli-
cably absent from morning meditation.

"She just went to check on Pan Igor," Alexis explained. "And to remind him
to expect the press."

"How do you know that?" I snapped, but Alexis didn't answer.

"Let's say a prayer," said Renata briskly, clapping her hands, but before we
could form a circle, someone pounded on the door.

"Chloe!" I said and rushed to open it for her.

"Stop!" ordered Schulz. I gaped at him as he marched around the chaise
longue, up to a window that looked onto Stoczek Street. "Scheiße," he said and
ducked down. For some reason, Alexis and I both ran up to the other window,
and for a second, our shoulders were touching, and for a second, I hoped it was
the archer—hoped he'd finally tracked us down and was about to take aim at
Alexis—but in fact it was a dozen or so photographers and cameramen standing
around in little groups. Piles of their equipment blocked the sidewalk; their cars
and vans clogged the street.

"Don't let them see you," Schulz whisper-yelled at us, still crouching, but it
was too late. Alexis's beauty had reached them, and they were already moving to
join their scout at our door—all of them but one, a woman who was—unlikely
as it seems—as beautiful as Alexis, who stood still. Alexis stared at her stupidly,
and the woman held up a microphone, staring back and seemingly entreating
Alexis to tell all.

"We cannot talk to them," Petra reminded us. "No matter what happens. We
are not authorized to speak to the press."

Some of our phones chimed. Mine didn't, but I extracted it from my pocket as if it had. It was a message to our Team Irena WhatsApp group, from Chloe, who wrote: "bogdan's been in touch. he called pan igor, who asked if he (b) knew for sure where irena was. bogdan seemed upset to learn she was not in białowieża."

"So either he's faking it," said Ostap, "or Bogdan didn't kidnap her."

"Wait," I said. "How do we get Chloe home?"

"Oh my God," Alexis said, and before I knew what was happening, she'd fired off multiple messages: "Press is everywhere!" "Are you okay?" "Shelter in place or come around back."

I wrote: "FWIW I was worried first," then went to unlock the back door.

Petra had never announced she'd changed her mind about leaving Białowieża, but she had unpacked her suitcase. Her things were arranged around the living room now, in neat but precarious stacks. I returned to the main room and sat between her shirts and her pants on the chaise longue and awkwardly tried to appear comfortable by leaning back on my hands.

"Oh gosh," said Ostap, who was staring into his computer screen.

"Is it Irena?!" I cried, but by the time I said her name, I was already standing behind him, reading the headline out loud: ROGUE ARCHER STRIKES AGAIN.

This time I was too fast for Alexis. "Chloe be careful!" I wrote.

"He didn't kill anyone, though," Alexis assured us, sounding almost disappointed as she set her iPhone down.

Chloe wrote, "?"

"It says he screamed, 'Keep invasive species out of Poland!'" I said as I skimmed the article. Then I took a step back because Ostap's neck, which had been doused in allspice, was making it hard for me to breathe.

Renata shivered and took up her knitting.

"He was arrested," Schulz said from behind his own silver laptop. "In Narewka. Isn't this all basically good news?"

"false alarm lol," wrote Alexis.

"I wonder what he meant," I said. "I mean, when he said 'invasive species.'"

"An invasive species is nonnative and capable of causing harm," droned Alexis.

"Right, but he wasn't talking about parrots," I said. "No offense," I added quickly, seeing the look on Petra's face. "You don't think . . ." I was embarrassed to ask, but it was starting to bother me too much for me to keep the question to myself. "Do you think we could be an invasive species?"

"We?" said Pavel. "Why?"

"You mean human beings?" said Petra. "Yes."

"I mean us, translators," I said.

"We are merely foreign," said Renata. "We're not doing any harm."

"Right," said Schulz. "It's not like we're altering the Polish literary ecosystem. It's not like we're colonizing the Americas." He glanced at Alexis. "No offense."

"She should take as much offense as me," Alexis said, pointing in my direction. I rolled my eyes.

"Well, maybe," said Freddie. "Maybe we're not altering the ecosystem, or maybe we're just not altering it much. After all, every reading is an action a person takes upon a book. Actions produce reactions."

"Right, but translations are like the next generation," said Schulz. "They don't retroactively impact their forebears."

"You're saying children don't change their parents?" Petra said.

"We *could* be considered an invasive species," said Alexis. "It really depends on how we do our jobs. All books are inherently collaborative experiences, as Freddie said. We take that collaboration and make it intercultural. We step in, and we expand the audience. We just have to make sure we're not taking up too much space. We need to tread carefully, and not only out of respect for the author."

"Yes, only out of respect for the author," I said. "And Freddie said nothing about experiences. Books are books. They're written by authors. Not readers, not critics, not us."

"Right, technically, yes. But focusing too much on the particular author is simply playing into the kind of destructive thinking I thought we all agreed even Irena is against in *Grey Eminence*. The Romantic cult of individual genius. That's what's anti-environment: that idea of authority."

"But authors deserve to be recognized!" I cried. "Irena *is* a genius!"

"Emi," sighed Alexis. Her look made me feel like an idiot, and I flushed. I pinched my arm, hard, to distract myself. Alexis was driving me to distraction, and I still wasn't sure I knew the answer to my original question: Did we, Irena's translators, no longer in the presence of Irena, have the potential to cause harm?

"everything ok?" Schulz wrote to Chloe, but we heard her phone receive this latest missive as she burst in from the hallway and collapsed onto the chaise longue, strewing Petra's sparkly shirts onto the indecipherable carpet below.

"What's wrong?" I half whispered, my face only inches from hers. With the archer arrested, our most imminent threats were journalists, but it was hard to imagine Chloe reacting this way to an interview request.

"Is it Irena?" asked Petra. "You didn't— She isn't— Is she—?"

But Chloe shook her head and said, "Straw wraps."

"Straw rats?" asked Freddie.

"Wraps," said Chloe.

"But it's hot," said Alexis.

"But it's October!" said Chloe. "Someone wrapped their saplings. I went up to Kamienne Bagno and started walking toward the cemetery, you know, just making sure no one was following, and I came to this house I'd never really noticed before, which I probably wouldn't have noticed this time, either, if it weren't for the garden, which was gorgeous, and the lilies, which were leaning out over the licheny fence, so much so that in order to continue on my circuitous journey I had to pause and gently sweep them back into the garden. That was when I started hearing music."

"From the house?" I asked.

"From the straw wraps!" Chloe cried.

"What are straw wraps?!" said Freddie desperately.

"They protect plants and saplings from frost," I told him. I only knew the word because of a scene in *The Wedding*, a play about a missed revolt, which also featured animate straw wraps. "What kind of music?" I asked.

"Kannel," she said. "Traditional Estonian kannel."

"How do you know that?" I asked.

"So the straw was being plucked?" asked Petra.

Chloe sighed. "The straw wraps were making the music on their own. And I spent a summer in Estonia once."

"What?!" I said. "When?"

Alexis moved to sit in the barrel chair closest to Chloe, stepping on Petra's red tank top.

"I believe you," she said, peering into the eyes of my former best friend and placing her ugly perfect hand atop her lap.

But I wasn't sure what to think. That is, I believed she'd spent a summer in Estonia, but zithering straw wraps did sound crazy, and it was crazy of Chloe to be friends with Alexis. It was out of character for Chloe to get ecstatic over some vision in a garden. But then again, given all the extreme unusuals that had occurred at our summit so far, I was loath to come to a final conclusion. Maybe this was a scene she was rehearsing, a chapter she was trying out for her graphic memoir—since she'd never recovered her red notebook, she might be on the lookout for new material to replace what she'd lost.

I remembered how, the previous evening, Ostap had gently assaulted Renata, pressing his snout to the back of her head. Maybe we were all out of character now.

THE NEXT DAY was October 5, and we gathered together at Our Lady of Literature at five, well before sunrise, in the hopes of making up for translation time lost to eluding literary journalists. We prayed to Saint Anthony, and we prayed to Saint Wenceslas, and we prayed to Saint Jerome.

"We also pray," concluded Renata, "that today Irena Rey will finally win the Nobel Prize."

"She's forty-two," Alexis scoffed, letting go of Chloe's and my hands. "I don't know that the word finally applies."

"She's not forty-two," I said. I couldn't believe I was the person who was pointing this out, but it hit me now, and I was unable to suppress it. "Pan Igor said that she was nine years old when her mother left. That means she's forty-eight." I looked at Pavel. "That means she was forty-four when she got pregnant."

"Fuck," said Pavel quietly, wincing and breaking away from Schulz and Petra to sit down.

"Can that be true?" said Ostap.

"She looks amazing for her age," said Alexis.

"Could be the fortifying Cordyceps," said Freddie.

I knew it was the acids, and likely also the black magic ring, but before I could proffer my insights, Alexis squealed.

"Oh my God!" she said. "I got an email from Irena!"

Everyone leaped up and began talking over one another and making sounds that weren't quite words. Before I even knew what I was doing I had torn the phone out of her hands. The message read:

*Darling Alexis, I know you've been working hard as always on translating
my new novel. Can you please send it to me as soon as possible? I need to
share it with the Swedish Academy. Don't say anything to anyone yet.
Kisses,
Irena*

Because I blacked out, I don't know what happened immediately after that.
I know that eventually it was decided that we would retreat to our working table
on the third floor, as far from the front door as possible, and collectively copy-
edit Alexis's translation of the first 175 pages of *Grey Eminence* so that she could
send them to Our Author before ten A.M.

I know that we all believed Our Author was getting the Nobel Prize. Even
Freddie, despite previously insisting she would never receive it. He said that that
was how it worked, that the Swedish Academy called the author before the year's
prize was announced. I wondered how she had known to answer her phone when
they called her, since she had always evaded our attempts, but then I figured she
had seen the country code and realized she needed to pick up. But then I wondered
why she hadn't picked up when Freddie had called, which I had witnessed him
do twice.

I would describe my mood that morning as a blend of elation and confusion
with some disgust, a little rage, and a little bit of wetness likely attributable to
the fact that I was sitting next to Freddie. I was disgusted that we were all setting
aside our own translations into our own equally important target languages in
the service of the already hyperprivileged English-language one. It was outrageous that Alexis even expected us to have a working knowledge of English in
the first place.

But it was wonderful that Irena was going to get the single most important
prize in all of literature, in all of culture, in all the world. It was wonderful that
Irena was talking to any of us again, even if it happened to be Alexis. It was
wonderful that Irena had not been killed by Russia, Poland, or Belarus, or any
other nation, nor by Bogdan, nor by the xenophobic archer, nor by us, accidentally, nor by anybody else. It was wonderful she wasn't sick, or so it seemed—she
was well enough, at any rate, to send an email. It was wonderful that she wanted
our translations of *Grey Eminence* because it meant things were going to go back
to normal: We would translate, she would come home, and the book would be

published in all nine or ten languages (depending on what happened when she saw Pavel, a reunion I couldn't even begin to imagine as I was already having to imagine so much), and we'd go home in triumph, like we always had.

We worked like mycelium, and Alexis sent her translation to Irena at 9:59 A.M. Then Alexis thanked us, showing too little gratitude, and completely ignoring the cacophony below, we turned back to our own manuscripts. I was on page 199 when Freddie jumped up and said, "It's starting!" and we all gathered around his computer, which buffered for a moment, and in that moment, we heard the journalists pounding at our door, and then the head of the Swedish Academy began to ramble, and the audio cut out, but then it came back just in time for the head of the Swedish Academy to announce that this year's Nobel Prize in Literature went to Kazuo Ishiguro. Not Irena Rey.

CHAPTER TWENTY

By the time we went downstairs and peeked out the front windows again, the reporters had all gone, leaving Stoczek Street even emptier than it had been before, when the only signs of life had been all the signs threatening dogs we couldn't see or hear or smell. We were surprised to be filled with nostalgia for the halcyon day and a half when our summiting place had been beset by paparazzi, journalists, and others who desired us—we who were sure we were about to get a Nobel Prize.

There was no satisfying explanation for what had happened. Had Irena herself been tricked? This struck us as unlikely. Nobel pranks had been played on authors in the past, but we knew no one would dare do something like that to Our Author, whose Bogdan they would have to assume would track them down and make them pay, unless they knew something we didn't—about her, about Bogdan—but we still took it for granted that no one in the world knew her better than we did. Even her father (we took it for granted) didn't know her better. He just knew her differently, from a more challenging, less interesting period in her life.

Had Irena merely jumped the gun, assumed she was going to win, and started getting her ducks in a row? In which case she might still be on her way back to us now that she seemed to have opted in favor of proceeding with the publication of her magnum opus. It was a fifteen-hour flight from Tokyo to Warsaw. It was a three-and-a-half-hour drive from Warsaw to here.

But there were more disturbing possibilities. What if she had won the Nobel Prize and, after some toing and froing, determined that she would turn it down?

In protest of the corrupt Swedish Academy (sexist, racist), in protest of literature itself. No protest boded well for the fate of *Grey Eminence*.

She could have even perished at some point between that initial call from the Swedish Academy and the announcement we had seen, forcing them to publicly offer the award to their second choice, since you could not win a Nobel Prize if you were dead already (assuming the Academy knew). Seemingly in support of this interpretation was the fact that she hadn't written Alexis back to acknowledge the receipt of her translation. Not in support of this interpretation was the fact that this was an awfully narrow window in which to be rekidnapped and killed. And why would the Swedish Academy learn of it before we did?

Unless the Swedish Academy had murdered Irena Rey, but for various reasons, we doubted it.

Chloe led us back to the house on Kamienne Bagno, which did have a beautiful garden, some of which was, as she'd said, already wrapped up in straw. But we waited a while at the fence and heard no noises, other than birds and bees and the very occasional car.

"Do you hear the music now?" Alexis said cautiously to Chloe after almost half an hour had passed.

Chloe rolled her eyes and led us home, where we ate a mostly silent lunch of beets and goat cheese with a little watercress. Some of us drizzled our plates with honey. I started to, then stopped.

"Borges never won a Nobel Prize," I muttered. Pavel blew his nose.

At the sink, I flipped through the pages of the calendar in the hopes of finding anything like a clue, but there was nothing, other than what we'd already seen in September, just *Translators* on the twentieth and *St Wenceslas* on the twenty-eighth. There was one other day that was blacked out, but we didn't know what had happened on January 13, either.

All progress had stalled. Yet at around three P.M., there was another knock at Irena's door. We were in the middle of trying to teach Quercus to say "cześć," which in Polish means both hello and goodbye, kind of like "ciao" in Italian. Quercus's feathers had mostly finished growing in over the past few days, and he was very handsome; we were all quite attached to him already and took turns providing him with snacks and branches to perch on and strengthen and hone his bright red beak. Petra and Renata had shown us how to pet his neck and how to tickle him—if and only if he was in a cuddling mood—and Freddie had come

up with a game to help Quercus be a better flyer, since his family hadn't taught
him before presumably migrating south. One of us would stand at the base of
the staircase, and one of us would stand by the front door, and we would "pass"
him back and forth by flicking him from our perching fingers and offer him seeds
or nuts when he landed on the other person's hand.

"Cześć," said Quercus now, and Renata lifted him up onto her index finger
and carried him upstairs.

Schulz started for the door, picking up the Roman caltrop and the giant
candelabra and setting them aside. He put his ear to the pale wood.

"Cześć," said a woman's voice.

Pavel stood.

No one said anything.

"I *know* you're there," said the voice, in the same tone you might use with a
toddler who was insisting on playing hide and seek at a hospital.

Pavel walked up behind Schulz.

"Barbara?" he said softly.

"Not Barbara as in . . . Bonk?" Schulz yell-whispered.

"Pavel, honey, let me in!"

WE ALL KNEW who she was, of course, but Pavel actually *knew* her, and we
could not imagine how, since Barbara Bonk was Our Author's least favorite
author in Poland, and even reading her—even thinking about reading her—was
forbidden to us. Yet here she was wrangling a rolling suitcase into Irena's
living room, gawking at our shrine and at the portraits and at the Bozdoğan
mace that now lay on the low alabaster table and, above all, at the massive, ancient-
looking chests.

Given everything—the extreme uncertainty of our situation, the invasive
species, the invisible guard dogs, Veles, Leshy, Perun—we had barely interacted
with anyone outside the safety of our summiting place, and we certainly hadn't
had anyone over. As this invader, Irena's intellectual inferior, loomed in our living
room, I saw for the first time the breathtaking mess we had made over the past
fifteen days.

From this angle, our shrine appeared preposterous, the aftermath of an arts
and crafts class in the Alzheimer's ward of a nursing home. Dust covered

everything, and cobwebs linked the chests. All the coffee-table books were stained with coffee. Near the fireplace and Our Lady of Literature lay the poker, a bulky laptop cord, the Byzantine lance we had found in the garage, and a pair of Bogdan's socks, yellow or yellowed. The red carpet with the illegible calligraphy was even more illegible now that it was splotched with mud. All the ornate bright cloths over our barrel chairs were hopelessly crumpled, and I was horrified to see that one of the blue ones had been torn.

I looked over the black-and-white photographs of Irena's mother, to whom we'd always said she bore such similarities. I squinted. Suddenly oblivious to the blond wrench in the room, I went and picked one of the pictures up. I pried its backing off. Sure enough, typed down the center of the photograph's reverse, were the words, "Jardin Majorelle, March 11, 2010." I flipped it over. It wasn't a picture of anybody's mom. It was a picture of Irena. On a footbridge between palm trees, gazing away from the camera, her lustrous hair cascading down her mostly naked back, her arms bare but for a pair of glimmering gold bangles.

I slapped her face down onto a small stack of books at Our Lady of Literature. My humiliation was making steady inroads into the limited part of my brain that was still capable of processing emotions. How had every single one of us failed to notice, again and again and again, that all the portraits of Irena's supposed ancestors were just pictures of her? Chloe had known about Irena's father, and therefore her mother, which meant Chloe must have noticed and simply chosen to perpetuate the lie—even to me. I glanced at a picture in the corner; it was actually a selfie, taken in the bathroom mirror at a fancy, vaguely Mediterranean-looking hotel. That explained the angle; that was why her right arm was cut off.

I turned and saw Chloe following Barbara and Pavel into the other room, or rather, Schulz's room, where, over our dining table, the three of them were making stupid jokes about how it was bound to be five o'clock somewhere, and more specifically, nine kilometers east of here, in Belarus, where it was 5:06. Like moths to a foul-smelling candle, the rest of us drifted their way.

That was when I made a decision that would have stunned my former self: I decided to have some beer, or wine, or whatever it was the rest of them were having. Between the old dad and the fake duel, not to mention the selfie, the time for me to drink had come. Pavel had the gall to leave us alone with Our Author's least favorite author as we listened to the crystalline music of cocktails being mixed, which intermingled with Quercus's chipper upstairs squawks and the occasional creaks of our chairs that none of us could remember ever making any kind of noise before.

"Well, don't be scared!" she called to the five of us clustered in the doorway. I was gripping the wall in my left hand and holding on to Freddie, who was standing behind me, with my right.

Needless to say, Alexis seemed to have no qualms about squeezing past us to sashay into the winter garden and extend her hand.

"Hi!" she said, with that unbearably symmetrical smile. "I'm Alexis!" Then they proceeded to *embrace* under the Czech chandelier as though it were mistletoe, as though this were a U.S. movie about leopards and bones.[47] Then, to my continued horror, Alexis turned to me.

"This is my wife, Emilia," she said.

I stared.

"What did she tell you all about me?" said Barbara. "I do not eat human flesh."

But as Barbara shed her gratuitous beige jacket and her ridiculously frilly scarf I saw that she was wearing Irena's black magic ring around her surgically lifted neck. All the muscles in my body became painfully taut. How could Barbara have acquired Irena's most precious possession, passed down to her through generations, other than by murder?

But then I shut my eyes and shook my head, for surely, just as the Swedish Academy did not go around knocking off authors, killings of literary celebrities by other literary celebrities were rare.

Alexis laughed again. Freddie gently pushed me forward by the waist.

"So it's that kind of household!" exclaimed Barbara, clapping her hands, where other, paler rings shone limpidly in the volatile afternoon sun.

Pavel brought in a tray of drinks.

"I've been translating Barbara for three years now," the turncoat told us. "Ever since Irena let me go."

---

47   A reference to 1938's *Bringing Up Baby*, which as far as I know features zero scenes under mistletoe (Trans.).

BARBARA BONK (NÉE Bąk and still Bąk, but only in Polish) was the Karl Ove Knausgård of Katowice. Born July 7, 1970—six months *after* Irena, we now knew—to a banker and a senior business analyst at the largest electric company in Poland, she had written eighteen autobiographical novels, along with countless articles and editorials and five travel books the Poles called "reportage." She believed it was dishonest for an author to write fiction or nonfiction without acknowledging her human biases and preferences—that there was no such thing as pure fiction or objective reporting, only experience, artfully retold.

A graduate of the Karol Szymanowski Academy of Music, Barbara played impeccable piano and, unlike Irena, had a hypnotizing singing voice. (Everyone had seen her on YouTube; the videos were ubiquitous, impossible to completely avoid if you were on the internet in Polish.) A petite, pert blonde with a taste for sexy stilettos and Karakalpak couture, she was a frequent guest on several talk shows, a situation that had not changed with the installment of the right-wing government (she pronounced herself "totally apolitical") or the advancement of her age. (She was fond of calling those opposed to cosmetic procedures luddites, depressives, and ingrates.)

Unlike our author, she had been translated into Japanese.

Irena loathed her. At our translation summits, she had called her the antithesis of literature, the epitome of bad taste, an enemy of erudition, and a prime exemplar of society's slide into an abyss of the imagination. From everything we knew about Barbara, we didn't doubt that Irena was right.

Except, of course, Alexis, who certainly seemed to be doubting it now. Sitting down next to Barbara, she served herself a glass.

"So are you just here for vacation?" she asked, in a high chirp that was horrible to hear.

The rest of us looked at each other in wonder or disgust as the two of them talked. Angling her chair so that it caught the massive leaf of a monstera, then pinned it to the windowsill, Barbara said that she was on her way east, that she had come here from Berlin with a Canadian journalist named Mackenzie Tremaine; together, they planned to cross into Belarus to meet a Belarusian journalist who had recently been arrested, fined, and brutalized but not dissuaded from reporting or creating more news. Most recently, he had entered his parakeet into a local council election by photoshopping her feathered image into his own human passport, which made us feel ashamed of Quercus, who had been apolitical so far, although we should have been more careful what we wished for.

"We plan to meet in Brest," Barbara was saying. "It isn't far from here. We're going to do an exposé on a new lead-acid battery factory, a coproduction between the U.S. and China, guaranteed to contaminate the whole area. Should be a lot of fun!"

Barbara seemed to enjoy talking, and once she had explained what we later learned was one of *two* terrible reasons for her appearance in Białowieża, she was happy to turn to whatever other subjects we pleased. Although I found myself unable to voice my alarm over the necklace—my throat closed up when I tried, perhaps the result of the ring's powerful black magic—this still meant that three key questions were answered in rapid succession that afternoon. The first had to do with the fate of the woman from Spain who had promised to translate *Lena* into Catalan and then disappeared. What had happened was that Barbara had poached her, although of course "poached" was not the word she used.

The second question was one we hadn't even thought to ask, namely, why Irena had forbidden us from ever translating anyone else. The answer was that when Pavel had let her know that he was going to start translating Barbara Bonk's Silesian saga, she had flown into a rage that she had taken out on us. Not that we minded, exactly, and not that we had found it strange at the time. In some ways, it, too, had come as a relief. We were in love with Irena, and we had no energy to be in love with anybody else, which meant our work might not have done them justice.

Nonetheless, Alexis confessed that she had started translating from German then, and even Ostap said he'd been translating from Russian for several years. Even Petra, bastion of devotion to Our Author, said then that she'd been translating from English, a revelation that made us all gasp in astonishment or, at the very least, surprise, except for Freddie, who shook his head and clicked his tongue at us, apparently awestruck at our gullibility. It was then that he first called us a cult, and when he did, I slapped him, seemingly, but not exactly, in jest. He was tipsy and didn't take much notice, but Petra, who was of course dead sober, looked at me like she knew.

The third question, which was the only question, but which we'd believed we'd all but answered, was seemingly actually answered just past nightfall, when the perfectly full moon cast its quicksilver pall over everything and filled the house with the spire-like shadows of trees that still refused—at the start of October, fifty-three degrees north of the equator—to degreen. Barbara was wrapping her scarf around and around her ensorcelling throat, already holding her purse as we stood uselessly around her, when Alexis took an unthinkable step.

"Hey," she crooned tipsily. "You wouldn't happen to know whether Irena's in Japan or Ukraine right now, would you?"

Barbara leaned in and looked around with stagy paranoia. "Promise you won't tell anyone?"

Vehemently, involuntarily, we all shook our heads: We would never tell a soul.

"It's top secret, and it has to stay that way. Irena isn't in Japan *or* Ukraine. She's in Brest!"

She scanned our faces. I was too stunned to compose myself. I glanced at Chloe, who was scowling in apparent disbelief.

"That's right!" Barbara exclaimed. "We're working together. We just got together and we realized that the next frontier in our careers—you know, at our *age*—would be *collaboration*. We'll be reporting side by side! Feminine solidarity. A reinvention, from the ground up. Two minds!"

"Two minds?" Chloe asked, narrowing her eyes. "*Irena* is writing something with you?"

"No," I said.

"Oh, yes," said Barbara. "With me and Mackenzie! You'd love her. She was here at the house a little earlier, but then Irena didn't win the Nobel Prize." Surreptitiously, I thought—though I'd already had three cocktails—I googled Mackenzie Tremaine. Sure enough, she was the gorgeous reporter who'd been making eyes at Alexis. I wondered if Alexis realized that yet. "Actually," said Barbara, and she put a hand flat to the side of her mouth like she was about to whisper something to us and then continued at exactly the same volume as before: "I'm glad she didn't win because I don't know what would have happened to our collaboration if she had. You know. With all the . . . How do you say it, Alexis? Junkets?"

Alexis nodded eagerly.

"You want us to believe Irena is in Belarus," Chloe said flatly, "waiting for you."

I was relieved Chloe agreed with me on the impossibility of this, and I assumed we all agreed, except perhaps Alexis. We all knew for a fact that Irena would rather die than collaborate with Barbara.

But then Barbara nodded, and Petra said, "Well, I guess that's good? As long as she's okay."

And Renata said in a starved tone, "Can we come with you?"

"Well," said Barbara, "the visa application takes a couple of weeks. Mackenzie had to wait a month for hers. Only Ostap here could get away without one." Here Barbara gave Ostap a wink.

Renata scowled and sat down in one of the threadbare barrel chairs.

"I have dual citizenship," Chloe said. Barbara regarded her blankly. "I'm a Polish citizen," she clarified.

"Oh, well, sure, if you want to come, you and Ostap," Barbara said, "although honestly it's not like we're going to be gone all that long. Two, three weeks tops. You're probably better off just waiting. I mean, you're probably better off working. Translating—isn't that what you're supposed to be doing right now?"

"I could go," said Petra.

"Oh?" said Barbara. "I thought you were Croatian."

"I'm Serbian," said Petra. "I wouldn't need a visa. But I don't want to go."

Barbara looked at Petra like she was seeing her for the first time: her red cotton V-neck that showed off her silver cross, her black cotton pants, her leather sandals.

"Well, you all just think about it," Barbara said. "It's a little on the late side now. Pavel, Alexis, would you be so kind as to escort me back to my hotel?"

"Wait," Renata said, in desperation. "We can't just wait. Can't you spare her? Can't you send her home?"

"If I were you," Barbara said, "I'd be more concerned about Irena coming home to unfinished translations. You don't want her to think you need her to supervise your every single sentence, do you? Surely you want her to know you're *brave* and independent—that you're capable of conveying her new book into . . ." She turned to me.

"Spanish," I said.

"Exactly," Barbara said. She smiled a forced smile, her lips almost inanimately rigid. Then she spun around and stood stock-still before the closed front door, waiting for Pavel or Alexis to open it for her. Eventually, Alexis did.

WE COULDN'T TRANSLATE while we waited up because we were all under various influences, even Petra and Schulz, who weren't drunk like the rest of us, but who couldn't let Barbara's ugly-pretty style contaminate their version of Irena. For a while we played cards. I tried to teach them truco, but it was too hard to explain the rules in Polish. Schulz did tarot readings for Petra and Chloe, who asked not to know their past or present. Petra drew Justice, Chloe the Tower. Ostap played piano, alone.

I tried to read *The Remains of the Day* in a Spanish translation from Spain, but I wasn't enjoying it because of Barbara and Alexis, and because it was a shitty PDF, and because Freddie kept muttering to himself, until finally I snapped, "Freddie? Do you mind?"

"Don't you want to know what I'm doing?" he asked.

"Not especially," Chloe said.

"Did you know that a quarter of the languages spoken on our planet are spoken in the planet's greatest forests?" said Freddie anyway. "The Amazon, for instance. The Congo. Australia's Daintree Forest. It's odd Irena never thought of that—the extinction of languages, it seems like she would care about that, too."

"Maybe she cares so much she doesn't want to mention it," said Chloe in a tone that strongly suggested she didn't mean what she'd just said.

"I don't know," said Schulz. "I don't really think so. I think she thinks of language itself as a necessary evil."

Chloe was scratching at a tiny mirror in the pink fabric that covered her chair. The mirror came off, and she looked up at me in surprise. We smiled, but there was a mournfulness to our exchange. Then she said to Freddie, "What does this have to do with what you're doing?"

"Aha!" Freddie cried, and I understood that he would devastate our friendliness—Chloe's and mine, I mean, not mine and his, which was so heavily reinforced by sex. "I knew you must be curious. I am compiling words from endangered languages to create poems in Swedish and English. I am going to save those words."

"Okay," said Chloe. Freddie looked around, expecting a follow-up question.

Schulz got up and went into the dining room, which was his room, only to return seconds later with Barbara's suitcase.

"Why would she leave it?" asked Chloe.

"What's in it?" asked Ostap.

"We can't—" Petra began, but already Schulz had unzipped it.

I expected clothes, and ridiculous shoes, and toiletries, but Barbara's suitcase was empty.

"Why would she bring an empty suitcase?" asked Ostap.

"We should fill it up with trash," I said.

"Emi," said Petra.

"Forest trash or trash trash?" said Chloe.

"Trash trash?" I said.

But Ostap said, "Irena!" And we jumped up and ran to take a peek at his screen.

It turned out Ostap, too, had received an email requesting his translation of *Grey Eminence*, but his had arrived hours after the announcement, at 4:47 P.M., and it had come to his teaching email, which he told us Irena never used. I read it once over his shoulder, and then I read it again. Then Schulz read it aloud for the benefit of those who had chosen to remain in their barrel chairs.

> *Hey man, I've been thinking about you lately, how's dear Daniela, how are you, how is your dog. Where are you in your translation? When you get a chance could you send it to me please thanks so much and can't wait to see you!*
> *Love,*
> *Irka*
>
> *P.S. I've misplaced my original manuscript, can you send that to me, too?*

"You don't call her Irka," I said softly, addressing the top of his dandruffy brown head, which was already turning from side to side by the time I added, "Do you?"

"She must have gotten me confused with Pavel," he said.

That sent chills down my spine. Surely Our Author would never have confused innocent Ostap with treacherous, sexual Pavel—unless Ostap really was a perfectly camouflaged creep.

But hearing the message out loud had made it feel both more and less real. It was real in the sense that it was another thing that was really happening to us: another trial. It was unreal in the sense that it could not be authentic. It didn't sound like any possible version of Irena in any possible version of anyone's story of what was happening in Białowieża that hot fall.

"Daniela is your wife?" asked Freddie.

Renata got up. "Please excuse me," she said. Petra followed her up the spiral staircase, and suddenly there were only five of us, out of nine.

I took Ostap's computer out of his lap, then said, "Can I see that?" And even before I had it at eye level, I had already found exactly what I'd feared.

"This is fake," I said to Ostap, Freddie, Chloe, and Schulz. "The account that wrote you isn't cogitatrey@earthlink.net. It's cogitahey@earthlink.net."

Chloe said, "But that means . . ."

But I couldn't let anyone else say it—it was mine to say. "It means Alexis sent the first one hundred seventy-five pages of Irena's secret masterpiece to a completely random stranger."

"No no no no no no no," said Ostap. Schulz punched the wall.

"It could be online by tomorrow," said Chloe.

"It could be online right now," I said. But we scoured the internet for any traces of *Grey Eminence* and thankfully, there were none.

I turned to Schulz and saw that he was crying, cradling his fist.

"We will get through this," Chloe said, looking at me like I should do something, too. We wrapped our arms around him. We stood like that for a little while, next to Our Lady of Literature, quietly infusing each other with kindness and calm. When I look back on it now, I think that that might be my fondest memory from that whole summit, the nicest moment we had together, and in a way, it was thanks to Alexis, or to her hastiness and hubris.

Then she and Pavel came home, and it was over.

THAT NIGHT, OF course, I slept with Freddie. But for a variety of reasons, I couldn't sleep. Freddie snored, and Petra woke up screaming, and I kept getting up to check on her, and every time I got back into bed and started to mentally prepare myself, I'd think about all the different lies I'd been told lately, seemingly by everyone, and wonder: What, if anything, was still true?

Whoever was sending us emails, one by one, like a serial killer, had done a good enough job of lying that they had gotten 20 percent of Grey Eminence served up to them on a silver platter, in English, which you would think would be the main thing—as much as I hated to admit it—if what they were after was cash. Then there was Chloe, who had lied and was likely still lying—but why? There was her other BFF besides Alexis, the centenarian, with his wartime tales, tales of abandonment, tales of Solidarity, and even Bogdan tales.

Since father and daughter seemed like two peas in a pod, who knew?

Pan Igor had told us that Irena was supposed to be in Ukraine but that she might instead be in Japan, while Barbara had assured us that Irena was in Belarus. If Barbara was really close enough with Irena that Irena had given her her grandfather's black magic necklace, then that meant another chapter of Irena's biography was fake. And if Barbara was also lying, then what was she really up to, here and in general and in Brest?

Could it be true that Bogdan was visiting his newfound brother? Did Bogdan actually have a brother, or a father, at all?

Freddie had been Skyping with his wife a lot, too much, I thought, for a woman with whom he claimed not to be in love. Unless he was lying—unless he was actually talking to a myriad of Polish singles in our area, although when I downloaded Tinder at four A.M. I was able to see that there were only three available women within twenty kilometers of us.

And yet—and it pains me to acknowledge it now, just as much as it pained me back then—it wasn't Barbara or Pan Igor or Bogdan or Göring or Freddie's phantom paramours who ultimately prevented me from falling asleep that night. It wasn't my conscience. It wasn't the fact that the Nobel Prize in Literature hadn't gone to Irena, nor that it had gone to a man who'd been born in Nagasaki but who didn't write in Japanese, which was no doubt why Our Author had none of his books on her shelves.

What actually kept me up that night was our reckless Alexis, and her translation, which I was sure—and there it was again, that dread—would be available to everyone on the planet who could read English. I had read only thirteen pages of it, although I had claimed to read my fair share, which was nineteen. But something about what I had read had so disturbed me that I was actually unable to go on. There was a relationship between Our Author's sentences and Alexis's, but *I didn't understand what kind of relationship it was.*

She'd been flirting with Barbara, and when she and Pavel had come back from Barbara's hotel at almost midnight, she had reeked of some new perfume, something that smelled like boxes—like glue and cardboard—and musk. It must have been Mackenzie's, I reasoned, which meant that she had been flirting with the Canadian model-reporter, too. What secrets had the two of them been whispering to one another, in English, while Barbara and Pavel caught up or made out in another corner of their room? Had all four of them had sex? Who had done what, and to whom?

What havoc had Alexis wreaked, with her lithe and flawless body, and her contorting, all-too-forceful mind, and what would she break next?

CHAPTER TWENTY-ONE

When I ran into your old friend Leszek, he suggested I send up a flare, to let you know we're looking for you. I've been thinking about it, and I think this is the closest I can get: an account about *Grey Eminence*, by us, your faithful translators, although for now it'll just be me because I don't yet know if this is dumb or not. #bialowieza #greyeminence
October 6

Freddie (aka Swedish) asked me if I would visit him when all of this was over.
I didn't know what to say. #bialowieza #greyeminence #wishyouwerehere
October 7

I cried myself to sleep last night, from sheer confusion. Irena, where are you???? Could you really be in Belarus? We decided to follow your (former?) enemy's advice, and Petra (Serbian) calculated that if we manage to translate twenty pages a day, we can get to the end of the world by mid-November. We've never translated twenty pages a day, and I don't know if we can or not. Will you even be back by mid-November? #bialowieza #greyeminence October 9

Alexis (aka the worst) broke your washing machine. We mopped it up with towels, but then we didn't have any way to wash the towels. All we could do was dry them. #whyalexis #bialowieza #greyeminence
October 10

All logging in the Białowieża Forest has been paused. Apparently an enormous oak fell over onto a logger the night before last, and he died. The complaints came flooding in then, all the people who never cared about the plants or animals or fungi couldn't believe a person had been killed. Whatever. The point is they've paused it, until "the safety of the relevant populations can be accurately assessed." #xl8 #bialowieza #greyeminence October 11

Most of the time, we translate. But we also need to feed ourselves, which
means that sometimes we go mushroom hunting in your honor. We've found
rydze, borowiki, podgrzybki, koźlarze, pieprzniki, czubajki, gołąbki, gąski,
opieńki.[48] I personally identify with the pat of butter melting on the surface of
a cast-iron skillet as we sauté the saffron milk caps. This is Alexis's fault.
#fungi #bialowieza #greyeminence #downwithalexis
October 14

---

48   The names of these species are so different in English (and in Latin) as to become utterly meaningless in translation—a rose by any other name just doesn't smell as sweet—which is why they are in Polish
here (not because I forgot, as my editor had the audacity to suggest) (Trans.).

Last night we learned from the news that the Czartoryski Museum thefts of
1987 have been partly resolved—not solved, but there's been an end to the
mystery disappearance part of their story: Three of the mummies that had
been housed in Kraków were repatriated to Cairo in early September! The
transfer was made anonymously, and no one knew about it until yesterday,
when Ryszard Krall,[49] who was on vacation in Sharm El-Sheikh, happened to
stop in Cairo for coffee with one of his government contacts, a minister of
culture who spilled the tea. I thought you might like to know that since you
wrote your first book about the Czartoryski guards who let that very theft
occur. But, Irena, there is so much more. The most shocking part of everything
is that one of those guards was Freddie's ugly wife!

. . .

---

49   I can't help but feel it is beneath me to annotate this author's Instagram captions, but here we are,
twice in a row: Ryszard (pronounced Ree-shard) Krall is one of Poland's finest untranslated authors; his
books of reportage almost rival those of Barbara Bonk's in popularity (Trans.).

When the story came on I sat bolt upright and kind of crashed back against the headboard, but when I turned to Freddie to apologize, I saw he was sitting up to pay attention, too. I couldn't imagine why he would care as much as I did since he has (I am very sorry to say) not fully familiarized himself with your bibliography and didn't know your first two books had been lost to history. But after the news was over, he explained: Bogdana was eighteen at the time—which means (?) she is/was the same age as you. Bogdana is from Kraków. That was her first job! Of course she got fired for it, and she was so humiliated and ashamed she moved clear to the other end of the country, to Gdańsk on the Baltic Sea.

. . .

From there she crossed the Baltic to settle in Sweden (this was 1994), where for a long time she worked illegally, waitressing and doing odd jobs. That's how she and Freddie wound up getting married. They dated a little while, and he just offered (as opposed to proposing!), and she said yes. #greyeminence #stillifewithstillife #bialowieza #mysterysolved

October 17

We made it to page 500 today. We knew we needed to get through the chimpanzee experiments (to end the gnawing dread), so we translated until after 11:00. It's almost midnight now. Freddie's still reciting, though we have to start every morning at 5:00. Petra says it's good preparation for having a baby again, never getting enough sleep. I just hope we are doing you justice. #greyeminence #bialowieza #torture

October 20

Too late, and out of nowhere, the leaves changed and fell, all at once, and I thought that maybe I would visit Freddie in Stockholm, even if you don't come back. I'm not saying I'm giving up on ever finding you. I'm just saying that maybe it's time for us to think about our own issues, too. Deal with Alexis. #bialowieza #greyeminence #thewritingonthewall

October 24

CHAPTER TWENTY-TWO

Nine things happened on October 26. The first was that the temperature, which had skyrocketed to heights that were unprecedented in the history of Białowieża, plummeted at last.

At seven A.M. on October 25, thirteen minutes before sunrise, it was an extremely unseasonable sixty-nine degrees.[50]

That night, as we struggled to get to page 626, where Amália falls in love with a Turkish software engineer, and then 627, and then the bottom of 627, where Amália falls out of love with the Turkish software engineer, the character of the air seemed to change, to grow dense as well as cold. The colder our fingers got, the harder it became to move. What had felt like a glorious high dive just two weeks earlier now felt like trying to force our way through concrete. For the first time, we fell short of our goal. That was the only thing that happened on October 25, a thing we didn't do.

Freddie and I had sex with sweaters on that night. I wore one of Irena's. It had nice pockets and looked vaguely like rusted chain mail. The wind was a perpetual howl in our ears, and it took Freddie a long time to finish, longer than ever before. Then he recited his poetry in bed, under the covers, instead of kneeling beside the bed as always before.

---

50   The average temperature for this time of day in late October would be around thirty-five degrees Fahrenheit (Trans.).

At seven A.M. on October 26, it was thirty-three degrees. The radiators seemed like they were trying hard to come alive, but they weren't producing any warmth yet.

"We could build a fire?" suggested Ostap. Out of all of us, Ostap was the most dejected: Bewilderingly—he said he could not explain his reasons—he had left his glasses outside overnight, where, in the freezing temperatures, one of his lenses had shattered, making it almost impossible for him to see.

"We'd need to gather wood," Pavel pointed out.

"Can we take wood from the forest?" Schulz asked.

"Good question," I said. "We could steal some wood from those areas that are marked forbidden, where all the trees that have already been chopped down are."

"Like Robin Hood!" exclaimed Alexis. She was wearing a burgundy dress that belonged to Irena, velvety with lace around the hemline, short.

"Not—" I started to say, before realizing it was pointless to debate her on the nature of the story of the day. She never listened to anyone, and besides, each of us had continued to operate in our own genre, coinciding only in the pages of *Grey Eminence*, which was literary fiction, in the traditional sense, like *The Magic Mountain* or *Sense and Sensibility*, except of course that it was better, and for now, anyway, most of it belonged exclusively to us.

"Is spruce a good wood to burn?" asked Ostap, covering his lensless eye with his palm.

"Why not?" asked Freddie.

"I think it's fine," said Pavel.

"I think oak might be better," said Schulz.

"We could burn the table," said Chloe, and everyone tried to smile politely at what we hoped was a joke. I watched the little triangle of shadow between Alexis's thighs. She was wearing a pair of hose she must have also borrowed from Irena, but still, I thought, she must have been cold, colder than was necessary, colder than me.

"Does anyone know what time the loggers arrive?" asked Pavel.

Ostap and Renata startled.

"The loggers are coming back today," I told them, as gently as I could. "We saw it on the news."

"I don't think we should profit from the fecklessness of the Polish government," said Petra. Her hand was on her abdomen. I knew from the conversations they kept having that her fetus was the size of a strawberry now.

"Has anyone noticed that one of the shrubs in the backyard is infested with moths?" asked Freddie. "The one with the wilted yellow leaves? Perhaps we could do her a favor and start by burning the affected canes from that."

"Fine with me," said Pavel, and the two of them marched out the back.

"I'll grab the shears!" Ostap offered. Then he ran out of the room, banging into the back door Freddie and Pavel hadn't held for him.

"We might be out of matches," Renata said, once he was gone. In fact, we had run out of a lot of things, almost everything, over the past twenty-one days. We'd been putting so much pressure on ourselves to finish our translations that we hadn't had enough time to replace anything but food, beer, wine, and toilet paper. We had consumed not only all her matches, but also all her matcha, her acids, her tinctures, and, each of us in semisecret, her self-help books. We'd exhausted her refrigerator, which now made a frantic chirping sound at unpredictable intervals, and we hadn't called anyone to come and fix it because we didn't want more people (more than Leszek and Barbara and Pan Igor) to realize she was gone. Irena had trained the village to expect a certain level of reclusion during her novel-writing times, but an extended absence risked upsetting them—upsetting the balance of Białowieża, as Leszek had said.

"Maybe we could try taking our laptops to the lobby of the Booted Eagle," Alexis said. "I bet it's warm there, and when Pavel and I went with Barbara—"

"Oh my God, Alexis, why are you still here?" I said. There was a collective groan, and I knew that everyone was sick of us, or maybe sick of me, but it wasn't my fault, and I knew that, too. Alexis kept trying to upend all of our traditions, impose her will on us and drive me insane. I just refused to fall for it, and that in turn made her try harder. Sometimes I genuinely wanted to kill her, not because I wanted to hurt her, but out of a perfectly natural need to protect my own brain.

"Fine," I said. "We can use our amadou." I went back to Pavel's or Irena's bedroom to retrieve the ferrocerium rod.

I lay down and spread out across Irena's bed, which I was surprised to find perfectly made. I flipped over onto all fours and tried to imagine it, being Irena, with Pavel, but then Schulz called from the living room that they were ready, and I had to get down from the bed.

It took just two tries to light the amadou, and the fire spread almost imme-diately to the infested shrub. That was the second significant thing that happened on October 26: Our amadou worked. Within minutes, the room had filled with smoke.

"Would someone open a window, please?" cried Petra, moving to shield her mouth and nose.

I leaped to the rescue, opening the window closest to the fireplace, watching tendrils of gray as they extended toward the frozen sun.

"No, I'm telling you, there's actual treasure. In chests,"[51] a voice said then, in English. I spun around and saw Alexis looking as stunned as I felt.

"Treasure," repeated the voice.

In the center of the room, Petra was gazing into the fire, backing away from it in horror.

"The shrub," she said. "It's on fire, but the fire is not consuming it! Exodus 3:2!"

I looked at Schulz. I could see the fire reflected in his eyes. " 'There the angel of the Lord appeared to him in flames of fire from within a bush. Moses saw that though the bush was on fire, it did not burn up,' " he murmured.

"A prophecy!" Renata cried. "It has to be!" She ran to place her hands on Our Lady of Literature.

Freddie and Pavel were already at the chests, meanwhile, trying to force them open with brute strength. That was the third thing that happened: Our trea-sure hunt was launched. Alexis was critiquing their efforts, admonishing them for not first helping her search for the keys, when she was interrupted by the unex-plained, possibly prophetic voice.

"No this is not going to be another Winnipeg," it said. "I swear."

She cocked her head. "Mackenzie?" she said loudly. Her voice was higher pitched than I had ever heard it.

"Alexis?" said the voice, which matched Alexis's.

"Oh my God!" Alexis said. "What are you doing back here?"

---

51   What to do with text that is already in English when translating into English has been the subject of perennial debate. However, although this is completely fictional, since I was there, I have opted for a more authentic version of this line, which in the original reads: "Actually there is a treasure in the chests" (Trans.).

"Hang on one second," Mackenzie said. Then, in a different tone, "Just send one cameraman. Just one. That's literally all I ask."

A few seconds later, there was a rap at the door.

AS IT TURNED out, Mackenzie had been trying to get back to Białowieża for most of the past two weeks. Poland had shut down the border with Belarus, however, due to a recent surge in unauthorized crossings. Everyone knew that once you got into Poland, you could go anywhere in the EU, Mackenzie blathered, including Germany, since within the Schengen Area—which included Germany and Poland—there were effectively no borders.

But for some reason, that morning, the government had reopened the Połowce-Peschatka crossing (which was, in any case, for foot traffic only). The guard she talked to, Mackenzie told us, said he thought it was because of the cold—that the government assumed the drop in temperature would send most would-be crossers home.

Some of this overlong monologue we all got directly from Mackenzie. Some of it had to be translated into Polish for Ostap and Renata, mostly by Alexis, who turned out to be not very good at interpreting without referencing Google Translate.[52]

"But where is Barbara?" asked Pavel, in English.

Mackenzie sighed. "She's still there. She still somehow believes Irena's going to show up in Brest, fully three weeks after their appointed meeting time."

"So Irena never went to Belarus?" said Petra, in English.

Mackenzie shook her perfectly coiffed head. "Nope. We sure never saw her, anyway."

Which was the fourth thing that happened: We learned from Canadian reporter Mackenzie Tremaine that Our Author had not, in fact, traveled east for a story she was writing with her archnemesis, Barbara Bonk.

"Did she just ghost you?" asked Alexis.

---

52   I've worked hard at my languages, but being banned from translating anyone but Irena has meant that my Polish vocabulary is exclusively composed of her words, the words she favors, likes the sound of, which means that of course when someone else is speaking it takes me some time to adjust (Trans.).

"No," said Mackenzie. "If she'd ghosted us I don't think Barbara would still be waiting. Every day she gets some dumb new email from Irena saying she's sorry that such and such came up and delayed her, but that she's on her way."

"On her way from where?" asked Schulz.

"That I don't know," said Mackenzie.

"But you're not in touch with Irena," said Chloe.

"No," Mackenzie said.

For a moment, we all got lost in thought. Then Mackenzie reminded us of that other, fresher mystery. "Did you guys know about the treasure?" When none of us spoke, she prompted us: "In the chests?"

I craned my neck. I had started dusting the chests after the embarrassment of Barbara's visit, but they still looked dilapidated, mottled and sunken, on the verge of rot.

Mackenzie tried again: "Have you ever seen them open?"

"I don't know that they can be opened," said Freddie. "Not without doing damage to whatever is supposed to be inside." Freddie's English was better than his Polish, which made me jealous of Alexis, even though I was sure Alexis wasn't attracted to Freddie—at least I thought I had decided that now. I took little steps sideways in his direction until our shoulders were touching.

"What type of treasure is it?" asked Alexis matter-of-factly.

Mackenzie groaned. "You sound like my producer. I don't know what kind of treasure, okay? All I know is that Barbara said there was treasure in there, and that she didn't know exactly what it was, but it was definitely big enough to make up for the story we lost in Brest."

"Wait, why did you lose the story?" I asked, although I loathed speaking English in front of Alexis.

Mackenzie sighed. "Because the battery factory wanted Irena, not Barbara. I'm sure she'll spin it some other way somehow, but that's what happened. They wouldn't let us in."

"But what kind of treasure *could* it be?" asked Alexis.

Petra stood up then, arms crossed, hands in her armpits, lips tight. She crossed the room. "How did it not occur to you that you can't just bring a cameraman into someone's house? That you can't broadcast from someone's private property without permission?!" she said. "How did it not occur to you that you can't just waltz around like this, rifling through people's things? Are you planning on searching our suitcases? Are you actually recording right now?"

I'd never seen Petra like this. It was exhilarating. But she had switched into Polish, and Alexis seemed reluctant to interpret for her. Bored, Mackenzie sat down on our chaise longue and started making a scrolling motion on her phone with her thumb.

"Alexis," she said. "I didn't realize you had already published a part of your translation. Congratulations!"

All of us fell silent. Alexis's face went white.

"Are you okay, Alexis?" asked Schulz, and Pavel said, "I'll go get you a glass of water."

"Alexis?" Freddie prompted her. "What is it? What are you thinking?"

And so the fifth thing that happened on October 26 was that Alexis's English translation of *Grey Eminence* exploded all over the internet, all over the world. The first twenty chapters that Alexis (and, in fairness, also the rest of us) had been conned into sending that hacker were released at ten A.M. New York time, four in the afternoon where we were—the exact moment Bogdan would have served Irena her *Cordyceps* tincture. *The Bucharest Review* was an achingly hip website without a print magazine that consisted of 70 percent white space, 25 percent prose in Akzidenz-Grotesk by authors without vowels in their names, and, now, 5 percent an extremely long excerpt from the magnum opus of Irena Rey. To reach it, you had to click on a photograph of a cast-iron skillet containing nine tiny critically endangered Macaya breast-spot frogs.

This happened at noon in Buenos Aires. At 12:13 (our 4:13), I received an email from my editor demanding my translation at once. At 4:15, I got an email from the head of publicity for Mexico, and by 4:30, I had messages from Ecuador, Colombia, Uruguay, and Spain. I even had one from a Spanish-language house I'd never heard of in New York.

By five P.M., we had all heard from our editors. With the exception of Alexis, who was in a slightly different position from the rest of us, we agreed not to respond until we could come up with a coordinated solution. Half of us felt it was more important to figure out a way to crack the treasure chests, by force (regardless of the consequences) or by key. But Mackenzie assured us that her cameraman would be arriving within forty-eight hours, and that we should wait until he got there so they could "capture the whole human drama" of the exact moment we all got to see what was inside. And she was so pretty, in a cold, North American sort of way, that the treasure-hunting half of us agreed to wait.

Alexis's editor was furious about the leak, and she was threatening to sue Alexis; at first, she was completely unsympathetic to Alexis's efforts to explain. Needless to say, we had to lie, and surprisingly, Alexis was not the best liar, which might also have weakened her case somewhat.

When the editor's fury subsided slightly, however, she asked Alexis about a certain Arabic-language translator, whether the Arabic version that was slated to come out in 2019 would be translated from Alexis's English or from Irena's original Polish. We knew, of course, absolutely nothing about an Arabic translator, but Alexis's editor said she had heard from Irena's own editor in Warsaw that Bogdan had traveled to Cairo in order to meet with the head of some major Arabic-language house, and that the meeting had gone well, and that the translation was already underway.

"Well, that's obviously false," said Chloe. "Bogdan's been with his brother."

"Perhaps Bogdan's brother is Egyptian," said Freddie. He seemed pleased with himself, and I didn't especially want to side with him against my old friend, but then I remembered the postcard from Cairo I had seen on Pan Igor's side table.

"It might be true about Bogdan." I said. "I think I saw the evidence next door. Not about the brother, necessarily—but Bogdan could be in Cairo."

But then that didn't really answer Alexis's editor's question, and instead of being grateful that I was still trying to help her after she had made such an incredibly stupid mistake, Alexis seemed almost annoyed that I was still talking, like she had someplace more important to be.

This was the first time in five weeks that I saw (or heard) Alexis actually call her partner, Romy Corona.[53] It was four in the morning in Sydney, so I wasn't surprised when Romy Corona sounded less helpful or supportive than she did confused. In the end, Alexis and Romy Corona decided to talk more about the legal ramifications of Alexis's idiotic action later that night, or more pertinently to the decision, later that morning.

---

53   This just shows the extent of this author's disconnect with (fictional) reality (Trans.).

Since the rest of us were nowhere near a coordinated solution, we all had a little time to burn, and the sixth thing that happened was that we conducted another, more complete search of Irena's computer after Mackenzie finally went back to her hotel. I wasn't the one who suggested it, but once Chloe had, I was, once more, willing to take the lead.

She said we were truly out of options now, that she got why some people were uncomfortable but that Irena had been gone for fully five weeks now, and she owed us some kind of explanation. Plus, some of us were still worried she might be in trouble or have come to some unknowable, unthinkable end, like falling off a very tall roof, as she almost had in Gdańsk in 2008, when we had saved her from that Veles-esque waiter (though I couldn't have picked up on the resemblance at the time).

But would she not have perished had we not been there? Could we not at least agree that we had not been there this time, given that we didn't know where there was?

I desperately hoped that the seventh thing to happen on October 26, 2017, would be conclusive evidence as to Irena's intentions and whereabouts, which we would find somewhere in the recesses of the computer part of her brain.

We began by returning to her email, where we found more tragic epistles from Bogdan—which did dwell, as Pan Igor had suggested, on also ascertaining her location, and which thus offered us no actionable clues—as well as emails from her editor, though these had now dwindled to an occasional question mark. There was one email from a person purporting to be a Lithuanian translator, someone who wrote as though they had spoken to Irena before, even as though they had been asked by Irena to translate *Grey Eminence*, which they claimed to want to do above all else, and which they said they would have done already, but for the fact that the manuscript had still not reached them.

When we googled their name, however, all we found was a disgraced Palanga schoolteacher who was currently in prison for murdering her sister over some stolen vimba.

"Has to be the hacker," said Ostap.

"Has to be," said Schulz.

And so from Irena's emails we moved on to her files. "ARCHIVES" didn't have much in it, mostly just some paperwork. Invoices, specific readings she had done at different festivals, that kind of thing. "Archive 2017" had some screenshots from Barbara Bonk's Facebook page, which neither proved nor disproved what Barbara had told us about them doing a project together, so we put a pin in Barbara and moved on.

There was a folder for each of her ten previous books, and one for ГОДЪ, her unfinished libretto. There was a folder for *Grey Eminence*, and inside it, folders for Amália, Amália's parents (gruesomely killed) and sister Celeste (killed even more gruesomely), and Nikau, and a folder for each of the following, recently extinct: Bennett's seaweed, Pensée de Cry, western black rhinoceros, passenger pigeon, Kaua'i blacksnakeroot, Eğirdir minnow, Tasmanian tiger, sooty crayfish, Christmas Island pipistrelle, kāma'o, Pyrenean ibex, Caribbean monk seal, Mauritius turtledove, Chile sandalwood, Pinta Island giant tortoise, golden toad, dodo, little flat-top snail, Chihuahuan dwarf crayfish, São Miguel ground beetle, Santa Cruz pupfish, Guam reed warbler, Bramble Cay melomys, Bermuda saw-whet owl, and on, and on, and on—hundreds of folders, one for every disappearance, some with sketches she'd scanned in, some with images she'd downloaded, each with a bio that included cause of extinction and, if possible, a little list of what the creature's favorite things had been before it vanished absolutely.

Aside from these, there was a folder called "Tś" that contained reproductions of the nineteen fragments preserved from Basel's fifteenth-century Dance of Death mural; a folder for photographs from Mexico's Day of the Dead; a folder of various artworks inspired by Obon, a Japanese festival that seemed similar to Mexico's Day of the Dead; a copy of a folder from *Future Moonscapes* that contained writings on extinction in general; a folder called "Beyoncé"; a folder called "Lena," which must have just been in the wrong place; a folder called "the pope"; and *Future Moonscapes of the Eocene* itself.

There were folders called "Books" that held PDFs of other people's works and "Taxes" that held subfolders called "deductions," "filed," and "future." As these seemed self-explanatory, we let them be.

Alexis yawned, showily, squeakily, and stretched out her arms. "I think I'll take a nap," she said. Then she gave an almost wink that almost seemed like it might be directed at my almost-boyfriend, but I thought: Surely that cannot be the case. Surely even Alexis has a lower limit, a bottom beneath that to which she cannot or will not go.

"It's seven o'clock," I said.

"I know, right?" said Alexis, as she floated out of the room.

"But we haven't found anything yet!" I called after her, hating myself for trying—in vain—to make Alexis stay.

"Oh, you know," said Freddie, making a swooping fist in the air. "I forgot I have to call Bogdana." He grimaced apologetically at me and disappeared.

Because Freddie and Bogdana only ever spoke in the early morning, I wondered if this apparently emergency conversation could be about the Czartoryski thefts. I even thought that maybe now that the case was semi-resolved Bogdana might be willing to return to Poland, leaving Freddie free for me.

Ostap and Pavel and Schulz adjourned to the winter garden to smoke and talk things over, and, in Ostap's and Pavel's cases, to drink. Chloe and Petra and Renata and I went up to Petra's and Renata's room on the third floor. I was hoping to take another lucky acorn from the glass bowl in their small sitting area, but when we reached it, I saw that the acorns had been replaced by pinecones, and I realized I had lost my chance.

And so the seventh significant thing to happen on October 26 was that while Chloe and Petra and Renata and I were debating what to do about our editors and whether Petra was showing yet or not—I said she wasn't really, Chloe and Petra and Renata said she was—the bad luck I had been having got significantly worse.

We had just come to a standstill in our brainstorm—we could send them everything we had; we could send them nothing (we could confess that Irena was gone, and that we didn't have her permission, or we could simply not respond, do to them what Our Author, our leader in all things, had been doing to us); we could password-protect the files and then give them the wrong passwords (we didn't think they were in touch with each other, so they would never know we had done it on purpose, and it might buy us some time); we could send them the first couple of chapters and say that was all we were authorized to show; we could send them random samples to excite them or confuse them or alarm them, depending on the samples we chose—and I said I wanted to step out onto the balcony and look at Belarus for a minute in order to clear my head.

"No!" cried Chloe.

I must have looked mystified, which I was, because she continued, haltingly, searchingly, "It's cold outside. Go get your coat first." Then she picked up her phone and started typing very quickly with both thumbs.

I told her I'd be okay for just a minute, and I stepped outside. I was stunned by the total transformation of the forest. The trees that had glowed so lushly throughout our stay in Białowieża were now completely bare, and all the paths had disappeared under red and brown and yellow that shivered in the icy, whistling wind.

I thought how good it was that we'd kept Quercus. I wasn't sure such a young bird from such a hot climate could have survived in this changed landscape. (Although later I read that lots of immigrant birds just like Quercus do.)

Then I looked down, and that was when I saw them: Freddie, the man I was having a passionate, almost even loving affair with, and Alexis, the person I hated more than anyone in the world.

I stared, squinting in the hopes it was my eyes that had betrayed me—but no, it was them, skulking up Stoczek, seemingly having the time of their lives. From the third floor of our summiting place, Alexis almost looked like she was skipping. As for Freddie, all I could see for sure was that he was wearing one of Bogdan's coats, but I felt sure from his gait and his posture that he was smiling in that slick, intimate way of his.

"What the fuck!" I shouted. Chloe came out and pretended to be concerned. I pointed at the evildoers. Yet she assured me I had nothing to worry about.

"Alexis said she's almost never into men, remember," she said.

But I didn't care, and I ran. I ran downstairs to my former room and ripped my suitcase out from under the bed I had formerly slept in and threw it on the bed scattering dust in every direction and unzipped it.

I had packed the white puffy coat I'd brought to Białowieża three years earlier, the one time we'd ever come over the holidays. Irena had held one summit in early spring, for *Matsuura*, but *Pompeii* was the first time we'd ever been to the forest in the dead of winter, and before I'd arrived I'd been terrified: I had read that the temperatures in December rarely rose over freezing, so I had invested in mittens, a lot of long underwear, Dutch knit caps, and Mapuche ponchos from the north of Argentina.

Then on the plane I had worried I would look overprepared to Irena, that she'd decide I was a fool and replace me. But in the end, my fears had been unfounded: It hadn't really snowed in the brief time we were there, and she had loved my winter gear, especially my new coat, which she had commented on, twice.

Now when I threw open my suitcase, however, it was gone. It had taken up the bulk of my luggage, and for a moment I just stared at all that empty space. I closed and opened my suitcase again. I got up and looked around, trying to remember if I could have hung it up somewhere. But I knew I hadn't. I always waited until it was really time for something before taking it out, which was maybe a translator's thing, responding rather than anticipating.

I had done nothing when my earrings and the house key disappeared. Keys and earrings are small things; however vital they may feel, they get lost all the time. Like the nuance of definite and indefinite articles lost in translations into languages like Polish that feature no such thing, their absence, while privately distressing, did little to alter the overall picture. Unlike a coat.

I took out my phone and sent a WhatsApp message to our Team Irena group. "Alexis stole my coat," I wrote. "YOUR COATS COULD BE NEXT!!!!!!!!!!!!!"

That was the eighth thing: I exposed my true hatred to everyone, in writing, resorting to all caps and exclamation marks.

A moment later, someone knocked on my door. I opened it, and Chloe came in.

"I don't think Alexis took your coat," she said softly. "Why would she?"

"Why are you defending her?" I shouted and stormed out of the room, slamming the door behind me.

In a frenzy, I flew downstairs to Freddie's room. My phone dinged. It was our Team Irena group. Alexis had written, "LOL."

The ninth significant thing that happened on October 26 was that I renounced the relative safety of Irena's house and went outside in Freddie's coat. I was a five-foot-two berserker in a giant's wool armor with a messy, slightly greasy ponytail, carrying the pistol-grip spotlight we kept by the back door, trying to track down Freddie and Alexis in order to kill them, or possibly only Alexis, depending on how I felt—or what they were doing—when I found them.

But they weren't on Stoczek Street, or Tropinka, or Kamienne Bagno, or any of the side streets that connected those three. On Kamienne Bagno, I shined Bogdan's light out over the fields and caught roe deer grazing, a whole family, but I couldn't find any trace of Freddie or Alexis, and not since she had laughed out loud at me had either of them responded to my messages or calls. Like Irena, they had disappeared into thin air.

By eight thirty P.M., my fury had congealed into grief at the thought of losing Freddie, and I couldn't feel my hands or feet. It occurred to me that maybe Freddie had finally decided to go back to Stockholm and Bogdana, and that Alexis, who had been undermining my sanity for well over a month now, had volunteered to drive him to the airport. I hadn't even thought to check the garage!

I forced myself to stomp around until eight forty-five or so, but then the most shocking thing that could have happened happened: I heard a deep and agitated barking, a sound that seemed to be coming from an actual living dog.

In the dark, I couldn't tell where it was coming from, or how far away it was, or whether it was a ghost, or a zombie, and I summoned what little energy I had left and took off at a run toward home, or rather, Irena's and Bogdan's garage.

But the car was there, and when I went into the house, I found Freddie and Alexis sitting in the living room. In fact, everyone but me was sitting in the living room. Somehow even Leszek was there, with his amadou bag in his lap, yammering on about beavers. There were packages of cookies called "little hedgehogs" scattered everywhere. Schulz had a piece of ground hazelnut stuck in his moustache.

They claimed they had just gone to the store. Needless to say, I didn't believe them. I had checked the store. That was the first place I had checked!

I seized a package of cookies and went upstairs. I'd never noticed our rooms didn't have locks; we simply hadn't needed them in Eden. I barricaded my door with my suitcase and then with my desk. I knew it was a fire hazard, but in the postlapsarian nightmare my life had become, zombie dogs and liars were more real to me than fire.

For four days, I refused to sleep with Freddie, and I did not address Alexis directly except for once on October 28, when I asked her to pass me the pepper.

On October 29, Irena's official Instagram started posting again. Some of us thought this was good news—I in particular thought that—but Pavel was quick to assure us that Irena had never once so much as opened Instagram, and that this was just Bogdan reacting to Alexis's publication, scrambling to keep up in the dark.

"Never?" I squeaked.

Pavel, who smelled of honeysuckle, shook his head. I experimented with flirting with him then, but he didn't notice, and I found it easiest, under the circumstances, to give up.

On October 30, I followed Freddie into Bogdan's room after dinner and pushed him, sort of gently, into Bogdan's dresser, pinning him to it by the throat. Unlike Pavel, Freddie took the hint.

CHAPTER TWENTY-THREE

By Halloween, I was sufficiently satisfied with Freddie's lust for me that I had resumed my (admittedly always strained) conversations with Alexis. We'd used some of the funds from our dwindling shared bank account to purchase snacks and mass quantities of alcohol, and Alexis had ordered a couple of (to my mind redundant) cardboard cutouts of skeletons and ghosts.

We'd created our own costumes based on some of our favorite characters from Irena's books. Alexis had insisted on dressing up as Zamenhof, the most ridiculous possible choice. It meant that she borrowed the suit Freddie had brought for our groundbreaking dinner, which in turn meant we had to explain to him who Zamenhof was: the real-life Russian Jewish creator of Esperanto—born in Białystok, site of Irena's youthful postcard caper, capital of the Podlaskie Voivodeship where we currently (still) were—who had also inspired Irena's fictional political movement in *Sedno II*. It meant that Ostap was cruelly recruited to fashion her a pair of spectacles out of the muselets Renata had been storing up on Irena's mantel and, occasionally, our shrine, despite the fact that Ostap's own spectacles were little more than a monocle now.

It meant she spent half the afternoon coloring a beard on herself with slightly sparkly gray eye shadow and putting her hair up in my silver swimming cap and playing and replaying pronunciation videos on YouTube so she could stand, head held high, in the living room doorway reading out at random from the handful of books in Esperanto she had found around Irena's library as "her" "guests" arrived.

It meant I got stuck with Sacher-Masoch's Wanda, from *Sedno I*. But since I was half-boycotting Halloween, a commercial U.S. holiday, I just borrowed

Chloe's gorgeous knee-high black leather boots that I'd been wanting to borrow anyway and the riding crop I found in Irena's room and a burgundy polyester blanket from the chaise longue that I fastened with an oversize safety pin (reluctantly borrowed from Alexis) over my swimsuit. I hadn't waxed in a while, but you couldn't really tell because I'd been shaving consistently, and anyway, we had agreed to dim the lights.

Unfortunately, Alexis and I were the first ones ready. Ostap and Renata had disappeared somewhere, and the three musketeers were in the summit room, now sadly sometimes called the game room, warming up with a round of Maßkrug-stemme, an endurance sport Schulz had introduced us to that consisted in holding a full stein of beer (or something similar) at arm's length until you absolutely had to put it down, or until it crashed and shattered and spilled on the floor. Pavel had successfully advocated for a slight modification of the rules that would enable their brains to disassociate from their biceps: Even after spending time with Barbara, they somehow still wanted to listen to her book of reportage about New Zealand, *A Little Lamb in Middle-earth*, narrated by Elżbieta Moszna, which they claimed was helping them refine the Nikau sections of *Grey Eminence*, although the snippets I'd overheard had been exhausting: densely written musings on phenomena neatly divvied up into profound- and unique-sounding categories that sooner or later would turn out to be the same one category, Things that Had to Do with Barbara, and I couldn't imagine how *we* could learn anything about *Grey Eminence* from *her*.

When Alexis began to ad-lib in what she thought was Esperanto I decided to retreat to the second floor. Quietly, I rapped on Chloe's door. She was sitting at her desk in front of her big mirror, carefully covering her face in diamond-shaped patches of eyeliner. She was wearing her dark pink minidress patterned a little bit like snakeskin, with a braided black leather belt at her waist and smooth Italian loafers.

"Do you have them?" she said, without taking her eyes off her reflection or interrupting the precise movements of the minuscule brush in her hand. Her nails were an immaculate white.

In all my loathing of Alexis, I had almost forgotten the fangs in my fist. Now I released them onto Chloe's desk. She dropped her brush and looked at me, and we laughed.

"Do you think he's going to be mad?" she asked.

"You mean because he once accidentally plunged his whole hand down a viper in front of Our Author?" I asked. I was still willing to make fun of Freddie if it made Chloe happy. I still wanted—pretty badly—to be her friend.

"You're right. He won't even get the reference. Alexis looks amazing, don't you think?"

She picked up the brush again and dipped its tip into the pot of black gel.

"You look extremely sexy," she said into the mirror.

There was a silence.

"I'm talking to you," she said, but she still didn't take her eyes off her reflection. I also didn't know if she was saying it because she meant it or because she realized she'd made a mistake in bringing up Alexis.

"Are you one hundred percent sure there's nothing going on between her and Freddie?" I asked. I didn't want to talk about Alexis, least of all with Chloe, but I couldn't resist.

"Between who?"

"*Alexis*," I groaned. "Between Alexis and Freddie."

"Oh my God, Emi, one thousand percent! No one but you likes Freddie." She glanced at me in the mirror as if alarmed by her own candor. "I hate to say this because I know this is important to you right now, but as your friend, I feel like it's also my duty to slip off your blinders for a sec."

I tried to laugh this off—at least she still considered us friends then—but I couldn't help saying, "Irena liked him."

"I'm not so sure she did. He's actually really annoying. He talks too much. His poems are *awful*. Half the time he calls me *Cleopatra*. He's always late to our group meditation, even when you aren't late. What is he doing that's so much more important than everything everyone else has to do?"

"He sometimes has to call Bogdana."

"Oh my God, Emi. The way you say that. Doesn't it bother you that he's married?"

"Not really."

"Really?"

I shrugged. There was a silence. I looked at Chloe in the mirror and saw that she was very far away, and I remembered an afternoon in high school when our biology teacher gave us a lecture about socks. Socks stretch, she had told us, every time you put them on. You put them on the first time, they look great. The next time, fine. And on and on, a thousand times, but then eventually, they stretch out. They wear at the toes and the balls of the feet. One day you're about to put your shoes on when you see your heel through a big old hole. You can darn them a few times. But you cannot infinitely mend a sock. At some point, you throw it out.

That's what happens to the heart, she had said. It expands and contracts and expands and contracts and then one day, it wears out.

I was fifteen then. I was sad for a week. Now, as Chloe poked her earrings through her ears, that memory devastated me. It felt like everything was ending: *Grey Eminence*, our summit, the world. Irena's works were eternal, but our translations were no more enduring than socks.

"Are you going to wear the black lipstick?" someone said in a voice that sounded like my voice except that it was thin as aluminum foil.

"Of course," Chloe said. "But first let me try on my teeth."

She snapped them in and scowled at me, testing out her costume. When I looked in her mirror again, I saw Alexis, looming over my shoulder like the ghost of Esperanto. For one split second, I thought I had turned into her. Then I caught a glimpse of my own stupid costume, wedged in between Chloe's and Alexis's reflections, and I turned, pushed past Alexis, and walked out of the room.

Chloe called after me, but I kept going down the stairs.

At the base of the stairs were a cardboard cutout of a ghost and Renata, who had dressed as the figure in the Flammarion engraving from the cover of *Ad Nauseam*, wearing a traveler's cloak. Petra had come to the party as *Lady with an Ermine*, from *Still Life with Still Life*, bringing Quercus as her ermine.[54]

Unsurprisingly Freddie was one of the miners from *Future Moonscapes*, wearing a leather jacket that looked so good on him it was hard to focus when he talked. I was grateful to Freddie, despite or in light of Chloe's critiques, for giving me love with no real future—the purest form of love—and I would have admitted to anyone that night, as I stood there staring, tapping my riding crop against my thigh, that I actually kind of loved him. I don't regret feeling that way even now.

---

54   This author's assumption is that both of these novels do in fact exist, although not a single reader of either has ever come forward, not even since Irena's Nobel (Trans.).

I don't regret loving you, either, Irena. Even now.

Chloe and Alexis came down, and Petra laughed.

"That's a very liberal interpretation of 8128," she said.

"What did you expect?" said Chloe, sounding funny through her fangs. "A laptop?"

"What was 8128 again?" asked Freddie, putting his arm around me.

Chloe looked at me accusingly and groaned.

"8128 is the protagonist of *Perfection*," I told him. "We couldn't figure out a good AI costume, so we went with an AI-generated costume instead."

"So what are you?" he asked her.

"A sexy snake," she said with a lisp.

"Fuck!"[55] said Freddie, jumping back, and for a second I couldn't tell if he was kidding. Then he hissed at her and winked at me, and that was when he pulled out the gun.

Renata screamed, and Ostap yelled, "No!" Chloe had her hands up, still standing on the knot on the third step, but she was smiling.

Freddie lowered the gun. "Don't worry," he said. "It isn't loaded."

"We took out the bullets," said Chloe.

"What are you talking about?" I said. How could she keep keeping secrets from me? Worse, keep keeping them with Freddie, the person I slept next to every night?

"It's just the reality of being in a Russian amber-mining gang." She shrugged.

"What are you talking about?" I repeated, louder this time. "Where did it come from? Where did you get a gun?"

He held it out to me. It was a revolver, and it had a star printed on it. It had a brown Bakelite grip that also looked like snakeskin, as if Freddie was infecting everything.

I took it from him. It was heavy. I had never held a gun before, and it was heavier than I had imagined. In a strange way, that weight was satisfying. It grounded an idea that had been abstract and even inchoate (not fully fledged in language) in my mind until that moment, an idea of death, or of killing.

---

55 I have translated "kurwa" as "fuck" throughout, though what it literally means is "whore" (Trans.).

I must have stared at it a while because the others started laughing, and when I looked up they were all gathered around me, in a circle, as though I were Our Author now.

PAVEL, FREDDIE, AND Schulz wanted to play beer pong, which they'd seen in movies and which Alexis helped them set up. Freddie and Ostap and I played against Schulz, Renata, and Pavel. Alexis and Chloe went downstairs to fence for an audience of Petra and Quercus. I would have preferred to fence with Chloe, and I resented them for not inviting me, and I played beer pong poorly and got drunk while they stayed relatively sober, except for Schulz, who was totally sober because the beer he was drinking was actually iced nettle-leaf tea.

Downstairs we played a game that had come in the mail to Alexis. It was called Twister, and playing it, Pavel, who was dressed as Nikau, seemed longer and more limber than I'd realized. As I watched him, it was easy for me to imagine him and Irena together, whereas it had always been difficult, if not impossible, to picture what happened between her and Bogdan behind closed doors.

Was it easier to imagine her with Freddie, on that first night? I pictured her standing naked in his bedroom (formerly Bogdan's). I pictured him coming up to her and placing a hand on her waist, another on her hip. I pictured her arching into him and then slamming her hands down on the grainy surface of the dresser, keeping her eyes on her own face in the mirror as he moved her, grunting and muttering in Swedish, like he did when he was with me.

Was it possible to imagine Bogdan with anyone? With Barbara? I squinted into the writhing mass of my colleagues on the floor. Since Barbara had always been in competition with Irena, she must have at least toyed with the idea over the years.

Barbara must have wanted to stop by when she did so she could gloat about Irena not getting picked for yet another year's Nobel Prize—on that point we all agreed, even if she really did also want to write something with Irena. So I was able to picture Barbara and Bogdan engaged in petty sex—the lowest form of love—essentially revenge, but ultimately just an impotent attempt, since they couldn't truly hamper her or even touch Irena's genius. But it all depended on what had happened between Bogdan and Irena, which we couldn't know. It depended on where Bogdan had gone after Cairo. Why wasn't Bogdan with Irena? Why wasn't Bogdan here?

At some point in that drunken conversation, Barbara had encouraged us all to cross over to her oeuvre whenever we were ready, as if it were an inevitable, retraceable step. As if Pavel had blazed a trail we would all have to zigzag down now. We'd be in excellent company, she assured us—aside from Catalan and Japanese, there was Arabic, and Hungarian, and Portuguese, and (she said with special relish) Swahili. When Ostap pointed out that she already had a Ukrainian translator, as well as, of course, an English one, she said not to worry, that we would "figure that out." But how could there be two translators of one author into one language? What would happen to Ostap? What would happen to Alexis? I might have wanted to kill her, but I couldn't imagine us without her, with some other English in her stead.

Schulz was trying to spin the gun around his trigger finger in the doorway. He'd put on music, loud and angry-sounding throbs that made it hard to keep track of my thoughts. Chloe was teaching Petra to parry. Freddie, Ostap, and Renata were in the kitchen teaching Quercus how to play basketball with a ping pong ball and part of an empty egg carton. Directly in front of me, Alexis rose on all fours and slowly raised her eyes from the big colored dots on the mat until they met mine.

"Ride me," she said.

"Pardon?" I said.

"Ride me," she said, without laughing. "Wanda would ride."

I squinted at her and took an involuntary step forward in Chloe's black leather boots. I raised my riding crop. She bit her lip and raised an eyebrow. Unthinking, I brought it down on her back.

"That's it," she said. "That's good."

I hit her again. Pavel had tumbled away and was watching us from a cross-legged position on the floor.

"Let me try," he said, holding his hand out in expectation of the riding crop.

"I want Emi," said Alexis in a soft and even tone. "I want Emi to do it."

I sank down on top of her and squeezed with my bare inner thighs, pressing into her with my pubis.[56] Freddie had noticed and was coming in from the kitchen.

"Chloe," he said. "Give me your phone."

---

56 Here I have preserved her ridiculous word (Trans.).

With my left hand, I reached forward and plunged my fingers into Alexis's hair. Slowly my fingertips made their way down her scalp and gathered her hair into a ponytail and pulled. With my right hand, I reached back with the riding crop and began to hit her, repeatedly, for Freddie's sake, or for Pavel's, or for mine. I could see my reflection in the sheen of Pavel's naked head. I liked what I saw.

That was, of course, the video that would make us so famous nine years later, after the announcement of the 2026 Nobel Prize. But of course it didn't represent us. Images can never capture the same things as words. By appearing more faithful, they're able to betray even more.[57]

---

57   This is fascinating because I would argue the exact same thing applies to this author's approach to translation (Trans.).

CHAPTER TWENTY-FOUR

November 1 was All Saints' Day, and we'd decided to honor that and take the whole day off. Polish tradition required us to pay our respects at the cemetery in the afternoon, once it was dark again, and all was awash in flickering candles, but until dusk, we'd be completely free of every obligation. I woke up around noon with a headache, took some pills from Irena's medicine cabinet, and saw out the backdoor window that a quasi-freezing fog had totally perfused the landscape, obscuring—far more than the flood of dead leaves had done—all its familiar features, like the shrubs, minus the sections we'd burned, or the scorched earth where Pavel's shed had been.

I slouched back to bed, and Freddie rolled over to hold me, but we didn't make love. He slept, and I finished reading *The Remains of the Day*. I got up again and made two slices of toast, which I ate at the kitchen counter. I sent a message to my mother, and then my father, carefully ignoring everything else on the screen of my phone.

I've never known what to do or even how to feel on days that are supposed to be important. But I'd worn my swimsuit to bed, and I thought that maybe that could be a clue—I was still wearing it, under Irena's crochet knit sweater that let in the cold and a pair of Chloe's sweatpants, although I couldn't remember why she'd given me her sweatpants, or when. I had not been swimming since we'd arrived this time—I hadn't had the energy, between Freddie and translating *Grey Eminence*—and it wasn't until I'd put on my suit the night before that it hit me how much I missed weighing nothing and dissolving. There was also the perverse pleasure of doing the opposite of what even I would expect me to do: In the cold, not camaraderie and not hot chocolate, but near-nudity, plunging, damp, and isolation.

I made my way to the Booted Eagle Hotel, where Pavel and Alexis had had their alleged foursome with Barbara Bonk and Mackenzie Tremaine,[58]

crossing from one side of Stoczek to the other, back and forth, slowly, hoping to exhaust my anxiety about it being All Saints' Day already and, I suppose, my grief. I came to the turn in front of the old brick orphanage, massive and covered in storks that looked like living gargoyles. Suddenly a convoy came speeding toward me. I leaped, lost my balance, and fell forward over the curb. As I was righting myself, slowly, painfully, I glimpsed the side of the last Jeep in the convoy, which said, in red capital letters, BORDER GUARDS. I brought my hands forward; they were red and scraped, but barely bleeding.

The storks should not have been here anymore, I realized. In the protraction of summer, the absence of signs that it was time to go, they must have missed their chance to migrate. Then again, I hated storks. I didn't mind if they all died.[59]

I reached the hotel and explained to the startled clerk what I wanted to do without trying to justify why. The empty pool was underground, as dimly lit as our Halloween party, with a glittering blue ceiling that my mind tried to pick out constellations from as I floated: the Southern Cross, Carina with its magnificent, eternal star. I was hungover, but some of my best ideas have come to me the morning after too much wine, and I assumed the same could be true of bison-grass vodka.

I washed off my hands and then tried in the relative silence, which was interrupted only by the rocking of the water, to think—to really think, in terms unclouded by her presence—about Alexis. She'd started wearing Irena's clothes and shoes exclusively now, and she'd stopped wearing her own gold necklace with the *A* on it, no doubt in an effort to trick us. She alternated between caring about us and forgetting our existence, enslaving our minds by making us wonder what she'd do next or how she might be feeling. The musketeers were always asking her what she was thinking. Every time I heard that question I wanted to scream.

---

58   Literally no one alleged this other than her (and she is insane) (Trans.).

59   This is so crazy and no, I did not invent it (Trans.).

Most importantly, she had violated our sacred translation honor code. Alexis was an evil changeling, the ultimate troll: someone who could work to undermine Our Author from within, subtweeting her *as she translated*, skewing every sentence so as to reject Our Author's supposed "selfishness" or "spurious ontology" or "formulaic prose." Every day when we sat down to translate she'd whine about some supposedly new thing. She said it openly: She thought translating was also editing; what this ultimately meant was that she trusted her own judgments more than she trusted Irena. She pretended it had to do with her "target audience," but Irena's work was already universal in the original Polish. None of the rest of us ever felt the need to change a word. That is, we changed every word, of course, but only outwardly, and not in spirit.

I couldn't comprehend why the others refused to take sides. Pavel had even called our relationship a "rivalry," and when Alexis and I agreed that was sexist and dumb, he responded, "How do you feel about 'catfight'?"

None of the rest of them even seemed to want to decide what they thought about the novel's main argument, whether art could ever be for good or whether even *Grey Eminence* had the potential to unleash catastrophe on us and on the Earth. It wasn't our place to weigh in, but I was curious, and sometimes I thought I detected indifference in Chloe's limpid French, a certain sluggishness in Ostap's Ukrainian which gleaned similarities to Polish and which had, in previous translations, at least to my eye, bounded from page to page.

I needed to know that they agreed with me that *Grey Eminence* was worth translating; I needed to know that publishing our translations would mean something. But for the past five and a half weeks, we'd been too mired in our confusion, and then Alexis and I had been mired in enmity, and it was all we could do to just keep going, keep sitting there every morning, keep meeting downstairs for dinner at dusk.

I dove down to the bottom of the pool and did a handstand. But what, I wondered, pressing my scraped hands to that rough concrete, could the border guards be doing? Where could they be going in such haste? Yet those were the wrong questions. They were going to the border, which meant that someone must have been trying to cross it illegally in spite of the cold, someone the Poles considered to be a member of an invasive species, someone from outside the European Union who would, they believed, destabilize that shriveling continent using powerful invasive magic, or simply slow hard work.

If my mother's grandparents hadn't immigrated to Argentina, assuming they'd even survived the Holodomor,[60] they would have been killed in concentration camps, along with my mother's father. I would never have been born. I surfaced. I dove down again.

And as for plants and animals and fungi, wasn't it only the invasive species that had avoided extinction into Amália's day? We had been harnessed by Our Author to describe in agonizing detail the extinguishing of life on Earth, and the truth was we still weren't totally sure why. I never stopped believing in Irena's fundamental goodness. I never doubted that the sadism that flowed so freely through *Grey Eminence*—like the torture of poor Lena in Irena's first bestseller, or the desultory devastation of *Pompeii*—was entirely, or at least primarily, in the service of the ultimate achievement of harmony and peace.

Irena's wisdom was greater than ours, and we could not presume to always understand her means. We were united in our muted confusion, but the translation of that muted confusion still pitted me against Alexis, who kept calling for "clarifications" or outright "improvements" as we worked: glosses, amendments, reworkings, even the occasional cut. Who kept calling, in other words, for an end to our silence, an admission, or a proclamation, of our bewilderment.

I knew that what she really wanted was to civilize Irena's text, exactly as you would expect a U.S. usurper to do. She wanted to tidy it up by eviscerating it, make it essentially her own. She claimed Irena had a "sad Japanese fetish" that it was our moral duty not to perpetuate, among other "problematic views."

To which I demanded to know why she had ever even translated Irena, to which she responded that she didn't get why I didn't get it, and the fact of the matter was I didn't know what "it" was. I did know that Alexis was trying to drive me insane because I was the only one who saw or understood what she was doing, and in order to ensure I couldn't stop her, she would keep tap-tap-tapping at my skull until it cracked.

What I needed to do, I realized now, as I began to run out of oxygen, was prove it. Surely if Petra and Renata and Chloe and Schulz and Ostap and even Pavel and Freddie understood that Alexis was being grossly unfaithful, they would be willing to get *involved*. Surely they'd agree that *Grey Eminence* deserved

---

60   A genocidal famine engineered by Joseph Stalin (Trans.).

to be read in every language the way Irena had written it—the way she'd wanted it to be read. Only in this way could it have the impact it needed to have in order to panic—and therefore save—the world.

I burst up out of the water, gasped, then blew the blue water out of my mouth and nose. I forced my eyes open. I got out of the pool.

On my way out of the hotel I paused in the lobby to look up at the trophies mounted just under the ceiling on all sides. There were boars, and deer, and there was a badger; there was even a bear. I pictured Freddie's head glued on to a wooden plaque, then Alexis's with that stupid, perfect, ridiculous grin, and that hair without a strand out of place except when my hands were in it. Then Chloe, then Petra, then Schulz, and so on, until they were all up there, even me.

A post from your father's house, since now I know you'll never see these, plus a little video from "Halloween." #toolittle #latergram

November 1

I had been hoping for snow before our summit ended. I was frightened of cold, but snow was something I felt I needed to experience here. It had snowed only once in the past century in Buenos Aires, in 2007, and we'd all gone out onto our balconies and snapped millions of ridiculous pictures, little pops of light that lasted longer than the flakes of snow, which were gone once they hit the ground, perfectly traceless—Amália's, perhaps Irena's nonliving ideal. (Our photographs had come to nothing, too; they had been only gray blurs, or other people's flashes.)

But outside, the light was already beginning to falter, and the wind had picked up, and although it felt freezing, according to my weather app, it was in fact still forty-five degrees—too warm, according to the internet, for snow. I went straight to the cemetery, where we were all to meet Leszek, and found it overwhelmed by the delicate flames of hundreds upon hundreds of devotional candles, lit on every grave, and despite the glass jars, it felt to me like a very real fire hazard, like the forests' undoing, like the dead were finally poised to exact their revenge upon the hornbeams that had failed to conceal them, the elk that had eluded them—all the abundance the forest had promised and withheld, and the prehistoric threats it had made good on, its ruthlessness and the devastating dread that resulted, endless, all-consuming. Now it felt as if the candle flames would leap from grave to leaf, and gone would be the toothwort, the mistletoe, the rue-leaved isopyrum, the froghoppers, the blue hares, the muskrats, the owls.

I'd been alone in the crowd for a few minutes when I got a text from Freddie saying they were running late. Circling our meeting point—the honey-hunter's grave—I opened our @amaliaearth account. People I no longer knew well kept sending me messages, people who wrote to me in Spanish, and I kept having to slide them off my screen, but in the end, I was able to scroll back and find one last picture to post, and to post it, together with the video Chloe had sent to everyone on Team Irena.

I called Leszek, but he didn't pick up. I waited a few more minutes, but in the snowless cold, surrounded by mourners, inundated by elogies, I began to feel I was at my own funeral, and I couldn't wait anymore. I zipped back out of the cemetery and onto the street. There, on the corner of Puszczańska and Kamienne Bagno, I heard the plaintive sound of something like a violin. But it wasn't a violin, exactly, and I followed it to find out what it was. This led me to the house with the beautiful garden, bare now but for the straw wraps that blanketed nearly all the shrubs and trees.

I was amazed to discover that the straw wraps *were* producing that music, exactly as Chloe had said. But Chloe had been in a hurry, and I was now a ghost. Time was nothing to me. I opened the wooden gate.

I pried the straw back from a young ash. Clipped to a thin wire around the trunk was a small speaker, marigold in color, with three almost invisible symbols. I pressed the triangle. The music stopped, though it continued around the rest of the garden. The instrument I'd first heard was now accompanied by a choir, and suddenly, too, the Apple ringtone.

It was Chloe. "Chloe!" I said. "You were right!" But I couldn't hear anything on the other end of the line. "Chloe?" I said, but there was nothing, and I realized my phone had switched over to the Belarusian carrier, and out of the corner of my eye I saw a flash of something, an animal in a rush, chasing or fleeing, and it turned out to be a woman in a leopard-print coat and ballet flats, her short dark hair half-veiled by something crimson, coming around from the back of the house. She was walking very quickly, almost running, and she didn't notice me—she just went out the side gate.

"Wait!" I called, but the woman didn't hear me, because of the music or because maybe no one could hear me anymore. I zoomed after her, back into the cemetery, and tried to catch up with her as she weaved her way through the maze of the graves and the weeds that were drooping in the semi-frigid air and the people who were visiting their dead, and only once did she glance back, and when she did, I saw that she had Amália's pale skin and big brown eyes and slightly cleft chin, Amália's mole on her right cheekbone, all exactly as Our Author had described.

A hand gripped my forearm, and suddenly I wasn't a ghost. I looked down and saw a heavy glove and tensed and looked up, startled, but it was only Leszek.

"Leszek!" I cried. "Who is that?!"

"Who is who?" he said, and I pointed, but the woman had disappeared into the crowd.

I closed my eyes and spun my thumbs. It couldn't have been Amália, I tried to reason with myself. But could it have been?

What if Irena's powers had finally exceeded the page? In writing such a compelling protagonist, could Irena not have conjured flesh and blood this time?

Could I have had something to do with this miracle, terrifying as it was? Not only through translation, but also Instagram?

"Come," Leszek said, and as usual, he took off without awaiting a response. Still looking around for any trace of Amália, nearly tripping over crouching villagers and their devotional candles, I struggled to keep up, and then he stopped, and I crashed into him, but he rebalanced quickly and just gestured at a row of graves. "This is Olga Smoktunowicz, 1891 to 1989. A felczer, which—" He held out his palm to stop me from posing the question. "Which means a person with medical expertise."

"Like a doctor," I said, and I closed my eyes again. Amália isn't real, I told myself.

"Not a doctor," Leszek said. "Felczer Smoktunowicz was a mentor to Irena's father, especially after the war. She single-handedly united all the human communities of the Białowieża Forest—Catholic, Orthodox, Muslim, Jewish, until the Jewish communities were gone—through the establishment of a makeshift hospital where everyone was warmly welcomed. Her husband was murdered by the Nazis, and Olga never got his body back, so when she died at the age of ninety-seven, Olga was buried next to her parents, Nestor and Yevdokiya, whose tombstones you see before you now."

I pictured my own grave again, this time sandwiched in between my parents'. But I knew my parents would be unable to stand one another in the hereafter just as they were unable to do so on our present plane. They weren't even able to bestir themselves to message me back, today of all days, and it was now nearly eleven A.M. in Buenos Aires—unless, I supposed, their messages had somehow gone astray in Belarus.

On the concrete between us and the Smoktunowiczes, there was a half-devoured caterpillar in a whirlpool of ants. I felt an unprecedented impulse, a desire to smash the whole candlelit tableau, to grind into nothingness the predators or the scavengers as they desecrated the squandered possibility of a butterfly. I might have done so, had it not been for Leszek, but then I looked again and saw it was a worm.

For all the relentlessness and sadism of human artifice that Irena addressed in *Grey Eminence*, wasn't the suffering that existed in nature unbearable as well? And wasn't it understandable that people tried to escape an endless cycle of oblivion and pain? The primeval forest was hardly a garden of Eden. Even the friendliest-seeming animals could be vicious, like the storks that intentionally starved half their chicks to death. Just compare a stork to Olga Smoktunowicz![61] Maybe it was glimpsing some shade or version of Irena's protagonist in real life, but I was suddenly feeling more sympathetic to people and to art.

"Sometimes we must create the community we wish to protect," said Leszek, and I nodded, but I hadn't been following and didn't know what he meant. "Have you heard from your friends?"

"Ugh, yes," I said. "All day."

"All—what?"

"Oh, you mean Irena's other translators."

Leszek looked confused, but then his phone dinged, and he opened his amadou satchel. "Ah," he said. "Good. It's from your boyfriend."

"Freddie?" I said faintly.

"Is there another one?"

"No, he's just not my—"

"Wow! Wow wow wow! But this is a *Buprestis splendens*! But this is impossible! But look at this!"

Leszek handed me the phone. On its screen was the russety green beetle I'd seen after almost being killed by the rogue archer. Freddie had told me he had seen it again, but I hadn't realized he had pictures. There was a bolt of lightning in the distance—Perun,[62] I thought—and then—I counted—just three seconds later, a clap, then a rumble of thunder.

"He's telling me I should come over. To ID it for sure."

I nodded. My own phone rang again. It was Chloe, again, and I picked up, expecting not to hear her, but this time her voice was crystal clear. "She's back!" she said, and she sounded excited—but also not quite like herself.

"Who's back?" I asked.

Chloe sighed. Then she said, "Irena. Our Author. She's back."

---

61   But compare a stork to Ilse Koch, aka the Beast of Buchenwald. Nor, of course, is humankind extricable from nature (Trans.).

62   This reference is clearer to the original reader: "piorun" means "lightning" in Polish and derives from the same Proto-Slavic source as Perun, the name of the ruling god of ancient Slavic mythology (Trans.).

CHAPTER TWENTY-FIVE

The clouds burst, unleashing universal panic as candle flames spluttered and hissed, umbrellas opened, and those without umbrellas ran for their cars or the church. Without exchanging a word, Leszek and I raced down Puszczańska, and the rain turned into hail, but all I could think was: Hallelujah! I flung the door open and threw myself inside.

I saw everyone standing in front of me, and I looked in every direction, expecting to see Irena's smiling face, or, if she'd been somewhere she hadn't wanted to go, maybe her crestfallen face, but in any case *her* face. For a millisecond, I thought I saw it, and my hands flew together, and I started to smile a wide-open smile only to realize the person I thought was Irena was in fact fucking *Alexis*—that Alexis had dyed her hair so that it was now as dark as Irena's, and she was wearing Irena's long forest-green dress, and her brown boots, and her amber bracelet, and her lipstick, and her petrichor perfume that collided with the real scent of the deluge, creating a fetid cloud.

I reeled back in disgust. There were Petra, and Renata, and Ostap, who was wearing a bright knitted eye patch that made him look like a pirate whose grandmother happened to be insane, and Chloe, and Schulz, and Pavel, and Freddie, all witness to my incredible error, and then there was Mackenzie and some grizzled-looking man, and for some reason, all of them were watching me, and Petra looked over showily at Our Lady of Literature, where I recognized her dilapidated laptop in between identical revolvers on what had formerly been the *Sedno* shelf, and there, pixelated, were my terrible parents, and just then, as the horror of the situation was beginning to wash over me, they all yelled in a more or less coordinated manner, in Polish and Spanish and *English*, "Surprise!"

Before I knew what I was doing, I had run back out into the rain.

They had betrayed me. They had all betrayed me, even Chloe—Chloe most of all.

Standing in the middle of the street, sopping wet, I watched as the years washed off me and all rushed down the street, into the gutters or on toward the river, everything I had ever had that I had failed to enjoy or appreciate, or that I had treasured and still lost. Thirty-five years, and the best thing I ever had, my relationship with Irena, and by extension my relationship with Irena's other translators—all of that was gone.

The wind moaned, and the hail felt like bullets raining down on my face and my hands that were trying in vain to protect my face, and I realized I had nowhere to go but back, and I turned and rolled over the doorknob, and I saw their concerned faces light up as if it might have just taken me a minute to realize that I was in fact delighted they'd decided to throw me a surprise party for my thirty-fifth birthday—delighted they had all been keeping an enormous secret from me, delighted they had lured me to the party by *lying to me about the single most important thing in my whole life.*

I shoved past them, parting Chloe and Alexis and coming to Ostap and Renata, who for some reason were *holding hands*, making it impossible to get past them, so that in order to resist the temptation to rip off Ostap's eye patch and crush his monocle with the Bozdoğan mace, I swerved around Renata and flew up the stairs into my room, where I barricaded the door with the corduroy dictionary and sank down to the floor and sobbed.

I know my mother and Chloe tried to call me. Freddie tried to force the door, but I pushed back, and he gave up. Petra sat down on the other side of the door and told me that they had found the keys to Irena's ancient chests while I was at the Booted Eagle inside Irena's *Complete Moomins*, which wasn't actually a book but a box, and that they had been waiting for me to open them, now that Mackenzie's cameraman was here.

Needless to say, I didn't believe her. Why would they wait for me? There must have been some other reason, something they wanted or needed from me. Then Renata joined Petra and told me that she hadn't told anyone else yet but that she wanted Petra and me to be the first to know that she and Ostap were going to get married, that he had finally left his wife. That they'd been seeing each other since *Matsuura*, but that they had never *fully* consummated their relationship until Ostap finally broke up with his wife over Skype that afternoon.

Perhaps what I had interpreted as hatred between them could have been love—but I didn't believe her, either. All I took from what she said was that she and Ostap had had sex that afternoon, and I couldn't help but picture it, but the picture—Ostap in his eye patch, Renata confused[63]—was so ungainly and unlikely that it knocked me out of my stunned grief just enough that I was able to open Instagram on my phone.

For the first time, @amaliaearth had actual notifications. It had a lot of notifications. And almost all of them, unbelievably, were from an account called @irenadembowska. @irenadembowska had liked every single one of my posts. She had commented on one! I clicked on it. It was the picture I'd just posted, my #latergram of the sign showing the dog and the gun on her father's front fence. Her comment was a skull emoji.

Her comment was a skull emoji!

Chloe was saying something on the other side of the door now, about how she hadn't wanted to trick me into coming back, that Alexis had put her up to it, and she hadn't realized that Freddie had already solved the problem by convincing Leszek to come over, but I didn't care about anything she had to tell me anymore because all I cared about was this Irena, not the hacker who emailed us or the phantom they had stupidly, cruelly conjured up for my birthday, which I hadn't wanted to celebrate or even remember was happening, but the Irena I had found on Instagram by sending up my flare.

Through the door, I said, "Get me Leszek."

"Okay!" said Chloe immediately, and I heard her footsteps fading down the stairs. A few minutes later, I heard his willowy voice. I cracked the door.

"Did you know about the party?"

"No," he said.

"Come in," I said, opening the door just wide enough and not looking at Chloe, who was leaning against the railing of the staircase, or Petra and Renata,

---

63 This is so rude and untrue—as *if* this author were the only one capable of lucidly spreading her legs for some middle-aged, slightly potbellied loser (Trans.).

who were huddled together on the floor, with Quercus on one of their shoulders—in my peripheral vision I couldn't make out which one.

I showed him my screen.

"Is that . . . ?"

"Yes," I whispered urgently. "I think it's real. I think it's real because they *liked* all my posts, but only *commented on* the one from her father's place, which only she could know was his."

"Has she posted? I mean, has this account posted?"

"Shh!" I said. "You can't tell *anyone* about this. Do you promise?"

He looked at me with the same confusion my colleagues had evinced downstairs. But after a second's hesitation, Leszek promised, and we shook hands, first right and then left, which came naturally to us, and which we didn't discuss in advance.

I clicked on @irenadembowska. She had posted. She had posted! Only minutes earlier she had posted a picture, in black and white, of a bird of prey. That meant that Irena was still in the forest! Part of me desperately wanted to just open the door and show Petra and Renata, who could fully decipher the clue, but I definitely couldn't trust them now. I showed my screen to Leszek again.

"Doesn't this mean she's still in Białowieża?" I said.

Leszek, studying the photograph, shook his head. "I don't know. I don't think so. This is a common kestrel, which is not so common here."

I winced at this. The wind bayed, like an army of zombie dogs.

"They don't have the *Buprestis splendens*, either," he told me, when the wind died down again. "They said they had it an hour ago but that it disappeared somewhere. Into the wall."

Suddenly there was an all-piercing siren that rose and fell like La Llorona in search of the children she had drowned. Then Leszek's phone howled, and he rummaged for it in his soaked amadou bag.

"Does it ever bother you that amadou is the product of a parasite?" I asked him, ignoring the siren and the howl.

"*Fomes fomentarius* starts its life as a parasite," he said, still searching. "But then it turns into a decomposer, helpful, converting the dead tree into life-giving soil. The ecosystem needs parasites like these. Unlike human parasites."

He extracted his phone then at last. His eyes got wide. "It's a tornado," he told me. "There has never been a tornado here before." He searched my blank face with frantic fervor. He flung open my door. "I have to go put up the bison! I'll be back tomorrow! We will locate the *Buprestis splendens*!"

"We need to get to the cellar!" I heard Alexis shout from down the hall, and in an oddly energizing mix of loathing and elation, I followed her order, marching down the spiral staircase and then the semisecret staircase beneath Freddie's room along with everyone else.

"What about Pan Igor?" Chloe asked me. Her eyes were enormous. I looked into them and said that I was sure Pan Igor's nurse Nina was shepherding him into a room with no windows as we spoke. That was all I knew about tornadoes, a detail I'd read in a strange book called *Snakes and Ladders* written for some reason in Argentine Spanish by the U.S. translator of Olga Tokarczuk.

Underground, the rain and hail were muffled, but the wind remained a low roar. Someone pulled the little cord that switched on the one bulb in the cellar. Something slithered somewhere, a snake or the tail of a field mouse or a rat. Chloe went and sat at the far end of the cellar, on top of the broken washer, and Alexis sat down next to her.

The cellar was mostly empty now. There were only a couple of books on a metal shelf that also held duct tape and gardening shears and something like a little scythe. I picked up one of the books; it was a history of Japan, written in English, a language Irena always claimed she didn't really read.

For the first time, I felt sorry for Our Author. Whatever her obsession with Japan was, it was pitiful. It had never fully occurred to me before that there were basic things Our Author didn't understand—and worse, that there were things she knew she didn't understand, that she was trying to understand, and that she maybe couldn't, no matter how hard she tried.

I opened the book, and a postcard fell out. I scraped it off the concrete floor and saw, lined up almost symmetrically against the wall, two dead frogs. I straightened. On the front of the postcard was a picture of a maple tree. It was artificially colored the way postcards used to be—not sumptuously printed like the postcards that had burned up in the shed. Slowly, I turned it over. Petra and Renata and Chloe came closer and peered over my shoulder.

The postcard had a little information box in the upper left-hand corner that explained it came from the island of Itsukushima. It was addressed to Irena Dembowska, dated December 3, 1995. It didn't communicate much—it was only an old postcard—but I passed it around, and Chloe and Alexis came up so that all of us could scrutinize it under the one bulb, trying to figure out the signature, which started with an *M* and turned into a short-lived cardiogram.

Together we gleaned, from the book, with Freddie and Alexis ridiculously vying over command of the English language, Freddie wedging himself in between Chloe and Alexis, that Itsukushima was an island where maple trees grew freely—no one was permitted to cut them down under any circumstances—and deer intermingled with the two thousand or so human inhabitants. Only one battle was ever fought there, in 1555; immediately afterward, the island was purified, and blood-soaked soil was removed.

"Wow," said Chloe and Schulz at the same time, though they pronounced it differently. One of them smelled like honeysuckle, cloyingly sweet.

"That's why we're still here," said Pavel.

"Why?" asked Freddie.

"I mean, you're right, of course," said Pavel. "We should have left by now. There's something here that's keeping us from leaving."

"Yeah," said Petra. "Irena."

"No," said Pavel. "That isn't all it is."

"What else is it?" Alexis asked. She batted her lashes at him, but he wasn't looking. She went back to her perch on the dryer, and Chloe followed.

"Blood-soaked soil," said Pavel. "Białowieża. Just think: This part of Europe used to be covered by forests. People destroyed them—all of them but this one. Why?"

"It's a beautiful place," said Renata simply. "With lots of birds in it."

"Białowieża's not a place," I told them. "Irena told us that on our first day. Białowieża's not a place, it's a network."

"What it is is a vicious circle of protection and aggression," Pavel responded. "Since it fell into the hands of the Polish king in the 1400s, those in power have protected it, but only because it served their purposes, and because it was entertaining to them. Did you know hunting bison was made punishable by death in 1538? But only if you were a peasant."

"Yes," said Freddie. "The forest is a tangled web of wanton violence. It holds power over us because it summons our animal selves from deep within us, where they have been repressed, and because it urges us toward destruction—our own and everything else's."

Schulz nodded. "Misery wants company. Violence wants company, too."

"You're still talking," I said, "about the special stress mushrooms you told us grow in Białowieża—"

"They're not talking about special stress mushrooms," said Chloe, slamming her heels into the dingy metal of the washing machine. "Don't be literal. They're saying it's overwhelming and toxic and weird here, and I definitely agree."

I made a child's face. I wasn't literal. But Chloe wasn't looking at me.

"What were the special stress mushrooms again? You mean like hallucinogens?" asked Pavel.

"I think they mean the murder mushrooms we were talking about that night in the garden at the pizzeria," said Petra. "Mushrooms that thrive on contaminated soil, after fires or in Chernobyl. Or here after the war."

I had never previously experienced claustrophobia, but nor had I ever had much of an opportunity. Then Alexis said, "What are we going to do about the loggers being back?"

"Good question," said Schulz. "What could we do?"

"I was thinking," said Alexis. "What if we took to social media?"

At this I began to be consumed by the nausea of dread. The last thing I wanted was for them to find my secret Instagram account, or to find out that Irena had just posted a picture of a common kestrel. I had worked hard for that clue, and I wanted it, unlike every solution we had ever come up with before, collectively, in our translations, to belong to me.

"We can't *take* to social media without Irena's permission," I said, and no one seemed to notice I was faking my indignation, maybe because they'd all gotten so comfortable lying to me.

"We do *not* need permission from Irena to get on Instagram," Alexis said, rolling her eyes.

"Yeah, I don't know, Alexis," Schulz said. "Could we make it a private account to start out?"

"That would defeat the whole purpose," said Alexis.

"Oh," said Schulz. "Yeah, I guess."

"But Alexis," said Petra. "We can't reveal anything more about *Grey Eminence*. And we can't reveal Our Author's disappearance."

"We won't," said Alexis. "This will be a continuation of the novel, not a tell-all. It would just be to get the word out about the possible deforestation and how dire the consequences would be."

"The question," said Renata, "is what would Irena do? We mustn't stray from the trails that she has blazed."

"True," said Petra. "True."

"Irena would write an essay," said Alexis. "We could do that, too."

"Write an essay?" asked Freddie, whose interest, as a translator who unthinkably also considered himself to be an author, was piqued.

"Yeah!" said Alexis. Even under the sickly faulty light of the one bulb I could see her green eyes getting brighter with every word that came out of her glistening mouth. "We could write on conservation, in general, and on that critically endangered beetle, and on Białowieża, and then we could publish it in her name, in our languages."

"Are you kidding?" I shrieked. "We can't write in her name! That is the absolute worst thing we could do as her translators."

"I just mean," said Alexis, "how else are we going to save the forest? We can't save it ourselves. We've been here six weeks and done nothing. We got that little reprieve, but now things are bound to get worse. They'll probably want to make up for lost time! Why don't we write an article about it and publish it so that a bunch of journalists come here to document the logging—then maybe the EU will get involved. Something like that, I don't know."

"Alexis is right," said Freddie. "What other option do we have? Irena left us here to deal with it ourselves, so let's deal with it. We don't have the platform she has. If we write an article in our own names about a Polish forest, who's going to publish it?"

"We literally wrote an article in our own names and got it published everywhere a year ago," I told him. I looked around at the rest of them. "And it worked! It got Irena out of jail! Are all of you insane?"

"Need I remind you," Freddie said to me, "that sanity has not exactly been the guiding principle since our arrival here?"

I wriggled out of his grasp and batted his arms away, but once again he seemed to think that I was being playful.

"That article was different, Emi," said Petra, and I could not believe that even Petra was taking Alexis's side. "Because it was about her. In other words, it continued to contain her name."

"We could confess in a month," suggested Ostap. "Or whenever they stop the logging."

"Next year, maybe," said Renata.

"How are you all on board with this?" I yelled.

I looked at Petra, imploringly. I looked at Schulz. Then I approached the laundry area and locked eyes with Alexis.

"I'll kill you if you do this," I said.

Alexis said nothing, and in her eyes I saw a blaze of defiance.

"If you do this," I repeated, "I will kill you."

No one said anything at first. Then Petra said, "Emi, when we get out of here, you should call your parents back. They were so disappointed when you fled our surprise."

My eyes bulged. How could *my parents* be what anyone cared about right now?

"Happy birthday, Emi," Renata said.

"Happy birthday," Ostap echoed in a whisper.

Chloe had said that some English-language authors kept their translators in bunkers, cut off from the outside world. At the time, I'd thought that sounded cruel. But in light of Alexis's suggestion that we try to fool the reading public into believing we—her translators—*were* Irena Rey, imprisonment felt like just what we deserved.

If we stayed down here, unable to communicate with anyone except each other, would we not be protecting Irena, her reputation, not to mention refusing to stain our whole profession by willingly transforming into the very traitors some readers had long suspected us to be?[64]

Squatting against the wall I idly prodded the four figurines on the lower metal shelf in front of me, small limestone vases with different heads. The nearest one was a bird of prey of some kind; next to it was a cat. Behind these were a person and a baboon. Their faces were painted in faded black. I picked up the two in the back and brought them out. Renata rushed over.

There was a crash aboveground. The lightbulb flickered.

"Canopic jars," Renata whispered. "These . . ." She picked up the cat. She leaned into it as though to kiss its sculpted nose, or its lined eyes, then said, "This is Duamutef, the jackal god, who represents the east." With his hand on the wall,

---

64 The reference here is to the superstition among certain readers who believe translations necessarily adulterate their originals, and thereby ruin them. (I think I have shown irrefutably throughout this novel that a translation is often superior to its original, but of course this is for you to decide) (Trans.).

Ostap tiptoed over. He tilted his head, and Renata replied, "Each of these jars holds an organ. The ancient Egyptians removed them before creating mummies, to keep them whole—to save them for the afterlife. This one," she continued, taking the monkey from me, "is Hapi, who represents the north. They put the lungs in here."

"But they're not . . ." Schulz squinted. "They can't be real," he half asked, half insisted.

"Wait," said Alexis. "Surely you're not saying—you can't be saying you think Irena's in there. You can't think Bogdan—" But she stopped herself before she said it.

Following on the heels of my fury was faintness; as the others closed in around Renata and the four figures and me, all the oxygen seemed to be absorbed by the cellar's stone walls. Alexis had come and was looming over me; then she had dropped to her knees, seizing the other receptacle out of my hands.

"That's Imsety," Renata said. "She represents the south and keeps the liver."

"Irena isn't dead!" I cried. "She can't be!"

But Alexis wasn't listening. Alexis was trying to pry the head off the jar. Moaning when she couldn't, she looked up at Freddie, and they made extended eye contact, and she held Imsety up to him; he hesitated for a fraction of a second, then reached out.

At the same time, Renata was raising the final figure, the bird of prey, which she said represented the west and contained the intestines, and when she said the word "falcon," Petra screamed.

In the confusion and concern that issued from that scream, someone turned the light off, or Irena's house lost power, and I sensed that all the ghosts who could be there with us then were. They were undulating greens, similar to the southern lights, ineffable, culminating cascades of deafening silence. The honey-hunter Filimon Waszkiewicz was there, and so was the noble Olga Smoktunowicz. There were the ghosts from just east of where we were, Yuriy Verbytsky, Nikolay Andrushchenko, Yevgeny Khamaganov, Dmitry Popkov, Georgiy Gongadze. I sensed the palest gleam that lay in wait for Pan Igor Dembowski, father of Irena, who was probably currently wishing Irena was with him right now, like we were, but who soon enough would be cascading, silently roaring, green.

Petra sobbed. "We forgot about Quercus!" she cried.

In spite of my faintness, my fury remained strong. I shoved everyone aside, especially Alexis, who slammed into the metal shelf, and I raced back up the stairs while everyone screamed at me not to.

Aboveground was dark but for the rumbling shadows, and the wind was like a freight train, like when, in Buenos Aires, I sometimes squeezed in between the gates at Juan B. Justo to feel the commuter trains slice by, knowing how many people were killed by those trains every year, and I understood that these could be my final moments, that I could die a tragic death, in glory, in the empty plenitude of Irena's home that might be about to be leveled, and there was nothing anyone could do to defend against that wantonness, that violence, that impending void that could return all Our Author's holdings to the Earth, even us.

I knew that Quercus was in Petra's and Renata's old room where neither of them slept. I did not pause at the lucky knot at the base of the staircase on the ground floor; I did not stop for anything in my room, or Chloe's, or Alexis's. I reached the third floor. Quercus was sitting at the bottom of his cage, his wings slightly raised and quaking, drowsy but in terror.

Barely seeing where I was going, I took Quercus down the two flights of stairs and into Freddie's bedroom. I heard a window shatter. I thought it must have been in the kitchen. I kept going.

The cellar was still plunged in chaos, completely dark except for someone's cell phone propped against the books on the metal shelf. Petra burst into tears and wrested Quercus's cage from me, wrapping her arms around it and turning toward the closest corner, where she murmured to him and kept crying.

I felt aloft, like I was no longer bound by the same rules of gravity that applied to everyone else. Then Alexis pushed me back against some empty boxes, so that one of them exploded, releasing a burst of soil. She looked perfect: perfectly poised, perfectly coiffed. Unscathed.

"Let's write it now," she said, and the others readied their phones.

They went sentence by sentence, in your language, Irena, everyone offering ideas that they rapidly polished into words that really could have been yours— that were yours, that they stole from the stockpile we'd created out of *Lena*, and *Matsuura*, and *Future Moonscapes of the Eocene*, where you'd written of the first time in the history of Earth that an *Ophiocordyceps* had infected an ant. You'd described how that fungus forced the ant to climb a foot above the forest floor, forced it to face north, and then, at noon exactly, sprouted out of the top of its head to shower down millions of spores that would land on the next generation of ants.

As I watched my colleagues write your op-ed, I was reminded of those ants.

CHAPTER TWENTY-SIX

I decided to type up my challenge to Alexis; it felt more professional that way. Because we had never figured out how to connect our computers to the printer, I sat down, for the third time, in the womb chair at Irena's desk. I realized as I stared into the blankness of her screen that I had never read an invitation to a duel, and that I didn't know the format. The storm had knocked out our internet again. Had I been able to look up some examples, I might have thought to specify that what I wanted was a duel to the death—not to first blood and certainly not the kind of duel where you can fire only a single shot. But without Wikipedia, I believed all I needed was the same information you'd find on any invitation: place (the meadow outside the strict reserve) and time (the following day, November 3, Saint Hubert Day,[65] at dawn).

I struggled to find the right conclusion. I began to type the traditional "Pozdrawiam serdecznie," which translates literally as "I heartfully salute you,"[66] but then I stopped because it occurred to me that this might come across as dishonest, or worse still, might confuse her as to my intentions, which were to kill her. I decided just to sign it, without any salutation. Let her infer from my signature that I had closed.

The first time I printed it, I picked it up too hastily and smudged the right side. The second time, it turned out perfectly. I slid it under her door and went

---

65 Saint Hubert is the patron saint of hunting, dogs, and archery (Trans.).

66 The Polish word "pozdrawiać" comes from the word for health, which is why I chose the word "salute," which comes from the Latin "salus," meaning health or welfare.

back downstairs to prepare the case I would present to everyone in favor of Alexis's demise.

Our Lady of Literature had not been destroyed in the tornado. I sat down at Petra's feet, grateful she was there, trying not to wake her. I wasn't planning on casing the house with the straw wraps. If I could mistake Alexis for Irena, then I had no doubt the woman I thought was Amália had been no one.

I saw *Sedno I*, and *Sedno II*; there was *Perfection*, and what was left of *ГОДЪ*, in Ukrainian and Russian and broken-off Polish; quotes from *Grey Eminence*, written in inky cap, were taped up the side of the shrine. We were a dozen or so pages from the end now. Amália was dead, and so was most of Portugal. So was much of Spain. The tsunami had triggered the release of an oceanic plague that was now infecting human beings, moving east from Western Europe and south from Northern Africa and west, back in the ocean, to Brazil. The novel's last gasp had to do with Nikau; the truth was they were among the finest pages in the book, and we'd said we wanted to take our time with them, though maybe that was just something we'd said. Maybe we weren't ready to go home yet, to face the fact that we had failed to find her, that she was gone from our translations, and probably our lives.

Gingerly, I opened my laptop. On the left half of my screen I arranged Irena's original file. On the right, Alexis's translation.

Alexis had persuaded everyone but me to write an op-ed in Irena's name, but surely they hadn't succumbed to her vile influence so totally that they would approve of infidelities in Irena's magnum opus—and if they disapproved of those, perhaps they could still be persuaded never to send out their counterfeit plea.

I had a hunch that Chloe might have been helping her new best friend to cover up her crimes, so I began with the chapters Chloe had been put in charge of proofreading on the day Irena hadn't won the Nobel Prize.

In those chapters, Amália's parents are driving her and her sister Celeste to Praia da Marinha when they are hit by a drunk truck driver. Celeste flies through the window, and her small body shatters into a hundred pieces while their car catches fire. Their father is trapped in the driver's seat, half consumed by flames, and Amália, only nine years old, is in shock. Her mother gets out of the car and starts picking up the pieces of Amália's sister from the road. Amália sees an arm, or part of one, and then she sees her sister's gold-brown hair.

But Alexis's translation was missing that chapter. I scrolled up and down several times. Chloe was an amazing close reader, and a fantastic editor—in fact, she moonlighted as an editor for an academic press in Vauvert when she wasn't too busy with Irena. There was no way it could have escaped her that an entire chapter of *Grey Eminence* was missing from the English.

I skipped to the next reference to Celeste. In the chapter that is supposed to follow the car crash, Alexis had added two sentences. "One day in July," she had written, "the whole family was on the road when their car was struck by a drunk driver. Amália's sister, alas, did not survive."

Alas!

I had it, I realized. I had my proof. I felt both overwhelmed by loathing and like a huge weight had been lifted off my shoulders. I couldn't wait to expose her while also announcing her imminent, honor-restoring demise.

The morning passed. Petra stirred, and I brought her toast with jam for breakfast. Freddie came out of his room, rubbing his eyes, reciting Emily Dickinson:

> Ashes denote that fire was;
> Respect the grayest pile
> For the departed creature's sake
> That hovered there awhile.

When Petra didn't react, I took the opportunity to change the subject. I suggested that we proofread our op-eds before taking any further steps, and they both agreed.

But there was still no sign of Alexis. I grew nervous not because of the duel but because I wondered whether the idea of a duel might not elicit mixed reactions, even if I knew they'd be on my side about Alexis's translation. I stepped out of the room again and made some coffee.

When I returned with Irena's small ceramic pot and two cups I found Ostap and Renata at the piano performing Chopin's Polish songs. When they were done, I told them we had decided not to send our op-ed yet. They agreed: It was essential to be careful, they said. They drank the coffee I had intended for Freddie and me. I made more coffee.

Chloe came down, and after going next door to check on her adoptive grandfather, who was fine, she taught us to greet each other in Wolof—not the more
widespread Arabic greeting she'd taught Pan Igor, but greetings that were actually in the indigenous language her own father had spoken at home.

"Mbaa yaa ngi ci jàmm?" Ostap and Renata asked, which meant, Are you in
peace? To which Chloe and Petra responded, "Jàmm rekk," which meant, Nothing
but peace.

"Mbaa yaa ngi ci jàmm?" Freddie asked me.

"Jàmm rekk," I said. In the glow of our togetherness, I almost started to think
that we *would* be in peace. That things might still turn out okay, that not all was
lost, that although I hadn't managed to prevent the act itself, it might still be
possible to reverse it, or to keep it a secret, and if so, to call off the duel, to retract
my challenge, to proceed as we had always done: finish the novel, send it to our
editors, go home. There was no real reason to believe Irena wouldn't eventually
return.

Having given my coffee to Chloe, I went back into the kitchen a third time.
There I was greeted by Quercus, perched on the towel rack, crunching on something. It took me a moment to process what I saw. Then, in abject horror, I froze.

Quercus's innocent red beak contained the telltale russety emerald shape of
the extremely endangered, in fact almost extinct, *Buprestis splendens* that Leszek
had been so desperate to find. I took action: I shouted and lunged forward, letting
go of my heavy Bolesławiec mug, which struck the floor and became blue enamel
flakes and thick, deadly-looking shards, but Quercus took flight and eluded me,
and by the time I'd caught up with him again, the beetle was gone.

"Oh no!" I cried. Freddie came loping up and squeezed my shoulder. "How
could I have let this happen?" I wailed, ignoring him. "Leszek's beetle. He's—
he's been swallowed!"

Petra and Renata came in, too. The refrigerator chirped.

"It's not your fault," Petra said.

"It's no one's fault," Renata said.

"Don't you care?" I shouted. "Doesn't it matter to you that what might have
been the only *Buprestis splendens* left in the entire world was just devoured by
our parrot?"

"He's more than just a parrot," said Chloe.

"Who even are you?" I shrieked at her accusingly, and Chloe recoiled, and Freddie leaned back against the counter.

"It makes you think," he said. "If we can forgive a parrot its natural impulse to consume . . ."

"What?" snapped Chloe. Her body was as rigid as a board. "If that, then what? Are you saying we should just pat ourselves on the backs for cutting down the forests?"

"How would you react if it was Irena?" I shrieked, as though echoing Chloe, although the fact of the matter was I hadn't fully understood what she'd said. What had happened was obviously my fault: I had heroically rescued Quercus only to be forced to watch him—an invasive species, like me, maybe—extinguish the last of the splendid—native—*Buprestis*, a forest jewel that might—would?— never glimmer again.

Schulz appeared in the doorway. Pavel was standing behind him with his hand on Schulz's waist. At another kind of summit, I might have been intrigued.

Instead, I blurted, "Alexis deleted a huge section of Chapter Ten! The car accident. She just deleted it!"

For a moment, I felt like I was finally on the path to victory. I felt comfortable, waiting for them to turn on her. But then Chloe took a step forward, standing very straight, too straight, and said, "That's because Irena stole that story."

I stared at her. "What are you talking about?"

"That time she came to Paris, when she messaged me to get together, just the two of us. At the time I was so flattered, and honored, and super happy, so it was relatively easy for her to get me to go into every detail of what happened—my dad's burns, how my mom left me there in the car to wander out onto the highway for Céline's head. The fact that some parts of her body were never found. That's my story. That was my sister."

Tears were rolling down her cheeks. I stared at her, at her tear tracks, then spun around to throw up in the sink. Uselessly, Freddie gathered my hair as he usually did during sex, just more gently, and I thought that probably even the sex would be sad now. Alexis put her arm around Chloe's baby-pink-swathed shoulders. Finally Petra said, "I already sent that section to my editor, of course, but I'll make sure they cut it, too, if you want, Chloe."

"Me too," said Renata.

"Me too," said Ostap.

There was another long hug, but this time, I wasn't a part of it. I didn't know what to do, what to think. I didn't know what to believe. There was a knock at the door, and I assumed it must be Leszek, which snapped me out of my stupor, adding to the already almost unbearable burden of my guilt. I braced myself, knowing how devastated he'd be.

But then Petra opened the door to Barbara and Mackenzie. Quercus said, "Cześć," and Barbara said, "Cześć," and Mackenzie looked at Barbara in disdain and sat down on the chaise longue and began tapping at her phone.

"Well," Barbara said to everyone, "I'm glad to see everyone is safe and sound! Or mostly, anyway," she qualified, with a glance at Ostap. "The tornado did quite a bit of damage to the village."

"Why the fuck are you here?" I said.

"Emi!" said Alexis.

Chloe sniffled and wiped her face with the sleeve of her delicate sweater, which had mauve satin ribbons that crossed over her back. She looked at Barbara. "Why *are* you here, though?"

"No one was killed," Petra said. "Right?"

"I don't know," said Barbara. "I'm here to retrieve some of what Irena stole from the Czartoryski Museum."

"Wait," Mackenzie said as she picked up a phone we hadn't realized was ringing and darted into the kitchen. If she had left the room in the interest of privacy, however, she had failed to go far enough. We heard her say, "Yes, now, Stoczek Street, it's the weird-looking house with the curvy sides, taller than all the other ones, light-colored wood. You can't miss it. It's like it landed from a different planet. It'll be on your right."

"Who is she talking to?" asked Schulz.

"Frank," said Barbara.

"Frank?!" I coughed.

"The cameraman," Petra said softly. "He came to your party."

"That was being filmed?!"

"What did Irena steal from the Czartoryski Museum?" asked Chloe before I could get an answer. I couldn't tell from her tone whether she was considering believing Barbara or not.

"Well, I'm surprised you never thought to check the chests," Barbara said. "I mean before Mackenzie told you. But then—well, the rest of it's right here in plain sight. The old armaments and armor, that snake table there, the alabaster one."

"How could you know all this?" asked Ostap. "If we've never heard a word about it."

"What happened here?" Barbara said, pointing at his eye patch and his monocle in turn.

"We had sex on top of my glasses," Ostap said simply, squeezing the plump upper arm of his paramour, whose face betrayed a certain mortification. So she had lied.

"We've always been Irena's closest confidants," Petra said, ignoring them. "At least, we always were."

"Well," said Barbara. She sat down in the barrel chair with the torn orange cover. "Last summer, I was in Kraków for an awards ceremony where Irena and I were both being honored. As generally happens, the ceremony went on and on. By the way, do you have any coffee you could spare? The stuff at the Booted Eagle is undrinkable."

She was addressing Pavel, and Pavel got up and disappeared.

"Anyway, like I was saying. The ceremony went on and on. Finally we got to the part with the drinks. Everyone was sort of milling about, toasting and complaining about the hors d'oeuvres, when out of the blue Irena just started *berating* Bogdan for something, for not ironing the right dress or the right shirt or something along those lines, and he just stood there and said nothing, but you could see he was embarrassed because a lot of their friends were there, and who knows what they did behind closed doors, but she didn't ever let her guard down like that when they were out."

Pavel returned with a tray that held coffee, cream, and sugar and presented it to her.

"Is this a vegetable milk?" asked Barbara.

Pavel shook his head, looking worried.

"Oh, thank God. Anyway. So Bogdan seemed to be under a lot of pressure because he just sank into a chair at the back of the room and drank about half a bottle of Wyborowa while she was schmoozing with the press, and at some point when everyone was talking about him and wondering what was going on, *I* actually went over there because I wanted to see that he was all right. Of course I did not intend to pry any secrets out of him."

"Of course you didn't," I muttered. Chloe suppressed a laugh, which shocked me, but I couldn't bring myself to look at her. She had lost a sister I never even knew existed. Where the fuck had I been?

"But Bogdan *needed* to talk. He just flat out told me that he had been living with a terrible secret all these years he had been with Irena. That the 1987 thefts had been her doing! That she had confessed it to him because they'd confessed everything to each other when they were newlyweds. She had some sort of justification for it, something *bizarre* like some inexplicable opposition to *art*, and even mummies, and he had gone along with it, but it had nagged at him—"

"Mummies?" Freddie had interrupted her.

"Mummies," Barbara confirmed. "That's what's in the chests."

"The canopic jars!" cried Petra, looking at Renata, whose hand was over her mouth.

"At any rate he had tried to agree with the stance she had taken, whatever it was, but in the end he just wasn't able to. After a while I stopped being able to understand what he was saying. He kept saying 'role model,' just that phrase, 'role model' over and over again. But I vowed to try to convince her, partly for his sake and partly for the sake of the nation of Poland, to return the stolen goods. I was going to offer to help her. Start by taking in a little bit of loot, see how it felt." She gestured at her oversize suitcase, which was still standing like a sentry at the far front window.

"Jesus," Pavel said, kicking one of the barrel chairs. "Ira. Goddammit."

"What else is stolen?" asked Schulz.

"The indecipherable carpet?" Chloe asked, and I realized they all believed what Barbara was saying. Then I remembered what Leszek had said that first day we had spoken at the cemetery: that in high school, Irena had stolen a postcard.

"Hey, Leszek," I messaged. "That postcard that Irena stole, was it valuable?"

"One of the only things that isn't stolen is the carpet," Barbara corrected Chloe. "You just think it's indecipherable because of context. Because nothing in this room makes sense. And you assume it's ancient and from elsewhere. But look closely, and you'll see it's only Bolesław Leśmian."

I felt my eyes bulging as I got down on my hands and knees on the carpet, still caked with dried mud, then backed away, then stood on the chaise longue staring down at it. Sure enough, it was one of the two untranslatable Polish poets Irena had given us license to translate, a stanza that read:

> Świat się trwali, ale tak niepewnie! . . .
> Drzewa szumią, ale pozadrzewnie! . . .
> A nad borem, nad dalekim borem
> Bóg porusza wichrem i przestworem.

I was sounding it out in my head when I heard the dread sound of Alexis, who had come down the stairs without my noticing. She opened the front door, and in walked the grizzled man from my "party," lugging two black cases of equipment. Staring at them, I lost my balance and fell onto the stanza's start, hitting my head against the hard base of the sofa.

It felt like she had already defeated me in our duel. Petra and Freddie and Chloe rushed toward me while the rest of them fixated on Frank, whom Barbara greeted as warmly as she had Quercus and then introduced to me in basic English: "This is Frank. He works with Mackenzie. He will record Alexis as she opens the chests."

"What?" I screamed, although my scream was half muffled by Freddie's flannel-covered arms. "Me estás jodiendo. You've got to be kidding, Alexis."

Alexis raised an eyebrow at me. "You know, I knew all along about the carpet. I just didn't know you didn't know."

"You didn't know about the carpet, you piece of—"

"But I did," said Alexis. "I even translated it because I knew it would make Irena happy:

> The world persists, but insecurely! . . .
> The rustling trees grow ultratreely! . . .
> And across the coniferous distance
> God moves in whirlwind and expanse."

"Wow!" said Chloe.

"I thought Irena said that you were not allowed to translate Leśmian?" asked Freddie.

"No," said Chloe. "She said Leśmian was untranslatable. Leśmian and Białoszewski. She said she didn't mind if we translated those two, but that both of them were also untranslatable."

I tried to imagine what possible response there could be to Alexis's off-handed admission that she, unlike the rest of us, or at least unlike me, had translated an untranslatable. There was something obscene about it. If Leśmian was in English, courtesy of *Alexis*, then what did "untranslatable" even mean?

I got a message from Leszek. "Priceless," it said. Then another: "It was the first postcard ever sent in Esperanto, written by Zamenhof himself." Then another: "Is everyone all right?"

But Alexis had already moved on to her next site of havoc, followed by Frank and his huge camera.

"In the middle of nowhere," Mackenzie was muttering, pacing between the fireplace and Our Lady of Literature. "In the middle of nowhere, in a town time forgot. In the middle of nowhere. Europe's most infamous author has hidden some of the greatest artifacts of the ancient world the world has ever— dammit! Some of the greatest—"

"Ready to roll," Frank called to her.

Alexis was kneeling in front of the chests, holding up three large brass keys and grinning like she was at an Arkansas beauty pageant.[67]

"Wait," she said. "Do I say anything?"

"No!" Mackenzie said. "I say everything."

"Got it," said Alexis.

"And, go," said Frank.

"Oh," said Alexis. "I thought you were going to say, 'Action.'"

Frank groaned and extricated his face from the viewfinder.

"Fine," he said. He reinserted his face. "Action."

Still grinning, Alexis inserted a key into the middle chest. I held my breath. What if there really was a mummy inside? What if that was the true reason Petra had been visited by all those ghosts? Not the logging—had Leszek even meant that, or had it been a joke?—but the fact that all along, three kidnapped corpses had been living in our living room?

---

67   Fuck you, Emilia Martini (Trans.).

"It's empty!" Alexis announced.

"Open the other ones, then," said Barbara, standing on a chair she had brought in from the winter garden so that she could see.

Alexis opened the chest on the right.

"This one's empty, too."

Ostap gave a loud sigh of relief. "Phew! For a second there—"

But Alexis was opening the left chest. We held our breath.

Alexis turned to the camera. She grinned.

"Empty," she said.

"Goddammit, Mackenzie," said the cameraman. "I left my wife in Mallorca for this." He continued muttering as he began packing up, but I could no longer understand what he was saying.

"Wait," said Mackenzie. She looked at Alexis with the same pleading kitten face Alexis always used on us.

"Alexis," said Pavel.

"What are you thinking?" I said in unison with him. He looked startled.

"Why not?" Alexis said.

"What are you talking about?" I said. A gelatinous foreboding was coloring the room.

"Nothing," said Alexis. "Mackenzie and I had just talked about how maybe I could read Irena's plea on behalf of the forest on camera. For the news."

"No!" I cried, but none of them seemed to hear me.

"Wait," said Petra, and I thought she might finally say out loud that she agreed with me. She was still standing over by the chests, but she was bending down over the pile of old boards. "Isn't this something?"

She turned over the top board and held it up to us. It was a portrait of a woman.

"What is that?" Ostap asked Renata. Alexis and Mackenzie were whispering beside me. Schulz and Pavel and Chloe came closer, drawn to the woman on the old board, and I moved closer, too.

"I think it's a Fayum portrait," she said, tiptoeing toward it as if afraid to wake the painted woman up. "It would have been attached to a mummy. They're very rare. Very few of them survived." She pointed at the pile, tallying. "This could be half of all that's left."

I went to stand in between Petra and Renata. The woman on the board was gorgeous. She had a long, sweet face, with big dark eyes and beautiful thick black eyebrows, and she was wearing pearl and obsidian earrings and a collar that looked like it was made of gold. There was no question that she was from a different, ancient world. Which meant that there was no question that Irena had taken her, and the missing mummies, and probably everything else.

"Wait!" I said. "I know where the mummies are."

Everyone turned to me, yet I didn't feel Alexis's evil eyes on my skin.

As if reading my mind, Chloe said, almost apologetically, "Alexis and Mackenzie and the cameraman went upstairs to her room to record 'Irena's' plea."

"Fuck!" I screamed. I started up the stairs, but Freddie grabbed me. "What the fuck?" I pushed him, hard, wresting my forearm from his grasp.

He blinked at me, from the base of the staircase, and for just a second I felt sorry, and I couldn't take my eyes off his. Then he turned and walked away, down the floral runner rug that led into his bedroom.

"What about the mummies?" Renata asked. "What happened to them?"

"They're in Egypt," I sighed. "Bogdan took them back."

"Motherfucker," said Barbara. She kicked over her empty suitcase, flung back the top and began filling it with instruments and figurines, whatever was on the nearest table. She stomped across the room and took the top Fayum portrait. Then she wheeled the half-filled suitcase into Schulz's room. I followed her. I saw her step up onto my chair and then onto our dining table. I watched as she marred our table with her stupid kitten heels.

"Could you give me a hand?" she asked, and I *did* it. I stepped up onto the table, and I helped Barbara hold the Czech chandelier as she unhooked its garlands of shinbones and thigh bones and skulls. They clattered as we lowered them into her suitcase. We tried to get it zipped up—she even crouched on top of it—but we couldn't, so when she stormed out of Irena's house, she was trailing a single tentacle of phalanges and metacarpals, a radius, and an ulna.

I closed the door behind her. When I turned around, in a daze, Alexis was spiraling down the staircase holding my invitation in her hand.

"You can't be serious," she said, not looking up from the page, but I knew she was talking to me.

"I'm dead serious," I said. I was surprised I wasn't nervous anymore. I was relishing the tautness of this new link between me and Alexis. The closer she was, the easier it might be for me to destroy her.

"She wants us to fight a duel," Alexis said, still halfway to the second floor.

I still thought they might protest—that duels in the Anthropocene were unthinkable, and I would have to explain that I had thought of it, and that therefore they were not unthinkable. Even in the Anthropocene, I would say, there could still be such a thing as honor. Maybe most things were going the way of the dodo, I'd say, but some of them we can still save, especially the ones that are fully under our control, like words and concepts, and I refuse to let Alexis get away with all these crimes against Irena—with the possible exception of the part Irena borrowed from Chloe without Chloe's permission—and by extension, against all authors and even against translators. Even against us.

But all Petra said was, "We'd need to go over the rules."

Alexis's jaw dropped. Her knuckles were even whiter than usual where she was gripping the railing.

"Are you talking about fencing?" Chloe asked me.

"Nope," I said.

"You mean Pan Igor's Russian revolvers?" Schulz asked warily.

I nodded.

"Fine," said Petra. "Now would be the moment for a sacrifice. To Perun. He's the most powerful god in the ancient Slavic pantheon, and we are almost out of time: The book will be done today or tomorrow. Alexis, choose your second."

"Chloe," said Alexis, and my excitement waned. Chloe didn't even look at me before accepting.

"Chloe," repeated Petra. "You and Alexis will spend tonight at the Booted Eagle Hotel."

"Why?" asked Chloe.

"The combatants can't see each other beforehand," said Petra, as though it should have been obvious. "It's bad luck."

"It's not a wedding," said Alexis.

"It's like a mystical divorce," said Chloe.

"Renata," I said.

As she looked up, Renata lost control of her knitting needles and jammed the left one into her right hand. In her lap lay most of a very small hat, for a baby or an animal.

"It seems like Petra is going to be our umpire," I told her. "So maybe you could be my second?" She stared back at me blankly, rubbing her hand. If she said no, I thought, not without panic, I'd be forced to appoint one of the men.

But as she picked up her little hat and started working the needles again, she nodded.

"What's going on?" asked Mackenzie from the stairs, in English, maybe sensing some sea change in our entourage. Frank went around her and knelt by his big black equipment cases by the door.

"Nothing," Alexis and I said in unison.

"Great," said Petra, in Polish. She went up to Alexis and pried the paper from her hand. "We'll all meet at six thirty sharp in front of the strict reserve. Chloe and Renata will carry the weapons. Ostap will have the first aid kit."

"But he's missing an eye!" cried Alexis. Petra shrugged.

"I'll have no part in this," Freddie said. He came around and leaned his shoulder against the doorway, looked at me. A tiny, childish part of me wanted him to implore me not to go through with it, if only to strengthen my resolve. But I could see that he was hurt—that I had hurt him—and all he said was, "I'm going home."

"See you guys later, then," called Mackenzie in English from the door.

"Bye," said Alexis, without turning.

"Fine," said Petra, while I was envisioning Freddie's joyful and then sexual reunion with his hideous wife. "Chloe and Renata will load the weapons together. They will place one bullet in each of the guns. Emi and Alexis will have one shot each, to be fired any time after Schulz has counted to three."

"On three or after three?" asked Alexis.

"Does it matter?" asked Pavel, who had drifted downstairs by now, too.

"It would matter to you if you were part of this," Chloe snapped at him.

"On three," said Petra. "You can rely on Schulz to count it evenly, and you can fire on three."

"How far apart are they supposed to stand?" Renata asked.

Petra put on her reading glasses and reached for her phone. There was a long pause as Petra searched for the answer to this question, until Schulz said, "Twenty paces."

Petra turned the page of her notebook. "Twenty paces."

"Twenty paces each, or twenty paces total?" asked Alexis.

"You meet and stand back-to-back and then each walk twenty paces," said Petra carefully, like she was teaching a class of kindergarteners how to be polite or recycle.

"This is a cult," said Freddie. "Don't you see that? Don't any of you see that? How ridiculous this is?"

"What if it's foggy," I said, as it suddenly occurred to me, "like it often is in the morning, and we can't see anything?"

"I guess we'll keep our fingers crossed for good weather," Alexis said in her most nasal voice. I couldn't look at her, but I could picture her smug, superior face. It was all I could do not to lunge at her again. I told myself I just had to wait until morning, when it could all be done.

"Are we still on for yoga later?" Pavel asked Alexis, who gave a vigorous nod.

"I'm in," said Chloe. Starting toward the stairs, she added, "Are we going to try and wrap the book today?"

"Sure," I said and followed her.

CHAPTER TWENTY-SEVEN

On the morning of the duel and the day after we finished translating *Grey Eminence*, I woke up without knowing what day it was, feeling cozy in my own bed. I stretched like a cat, and from my window, I saw a delicious cloud of dots rise and sway from side to side. It was an angular sway, maybe more like a swerve, starlings in a murmuration, I realized, and I rolled over onto my belly and buried my head in soft flannel. Being in my own bed instead of Freddie's reminded me of a time when we were all in unison, ourselves but inextricably linked, and that memory gave me the strength to think that something good was bound to happen soon, that I had right on my side, after all, and justice, and justice would be bound to bring Irena back—it had to. Only when I turned my head, and a single ray of light came glancing in across the low-pile carpet, did it dawn on me: She had broken everything, and I was probably about to die.[68]

I didn't want to die, and when it came down to it, I didn't really want to kill, but some force was urging me indefensibly on. Maybe it wasn't translation. Maybe it had more to do with blood or lust or Białowieża. Whatever the case, I got up.

I smoked a cigarette and noticed my hands were shaking. I remembered that Alexis wasn't there. I went out and opened the door to her room and stepped on the switch for her floor lamp. I picked up and held each of the things she kept by the side of her bed: a shiny copper tube of hand cream, a couple of undiscarded

---

68   Whether she means me or Irena here it is impossible to say; per her own "philosophy" of refusing to improve upon an author's original, I have kept this one minor ambiguity in (Trans.).

cotton rounds, frayed and blood-orange, as though my palm were bleeding. A wrinkled copy of *Lena* in English.

I opened her copy of *Lena* and saw that it was signed by both her and Irena, dedicated to someone named Sam. Who was Sam? The intrusion of some prior, other life of Alexis's set off the faintest tenderness somewhere inside me, but I squelched it. There was a packet of 2Fast2Thin pills and a mug with a green ring that would have been sickening on any other day. There was a keychain with an unlikely brown teddy bear holding a red heart that said, in tiny letters, I LUV U.[69]

I turned on the water in the glass case in the center of her room. Steam started to rise and to billow, and I undid the buttons of my pajama top and shrugged it off my shoulders and onto the shiny wood floor. I stepped onto her bath mat and out of my slippers and pushed down my pants and underwear. I showered, learning at last how it felt to stand warm and naked in the center of a room, and I felt calm, like I was a fish in an aquarium with nowhere to go but around.

Even enveloped in the steam of her shower, however, the adrenaline was making my fingers hurt, and I couldn't see how I'd be able to pull a trigger, although I would—I knew I would; I never doubted that.

I went back to my room. I didn't spend too much time in front of the mirror. I did not crave a beautiful demise. For the first time in my life, I didn't care

---

69   At this point it would be natural for the reader to wonder why I agreed to translate this book. My editor refused to let me have an afterword, as did this author, so I will talk about it here since not even my editor's assistant is reading the footnotes at this point.

The most pressing thing was that if I hadn't agreed to translate *Amadou*, someone else would have. Any translator (including this author) will tell you that one of the primary tenets of translation is to keep friends close and enemies closer. By translating *Amadou*, I was able to reclaim my identity as not 100 percent evil.

Also, maybe, as Robert Frost said, poetry is what gets lost in translation. People have interpreted that phrase to mean translation is necessarily flawed and flawing, but I understand it in a different way. To me, poetry is concision, refinement—the effect of considerable loss. Lose, from any page that's filled with words, all the ones that do not matter, and you may find a kind of poem.

I'd like to think I've made at least a little of that contribution here. Not to say that this is poetry—it obviously isn't—but I do believe or dare to hope I have improved it. Yes, I have deleted certain scenes. But as you can see right here, and everywhere, I have not acted in the interest of self-preservation. I have acted, always, in the best interests of my ideal reader: you (Trans.).

how I looked. I put on an ordinary brown sweater, jeans, and one of Bogdan's coats. I checked to make sure my amadou amulet was still in my wallet, then tucked my wallet in my pocket and went downstairs. Everyone was sitting in the living room except for Chloe and Alexis and Freddie, as well as Pavel, who stumbled out of Irena's room still buttoning up his shirt as I reached the third step from the bottom. I prayed. The others rose, and without exchanging any words, we went outside.

Past the door it was dazzling. The first snow of that year had fallen overnight, a foot of it or more, fresh and crisp and like nothing I had ever seen in real life. I thought that if I did die that morning, I'd die having lost everyone I'd ever loved but having seen everything I'd ever wanted to see in the world, having experienced so much more than I deserved. All around us it was silent, which made every motion we made as we approached the strict reserve a sacred motion. I could feel us transforming, and I felt that just as the landscape had been reborn in the snow, whoever didn't die in the duel would rise like the mythical żar-ptak, knowing the ultimate secret—the secret of this cleanness and this crystal world, and the secret of its shadow.

When we reached the big field, the air was so clear it was almost painful to take in the sweep of the trees. Chloe and Alexis came up behind us, and I couldn't look, so I took off my gloves and focused on the gun that was wavering over the snow, floating my direction, already barely in my second's hand when I grabbed it. My hands were sweating. I told myself to get a grip, but I couldn't; I couldn't get a grip.

Alexis started off for the middle of the field, and I followed. I kept my eyes on the ground and took one step with my left foot and watched my shoe tamp down the snow for a split second before shattering its invisible crust, sinking and then rising carrying crystals with it that looked like miniature ephemeral diamonds, and everything seemed so small and so significant, so filled with purpose. Then we stopped.

Alexis turned away from me, showing me her dark Irena-imitating hair until I turned away from her. Even facing the opposite direction, I could smell her yuzu perfume, and some new fragrance, too, maybe the shampoo at the Booted Eagle, or something else, something like rosemary, and I could feel the dawn straining to fully grasp us, to break through our almost-conjoined figure, the sliver of distance between our backs.

Out of the corner of my eye I could see Schulz coming toward us, and Ostap, with his little first aid kit, and Petra, with her hands over her ever-so-slightly swollen belly, and Schulz said, "Are you sure?"

I looked to my right as Alexis turned her fake-Irena-head left, and we were so close we could have kissed, and I wanted to kiss her, to force my tongue into her mouth, but then she nodded, grim and determined, and I turned away from her again, and Petra said, "Walk."

Glittering crystalline rainbows extended in every direction, while gentle gold beams swept between the softened trees that sparkled and beckoned and forbade. I was approaching a stark towering ash that looked almost exactly like Irena as we'd seen her in September. How had I never noticed it before?

A white-backed woodpecker investigated all that underlay the snow, bobbing its scarlet cap; a willow warbler that ought to have departed by now for Tanzania hopped from branch to branch flicking the snow off a spruce with its beak. I immediately lost track of how many steps I had taken and how many I had left. I just kept walking, taking ever-smaller steps. The gun was in my right hand. It dangled from my trigger finger the way a shopping bag with tomatoes in it might. I heard the guttural trill of a boreal owl.

"Stop," said Schulz, and I stopped. I stood at the very edge of the forest. Shouldering the snow, the ferns were so beautiful they seemed eternal.

I was sure I could not turn to face Alexis, that I would not be able to point my gun at her or even raise it from the snow on the ground. But from inside the forest I heard a crackling, and my eyes darted up, and I hoped I would see Freddie, and my mind flooded with gratitude, gratitude that he hadn't yet found his way back to Bogdana, who would eventually cause him to lose the physical memory of me, but instead I saw Leshy, reduced to the size of a pine marten, here to protect us or protect the forest from us or just to watch us, to be able to tell Irena what had happened in case one or both or all of us perished in the snow. I was struck by a feeling of pride: I was here to defend Our Author's honor, and perhaps by extension, my own.

Petra was counting now, and she said, "One," and I turned around, and her voice was a little bit unsteady, but still she said, "Two," and I fixed my gaze on Alexis's dark and shimmering head, and as Petra's lips rounded and protruded to launch an uncertain pronouncement of the magic word that might signify the end of us, I looked up, and it was infinite, it was a light blue, pure, with many other colors in it, every feeling, every depth. It did not have a temperature. It sounded like the glaciers of Patagonia that I had always admired on TV; in the distance the tiny, all-involving impact of a droplet of water, glacial, but not anymore, now an active participant in the rest of the world, and I understood that there were no exceptions, that everything always had to become a part of everything, that destiny was loss, but also luster, and as I looked into the blue, I released my shoulders, and my jaw relaxed, and I was gripped by an urge to inscribe our existence, the existence and significance of us as translators, how we mattered, and how we dissolved, which came to the same, like the horizon at sea. I was soothed, and I raised the soothing instrument in my hand, and as Petra was saying, "Three," and my fingers were curling back into my hand, I saw a row of Caterpillars making their way into the strict reserve, followed by some other large vehicle that bore on its roof a giant satellite, and I fired, and Alexis fired, too.

CHAPTER TWENTY-EIGHT

Then it was over, and everyone but me agreed to head into the strict reserve. Both of us had missed, Alexis intentionally, firing into the forest,[70] an outrageous offense that no one but me seemed to register. Nobody but me seemed to care. They all insisted it was over, despite nothing having changed. They began moving away from me, but Schulz ran back, and for a second I thought he might tell me that he was on my side, that we would redo the duel, just later, once the forest had been saved, but instead, he reached down for my gun.

After a long time that was scored by the snow-muffled din of chants and chainsaws, I crawled a little ways on hands and knees, then looked around in the brighter sunshine, then picked myself up and went home. It was going to be my first time inside her house alone, and I tried to think what I could do with that before the rest of them returned. I could just take a nap, I thought. I could do it in anyone's bedroom. I could wash the moldy mug on Alexis's bedside table, or I could smash it, leave the pieces all over her floor. I could go out on Petra's and Renata's balcony and try to discern the border between Belarus and Poland, visualize that invisible line. I could do anything. But that surfeit of possibilities only pushed me closer to a point of no return that I had always known existed but never really sensed the nearness of before.

---

70 See next page (Trans.).

Nothing had changed. My great solution to Alexis's distortions had failed. She had shot an innocent tree.[71]

I found a huge beige van parked in Irena's driveway, blocking the sidewalk and a third of the street. I pressed my face against a window. There was nothing inside, and no driver. I checked Irena's secret Instagram. She had posted:

---

71 *If* I had agreed to fight a duel with this author, which *obviously* I wouldn't, then I am sure I would have fired into the air, and not *at the forest*, given that, like everyone else, I wanted to protect rather than abuse the trees and their various wild associates. As to my own motivations to fight such a hypothetical duel, perhaps there was something so powerful about the forest itself—so powerful and so violent—that a duel would make sense to transplants who'd been trapped there for some extended period, say, seven weeks. Perhaps I simply wanted to make Emi be my friend. Perhaps I never understood why she felt as strongly as she did about me, and even after reading this account, I still don't. But obviously none of us would have agreed to fight a duel, and Irena is fine (Trans.).

Leave Lena.

November 3

Leave Lena? Did she mean her breakout novel *Lena*? The caption was in Polish, but the image itself featured Alexis's language, which chilled me. Could Irena be in Alexis's country? But if so, why?

There was no one in the house but the murderous Quercus, who cocked his head when he saw me and half chirped, "Cześć!" I poured him a teacup of water and set it on the mantel. I lay all the frames face down. Then I locked myself inside Irena's office.

Hell had frozen over. It was time for me to act.

The first two times we'd gotten into her computer, we'd turned up nothing, or what amounted to nothing. The last time, typing my challenge to Alexis, I hadn't even had the energy to try. Now I quickly checked her email and, seeing no new messages of any interest, began to go through every application she had. I went through her podcasts, her PowerPoints, even her system preferences. I opened Photo Booth and took a picture of myself, and behind and around me, her red womb chair, and farther back, her books.

I thought for a moment, and then, for want of a better idea, I went back over the files we hadn't bothered with before: the several spreadsheets (nothing of interest), the downloads (nothing of interest), the photos (surprisingly, nothing—just a couple of snapshots that showed the old her and Bogdan; the vague outline of a rhinoceros, black on a brown background, titled "Coliboaia," which turned out to be a cave in Romania; and a black-and-white picture of children on a dirty snowy hillock, all looking up at an approaching plane). I opened "Taxes." Neither "filed" nor "future" contained anything other than documents and PDFs pertaining to her taxes. "Deductions," however, was protected by a password that was no permutation of Pavel's name.

I tried all the words I could think of that were connected with *Grey Eminence*: "amadou," "Amália," "Nikau," "art," "extinction," "sex." I tried all the words I could think of that were connected with ГОДЪ and *Matsuura* and *Pompeii Catalog*. I tried "Czartoryski," "breakdown," "Białowieża," "Bogdan." I tried "Putin." I tried "Petra," "Renata," Ostap," "Schulz," and "Chloe" and "Alexis." I even tried my own name, knowing perfectly well that my name wouldn't be Irena's password. I tried "amadou" again in case I'd misspelled it and then lay down on the floor among her books and papers—all her papers were just pages from short stories by Bruno Schulz, in different fonts, with occasional illustrations—and the desk lamp we had righted but never removed from the floor, and I shut my eyes and tried to remember or invoke her, tried to bring her back.

In the dark, she came back to me in swirls, her black hair long and wild and luminous, almost on fire, while the rest of her was snow-white, spinning, around and around to a Belarusian myatselitsa, and I thought about the impossible-to-translate poet Miron Białoszewski, wondering whether Alexis had translated him, too. I thought about the poem "My bottomless ode to joy," which ends with:

> szara naga jama[72]
> szara naga jama
> sza-ra- na-ga- ja-ma
> szaranagajama.

The word "szara" means gray, as in *Grey Eminence*: *Szara eminencja*. The word "naga" means naked. The word "jama" means hole or pit or cavity or cave or burrow or even ventricle. Which could be:

> bare gray pit
> bare gray pit
> baregraypit

Without the third line, because each word in English[73] takes up only one syllable, broaching no division, and "naked grayish burrow" doesn't pack any punch, so although poetry itself is not untranslatable, twirling and spiraling might be, and with my eyes still closed I saw Irena dancing, chanting: szaranagajama, szaranaga-jama, szaranagajama, and it has been said by many that this is the closest Polish can come to Japanese—"sharanagayama" sounds like Japanese to Poles—and with Irena still twirling, I leaped up and typed *szaranagajama* into her computer—and I was in.

"Deductions" contained two subfolders. The first was titled "To Mama." I clicked on it. It contained two documents. One was called "adres" and was just

---

72   Pronounced "shara naga yama" (Trans.).

73   The Spanish examples of impossibility given by the author here are not especially illuminating, so I have substituted my own (Trans.).

the address of someone named Katarzyna Mori, 365-1262, Tanaka Harunacho, Sakyo-ku Kyoto-shi, Kyoto, 606-8234, Japan. Underneath the address was a character that looked like a fraction of a forest:

THE OTHER DOCUMENT was called "To Mama" again. It was a sequence of forty longish letters from Our Author to her mother, each written on a November 3. The letters began in 1978 and ended in 2017—November 3, 2017, the day of my duel with Alexis, and yet, how could Irena have written her mother a letter on her computer that day? What if, I thought, my throat tightening, she hadn't actually left us—what if she had been here all along?

But that was impossible, I assured myself. We would have seen her. We would have sensed that she was there.

At the very least, she would have visited her father. She would have retrieved some of her things.

I read the first letter. Irena was just turning nine. She describes the confusion of waking up from a nightmare about a huge shaggy monster chasing her into a river and pushing her down until she was all the way under the riverbed, stuck in some other world, and she cried out for her mother, who had always come, only to be met with stillness and silence as the darkness of the room congealed and became suffocating, terrifying, until finally she screwed up her courage and went out into the enormous-seeming house (in hindsight, quite modest, not the house where her father lived now). She began to search for her, everywhere, in the cupboard, in the cabinets, in the shower, on the sideboard—only to realize, eventually, that her mother wasn't there.

It is hard to describe how I felt as I was reading "To Mama." In hindsight, I think it was what made me capable of losing you, Irena—experiencing that grief through you, that loss of everything, and finding myself still intact. All hollowed out, but whole.

I had always maintained that *Grey Eminence* was a masterpiece. But I felt as I read those letters that they were your true magnum opus. They were certainly your life's work, and they were totally honest, and in a way, they explained every other thing you'd ever done as far as I knew when I read them, making your eleven books, and your libretto, and your essays all feel a little bit beside the point, like the adornments on a khopesh (the point of which is less to dazzle than it is to kill), although of course that didn't mean your published works were not worth reading. I spent a long time with those letters, and I still remember parts of them, but unlike what I found next, I never shared them with anyone and never will. For whatever reason, I still feel I owe you that.

It was called "metamorfoza," and it contained a document called "novel" that I saw when I opened it was titled *The Translators*.

"Every original work of literature," I read, *"is a Pasiphaë that bathes the world in light. Yet cursed with an insuperable desire for the Reader, a white bull, the text is doomed to engender a Minotaur, over and over again.*

"I am Ariadne falling to her knees on Naxos, stricken by the folly of my kindness."

I had to reread the opening twice before I understood what she meant, in part because Ariadne was the daughter of Pasiphaë, and I was surprised to learn she thought of herself as the offspring of her work.[74]

Then I realized Irena was saying that translators were Minotaurs, and frantically I googled in the hopes of discovering I misremembered everything about the ancient myth. But no: I remembered it perfectly. The Minotaur was a vile half-human monster who feasted on the flesh of full, beautiful humans.

I felt sick. I know no one will believe me, but I didn't read any more of *The Translators*. I knew I would never be able to unread whatever I read, and that it could haunt me for the rest of my life. Instead, I wandered into more sickening territory still: the nine subfolders contained in "metamorfoza." One for each of us.

We had accepted the fact that when she was eighteen, Irena had stolen half of Poland's best museum. We had talked about it a lot since Barbara unstole the Czech chandelier, and we had come to the conclusion that Our Author had taken the ancient artifacts because she was morally opposed to the display of human remains, particularly the Western display of Eastern human remains. As she matured, this opposition became a hatred of preservation tout court.

We believed she'd taken all the weapons because she hated the idea of violence, and she wanted to contain it where she could. But as I started to open the items

---

74   Lest there be any confusion at all, these lines could not possibly be the work of the great Irena Rey. It astonishes me that this author believes her readers will not think to wonder who her fictional Irena envisions as her Theseus. Surely she cannot think it would be Bogdan (Trans.).

in Alexis's file, it occurred to me that maybe she had taken all these things, and Chloe's horrific trauma, not because of any noble concept, but because she wanted to have them, and because she could.

There, in chronological order, was the sad procession of my enemy's earliest life: a picture of a trailer labeled "Outside Three Forks, Arkansas, near Gibson Bayou Cemetery"; a 1982 newspaper article about a domestic dispute between her parents; a 1983 newspaper article about her father's arrest; a reproduction of a letter, written in crayon, that Alexis had sent to her father in prison.

There was a sub-subfolder called "Child Beauty Pageants," but I didn't have the heart.

At first his folder didn't seem to contain as much material as the others: just a couple of pictures of him, a couple of his ugly wife, a couple of what I assumed to be their neighborhood in Sweden. But there was also a series of newspaper articles copied and pasted into a document called "parents." Each of the articles had been run through something like Google Translate, anathema to us, and between the poverty of the resulting Polish and my own occasional gaps, it took me a while to piece together what had happened.

What had happened was that Irena had chosen Freddie not because of the prestige of his language or the loveliness of his eyes, but rather the great tragedy of his childhood, when he and his mother had been hiking the Gullmarsvik mudflats of Västra Götaland on a summer afternoon as the tide had begun to come in. The only witness was a six-year-old Freddie, which meant that the timeline was a little bit confused, but somehow his mother got stuck in the softened mud that resolidified as the water rose, attaining the consistency of cement; Freddie had run to get his father, who stumbled out of their rented cottage drunk, and whose efforts to save his wife resulted only in him drowning, too.

It was how Amália's parents had died, after the accident that killed her sister. Maybe Irena's eagerness to use these stories had outweighed her hopes for her novel about us, or maybe she planned to rewrite them in *The Translators*. Maybe she'd been harvesting our stories one by one for use in all her novels since *Lena*, and I'd just never noticed. Maybe that was why she'd never let us get to know each other very well at other summits. Maybe *The Translators* would be about that: about our gullibility, our inability to understand even what was right before our eyes.

She'd found Freddie through Bogdana, who'd moonlighted as a Polish-Swedish interpreter. She might have planned to use Bogdana's story, but Freddie's was just better, and besides, with Freddie there was no risk of recognition, no risk of having to surrender her Czartoryski spoils.

I had thought Irena chose us to be her translators because we were good at our jobs. I had thought we might be the best Polish translators in the world, since she had chosen us. But now, as I clicked through the other subfolders, I understood that she had chosen us not because we were good translators, but because we made good characters.

"Leave Lena," I said out loud, suddenly recalling that inside the folder for *Grey Eminence* there'd been a subfolder called "Lena" that we hadn't opened, thinking it was just old material misplaced. But sure enough, when I opened it, I saw dozens of photographs of the woman I'd seen emerging from the straw wraps house, weaving in and out of the All Saints' Day crowds. In two of the pictures, Amália-Lena was wearing her leopard-print coat. In five of the pictures, she wasn't wearing anything. In one of the pictures, she was sitting cross-legged on the twin bed in the shed that had stood in Irena's backyard, wearing a big Jagiellonian University sweatshirt and a pair of boxer shorts.

I reached for the wastebasket and threw up without taking my eyes off the screen. I navigated back to "metamorfoza." I had no idea what I would find in my own folder. What if there were things in my parents' past that would further unravel my relationships with them, perhaps even cast doubt on my identity? What if I was adopted? What if something terrible had happened to me when I was a child, and everybody around me knew about it, but I'd suppressed the memory? What if I had terminal cancer, and my doctors had told only Irena so as not to spoil my final months on Earth?

That made no sense—I knew that made no sense. I hadn't bothered to see a doctor in years. But I could have been the daughter of my dad's disappeared sister. I didn't look that much like my mom. I knew I needed to open the folder, but at first I couldn't make my fingers work. Finally, I clicked.

I found pictures lifted from my Facebook page, a file with a selection of my ex's tweets, along with foul AI translations of them into Polish, my mother's LinkedIn profile, pictures of the inside of my father's factory off General Paz, pictures of our old apartment in Recoleta, pictures of my dad's new wife.

I found Irena's notes from the few conversations we had ever had. I realized we had never spoken one-on-one.

There was a page-and-a-half portrait of me as a character, outlining my weaknesses, my habits, what I wanted without realizing I wanted it. According to Irena, I was "a semi-soulless follower": I had dated a director because I needed direction, and I had driven him away by bending to his will until I was flat on the ground, someone he had no choice but to walk over.

It was a relief, of course. But reading those notes I couldn't help but feel she had misrepresented me severely; she made me sound far more pathetic than I had ever even accused myself of being. To her I was eternally adrift. I'd sleep with anyone who took the trouble to say any reasonably kind thing to me and then become them by adopting all their tastes and habits. In and of myself, I wasn't really anything. Instead of a cobbled-together creature like a chimera, nothing.

Or rather, without the riveting traumas of someone like Chloe or Freddie or Alexis, all I really was was a loser, present in the novel solely to provide the reader with some occasional comic relief.

I stood up from Irena's red womb chair and was unsteady on my feet. Confronted with Irena's color-coded bookshelves, I thought that if I didn't eat or drink something with sugar in it, I'd pass out, and no one would be able to get into her office to revive me. I unlocked the door and went into the kitchen. I poured myself a glass of juice and brought it to my mouth just as Freddie came up behind me and nearly crushed me, sending sticky orange rivulets down my camel-colored front.

"You're alive!" he cried. Then he picked me up and set me down on the same counter where, six and a half weeks earlier, Petra and Renata had sliced up inky caps to make Irena her last supper, at least her last with us. Freddie slipped his hands under the thin wool of my sweater and encircled me again to unfasten my bra. He crouched down and slowly untied my boots, slipping them off and placing them in front of the oven. Then he rose and wrapped his hands around my thighs, fingering the denim as he bit into my neck, and I cried out and jumped down and took everything off and turned to let him shove my face into the cold white tiles as he gripped my hip with his other hand, until he came.

When the others returned, accompanied by Leszek, who wasn't the size of a pine marten, Freddie and I were sitting side by side on the floor of the kitchen.

We had put our clothes back on. His French Brazilian sneakers were falling apart. Both of us were smoking cigarettes. Freddie was on his Nokia. I glanced at the screen of my own phone and was amazed to see that it was seven thirty in the morning. It felt like my duel with Alexis had taken place lifetimes earlier, in some other story in a language I could no longer read.

The others stood in the doorway, staring, until Alexis shoved her way into the kitchen and, voice raised, cheeks rosy, said, "Irena's piece about the forest—about protecting the forest—was published in the *Times* late last night."

Everyone watched me, as if expecting some violent reaction, as if they thought I might care. When I didn't lunge at Alexis or move at all except to breathe, Schulz spoke. "Thanks to Alexis, President Duda or someone in the government—"

"—someone high up—" interjected Petra.

"—must have told Szyszko to call off the dogs because everyone just left. We didn't even need to shoot."

Freddie, who was half asleep, looked from Petra to Alexis to Schulz. "Dogs?" he said.

"Loggers entered the strict reserve this morning," Schulz told him. "What are you still doing here?"

"RTL sent a news van," added Ostap. "That's a German TV station. They were ready to live broadcast the catastrophe."

"Just like in *Grey Eminence*," said Renata.

"Well maybe not just like," said Alexis. "But close, definitely close."

I was happy for the forest, but I was unable to pretend I gave a shit about any other microelement of this drawling conversation. I rose and pushed through them. "Follow me," I said, and it might have been the first time I ever said it, in any language, to anyone, and they did. As we walked into Irena's office, Leszek said, "She just posted." He gave me a meaningful look. "She's definitely not near here."

"Who?" asked Freddie.

"Irena," Leszek said. He was wearing all black. He looked like he'd aged twenty years since All Saints' Day. I learned later that he'd lost seven bison in the storm, a third of his herd. But he didn't mention that then. He only said, "Irena cannot be allowed to leave the forest. She is as much a part of the forest as the forest is part of her. She knows that. You must go and retrieve her. All of you."

He paused. It looked like he was swiping through more pictures.

"Whatever the cost," he said.

"Whatever the— What are you talking about?" said Alexis.

"Haven't we done enough?" Chloe echoed. "I want to go home."

"Not yet!" said Leszek shrilly, handing around his phone.

"Okay," I said. "This isn't what I want to show you. But I started an Instagram account a long time ago, and I used it to kind of find Irena."

"Kind of find—?" Chloe said.

"We don't really know where she is yet," I clarified. "We only know she isn't here."

Stop.[75]

November 3

---

75   Plural, informal (Trans.).

"Stop what?" asked Chloe.

"Do you think she means the translation?" asked Renata.

"You mean all we have to do is figure out where this photo was taken, and we'll be able to go get her?" asked Alexis. Then she looked at me in fear, but when she saw the exhaustion that had replaced the rage on my face, she relaxed again.

"This is Tempelhof," said Schulz, who had pulled up the pictures on his own phone, too, and was using his fingers to zoom in.

"The airport?" asked Petra.

"Former," said Freddie.

"Former?" asked Chloe.

"It used to be an airport," I said. "None of that matters now." They all looked at me. I had sat back down at her desk and was opening "metamorfoza."

"Shouldn't we go to Tempelhof?" asked Ostap. "Right now?"

"How long would it take to get there?" Renata asked Schulz.

"It's an eight-hour drive. If we left now"—he glanced at his watch—"we could probably still get there by sunset."

"Sorry," I said. "But she cannot have gone to Tempelhof. Tempelhof is the exact opposite of Białowieża."

I assumed that, to Irena, Tempelhof was the worst-case scenario: a mysteriously powerful landscape that had, over successive generations, been depleted and destroyed by mankind. Tempelhof was an aleph[76] that seemed to hold every possible moment of Białowieża's bad future in its palimpsest present. If Białowieża was the original, Tempelhof was the motliest possible translation. It was everything to everyone: concentration camp; Prussian parade ground; the primary site of the Berlin airlifts, which provided the city with 395,000 tons of mostly U.S. food, coal, and supplies over the course of a Soviet blockade; briefly, Europe's largest emergency refugee shelter; a public park.

"If Tempelhof is the opposite of Białowieża," said Chloe, "then maybe that's exactly why she went."

"Plus it was where her mother abandoned her," said Petra.

"True!" cried Alexis. "She could have gone in search of her mother!"

---

76 A magical marble containing all points in the universe (i.e., in both space and time). The reference is to a short story by Jorge Luis Borges, to whom this author has already referred (Trans.).

"You mean, like, spiritually?" said Chloe. "Like she might be writing an *Eat Pray Love* about her mom?"

"Who cares?!" I cried. They turned to me in shock. "Irena has been writing a novel about us," I said. I had opened all the sub-subfolders, all the little portals to our darkest hours or most shameful behavior or, in my case, just the reminders of our humdrum existence, our meaninglessness on this earth. "All this time."

"What do you mean?" asked Ostap.

"Just look," I said. I got up and motioned to Alexis to sit down.

CHAPTER TWENTY-NINE

The roads were not as perilous as we expected; had we hit a patch of ice, Our Author might still be alive.

It was the first time we had left the forest in forty-five days. Arboreal days, some fungal days, when we felt like decomposing, some animal days, when we felt like giving up, or locking horns, or coupling. We had grown used to the sounds of the wild and the sounds of our keyboards and had unlearned how to hear anything else.

Now the back of the van Freddie had rented to go to the airport was loaded with weapons and other brandishable objects from Irena's home: the nine-armed candelabra; Pan Igor's old Russian revolvers; the caltrop; the three reeds; the old Polish-Spanish dictionary with the corduroy cover. Our toy swords, modeled on the famous Szczerbiec, symbol of the greatness of the nation of Poland and the bravery of the Poles.

Throughout our summit, we had fixated on the border closest to us, the country we could see from Renata's balcony—partly because Barbara told us to expect Irena to return from there, and partly because we had learned it contained the majority of the forest—but now Freddie drove west, away from Belarus, past Hajnówka, past Bielsk Podlaski, into clarity or emptiness, whatever wasn't forest, and when we stopped to get gas a few miles east of Warsaw, we all piled out of the van in a daze, like newborns, like we were being forced to breathe.

Most of us went in for coffee, tiny paper cups of strong, bitter espresso, and chocolate bars or chips. Alexis, my former enemy, bought a banana. I was the first to return to the van and caught Petra fiddling with the rearview mirror; I

looked closer and saw she had hung up a silver-toned medallion that read SAINT
ANTHONY PRAY FOR US.

"Emi," she said. "I forgot to give you this." She held out an acorn. I thought
about swallowing it, to keep it from falling out of my pocket, but I was afraid of
choking to death before we tracked down Irena.

Schulz took over from Freddie, who came back and sat with his hand on
my knee. Schulz drove fast, but by the time we entered Berlin, the sun we'd
been driving directly into for over an hour was low and pale. It was 3:19 P.M.
By four, I knew, it would be dark, which meant we didn't have much time to
find her.

The parking lot in front of Tempelhof was vacant but for a few piles of snow.
Schulz pulled up to a long colonnade with a sign that said ZENTRALE
FUNDBÜRO.

"What's this?" I asked.

"Lost and Found," said Schulz. He turned the engine off, and for a moment,
we all just sat there, reluctant, as the van slowly exuded its heat.

Then we all spilled out, each of us taking one weapon. I picked up my Szczerbiec, thought better of it, and took the dictionary instead.

"We must risk everything," I reminded myself under my breath, "in order to
respectfully obtain our goals. And protect the community we need to create."

"It's a good thing my husband sent the spare keys," murmured Schulz as he
unlocked a set of glass doors, and we drifted into the old arrivals and departures
hall of Tempelhof, quiet as a crypt and dripping with refinement, its coral-colored
ceiling sixty feet high, supported by pillars of Jura limestone that connected it
to a vast, perfectly polished floor that extended from the counters of airlines that
no longer existed to the perfectly still escalators to defunct gates. Looming over
everything was a monumental clock, with twelve white typewriter apostrophes
and forty-eight white beads. In its center, two black-and-white drumsticks,
stopped.

We poured into the hall. We scattered, ransacking the counters, shoving and
striking and howling at whatever we found that was locked. There was no sign
of her upon the frozen baggage carousel. She eluded us at every counter. It felt
like we had leaped into a movie that someone else had paused. I tried to force a
heavy door with an angry eagle on it, black and red. Seeing I was getting nowhere,
caught up in our fervor, Freddie ran over and thrust his bronze candelabra

through the window. We peered inside but saw only an empty desk, neat rows of red and blue binders, and broken glass.

As the light outside flared and changed shades, the monumental airport's face grew more forbidding and more awesome, its enormous windows stark reminders of our guilt, and our anger, and our urgency, our wasted love. We entered an incomprehensible room with an altar and some stained-glass windows, somber amber and mauve. Beneath the octopus chandeliers of wrought iron, their glimmering glass globes like tennis balls, Petra prayed, holding the tips of the three reeds between her palms. At first I thought Freddie was praying, too, but then Chloe said, "What are you saying?"

And Freddie said, "I'm reciting my latest elegy. It's called 'My Girlfriend Isn't Sure She Wants to Visit Me in Stockholm.' It's about climate change and abolition. Would you like to hear it?"

"That's okay," said Chloe, and we heard the deafening din of a monster and ran back outside. The sky was an almost blinding tangerine. We caught a quick glimpse of a garbage truck before it disappeared around the bend. We looked everywhere, but there was nothing else that moved, except our shadows, which lurched in all directions, and nine desperate figures in the glass.

Schulz made a phone call in German while Alexis darted over to a gigantic glass case. I expected it to hold a huge map of Tempelhof, but instead—I joined Alexis—all it had in it was a postcard, longer than most postcards but dwarfed by the blocks of flushing stone.

The case was unlocked. I slid it open by a flat steel knob and took out the postcard. It showed a row of bluish people, a baby, a dog, a god or a goddess, some scrambling kittens, a dreaded stork. I flipped it over. The caption read, *"D'où venons-nous? Que sommes-nous? Où allons-nous?"* and then, in English, *"Where Do We Come From? What Are We? Where Are We Going?"* *D'où*, I thought, like *amadou*?

We had seen this postcard before, in Pavel's shed; I hadn't had the chance to examine it then, but I recognized it. It was a dream of human beings as primordially connected to every other constituent of Earth: its rock, its twilight, its serpents, its apples, its gods. It was the fantasy that original was right, and that whatever came after was too late.

Gratuitously, Freddie broke the case, losing control of his candelabra, which flew into our entourage, nearly striking Renata, then clattered onto several of its arms. Chloe grabbed the postcard, flipped it over, saw that there was nothing handwritten on it, and tossed it on the ground. Schulz picked it up, took off down a driveway, across a small plaza, pausing at a trash can to throw the card away, and down a steep dark staircase with a thin, wobbly rail. We came to a simple white room with large caricatures of people, whimsical Germans caught up in a storm; in the corner of the room, there was an empty cabinet of human proportions, but we didn't stop to examine it; we kept going into an echoing hall with chalky concrete arches, a convex mirror at the end. Each of the arches was labeled with a number in black; along the edges of the hall there were rows of pipes in different colors, some labeled, all manner of cracks and depressions in the walls, occasional graffiti, crooked metal hooks.

We turned and went down another set of stairs, into darker darkness; Schulz and Alexis, with her spotlight, led the way. We came to a frigid and cavernous place, and as our eyes adjusted, we saw that whatever inhabited this realm was sepia, scratched, damp. Schulz said, "This is the Hansa lab. The Nazis kept their surveillance photography in here. When the Soviets entered Berlin, the contents of this image vault were set on fire. Everything burned, without exception. This is why the walls look how they do: ruined, hideously scarred."

Petra set the three reeds in a corner of the room. The rest of us trailed our free fingertips along the masses of plaster, the faded rough brick. Each of the letters and the numbers carved into every wall received a fingertip; we found the site of her Instagram post, and without intending to, I touched my forehead, then my lips to the cold-soaked walls. Then I hit it with my fist.

In the last room we came to, we found a pallet, draped in a filthy blue blanket, covered with various items.

Freddie said, "Cleo! Your little red notebook!"

Chloe reached for it and said, "Alexis, your necklace with your initial on it."

"I think those are my keys," I said and scraped them off the concrete floor, revealing a little white card.

"My car insurance," said Ostap.

"My underwear!" cried Renata, rushing to pocket them. She wasn't fast enough: I could see that they were full-coverage, floral, worn.

We found several more postcards; we found, in the next room, two vials of a tincture labeled LION'S MANE on the upper rung of a ladder. We found a phone, but when I called myself from it, we saw that it wasn't her number. We found a passport confirming that her real name was Irena Dembowska, and that her real birthday was November 3. She wasn't a fire sign, though we would always think of her that way. We couldn't find her clothes or laptop. We couldn't find her.

Schulz showed us his name on the wall, inscribed, he said, at some wild party in 1986, and we knew that if Irena had posted a clear picture sooner, it would never have come to this. We would have found her in time not to find out what kind of person she was: not noble, but cheap, thieving. Base. Her genius wasn't hers: It was everybody else's.

We came to another room, where in the devastated concrete we made out a graceful shape that could have been Our Author, the one we had believed in before. Pictured as an ancient Egyptian goddess, she looked ready for battle. Petra cried, "Irena!" But the goddess was silent, and we realized she was just graffiti and fire damage on a cold old wall.

I was the one who alerted Irena to our presence. I believed she would want to know that we were there. I took a picture and posted it to Instagram as soon as we were back aboveground.

November 3

"Come," Schulz said. "Let's just try the Lost and Found."

We marched back toward the car. Schulz unlocked the Zentrale Fundbüro, and we streamed past the desk, where we deposited our armaments, and into a warehouse. Schulz flipped on the fluorescent lights.

Each of us took a different category. Of all of us, Petra was least qualified to make any sense of "Electronics and technology," but that was the category she searched. "ID cards, documents, and plastic cards" went to Chloe; "Vehicles, bicycles, and strollers" to Pavel; "Keys" to Freddie, who took pictures and notes he later published as an eleven-page illuminated prose poem titled "I Can Open You." We entrusted Ostap with "Medical items," but he got stuck on the "Glasses" subcategory, trying on every pair in the box until he found one that approximated his prescription.

I took "Jewelry, watches, valuables," where among the Patek Philippes I came across one of my missing earrings. It was more intricate than I'd remembered, its indented spiracles glinting in the fluorescent lights, its tilted abdomen, its little mandible that looked like it ought to have snapped off by now, at some point in its travels over the past twenty years. I rummaged frantically for its mate but gave up, grateful to have at least this back, and slid it into my right lobe.

For a long time, we found nothing. Or rather, we found everything but her. We confiscated candy and passed it around. We found alcohol, and most of us drank it. Freddie found an old-fashioned xylophone he struck into vague, unpleasant melodies. Schulz and Pavel confiscated a soccer ball and started to play.

After half an hour, we were ready to try elsewhere when we finally found something of hers.

"Isn't this . . . ?" Alexis held up a glinting onyx ring, and all of us squinted; Ostap took off his new glasses.

It was Irena's grandfather's black magic ring.

"But Barbara had it," said Renata. "Didn't she?"

"Maybe Barbara's was fake," Chloe said.

Pavel shrugged. "She probably has them stockpiled. They're probably all fake."

"But what about her grandfather, the local black magician?" Renata asked.

"That was probably somebody else's grandfather," said Ostap gently.

"Or nobody's grandfather," Freddie said.

We didn't have time this time to be disappointed in her. Right away Schulz intervened, asking, "Shall we try the grounds?"

Outside was another world, an enormity; there was not a single one of us who didn't despair over our odds. We would never find her.

The moon was the fullest we'd seen, but it was constantly being barreled over by snow clouds that hid it and the world from us. The cold stung my face and made me brace against it, a pain and a tension I had never felt until now.

Parts of the sidewalk were solid ice. Petra nearly fell as we rushed out the back of the building. I nearly fell when I rushed to her side. We struggled to keep up with the others, who were racing ahead. Within the infinite hangar, the world was black and abandoned, a mock-up of Irena's brain. I posted my last picture.

#mama #irenadembowska
November 3

We wandered out onto the field. Here and there it was studded by subtle rises that could have been kurgans containing every possible manner of death. Where the field was flat, it was delineated by a vast cage that held little human houses, maybe for the refugees. It stretched as far as we could see with our cell phones and our spotlight. To keep it from getting wet, I set my dictionary on top of my feet and hung my frozen fingers from the small freezing squares of the cage.

"And across the coniferous distance," I whispered, "God moves in whirlwind and expanse."

An arrow burst the corduroy atop my feet. It was a thousand pages away from my skin and my bones but I screamed anyway, and leaped back, and everyone ran for cover, back to the hangar, except for Chloe, who stood frozen, and I grabbed her arm and tried to pull her, but then I saw that she was staring at something, but it was dark, and I couldn't see, and my eyes tried to trace the arc of that arrow, the thread that had tied us to Irena since *Kernel of Light*, for ten years, and the clouds parted and silvered the snow, and I still couldn't see anything, but I was filled with a warmth that verged on fury, and suddenly, sure enough, there she was.

There was Irena, standing on the roof of the abandoned hangar, 150 feet up, overlooking all of Tempelhof: parade ground, concentration camp, once and maybe future bison land. She was there. There was no mistaking it this time.

No one has ever been as glorious as you, Irena, and no one ever will be. That split second of seeing you after seven weeks, feeling your pull and being the only one to see you, in that palimpsest place that was in fact no less original than Białowieża—it felt like so much that some days I go back to it, dwell in it for as long as I possibly can, just that still, all-dimensional split second, before our story, the story of our desperate quest, the story of your disappearance, reached its end.

"She's there," I screamed to the others who were crouching under the hangar. "She's on the roof. Up there!"

We climbed a concrete stairwell and emerged inside an airmen's lounge with a bar and then in the next room a series of drawings included the one Irena had posted before. At the window we could see the rest of the refugee camp, where some men were playing basketball, and over the corner of the door, as we exited the lounge, was a painting of a ship that said, on its hull, POLAND IS NOT YET LOST.

We climbed another flight of stairs, then another, then we reached the very pinnacle of Tempelhof. Between the three of them, Chloe and Alexis and Renata shoved open the thick steel door to the roof.

Pacing in the distance, a beam of full moonlight rewilding her dark hair, one hand across her back gripping her elbow, was Our Author, the woman we were all in love with once. Pavel dropped his fire extinguisher. At the sound, Irena stopped.

Our Author turned only partly toward us. It was enough for us to see the quiver slung over her right shoulder. Her bow was lying on the icy surface of the roof. "Welcome," she said in a perfectly ordinary tone, as though it were September, as though 150 feet up on a snow-encrusted hangar in Berlin were our summiting place.

A black hole is an astronomical monster, capable of devouring stars and even galaxies, along with all their light. The closer you get to a black hole, the more time slows, until it actually seems to stop.

Once we saw her, all we could see was her. For a moment, each of us was imprisoned in the extreme emotion of being in her presence again. Finally, the nine of us looked at each other, and I managed to step forward, unarmed.

"Are you writing a novel about us?" I asked. My voice shook when I got to the word "novel," and her face changed, but she said nothing.

Alexis stepped up next to me, shining her spotlight on Our Author's feet. "Are you working on a book called *The Translators*?" When Irena didn't answer, Alexis went on: "How did you find all those pictures? The trailer park, the pageants . . . Some of them I've never even seen." Then her voice broke. "It hurts," she said, but I don't know if Irena could hear her. I'd never seen Alexis get emotional before. I'd never seen her open up.

I followed the beam of Alexis's spotlight to Irena's too-big, dilapidated boots. From where I was standing, she actually seemed to be wearing them on the wrong feet. The woman we had worshipped looked almost clownish now. I tried unsuccessfully to suppress a sneeze.

Chloe, Alexis's second, was still carrying Pan Igor's old revolvers. Now she passed the right one to me, slipping it slowly into the oversize pocket of Irena's rusted chain-mail sweater. I could feel Alexis's eyes.

"Irena," said Petra. "We've worked really hard for you. We've tried our best to be faithful to your work. We've arguably gone above and beyond."

"Inarguably," Freddie said. "So it seems to me. You all have," he clarified. And then, under his breath, "This isn't my cult."

"So we just need to know," Petra continued. "What are you planning on doing with our lives?"

Irena looked back out over Tempelhof. She took a step toward the edge, surveyed the field again. The nine of us spread out into an almost-straight line along the building.

"Do you actually care about Białowieża?" Chloe called out.

"Do you care about us?" asked Schulz.

"You owe us this," I said. "You owe us an explanation."

Irena spun around again.

"I don't owe you anything," she said.

Those were her only other words to us, besides "Welcome."

Welcome. I don't owe you anything. The way to say "I do not owe" in Polish is the same as the way to say "I am not guilty." But Irena was guilty. She did owe us something. Maybe many things.

One of us took a step forward, and then the rest of us did, too. I ran my thumb over the safety of Pan Igor's old revolver. I raised it from my pocket, which was her pocket, and I pointed it at her. She glanced at her bow that was lying in the ice. She glanced at me. We all took another step forward.

It took us a couple more steps before Irena fully understood the danger. By then it was too late.

There was a muffled thud when she hit the ground. Freddie hoisted the giant candelabra with its dented arms and tossed it down after her. Now there was the sound of a little explosion. We ran back down the seemingly infinite set of concrete stairs.

Eventually, black holes pop out of existence, though recent research suggests they may leave a small nugget of information behind. This nugget has no event horizon, meaning that it devours nothing: no light, no stars, no galaxies. It has no effect on time.

A little while later the clouds came apart, and the moon glinted the fractured bronze and bared patches of snow on the ice that were spattered with something darker. We stood in a circle over her: Irena Rey, Our Author, ours again, gone. She couldn't be dead, and yet, she was.

We had made our sacrifice. The slate was clean.

CHAPTER THIRTY

I was the one who drove us home. I went slower than Schulz and Freddie had, out of deference or simply caution, and we arrived at our summiting place a quarter of an hour before four.

I got down from the van and lit a cigarette. It was so cold I couldn't think about anything except the cold, and then that craving. I went into the house and continued to smoke at our altar, ashing on the coniferous carpet, letting my eyes relax, until Ostap and Schulz came in carrying the body of Our Author.

They arranged her on the chaise longue, covering her up with torn orange and blue Punjabi patterns, positioning a first edition of *Lena* on what looked to be her lap. From the alabaster snake table, Renata picked up an empty glass inkwell, which she briefly cradled, then set at Our Author's feet.

"I guess we really are a murder of translators," said Alexis, in English, biting a glistening nail. No one said anything. Alexis was the worst, but she was one of us. I understood that no matter what, it would have been impossible for me to kill Alexis because I was Alexis, or Alexis was as much a part of me as I was.

Those of us who hadn't submitted our completed manuscripts submitted them now. We checked Irena's email, one last time, but all we found was an email from Bogdan telling Irena he'd been arrested in New Jersey for "fraud by wire, radio, or television." He said his bail had been set at twenty thousand dollars, and could she please wire it over as soon as she saw this, which of course she couldn't, and we didn't, so I don't actually know, even now, how long he spent in U.S. jail.

We gleaned from this that Bogdan had been the one sending us emails from Irena, trying to access her works. We agreed we couldn't blame him. We also were not in a position to cast stones.

We collected our things from our quarters—the ones that had been assigned to us and the ones we had adopted—and I gathered up all my notes that would slowly metamorphose into *The Extinction of Irena Rey*. Maybe *Grey Eminence* was right that writing has to be an engine of extinction. But the first to inhabit a traumatized landscape are often fungi, lichen, slime molds, and species of plants known as "ruderal," a word that derives from the Latin word for "rubble." Maybe the extinction of Irena Rey made the space for a ruderal art, like a book about what happened to her translators.

We each—even Freddie—kissed the knot at the base of the staircase, in gratitude, and to say goodbye. Schulz and Ostap and Renata transferred the ferns and the prayer plants from the winter garden to the rental van, which they drove a few blocks down the street.

The rest of us built a pyre in her living room, pushing the barrel chairs in around the chaise longue to create the shape of a seven-point star. Before lighting Our Author on fire, we uncovered her just to her shoulders. I find that even now I am unable to describe her indescribable beauty. She was wearing the white coat that had gone missing from under my bed. It was gray now, but that wouldn't matter for much longer. She was wearing the other bee. I stared at her face for a little while, in animal sorrow. Then I transferred my bee to her empty ear. I wanted her to have it, and I wanted not to be connected to her anymore.

Schulz took the ferrocerium rod off the mantel, and one by one we deposited our amadou. Schulz scraped the rod with the back of a knife, scattering a smattering of sparks. For a second, nothing much became of them. Then, bit by bit, as before, our amadou—our origin—began to glow.

Chloe stepped forward and peeled a quote off Our Lady of Literature, touching its edges to the tinder. Once it was on fire, she used it to ignite the splayed pages of *Perfection* where I'd put out my cigarette. We saw Irena's words with short-lived halos, blue and orange; we saw her pages stiffen and contract, then blacken.

Tears streamed down Pavel's cheeks as he added a couple of postcards to the pyre, then, with his arms crossed, watched them be consumed. Renata went into

Irena's office and came back with an armful of books. The fire was spreading: Already the carpet had started to burn. The room was getting warmer.

We fed the fire her library, book by book, starting with the purple ones, then indiscriminately, armful by armful. We fed the fire the portraits of her ancestors, probably stolen and probably of strangers; we fed the fire her clothes. We fed the fire our red velvet pouches, with their perfectly stitched executioners' axes—a random symbol that had nothing to do with the Dembowski coat of arms.

It was beginning to get hard to see. Ostap coughed, and then we were all coughing in the hot gray air, and as the flames engulfed more of the house and her body, I made the suggestion that we wrap Quercus in a blanket and depart.

"Shouldn't we sacrifice ourselves?" Renata asked earnestly as we stumbled out the door. "Like when a warrior's horses would be killed so they could be buried with their master?"

"Petra is pregnant," I said. "We're already sacrificing our summiting place."

"What if we cut off her fingers?" asked Petra. "We could keep them in jars, as relics."

"It's too late," said Alexis.

"Yeah," I said. "I agree." Our eyes met across the blaze. In the orange haze, her face was splendid, her cheekbones aglow, her eyes flickering, her gold *A* glinting at her throat. She was beautiful; I'd never thought otherwise. Beauty didn't mitigate destructiveness; Irena had more than proven that.

We turned to look back as we walked to our hotel. There was the sound of a siren in the distance, and then another. There was nothing they could do, of course. Word by word, thanks to our amadou, Our Author had turned into ash, curling, erupting, vanishing without a trace.

Suddenly Renata cawed. "Caw! Caw!" she cried into her hands cupped around her mouth, facing up into the pale cerulean-gray sky. Petra tightened her grip around Quercus. "Caw!" Petra cried.

Then all of us were doing it, even Quercus, crowing at the dawn, and that was her only funeral, the opposite of Amália's, drowned out by fire trucks, lasting only a block and a half.

LATER THAT MORNING, Irena's official Instagram posted a picture of Irena onstage, wearing a red dress, strappy heels, and an orange shawl that she spread out like wings. She was standing in front of a spotlight, and her outline glowed, and in its fineness, the image of her shawl was made up almost exclusively of light.

THAT AFTERNOON, IN our various languages, from the lobby of the Booted Eagle Hotel, we spread the word that Irena Rey's home had been burned by the government of Poland, in an effort to silence her. But she would never be silenced, we said. She was elsewhere, safe now, and the world would be hearing from her soon.

ACKNOWLEDGMENTS

Although I began this novel in Białowieża, I wrote almost all of it in the small Swiss town of Montricher, at the Fondation Jan Michalski, in a sumptuous tree house designed by Sami Rintala, Dagur Eggertsson, and Vibeke Jenssen, thanks to the extraordinary generosity of Vera Michalski-Hoffmann. Piotr Sommer and Anna Bikont were my companions during this time, and even now, several years later, I continue to draw on the intense happiness I felt when I was with them, gathering saffron milk caps in the foothills of the Jura Mountains, drinking cappuccinos, coming up with wild ideas for books.

Boris Dralyuk's exquisite translations and boundless curiosity about the lives of artists and the histories of places have been shaping and reshaping my attitude toward literature since that first afternoon when we met at the Crossroads of the World. So many people are indebted to Boris, who forgives all debts, but were he keeping track I'd owe him more than everybody else combined. Thank you for being the most sensitive, most empathetic person I have ever known, and thank you for being the greatest father, and thank you for marrying me.

I'm grateful to the Robert B. Silvers Foundation and Daniel Mendelsohn for an early grant to explore the relationships between translators, and to Sean Cotter, whose tales of Romanian translators fueled some of the delirium here. The origin of my obsession with translation communities is Olga Tokarczuk, an author utterly adored by her translators into all languages, and for good reason: Olga is a great writer (and it's a lot more fun to translate a great writer than a not-so-great writer), and her support of translators and translation has been, from the beginning, absolute.

I am thankful to James R. Monaghan and the Hermitage Artist Retreat for giving me the time and space to revise, and to MacDowell, for those beautiful red womb chairs in the James Baldwin Library where I sat and edited and watched the snow. Vu Tran and the University of Chicago's Literary Arts Lab offered a big dose of encouragement at just the right time. This book is one of many things made possible by the Tulsa Artist Fellowship and the University of Tulsa, and in particular its president, Brad Carson.

Merlin Sheldrake's gorgeous *Entangled Life: How Fungi Make Our Worlds, Change Our Minds & Shape Our Futures* was a major source of inspiration, as was an album titled *The Suspended Harp of Babel* by Vox Clamantis (an Estonian choir) and Jaan-Eik Tulve (who directed the choir), which I must have listened to ten thousand times over the course of creating *The Extinction of Irena Rey*. Henrik Sunde Wilberg told me about a Norwegian translator named Anne-Lisa Amadou, and he and Lucy McKeon and Nathan Jeffers gave helpful feedback on the manuscript at different stages. Elisabeth Ross has been a magnificent friend since the moment I met her, and she has helped me in every realm of my life while also publicly humiliating me by making me snort-laugh.

It was in translating the dazzling work of Roma Sendyka that I first considered the relationship between human trauma and the natural landscapes of Central Europe. Mateusz Szymura alerted me to the presence of tinder polypores in the Białowieża Forest, and subsequent visits were greatly enriched by the guidance of Renata Kosińska, Sylwia Iwanowska, and Mieczysław Piotrowski. Long before the existence of a first draft, I shared the kernel of this novel as a keynote lecture at Wrocław University. I remain surprised, and very grateful, that the organizer of that fascinating conference, Dorota Kołodziejczyk, permitted me to do so. The lovely and erudite Reinhard Bernbeck showed me the almost inscrutable traces of the concentration camp that briefly existed at Tempelhofer Feld in Berlin.

The stories of those buried in the Białowieża Cemetery are true, and they were compiled by Piotr Bajko for the online *Encyklopedia Puszczy Białowieskiej*. Igor Dembowski's story was inspired by the life of Jan Potoka, beautifully told by Anna Kamińska in *Białowieża szeptem: Historie z Puszczy Białowieskiej*.

The John Simon Guggenheim Memorial Foundation provided very much needed support for this novel, and I remain absolutely astonished that I was chosen to receive such an outsize gift.

I can't imagine what my life (let alone my career) would be like without my brilliant and indefatigable agent, Katie Grimm. At Bloomsbury, Ragavendra Maripudi's insightful reading of this manuscript helped shape its evolution, and my editor, Daniel Loedel, has amazed me over and over with his absolute clarity of vision, openness to discussion, attention to detail, and enthusiasm for this project.

Finally, I am thankful to my family. My mother taught me to be in nature at an early age, and my father taught me to be in the world. My sister went mushroom hunting with me, celebrated and commiserated with me, served as my sounding board, and helped me take care of my twins, who were born, by emergency C-section, between the second and third drafts of this novel, but who haven't read it yet.

A NOTE ON THE AUTHOR

JENNIFER CROFT won a Guggenheim Fellowship for this novel, the William Saroyan International Prize for Writing for her memoir, *Homesick*, and the Man Booker International Prize for her translation of Nobel laureate Olga Tokarczuk's *Flights*. She is also the translator of Federico Falco's *A Perfect Cemetery*, Romina Paula's *August*, Pedro Mairal's *The Woman from Uruguay*, and Olga Tokarczuk's *The Books of Jacob*. She lives in Tulsa and Los Angeles.

Date Due

	MAR 27 2024		
JUN 21 2024			

BRODART, CO.   Cat. No. 23-233   Printed in U.S.A.